"YEA, LADY FAIR, NAME YOUR TERMS."

She affected an alluring smile that felt stiff on her lips, and hid the tremor of her hand by gripping his. Not too much said, nor too little, or the ploy would be for nought.

"Twelve labors, as those performed by Hercules, would be too great a request. . . ." His amused snort was evidence that he agreed. "But perhaps a few lesser tasks would be sufficient to win my attentions for an evening, dread knight."

"Ah, and what happens if I perform my labor, but you grow too shy to settle the debt, fair lady? I caution you— I always keep my sworn word, and deal rudely with those who do not."

He was smiling, but there was a steely warning couched in his words that left her slightly dizzy. She must secure his pledge to help her, yet the resort to trickery was growing increasingly nerve-wracking.

"La, sir, do you think I would play you false? First, the evening of entertainment, and then the labor performed. There, you see? You risk nothing, lose only what you will, and gain . . ."

Leaning against him, pressing her breasts against his chest, she mimicked every woman she'd ever observed entice a man. She drew one hand over his mouth in a soft, lingering glide. His lips closed on her fingertips . . .

Also by Juliana Garnett:

The Quest

The Magic

Juliana Garnett

FANFARE ™

BANTAM BOOKS
NEW YORK   TORONTO   LONDON   SYDNEY   AUCKLAND

The Magic
A Bantam Fanfare Book / July 1996

ISBN 0-553-56862-0

Published simultaneously in the United States and Canada

PRINTED IN THE UNITED STATES OF AMERICA

OPM   0 9 8 7 6 5 4 3 2 1

To Evan Marshall, who hung the moon and threw the stars—I'm so grateful to be in your constellation.

To Amelia Bomar for actually going to Wales and bringing back tons of great stuff—and sharing it—and to her daughter Allison Lee for a love of medieval magic.

To Lisa Turner for rescuing me as always with her own special herbs and magic.

To Lisa Higdon for love and hours of patient listening, and to beautiful Farah Farooq for giving me a glimpse of Sasha . . . thank you one and all.

And last, but not least, to Sir Reginald Puppytoes, who gave me fifteen years of loyalty and love. You've left behind an empty space, Reggie, but I know you're where the sun is always shining, the grass is always green, and the squirrels are always just a little bit faster.

The magic of the spring returns
When flowers in painted meads unclose,
And man on earth's new face discerns
A smile of sympathy for those
Who see in love a restful thing,
A banquet for the famishing.

—Walter of Chatillon, Twelfth Century

The Magic

CHAPTER ONE

☙❧

England, 1192

"Did you hear that?" A mailed knight jerked nervously at the reins of his mount and cast quick, furtive glances into the gloom. A mist had begun to rise like smoke, drifting along the ground in vaporish wisps. It was too quiet—too ghostly in the dim, dusky silence of the forest. Tangled tree branches of ancient oaks formed a high ceiling overhead, as ribbed and vaulted as a French cathedral. Diffused sunlight pierced the tight-knit canopy of new leaves in thready streamers to light the narrow road, a hazy contrast to the air of expectant darkness looming beyond.

A faint tinkling sound like tiny bells carried on the wind. It faded so swiftly Rhys ap Griffyn wasn't certain he heard it. He pulled off his helmet to listen; light gleamed on blond hair, catching in thick strands dampened from the weight and heat of his helmet. Gray eyes narrowed to steely slits as he surveyed the road and dense weald around them. Nothing. No sound but the muffled thud of hooves on soft ground and the clink of harness.

The mailed knight rode closer to Rhys, looking around uneasily. "Did you hear it?"

"I heard nothing, Brian. 'Tis only the wind."

"Nay, this was different. It was . . . strange. Like . . . faerie bells." Brian seemed locked in the grip of fear. His back was stiff, and one hand tightly gripped the loop of leather reins. His mount danced nervously at the strangling hold.

Knowing better than to let the idea of faeries take hold of his men, Rhys said, "It's footsteps—the sound of our horseshoes on stones."

Brian blanched; his face paled beneath the lifted visor of his helmet. "Don't look behind us, for the footsteps will be those of dead men."

Rhys nudged his mount close and spoke low so only Brian would hear. "There are no footsteps. 'Tis the wind through tree branches you hear."

"Holy Mary—we should have stayed at the village inn for the night." Freckles stood out like splotches of mud against pale skin stretched taut over Brian's cheekbones and nose. "It's Beltane Eve, and we shouldn't be out. Spirits roam on the borderline eve between spring and summer, when it's not one season or the other." He paused to take a deep breath. "And it's a borderline hour, neither day nor night, the time when the faeries and spirits roam most freely."

Several of the soldiers within earshot began to mutter uneasily. Silently cursing Brian's superstitions, Rhys leaned on the pommel of his saddle to gaze at him with mock amusement. "Big as you are, do you think the Tylwyth Teg will be strong enough to carry you with them, Sir Brian?"

One of the Welsh soldiers laughed, though the sound was strained. When he added in a tense mutter, "Vsbryd-nos," the Welsh name for "spirit night" did nothing to calm the other Welshmen. A murmur ran through the ranks of mounted men.

Rhys sat up straight, shaking his head. "The spirit night will not harm us. Nor will the Tylwyth Teg."

"In Ireland," Brian said darkly, "we call them the Daoine Sidhe. And it's been said about more than one man that the faeries captured him."

"Yea, but it's my belief that more than one wayward husband had to invent an excuse for his angry wife," Rhys retorted with a grin. "Claiming capture by the faeries would be enough to convince almost any goodwife that her husband was detained beyond his will."

"You mock me," Brian said irritably when several of the men laughed. He glanced around, tugging off his helmet. Sweat plastered his red hair to his head. Splinters of light filtered through the roof of leaves, providing enough illumination to see the narrow road, but in the trees beyond, it had grown dark. Looking back at Rhys, he complained, "We should have lingered in the village, I tell you. The maypole was lifted on the green, and there's feasting and merrymaking."

"And winsome maids to go a'maying with—perhaps to get lost in the woods with while picking whitethorn flowers?" He grinned when color flushed Brian's face. "Nay, I know your way with the ladies. If we'd lingered, we'd not get to Coventry by Saint John's Eve, much less by the day after May Day."

Brian turned his mount on the close road, scowling at Rhys. Before he could speak, his horse gave a shrill whinny and half reared, huge hooves thrashing in the air. Leaves shuddered as the animal backed into a hawthorn hedge thick with white flowers and thorns, and Brian cursed loudly.

It was infectious. Suddenly all the horses began to plunge and snort, throwing the knights into turmoil. When his own stallion threw up his head and snorted, Rhys drew his sword and adjusted his shield. He'd been too long a soldier and knight not to trust the instincts of his warhorse.

Brian's sword flashed in the gloom, as did those of the other men. Some muttered curses, others offered prayers as they tried to calm their mounts without being unhorsed. Then one of the men gave a shout.

Rhys looked up. The hair on the back of his neck prickled a warning, and he fought his destrier to a standstill before he was able to focus on the object of this terror. His blood chilled, and he choked back a curse.

In the middle of the road just ahead stood a small figure, wreathed in shreds of mist as if newly sprung from the very ground. Flowing robes of deepest purple completely draped the motionless form. Rhys made the sign of the cross over his chest before he could stop himself. A light peal of mocking laughter greeted his instinctive movement, and he clenched his fist. Embarrassed anger replaced the irrational spurt of fear.

He curbed his plunging mount and spurred forward a few steps. "Move from the road," he ordered. Instead of immediately yielding, there was the sound of more amusement, and a brittle tinkle like tiny bells.

"*In nomine Patris,*" Brian moaned, crossing himself in a clink of chain mail that was echoed by the others. "*Confiteor Deo omnipoténti, beátae María semper Vírgini . . .*"

His prayer faded into silence.

Rhys lifted his sword; a runnel of sunlight skittered along the wicked edge of the blade. Light splinters reflected from chain mail and shield in glittering sparks. "Did you not hear me?" he demanded.

Again, he was greeted with open amusement. His jaw clenched. He tried to see the face, but the hood was pulled too far forward, leaving only a dark blur beneath. He considered putting an end to the mockery with a quick thrust of his sword, but something made him hesitate.

"*. . . beáto Michaéli Archángelo, beáto Joánni Baptíste,*" Brian wheezed.

Enough. If he didn't halt this, his men would be scattered through the weald like crows. He kneed his mount forward, but Turk only pranced nervously, tossing his head and snorting instead of charging. Rhys swore, uncertain if he was more angry or amazed at the horse's refusal to obey a command. Finally, the figure moved. One arm lifted slowly. A small hand was barely noticeable beneath the flowing garment. Rhys saw only a deep shimmering green on the underside; no weapon was visible in the folds.

The horses grew still, and an unnerving hush descended

on the forest road. Tiny bells tinkled on the wind, and from the shadows of the hooded cloak came words in an exotic language Rhys had never heard—high, soft, and mysterious.

Again the stallion shuddered, sleek black muscles rippling as he pranced in quick, mincing steps. Rhys tried to control the animal, but with a jangle of curb chain and bridle bit, the great head shook hard enough to whip the long mane about in a stinging brush. It wasn't until the figure spoke again that the stallion calmed, but the voice was almost drowned out by Brian's droning Latin prayer.

"... *sanctis Apóstolis Petro et Paulo, ómnibus sanctis, et tibi pater ...*"

Brian's confessional entreaty grated on Rhys's already raw temper. Devil, faerie, or enemy, this creature would not be allowed to make a mockery of him.

Clenching his teeth hard, he snarled, "Move from the path, or be ridden over. I have no time for this foolishness."

A snort of unfaerielike laughter greeted his command, and a gust of wind blew, shaking tree limbs. His eyes narrowed. No mystical faerie bells, just the wind.

"... *quia peccávi nimis cogitatióne, verbo et ópere ...*"

"Enough, Sir Brian." Rhys glanced over his shoulder in exasperation. When he turned back, the purple robe was gliding toward him. He tightened his grip on the hilt of his sword. Nay, this was no reckless man barring the road, but a woman. There was a fluid grace and fragility to the dainty form that could not be achieved by any man he'd ever seen. It was almost as if this were a faerie on winged feet.

His mouth tightened. Curse Brian's talk of elves and faeries—he had no intention of allowing those superstitions to affect him.

None of the men had moved after the horses quieted, and Rhys felt their gazes on him as they waited tensely to see what he would do. Wind rustled tree branches overhead with an eerie clacking sound, then it grew very still. No birds chirped, no normal forest sounds could be heard.

Mist crawled along the ground, rising slowly, curling around the specter.

Irritated by an unexpected chill coiling down his spine, Rhys stared coldly at the robed figure barring his way. "Why do you block the road?" he demanded, switching from French to English. "We would pass."

A sudden wind eddy lifted a spiral of dry leaves into the air in a slight whisper, and the figure stepped forward. A graceful lift of one hand pushed back the hood of her cloak. Rhys stared at her.

She was beautiful. Faerie-fragile and as luminous as moonlight on dark water, the maid staring up at him with a faint smile left him speechless. Lustrous hair, black as a raven's wings, straight and shining, fell around her dusky face, and her eyes—Jésu, but her eyes were as deep and dark as the night. She stared directly at him, and he was caught by the intensity of the eyes holding mysterious promises in their depths.

For what seemed like hours but in truth could only have been a moment, he stared into that liquid gaze. Until she broke the spell.

"Greetings, fair knight," she said in soft, perfect French. "I bar your path only to warn you. The bridge ahead has been washed away, and is not easily seen until too late to stop. I thought you should know of the danger."

"God's mercy on you for the warning." He cleared his throat and gestured with his sword. "I barely saw you in the road. Did we frighten you?"

A burst of laughter was accompanied by the tinkling of tiny bells as she shook her head. The movement dislodged a skein of her unbound hair; it fell in a gleaming ribbon over one shoulder to her waist.

"Nay, brave knight. I was not frightened. Were you?"

"Frightened? By a wisp of a maid? Do you think we are children?"

"I thought perhaps you would fear the Beltane Eve, as many do."

Christ above, but she was bold to taunt him with a subtle, feline smile and sly words. "I fear nothing," he said shortly.

"Is that so? Courage is always needed in these fearsome times." She took a step to one side, scattering shreds of mist that curled up around her like smoke. The mocking smile still played at the corners of her mouth.

Provoked, he said, "Times would be fearsome indeed, if the king's knights were to fear a simple maiden in the midst of the road."

The maid paused. Her gaze was eloquent, and rich with scorn. "Yea, English knights are valorous indeed, as courageous as the king is said to be. Yet I've heard that Richard slaughters children."

Rhys swung his shield over his shoulder again. A sharp ray of sunlight caught the metallic edge and flashed into his eyes. Blinking, he looked back at her. He could hardly deny it when it was true, but it didn't sweeten his temper to be reminded of it. "Are you Richard's enemy?"

The air grew radiantly bright. A thin shaft of light speared the gloom to fall directly on the maid's face. She waved an imperious hand, and the sunlight shifted from her eyes as if commanded away.

"Mea culpa, mea culpa, mea maxima culpa," Brian choked out, striking his chest with a mailed fist, and Rhys turned to give him a quelling glance.

When he turned back, the maid had faded into the shade of an ancient hawthorn; snow-white flower petals trembled delicately. Shadows darkened, obscuring all but her voice. "I am no man's enemy. And I fear no man."

Rhys blinked again, and the dwindling sunlight disappeared with a startling swiftness, as if an oil lamp had been doused. Staring into the black void, his first instinct was to call her back. "Demoiselle—come here. You should not be alone in the night."

Faint laughter drifted back on a sudden gust of wind. The sweet scent of hawthorn blended with a vaguely familiar, intriguing fragrance. In a trice, Rhys dismounted to follow her. His spurs chinked softly as he strode toward the trees.

Despite his fear, Brian flung himself from his horse, catching up to Rhys to tug frantically at his mantle. "Nay,

Rhys—do not! If you follow her, she will take you into the faerie world and you will never escape."

Rhys shook his arm loose impatiently. "Don't be a fool, Brian."

But when he moved close to the line of trees into which the maid had disappeared, he saw no sign of her presence. No broken branch gave indication of her passage. Only the faintly familiar whiff of fragrance remained as a teasing reminder. He jerked at a handful of hawthorn flowers, and swore softly when a barb found its way through the metal links of his gauntlets to prick him. No one could just disappear like that, like—like mist.

Brian nudged close to him, his voice rough with fear. "I cannot say if the maid was elf or faerie, but whatever, she has frightening powers."

"Do you think she summoned the dark?" Rhys mocked to hide his own misgivings. "She's only a simple maiden warning us of danger ahead. If she has any sense, she's wise enough not to become too friendly with roaming knights."

"Still, I cannot like this," Brian muttered. Rhys fell silent. There was no point in arguing deeply held superstitions. Pointing out to Brian now that dark oft came abruptly in the deep forests would do nothing to abate his belief that the maid had summoned the night. Nay, it would be a waste of breath even to attempt it.

The maid certainly wasn't a faerie. But who was she? If she was from the village they had left, she was too far from home and safety. No young maiden should be alone in the forest, day or night. But was she alone? She could be a ruse, a distraction, while villains lay in the trees ahead to fall upon them. Mercenaries could always set upon them, for the forests were thick with thieves on the roads leading to Wales.

Yet it was not a mortal enemy his men feared. . . .

Just a glance at their strained faces and wide eyes was enough to convince him they would be worthless the rest of the night. It would take a miracle to put them at ease— or more magic to counter what they feared.

He managed a tight smile. "There's a clearing not far

behind. We'll halt and light a *coelcerth* for the Beltane Eve."

Some of the Welsh soldiers nodded in relief. Rhys hoped it worked. A ritual bonfire to chase away the demons should restore their courage, so that the morrow would find the men free of the numbing fear that seemed to grip them now. When they returned to the clearing, the sounds of making camp lent a reassuring normalcy to the night. Welshmen readied themselves to gather the sticks from nine different kinds of trees to perform their ceremony, removing all metal from their bodies, including mail and swords.

Rhys looked down. He still held his naked sword. Slowly, he sheathed it. This sword had been used on the field of battle at Acre, and was forged of the finest steel, with a hilt of carved copper and bronze. He had captured it while on the Crusades with Richard, and it had served him well.

He thought of those distant, sun-drenched lands where towering stone fortresses stood stark against barren hills. It hit him then, as he stared into the enveloping darkness, that the intriguing fragrance he had detected was Turkish jasmine.

"That was foolish," Elspeth said sourly.

Sasha flushed with indignation. Her chin came up instinctively as she caught Elspeth's unspoken words *Reckless—and proud as Lucifer's own daughter . . .*

Ignoring the thought and addressing the spoken reprimand, Sasha said, "What, to warn the knights of the bridge? Nay, 'twas only kindness."

"They could have killed you. I've noticed no kindness from wandering knights to solitary maidens." Elspeth shook her head. A long shadow wavered on the cave wall. "Your Gift won't protect you from folly. It was foolish."

Sasha didn't want to admit how unsettled the encounter had left her. She managed a careless shrug as she seated herself before the fire and held her hands out to warm them. She was still shaking with reaction. Faintly amazed at her own daring, she'd not expected to have such an effect on the knights. She couldn't say she was sorry for frightening them, but she had expected the full use of her Gift to learn how best to approach the tall, lean knight who was their leader.

Instead, she'd encountered only a brilliant silence when she bent her talent toward the knight. No identity, unspoken words, or images had come to her when bid, only that bright, brittle band of silence. Alarmed, she'd turned her talent to the two-score men ranging behind the blond giant. Jumbled impressions couched in foreign languages had come from the armed men with him, restoring a shaky faith in her Gift. It was not gone, only powerless with this one man. She'd found the lack bewildering, then frightening.

Why couldn't she read his thoughts? It had never happened to her before. So she'd stood staring up at him while mist coiled along the ground in annoying shreds, dampening her cloak and veiling the knight in gauzy streamers. And then, bright and swift as a bolt of lightning had come the illuminating explanation: He must be the answer to the prophecy.

Elspeth made a soft clucking sound in the back of her throat, and Sasha looked up. Firelight danced over craggy walls and ceiling. Tucked beneath a shelf of rock and heavy brush not far from the road, the cave was well hidden and not easily seen, a perfect spot for travelers seeking safe shelter for a night. The low roof grew higher toward the back, and a bone-deep chill emanated from the rock walls. She also felt the chill of Elspeth's disapproval, and Sasha answered her at last.

"Not so foolish, if you will. My Gift has always given me the ability to see the true nature of men. The blond knight is not evil. I knew that when I spoke with him, even without using my Gift."

"Bah. He is arrogant and proud," Elspeth grumbled. "You should have fled, as did Biagio and I."

"Biagio fled with you?" she murmured. " 'Twould be the first time that brash youth abandoned danger."

Elspeth shrugged. "I did not say he came with me willingly. But at least *he* gave heed to my warnings. If those men had taken you . . ."

She let her voice fade, but Sasha did not need to hear thoughts or spoken words to know what she meant. Outlaw knights had little compunction about taking a woman against her will, even killing her. Richard was on his Crusades, and all of England had been left in the hands of his brother Prince John. With a villain as their ruler, villains roamed freely.

"Where is Biagio now?" she asked to avoid more censure from Elspeth. "We must re-pack the cart for the morrow."

"He went back to look for you."

Elspeth turned her head, but Sasha intercepted a brief mental vision of Biagio's face, contorted and angry, his words sharp. *Dio—I am going back . . . I will find her . . . should not have left . . .* Then Elspeth firmly focused on the leaping flames of the fire, and her mental images of Biagio disappeared to be replaced by a resolute study of the flames.

Sasha's cheeks puffed out in a sigh. Elspeth and Biagio worried unduly. But she couldn't change that. And in truth, there was often reason for apprehension. "I hope Biagio is careful," was all she said.

Biagio could take care of himself well enough. The young Italian seemed to have a multitude of talents, none of them fully developed, some of them irritating, but all accompanied by a strong sense of self-preservation. He was reckless and insolent, and though she would never have admitted it to him for fear his head would swell with conceit, she blessed the day he had joined them. And she was infinitely grateful that he had not interfered in the weald.

She thought again of the knight who had resented her warning. Having newly come from the ruined bridge, they'd had only enough time to hide in the trees upon first sighting the approaching knights, peering out at them through thorny branches. The men made no effort to be quiet, and Sasha found herself greatly amused by the man named Rhys's disbelief in superstitions. His arrogant denials had prompted her to mischief, to tweak him a little. It was easy for her to frighten their horses. And it had been worth it to see Richard's stalwart knights struggle with uncontrollable mounts, swearing and praying and sweating. She'd not been able to contain her laughter. There was a deep-seated belief in the world of elves and faeries in all men, whether they wished to acknowledge it or not.

But then the leader had shifted his shield and she'd glimpsed a mythical beast on the hammered metal surface. The griffyn—it was the sign she had sought.

Half-closing her eyes, Sasha gazed into the leaping flames. She'd not expected the answer to the prophecy to be so young. She'd envisioned a grizzled warrior with battle scars aplenty, savage and impressive, bellowing threats and even defying the heavens. But not this, not a man who looked more like a princely knight in a chansons de geste than a fierce fighter. She didn't want a romantic hero. She wanted a proficient warrior. That was what it would take to succeed.

Elspeth was right. It had been very foolish to stand in the midst of the forest road gazing up at an angry knight and gaping like a lackwit, but she'd been so startled by the lack of her Gift that she couldn't react. And then she'd seen the emblem he wore, and really looked at him. That had almost been her undoing. He could have been Apollo stepped down from the sun—as blinding, blond and beautiful as the Greek god. No helmet hid his bright hair or clean-shaven features, and she'd found herself staring at him as if struck dumb, thinking that he couldn't be the man for whom she'd searched so long.

But perhaps he was. . . .

There was character in his noble visage, in high cheekbones not at all marred by the scar curving from one temple, integrity in the cool gray eyes beneath a slash of dark brows, strength in the hard, arrogant set of his jaw. The very air had seemed to shimmer, as it did in the midst of a summer storm, when lightning charged the air . . . Yea, perhaps he was the man she'd been promised, the champion who would fulfill the prophecy . . .

Sasha.

Drifting to her through leaping flame and smoke, the unspoken word had all the raw power of a scream. Sasha looked up from the fire, reluctantly meeting Elspeth's eyes. As usual, she knew what the older woman was thinking. She slowly shook her head, and the tiny bells sewn into the lining of her cloak tinkled lightly.

"Elspeth, I must confess. His mind is closed to me. But this is the one—I'm certain that he is the man of the prophecy."

Elspeth stared at her. A frail hand moved up to her throat with a small flutter. "The prophecy . . . child, child, you were only eight years old when Rina told you of it. She was just a crazy Russian Gypsy. Who could know if this prophecy is true?"

"It's true. Nothing else makes sense." She drew in a deep breath. "It has to be true. I have searched so long for my champion, and now he is come."

Elspeth moaned. "Nay, Sasha, he's a rogue knight. He cannot be the one. You said yourself his mind is closed to you. It must be a mistake. We shall yet find the one who was promised. Perhaps when we get to my village—"

"It's this one. I'm certain of it. Do not ask me how I know. It's a feeling . . . think of the prophecy, the chance meeting with a fierce knight who is half eagle, half lion."

"How can you be so certain it's this one?" Elspeth's veined hands shook as she held them out. "Your Gift cannot foretell the future—"

"You didn't see his crest before you fled." Sasha's eyes began to burn, and she closed them against the smoke and doubt. "He wore the sign of the griffyn on his shield and surcoat. It was the half eagle, half lion that has haunted my dreams since I was only a child. 'Tis he, I know it. I cannot be wrong—"

"Because he wears the griffyn? Perchance, it's only his overlord's colors he wears, and not his."

"That's a possibility, of course, but it doesn't matter. He wears the sign. This is the one. I feel it, Elspeth."

"Holy Mary, child." Her voice quavered. "What if

you're wrong? You know your Gift is truly useful, but it cannot save you from disaster."

"Yea, I know that well. Too well. There are times this Gift is a curse, though it's often helped me learn truths others cannot see. He must be the one, Elspeth, he must— or I would be able to see in his mind as I can all others. He's too strong for me to penetrate the wall of light around him, too powerful for my Gift." She opened her eyes. "I intend to ask him to help us."

"Aiee! Child, you frighten me. Have you no regard for your own safety?" Elspeth rocked back and forth, her arms crossed over her bony chest in a gesture of grief. "I fear for you if you deal with rogue knights. They're evil men, with no regard for others, devouring all in their paths. If it's meant to be, it will happen. Do not ask him, I beg of you."

"But this knight is different." She searched for the words to explain herself, to make Elspeth understand. "When I look at him, I *see* a griffyn. We need such a fabled beast, need a man with the strength of a lion and the fierce courage of an eagle. Take heart. He's the knight that was promised, and he'll help us. I know he will."

Elspeth subsided, but the discussion was not ended. Sasha knew better. In truth, she had misgivings of her own. What if Elspeth was right? What if she'd made a mistake? But even if she had, wasn't anything better than what yawned before her—living out her years in a remote English village so far from everything? In a moment of despair and weakness she had yielded to Elspeth's pleas, and now they were so close to the village where Elspeth had been born, so close to the end of their long journey across most of Europe and all of England. Years of wandering, from gilded palaces to burning desert sands, over towering mountain heights and down into valleys beautiful enough to hurt the eyes, would soon be over. It hadn't all been wonderful. There had been terrifying times, times when she was certain they would be killed and their bodies left in a desolate wilderness, but they'd survived. She had done what she must—donned disguises, foretold futures at country fairs, even danced with a bear once on frozen tundra. She'd perched atop the bare backs of racing horses and won the admiration of a French count—the most dangerous kind of attention for a maiden, and one that had sent them scurrying from the chateau in midnight hours. Yea, she had not spent the past thirteen years idly.

But for what? If she gave up now, what would have been the purpose of surviving when those she loved had not?

"Remember," Elspeth said softly, coming to stand in front of the fire, "that you are a princess. Men oft grow greedy, or swollen with the lust for power. Do not trust too readily, child."

Sasha's mouth twisted wryly. "A princess without a throne or a country, hunted by those who would slay me for an accident of birth. I have riches but not enough to buy an army, royal blood but no title. Not even the name I use is my own. No, you don't have to remind me. It would be impossible to forget who I am. Or who I once was. . . ."

Those days were gone, vanished in the uprising of fierce men who had swept over her father's land, seizing the white-washed towers and minarets, slaying all those in their path. Her mother, the fair English rose renowned for beauty and wisdom, had been slain as well. Dark days, dark memories . . . The inherited Gift, passed from mother to daughter, had not been enough to save Elfreda from death. It had only allowed her to see her daughter and maidservant safely away, forfeiting her life to ensure theirs. That was the ultimate gift, the ultimate sacrifice, and it had been for love of her child. No, she would not allow that sacrifice to be in vain, not allow the murderer of her parents to go unpunished. And she would take back that which was hers.

Al-Hamin would not be allowed to keep what he'd stolen, neither would he succeed in annihilating all of Ben-Al Farouk's heirs, for she was still alive, the last one. And if her enemies knew it, she would die as well.

Rising, Sasha removed her cloak, laying aside the useful garment. It was royal purple on one side, green on the other, suiting whichever mood was on her, as changeable as she needed it to be. She moved to a bundle and rummaged inside until she found what she sought. Then she returned to the fire and knelt before it. After carefully inscribing a few words on a chip of sandalwood, she placed it in a brass censer.

"What do you wish for?" Elspeth asked.

Sasha looked up, pausing. "Only for an answer to the prophecy. What is meant to be, will come to us. I wish for another sign to prove that I am not wrong."

She lit the sandalwood with a burning twig; a fragrant coil of smoke rose to mingle with the scent of burning oak. She closed her eyes. Joy and peace, all the things that eluded her, were written on the sandalwood. The prophecy would come true. Opening her eyes, she stared intently at the brass censer, thinking hard of the wish rising with the smoke, repeating it over and over, until the wood was nothing but ash.

Eyes half-closed, she turned her head to stare into the fire. Among the leaping flames and curling smoke she saw a land of sunshine and warmth, peace and beauty—and the knight who could win it all back for her.

CHAPTER TWO

❧

Mist rose above the woodland pool in soft gray wisps, hovering in the windless chill of dawn. Rhys knelt at the edge, bare-chested and prickled with cold, one knee pressed into damp mud and fallen leaves. Avoiding tiny swimming creatures, he scooped up a handful of water to drink. It eased his parched throat and dripped down his chest to wet the waist of his chausses. He raked his dripping hand through his hair and stood up. It was quiet here in this small copse of trees. He was alone, none of his men brave enough to dare faeries, nor fool enough to admit their fear. These were the same men, of course, who thought little of fighting screaming infidels that were armed to the teeth and flinging Greek fire at them. Good soldiers and worthy men, but mindless idiots in the face of the unexplained. He grimaced. Brian was the worst of the lot when it came to believing tales of faeries and elves.

Rhys had outgrown those fears with his milk teeth. There was no room for intangible worries in a world too full of harsh realities. He'd learned that early enough. By

twenty, he'd been knighted. At twenty-nine, he was a bat-
tle-scarred veteran of several French wars—and of his
most recent exploit, the grandly named Crusades to con-
vert infidels who had no desire to abandon their pagan
beliefs. Not that it mattered. King Richard gave them little
chance to consider conversion, preferring the sanction of
the sword to that of the priest. But that was Richard. Magnificent, courageous, and as utterly ruthless a man as Rhys
had ever met.

Not that Richard was without a streak of mercy when
he wished to display it. When news of Griffyn ap Griffyd's
untimely death had finally reached Rhys in Jerusalem,
Richard had insisted he leave the Crusades and go home
to Wales. This act of kindness was only slightly tarnished
by Richard's expectation that Rhys would hold for England the Marcher lands that Rhys's father had be-
queathed him. Or—more important to an always
financially needy Richard—the coffers this inheritance
would bring. Crusades were expensive. Money was always
short. And so Rhys was summarily sent home with Richard's best wishes ringing in his ears. He fully expected
the king's tax agent to beat him to the gates of Glenlyon.

A distinct probability, as Rhys had been in England over
a month and was just now able to make his way toward
Wales. Immediately upon docking at Dover, he had been
handed a summons from Richard's brother John, a command he dared not ignore. After a frustrating fortnight
waiting in John's antechamber and hurling silent oaths at
a closed door, Rhys was finally granted an audience.

Ignoring the new lord of Glenlyon's request to be allowed to make haste for Wales, John had soothed Rhys's
concerns with a reminder that Glenlyon's steward held the
keep for him and was no doubt equal to the task—then
sent him on an errand in the opposite direction. A messenger had caught up with Rhys on the way back from
completing the task. The familiar signet of Glenlyon sealed
the letter from his father's steward. Written in Owain's
shaky scrawl, the letter directed Rhys to go to the church
in Coventry and wait for the messenger he would send to
meet him on the morning after May Day. Though terse,

the rest of Owain's message was clear—Rhys had enemies who threatened Glenlyon.

An understatement. The rebellion that had seen his father killed, had also claimed two older brothers, leaving Rhys as heir. Never had he thought he would return; now all was changed. He could finally return to Wales after twenty-one bitter years away, but it was as lord of Glenlyon.

Glenlyon . . . Lost by treachery. Gained by death. A trick, an illusion, a sleight of hand, and it was his after all these dark years . . . as if magic.

Rhys thought again of the maiden who had warned them of danger and then faded into the night like a shadow. She was not English. But neither was she French, though she spoke the tongue well. Too well, with insolence and mockery. If he saw her again . . .

A breeze sprang up, and he reached for the linen undertunic he wore beneath his leather gambeson. There were red welts on his body where the metal rubbed against bare skin even through leather and linen. He'd been so long in his armor that it had seemed grown to his skin when he peeled it away to wash. Even now, the cuts and abrasions pricked him more than the cold.

Rising to his feet, he hesitated, loathe to don the heavy mail again. This brief respite was sweet and welcome. Peaceful. An eddy of wind lifted a tattered shred of mist and whirled it across the water's surface. There was a distant, muted sound, like that of church bells echoing across a valley. Rhys lifted his head to listen, and the hair on the back of his neck prickled a warning that he was not alone.

"Who is there?" he asked sharply in French, then English. There was no answer, only the faint whisper of the wind through the tree branches overhead. He looked around, reaching for his sword.

A high, rocky ledge glowered across from the pond, half-hidden by hawthorn bushes and thick-trunked oaks. Ancient, painted men had extolled the deity of oaks at one time, preaching that the trees had souls. There was a time he'd thought it true, for oft could he swear primeval faces peered at him from twisted limbs and rough-barked trunks.

Quickly, he donned his linen tunic, cursing the clumsiness of his cold-numbed fingers. His sword clanked softly against a lightning-blasted stump when he lifted it. Again, he had the inescapable feeling that he was not alone. In a casual gesture meant to be a warning, he hefted the sword and gave a few expansive swings at an imaginary foe. Deadly light glittered along the length of the blade.

"Brave warrior," came a soft, mocking voice in perfect French, "do you fight the wind?"

Rhys recognized the accent at once. It belonged to the maid who had warned them of the bridge's ruin. He straightened swiftly, eyes searching for her in the mist-tricked wood.

"Show yourself, good lady, so I may thank you for the warning."

There was a slight rustle of leaves and bushes at one side, but no sign of her. Only her voice, soft and mocking. "Did you trust my warning, or did you go to see the bridge for yourself?"

"Neither. I sent a man to verify its condition." He paused. "In the near-dark we likely would have come to grief if not for your warning."

Silence fell, save for the whisper of leaves and wind. Rhys narrowed his eyes at the leafy gloom and waited. When she spoke again, it was farther from where he'd first thought her, but much closer to him. He turned slightly toward the sound of her voice.

"Come out where I can see you, or do you intend to dismiss the sun again?" He made a show of peering up at the early light streaming through tree branches. "No. It still shines. Show yourself."

"I go where I wish. And it amused me to dismiss the sunlight. It might not be so amusing on this day."

"Ah, an easy explanation to deceive only fools. Why are you afraid?"

"If I recall,'twas not me bleating prayers and shaking at shadows. Why would you think I'm afraid?"

"If you weren't, you would show yourself instead of hiding behind trees like a child or a wood sprite."

Laughter sounded softly. He caught a teasing hint of fragrance again: jasmine. It drifted to him on a gentle breeze, seeming to surround him.

"I fear no man," came the formless reply, and he remembered that she'd said the same words the night before.

"No? Yet you quiver in the brush like a hare. Am I so grim a knight that you fear to come too near?" Deliberately, hoping to coax her from hiding, he stabbed the tip of his sword into the damp ground between his splayed feet. The hilt swung gently back and forth.

Silence fell again, then branches rustled and leaves shivered. For a moment, Rhys could not see her, so perfectly did she blend into the green leaves around her. Then she was visible, a graceful glide across fallen leaves and limbs, jasmine and beauty and mystery approaching with a smile.

He'd not forgotten how lovely she was. High cheekbones accented wide black eyes lined by even blacker lashes, and her dusky skin had the rich texture of a dark rose. Arrogance teased the curve of her lips, softened by a slight dimple at one corner. This time, he registered trivial details: Her garb was simple. The long gown and mantle were of finely woven wool, yet without elegant fur trimming the edges. No embroidery adorned the deep green wool, nor gold brooches held the mantle closed.

Though her garments were worn and frayed, her demeanor was that of a queen as she approached with regal solemnity. No highborn lady perhaps, but neither was she a milkmaid.

When she paused beneath the prickly branches of a hawthorn, a ray of sunlight broke through the leaves and pierced the mist to lend a luminescent flush to her face. Rhys moved forward. He held out his palm with all the practiced gallantry of a knight at court, bowing over her hand when she placed it in his. Long, slender fingers trembled slightly in his grasp, soft, fine-boned, and delicate. Yea, a burgher's daughter wandering the wood with seductive eyes . . . Rhys looked up at her and smiled.

Her mouth curved in response. There was a glow in her

night-dark eyes—moonlight behind clouds, soft, shadowed, and promising. A light breeze teased a dark skein
of her hair. The scent of jasmine was heady, and he
dragged in another deep breath.

Her head tilted to one side, eyes sweeping him with a
long, considering gaze. "Dread knight, do you wish to
dance?"

Amused, he looked around them, then back at her.
"Dance? Here?"

"Aye. 'Tis May Day, a time of feasting and celebration.
We have whitethorn as decoration, the wind in the trees
for flutes, and the rush of water for a harp. You can dance,
can you not?"

"I learned to dance when still a squire," he replied,
"though 'twas in great halls, and not a weald."

"Then you may be a worthy partner." She held out her
other hand. Her gaze was challenging, her smile alluring.

Brian would have declared him moon-mad, and indeed,
he wasn't too sure of his sanity at that moment. But the
sun was shining, the wind soft through the trees, and there
was a fey quality about the maid that was elusive and
powerful and heady. Feeling suddenly reckless and much
younger than his years, he smiled. Then he took both her
hands and swung her around, his feet finding the rhythm
of a silent dance. She laughed softly. Delicate bells tinkled
lightly in the wind.

Dew wet his feet, glistening on his boots with a silvery
sheen. The hem of the lady's cloak grew damp, dragging
through grass to leave a darker trail where the morning
sun had not burned away the night's dewy residue. He lost
track of time as they danced, making up steps as they
went, playing children's games, careless of anything but
the pleasure of the day and laughter.

Sunlight warmed his face, and whitethorn scented the
air. Soft, balmy days had come to England, a time when
men's thoughts turned to other pursuits than war. Jésu, it
had been months since he'd taken time to linger with a
woman, and never with one as lovely as this. She was intoxicating, teasing, drawing close to him, then stepping
lightly away when he tried to hold her, shy and alluring

at the same time. Sly vixen. Sweet temptress. Diana the huntress and Venus the goddess of love and beauty in one small form.

Rhys drew her closer, sliding an arm around her waist, pressing his body against hers. She was slender but firm, definitely not a mist-maid as Brian had gloomily warned. Ah, she was flesh and blood, warm in his arms, her mouth soft, a contrast of fire and ice with heated skin and cool glances. She sparked a fire that threatened to engulf him.

Breathless, laughing, with limbs grown weary from their exertions, they stopped at last beneath a tree. Her head tilted back against the trunk, laughter parting her lips. Rhys bent to kiss her. His hand moved behind her head, fingers tangled in her hair to hold her still. His mouth hovered over hers, waiting. Her breath came swiftly, rising and falling with rapid movements that lifted her breasts. His grip tightened in her hair, fingers sliding through silken strands in a leisurely glide. She didn't draw away, and his hand slid low to rest on the thrust of slender hip cushioned by her bulky cloak.

Impatient with this barrier between them, he pulled it aside, slid his hand beneath the folds of wool. His palm caressed the slender span of rib cage and waist, then moved to the small of her back. With his mouth still barely grazing her parted lips, he pulled her fiercely forward, an abrupt motion that brought her hard into the angle of his thighs and hip. Without his mail and her voluminous cloak, he could feel the heat of her thighs against him, and his physical response was instant.

But then she turned, a graceful twist that evolved into a retreat, and he let her go. His hand was still beneath the cloak, holding a wad of green and purple wool in his fist. He smiled slightly. She hesitated, looking up at him, and he saw the indecision in her eyes and reached out for her again, slowly drawing her back into his embrace.

"Sweet flower," he whispered, and buried his face in the curve of her neck to drink deeply of her perfumed hair; she shivered. The blood pounded in his ears, the beat rapid and loud, drowning out any lingering qualms he might have.

Rhys stepped back to draw her with him down into the grass beneath the tree. With a few deft motions, he loosened her cloak and spread it for them, then eased her down to the wool and grass cushion. She sat gracefully, her hand still clinging to his arm, a tentative smile on her lips.

Stretching out beside her, he kissed her softly. She didn't protest or move away, and he drew one hand down her side, his fingertips sliding over her gown and curves to come to rest on the swell of her hip. Still kissing her, he urged her down with firm pressure, until she lay beside him. He lifted his head, regarding her for a long moment. She looked up at him with a gleaming promise in her eyes. He wound a long strand of her hair around his finger, then released it, brushing the tips of dark hair against the dewy slope of her cheek.

Neither of them spoke. It would ruin the spell, break the bonds of enchantment that held them, set the stars out of alignment and shatter the heavens—he kissed her again, mouth tracing the outline of her lips, his tongue coaxing them apart to allow entry.

Her lips parted for him. At the touch of his tongue to hers, she made a small sound in the back of her throat, one of those soft animal noises that was so inherently female, and so seductive. His desire grew hot and sharp, nudging him hard, and he reached down to loosen the laces to his chausses. He managed it with one hand, easing the heavy burden, shuddering at the sensual slide of her so close to him. Still kissing her, he spread his palm over the sweet curve of her breast. She drew in a sharp breath but didn't try to move his hand. Encouraged, Rhys dragged his thumb over the small bud he could feel through the wool. It grew harder beneath his touch, a beckoning lure that took his fingers to the neckline of her tunic.

She caught his hand, and he looked up at her flushed face. Her lips were slightly parted and her breath was erratic and swift. A pulse beat wildly in the hollow of her throat.

"Nay," she whispered, shattering the spell, tilting the

world, scattering his thoughts so he could only stare at her, "it's not right that we should—"

His throat was thick, and he cleared it to mutter hoarsely, "I think it well meet, sweet maid. You are the fairest flower I've yet seen."

A smile trembled on her lips, but her grip didn't relax on his hand. "And you, dread knight," she said softly, "are the most valiant and courteous of men." As his head lowered toward her, she added, "A man who would never forswear an oath of chivalry."

Unfair, to remind him of his knight's oath at a time like this. Discouragement cooled only a small bit of his ardor. It was a game, after all, such as those played by the sly ladies at court. They teased and tempted, feigned reluctance until he had met whatever whim they sought to appease before their inevitable yielding. But he was no novice at love play. Years of experience had taught him to play the game too, and he knew that persistence often gained a man great rewards.

Smiling, he murmured, "I will do nothing that you don't want me to do, sweet maid."

"You are a gallant knight," she murmured, but Rhys barely heard her over the staccato beat of his heart and the effort it took to breathe steadily. It had been too long. Much too long. She was much fairer than any maid he'd seen since his return, and she was here and willing, even if wavering a bit. He had to be in Coventry on the morrow: anything could happen there, and he might not have another opportunity.

And she was truly soft and sweet, and would be well worth the extra effort. He curbed his desire with a brief struggle, and drew a hand idly along the curve of her cheek. His fingers drifted lightly over her mouth. The blood raged in his veins, and he clung tightly to his impatience, determined to overcome her resistance by slow and relentless persuasion. Caressing her, he pressed light kisses along her smooth brow. Then his mouth strayed to the curve of her ear, and he breathed softly until he felt her shudder. When her breath came in unsteady gulps of air, he bent to take her lips again, sensing victory near.

But he had done no more than press his lips to the dimple at the corner of her mouth when Rhys heard a voice calling his name, far away and insistent. He tried to ignore it, but the persistent sound grew too near. Halting, he looked up with a scowl at the interruption. It took a moment for his surroundings to come fully into focus, then he saw with some surprise that he was far from the wooded pool where he'd first met her. An alder sheltered them beneath its branches, and a small burn trickled merrily by, water splashing over the rocks. A grassy meadow sloped downward from the trees.

She shifted, then lay her fingers against his cheek; her eyes glowed softly when he glanced back down at her. "I must go," she murmured. "It grows late."

He caught her hand, holding it. "Nay, wait. 'Tis only Brian. I'll send him away."

She slowly withdrew her hand and rose to her feet, and he followed reluctantly. "I cannot . . ." She cast a glance over her shoulder as Brian's voice grew louder and nearer. Gathering her cloak around her, she took a step away from him, repeating, "I must go."

He grabbed her hand again, fingers digging into her tender skin with shameless urgency. "Wait. Tell me your name, and where you reside. We'll meet again once I send Brian away."

Her smile deepened as she removed her hand from his clasp and took a backward step. "Yea, we shall meet again."

He started to reach for her anew, determined not to let her go so easily, but Brian's voice made him pause. "Rhys!" came the strident call, followed by pained yowls that dwindled into rough curses directed at a clump of brambles.

Curse Brian. He glanced away and shouted impatiently that he would be there in a moment. When he turned back, the maid was gone. Jésu. She'd been there one moment, standing near the crowded branches of flowering hawthorns, but now was not to be seen. He looked around, dumbfounded and furious.

"Rhys," came Brian's voice again, sounding relieved,

and breathless as he crashed toward him through a rasp-
berry patch. "Where have you been all day?"

"All day?" Rhys dragged his gaze away from the spot
where the maid had last stood and spun to face his knight.
" 'Tis but early morn. What's the matter with you? Did
you not mark that I was occupied—?"

The snarled oath that accompanied this demand made
Brian swallow hard. "Yea, lord," he said, looking down,
"I marked it well, yet—"

"Yet you chose to ignore it." He shook his head irritably. "Now she has fled, and God only knows if I'll ever
see her again."

"She?" Brian looked up from plucking a thorn from his
arm, blinking rapidly. "You were with a woman, my
lord?"

"Did you not say you marked it well? By all the saints,
Brian, I begin to think you wine mazed."

"Nay, lord, I've been searching for you. We thought ill
had befallen when we couldn't find you."

Rhys jerked at the ties of his loosened chausses. Damn
the ache. "I went to bathe at the pond—" He broke off
suddenly and looked up. "My armor and helm. I must
have left them off, but I don't remember. . . ."

Brian was looking at him strangely, and Rhys narrowed
his eyes. "Why do you look at me like that?"

"We found your armor and helmet by the pool earlier."
Brian swallowed heavily. " 'Tis near midday, and we de-
spaired of finding you . . . You've been with her, haven't
you? The Elf Queen?"

"I fully intend to check the wineskins when I return to
camp. I've a notion they will be much lighter than when I
left."

Catching his arm when he would have pushed past,
Brian said hoarsely, " 'Tis said that time is lost when one
dances with the faeries. Sometimes, men never come back
at all."

Rhys jerked away, angry at the unsettled ache inside
him. "Faerie? Are you entirely mad? More like a burgher's
daughter, is my guess." He drew in a deep breath when
Brian's face flushed as red as his hair, and said calmly,

"Time may have passed more swiftly than I thought, but
would you forget that prattle about elves and faerie
queens? We—" He broke off, appalled that he had been
about to admit they had danced like children at a May
festival. Brian would again leap to the conclusion that he'd
been dancing with faeries. He shook his head. "I was with
a maid until you frightened her away, though I confess I
don't know how she fled so quickly."

Brian's gaze had moved past Rhys to the thick branches
of a hawthorn, then riveted on a nearby copse of trees. He
made a strangled sound and croaked, "Look, the trees!
Oak, Ash, and Thorn—'tis the faerie triad. Your maid is
a witch who has turned herself into a hawthorn to escape."

"Devil take you, Brian. Make up your mind. Is she witch
or faerie?" He gave an impatient motion of one hand.
"You confuse your superstitions too freely, not that it matters now. She's gone, and it may be for the best. We'll
have to ride swiftly for Coventry to make up the time I've
wasted here. A hard ride should cure any more talk of
elves. Do you see dragons behind every bush, and goblins
under all the bridges?"

Brian didn't reply, but Rhys was well aware of his fear
and disapproval. It didn't help to find that time had, indeed, passed while he was dancing in the glen. Midday
sun shone brightly when they reached camp, and his men
looked at him strangely, as if fearing that he bore the taint
of the faerie world.

Even his Welsh squire, steadfast Morgan, who had been
with him since he first left Wales, looked at him askance
as he held out Rhys's missing mail and sword. This disapproval he deserved. It was bad enough to be thought in
dalliance with a faerie, but for a seasoned knight to abandon his mail and sword without a thought for his own
safety bordered on idiocy.

"Bring my horse," he said as he took his armor and
sword from Morgan. "We ride for Coventry."

Morgan slanted a glance toward the sun in the noon sky
but wisely did not offer any comment beyond a murmured
"*Ydi*, m'lord."

Rhys twisted his mouth into a grim smile. Brian silently aided him in donning his mail, his very silence as telling as any accusation. Tension simmered. Rhys buckled on his sword as Morgan brought up his mount. He'd show them he was untouched by anything but a determination to ride hard. He was to meet Owain's messenger in Coventry, and he'd already delayed much too long.

Mounting the restless stallion, he swung the horse around and spurred him forward. Dirt clods flew from Turk's hooves in spattering arcs. Hoof-beats sounded like thunder. He could hear his men struggle to keep up with the relentless pace he set. A pace that did much to silence his men, but nothing to ease the aching need the maid had sparked in him.

"So," Elspeth said as she stuffed clothing into a leather bag, "you danced with him. Is that all?"

A flush heated her cheeks before Sasha could avoid Elspeth's quick stare. It seemed to her that the old woman had the Gift as well, for she guessed Sasha's thoughts and deeds much too often for comfort.

"Nay," Sasha said, "it's not quite all." She met Biagio's sudden glance of interest with a lifted brow. "We . . . kissed."

"Oh no, not another like the French troubadour." He groaned in disgust. "Shall I just slit the knight's throat now and save us the pain of having to listen to his sighs and moans of everlasting love?"

She smiled sweetly. "If you think you can, Biagio."

Sasha ignored his muffled curse. A thin ribbon of smoke curled up from the fire in the cave floor. Bundles were packed, and the donkey brayed softly in the sudden silence. She looked back at Elspeth.

Her lips were pressed into a taut line. "So you kissed, did you? And you a chaste maid—"

"By my own choice, you might recall. If I had wanted to lose my maidenhead, I'd have done so by now. It's not as if I haven't had offers." Biagio snorted, and she shot him a dark glance. "I've seen nothing to recommend a

wrestle in the hay or clumsy gropings in the dark, whether
prince or peasant. It seems a sordid business to me, and
not worth my trouble."

Elspeth's lips pursed. "That's not the point. For once, I
agree with Biagio. Your wonderful champion is but a
hedge knight, and more likely to end up a nuisance than
a worker of miracles."

"A few kisses are not likely to turn him into Tristan,"
she said tartly. "Though if I knew of a love potion guar-
anteed to make a knight fall at my feet, I'd try it on him.
And not for the reason you might think."

It was a wonder the ground didn't open up and swallow
her for telling such a lie. Not that she truly wanted him
to fall in love with her, but it would make it much easier
to solicit his aid if he wanted more from her than just a
tussle on the ground. Worse, she didn't dare admit just
how arousing she'd found the tussle on the ground.

Elspeth gave her another hard look. "I hope you don't
think a few chaste kisses are enough to lure him to a war."

"Are you suggesting I yield more?" Sasha smiled at her
mutters of outrage. "Oh, Elspeth, you must know I'll be
cautious. I want nothing more from him than the use of
his sword and an army."

"Oh aye," Biagio muttered, "only an army. If you think
the two score men I saw quaking in the trees at the mere
mention of faeries can win back your land and avenge
your wrongs, you dream."

"I didn't say I knew how he'd manage it, only that he
will. He's the promised knight, the fierce warrior of—"

"The prophecy," he finished for her, irritable and glaring. "I've only known you for five years, and I'm weary
of hearing about this famous prophecy. I quake to think
how Elspeth must feel."

"Nay," Elspeth said. " 'Tis beyond thought. But changing the course of the Nile would be easier than changing
Sasha's mind once she's determined to do something. I can
only hope that this time, it won't cause disaster."

Draping his lean body over a rock shelf, Biagio nodded.
"Yea,'tis a gloomy thought. Until now, I thought the worst

notion she's had was that we all masquerade as rope dancers for that Austrian duke, but this is—"

"It was a good idea," Sasha said coldly. "A brilliant idea. We would have been greatly rewarded—if you had followed simple instructions."

Looking pained, he straightened. "Simple? Flying from the musician's gallery of a great hall to swing over the heads of dining noblemen is simple?"

"It would have worked. I've seen it done. There are gears and pulleys and a series of ropes, but one has to have the good sense to listen to how they're used. You didn't listen. It ruined everything."

"Say that to someone who hasn't fallen in the midst of a table of pies filled with live birds," he retorted. "The carnage was worse than the sacking of Rome. Blood, feathers, and birds everywhere, darting about, pecking at me. . . . Most of the blood was mine, you know."

Studying his sulky expression, Sasha smiled. "The peak of the evening. The duke was most entertained. He said he'd rarely laughed so heartily. And the reward was adequate, considering the botch you'd made of it."

Biagio's rude comment was to be expected, and she didn't begrudge him his rebuttal. It was only fair.

Elspeth wouldn't look at her but continued stuffing linen into the leather bag without regard for Sasha's neat folding. Tension settled, lying like shrouds of smoke in the dank air of the cave. After a moment, Biagio sullenly withdrew to the front of the cavern to pack the small wooden cart with their belongings. Sasha waited.

Turning at last, Elspeth met her gaze. "How do you know this is the man? How do you know he can be trusted? I fear him. I fear for you."

She'd been expecting this. The only weapon she had was the truth. "I don't know for certain, Elspeth. I only know I must follow the knight to Coventry. Do you know where that is, perchance?"

A wave of dismay emanated from Elspeth. "Coventry. Twenty leagues from here . . ." Her eyes narrowed suddenly. *But much closer to . . .*

Sasha stared suspiciously when Elspeth suddenly began

to think of spring flowers and a wonderful invention she had once seen in Byzantium. She knew this trick. And she had no intention of being distracted with the memory of an amazing mechanical angel that blew a trumpet. Her eyes narrowed.

"What are you planning, Elspeth? You might as well tell me, for I'll learn of it swiftly enough when you're not so guarded."

"Forsooth, but you are a rude child at times. Haven't I tried to teach you that it's impolite to meddle in people's minds?" Elspeth smiled slightly. *If you are rude enough to listen to my thoughts, then hear this: If the knight refuses your request, you must go with me to my village, and we'll hear no more of the prophecy... Swear it, Sasha, for I am getting old and I must see you safe... Swear it this time, for my sake...*

There it was, the plea that she'd always feared would come. The end to it all, the forsaking of the prophecy. But Elspeth was getting older, with gray streaking the hair beneath her kerchief, lines of worry creasing her dear face, and a slower step. It would be cruel to continue dragging her from one place to another much longer, heartless to abandon her after all these years, even in her own village.

"If I cannot get the knight to agree," she said slowly, feeling as if each word was torturously pulled from her lips, "I will speak no more of the prophecy."

"And you'll stay with me in my village? Swear it, swear..."

Closing her eyes, Sasha nodded. "Yea, I swear it."

"Shall I offer Master Beakins more?" Elspeth murmured.

Sasha pulled up the hood to her cloak despite the warmth of sunshine on her face. She looked over at the tradesman who had just refused their offer and was demanding a much higher price. Beefy and grinning, he waited confidently.

Oafish peasant... yea, I can 'ardly wait ta tell Walter Pinchbeck 'ow I sold tha' crazy beastie for two crowns...

'is eyes'll fair drop outa 'is 'ead, they will . . . 'im wi' tha' nag 'e wants only a crown fer . . . aye, 'e'll be fit ta' bury . . .

Smiling, Sasha ran a light hand down the neck of the bay mare quivering by the fence post. "Nay. Beakins will take what we offer, and think himself shrewd for getting so much. Mention that Walter Pinchbeck has another horse much finer than this one for only a crown."

Elspeth returned to bargain with Beakins, speaking her native English fluently as she haggled with him. Half-listening, Sasha knew when Biagio approached, hearing the familiar cadence of his steps before he reached her.

Leaning on the fence post, he stared thoughtfully at the bay. "The collier said that Beakins is the kind of man 'twould sell you a white-oak cheese in place of a real one. He also said this horse is dangerous."

"Not dangerous, just misunderstood."

A frown creased Biagio's darkly handsome face. "Why do you want a horse when we have a placid beast like Socrates to draw our cart?"

"Because until now, I had not met this horse."

Biagio muttered something in Italian, shaking his head. Sasha laughed at the brief image that flashed through his mind. She couldn't blame him at times. But once she'd seen this mare, there was no other choice. She had to purchase the horse. Coventry was still several leagues away, and a broken cart axle was proving a frustrating delay. Now, she could ride on alone to find Rhys, though it would be difficult to escape Elspeth's close eye.

Murmuring softly to the quivering mare, she scratched between her ears. The nostrils flared open like pink blossoms. Sunlight glittered on the deep brown hide that had been oiled to make it gleam. Horses were easily drawn to her. She sensed their moods and could soothe them when agitated. And agitate them when necessary.

Elspeth returned in triumph, and Sasha eyed her with growing amusement. Her tall, bony frame was clad in a rough wool tunic with a hood, a leather jerkin, baggy hose, boots, and a wide belt. She looked for all the world like a freeman. Which was their intention. It was a masquerade they frequently employed as they traveled. Few tradesmen would bargain fairly with a youthful foreigner or a woman, but found it easy to haggle with a freeman. And it gave Elspeth such great satisfaction to best them.

"*Dieu merci*," Elspeth said wryly in French when she reached the fence, "the mention of Walter of Pinchbeck had a most rapid effect on Beakins's price. So, we have a horse to feed now, as well as the donkey."

Sasha laughed. "Beakins has a private feud with Master Pinchbeck, and must outdo him at everything. I hoped that would help." She stroked the animal's fine head, murmuring, "Beakins thinks 'twill kill us before we take her far. But I know better."

To the horse, she whispered in the secret language, "We shall call you Bayosha, and you will run like the wind."

Snorting nervously, Bayosha pranced at the end of a lead rope as Sasha led her out of the fenced yard, hooves dancing along the hard packed mud. Elspeth kept close to the donkey and cart and out of the way of Bayosha's hooves, which had earlier kicked a hole in the gate. The agitated horse was given a wide berth by the Wytham villagers, some laughing to themselves that Beakins was finally rid of the worthless animal.

Sasha ignored the jumble of half-formed thoughts whirling around her in a blend of rough English and occasional French. She focused her talent on the blank fear controlling the mare. This was nothing like the use of her Gift on people, for animals were guided by unformed impressions and vague images. There was no fear of death, for it was too abstract for the simple animal mind, but there was a very real fear of pain, for that was a familiar experience.

As she focused on the horse, she began to absorb some of its fear. She channeled it as she had learned to do long ago, letting it flow through her without affecting her.

"Beakins abused her," she told Elspeth when they reached the yard of the Boar's Head Inn at the north end of Wytham. "That's why she's so afraid."

Elspeth nodded, not surprised by this revelation. "Easily believed."

Relinquishing the horse into Biagio's custody with strict

instructions for his care, Sasha gave Bayosha a pat on her soft nose and followed Elspeth into the inn. The common room was smoky and dark, filled with a clash of conflicting emotions that she quickly blocked from her mind. They found a table near the rear of the room away from the worst of the smoke and noise, and sat upon hard wooden benches.

From across the table, Elspeth eyed her gravely. Sasha tucked her hands into the loose sleeves beneath her cloak and shrugged. Elspeth's opinion of her determined pursuit couldn't be helped. Seven days of torturously slow travel had been hard on all of them. Especially on her. What if Rhys had already left Coventry? How would she ever find him? It would be hard but not impossible. He was no hedge knight as Elspeth thought, for she had heard the man named Brian call him my lord. No hedge knight was a lord. Nay, he was much more, though he traveled simply, apparently not wanting his identity known. If not for the conversation overheard between Rhys and Brian— whose fevered brain had contained little but a blank fear of faeries—she wouldn't even have known they were traveling to Coventry. Mounted horsemen traveled swiftly. He could be anywhere by now.

Immersed in thought, Sasha looked up with a start when the innkeeper's daughter paused at their table. The maid's eyes briefly met hers, and unbidden, Sasha had a swift impression of a recent scene in the back room. Quickly, she looked down and let Elspeth order them a meal and some ale. When the maid departed, Sasha leaned across the table, a wicked smile tugging at her mouth. "Would you like to know what yon frowsy kitchen wench was doing not a long time past?"

Lips twitching, Elspeth said, "From the looks of her untied bodice laces, one does not need a special gift to know she's made close acquaintance with a young man recently."

Sasha laughed. "The miller's son. Flour was everywhere."

"Sasha." Elspeth pressed her lips tightly together in a reasonable mimicry of disapproval, but a slight quiver at the corners of her mouth betrayed her amusement. Sasha wiggled her eyebrows, and Elspeth hid her laughter behind the bony curve of a hand. Neither of them could look at the maid when she returned with a tray of boiled beef and trenchers of bread.

The beef was stringy, the trenchers of bread hard enough to use as paving stones, and Sasha lost interest in the meal rather quickly. Did the rural English ever prepare food with any method but boiling water, or with a blazing fire that charred meat on the outside and left it dripping pink inside? If so, she hadn't yet found an inn that employed such a method.

"Are you going to eat that turnip?" Elspeth asked, pointing with the tip of her knife to Sasha's trencher. Sasha shook her head, pushing it toward Elspeth.

"You're welcome to it. I'm not very hungry."

"If you intend to find that hedge knight," Elspeth said shortly, "you'd best keep up your strength."

"His name is Rhys," she said absently. "And I'm certain he's more than a hedge knight."

"Rhys," Elspeth repeated with a snort. "If he's more than a hedge knight, he won't be eager to do your bidding, my girl. You'd best look elsewhere for your champion."

She frowned. That might be true. A lord with lands would be none too eager to leave England. Unless she could convince him 'twas for as grand a quest as the Crusades. That was possible.

Rhys . . . Just his name conjured up images: a sunlit glen, and eyes a smoky gray, gazing at her with frustrated desire. It had been easy to read him, even without the aid of her Gift. He'd wanted much more than a few kisses beneath an alder tree.

She was just glad that Elspeth couldn't read minds. There would be more than merely a severe tongue-lashing were she to know how enticing those few kisses had been. It was irritating, the way she found herself thinking about the sunlight in his bright hair, or his high, stark cheekbones and square jaw. Infuriating to recall the pale etch of the scar that curved from his left temple along the slash of cheekbone, and eyes that were fringed with such thick, dark lashes they were almost feminine. And the smile that slanted his hard mouth . . .

They were almost through with their meal when Sasha felt the touch of a familiar name, flicking across her dreaming mind like the sting of a carter's whip. *Rhys* . . . She glanced up sharply, and when the door swung open, wasn't surprised to see flame-haired Brian.

The mail-clad knight who had first sensed her presence in the weald ducked through the doorway and strode into the room, then jerked to a sudden halt. His head turned, and he reached up to drag away his helmet as he surveyed the common room with a slow, narrowed gaze. Sasha bent her head, unwilling to face him. He feared her. That fear could be dangerous, even more so than open hate.

When Elspeth made a soft, choked sound, Sasha lifted her head. Recognition flashed through the old woman's eyes, and she darted a quick glance at Sasha to see if she had sensed it. *Rogue knights*, was Elspeth's foremost thought. *Do not let them see us.*

Ignoring that, Sasha opened her Gift to Brian. If Rhys was nearby, Brian would reveal his leader's presence without knowing it. Yet the words that came to her were strange and unfamiliar, a language she didn't know. A brief image flickered, but it was of dark trees and shadows and a robed figure that she knew to be herself. That image was quickly followed by a wrenching fear and rapid visions of flight, churning hooves and urgency, before his thoughts swung back to the common room with dizzying speed to focus on heightened awareness and distrust. Did Brian have the perception to divine her presence? He must have some sort of sensitivity, or he would not be scanning the room for her now.

Sasha turned deliberately so that her profile would be visible. A rush of fear filled Brian, and his heavy boots scuffed across the inn floor as he bolted for the door. Words in the unfamiliar language assaulted her, rushed and tumbling and afraid, punctuated by Rhys's name. Then the door banged shut, and she looked up to see that he was gone.

Is it the rogue knight from the weald? Elspeth's hands

were knotted tightly around the hilt of her eating knife. Sasha nodded.

Yea, Rhys was close by, and his knight had gone to warn him. Dismay filled her. Would Red Brian stop him from coming in? She surged up from the bench and ran to the shuttered window, opening it to peer out. Where was he? A dusty band of mounted and dismounted knights milled in the courtyard. Then she saw Brian move to a familiar horse, and Rhys straightened from examining the great hooves to talk to him. After a moment, he glanced toward the inn and she quickly closed the shutter before he saw her peering out at him like a common goose maid. Did he mean to come inside?

Saints above, what if he did? Her hair was windblown, she smelled like a horse, and why hadn't she worn a better gown?

Sasha, what are you doing, child? Where are you going . . . ?

As the door to the common room swung open, Sasha lifted her skirts in both hands and fled.

CHAPTER THREE

"**S**he's here, I tell you." Brian tugged at Rhys's arm with frantic motions. "The Elf Queen is close. Mount. Let's ride on."

Rhys hid his quick, keen flare of interest behind mockery. "Brian, did you see her, or just hear faerie bells again?"

When Brian hesitated, Rhys lifted a mocking brow at the emotions passing across his expressive face. "Nay, don't answer, for fear you'll perjure yourself. I'll see with my own eyes if the dangerous Elf Queen loiters inside the common room of an inn. Mayhap, she's sprinkling faerie dust in the ale, and should be stopped before we all turn into toads."

Thrusting Turk's reins into Brian's hand, Rhys brushed past his friend. A cloud passed over the sun, darkening the sky, and a brisk wind sprang up. He heard Brian's muttered prayer but ignored it. Ducking under the low doorway of the inn, Rhys paused just inside the door. Thick smoke hung in layers over the large room. Other patrons looked up, one of them muttering about the door left open to allow in damp winds. Rhys slammed it shut, squinting in the dim light.

He didn't see her. No dark-haired maid lurked in shadowy corners or in the brightness by the fire. Only a few travelers and tradesmen dined at the long oaken tables or sat on benches drinking ale. A boar's head carved in wood leered down at him from a soot-streaked wall, and the smell of roast meat and hot bread made his stomach growl, reminding him he hadn't eaten since leaving Coventry at sunrise.

But there was no maid. No laughing eyes and teasing smile, no exotic perfume—though he could almost swear there were traces of jasmine among the scents of smoke and roast meat, which only went to prove that the mind could play powerful tricks on a man at times. Nay, Brian had been mistaken. Again. Since that day in the weald, every time Brian heard bells, he clutched at a charm he'd purchased from a wizened crone ugly enough to frighten the hair off a dog, then began muttering a chant.

There was no Elf Queen loitering among the smoky denizens of a village inn, nor even a gaceful maid with dark, mysterious eyes and a penchant for dancing in meadows. Which was probably for the best. Jésu, he had enough things to think about without fanciful dreams clouding his attention. Yet the past sennight had been spent turning restlessly at night while vague images of the maid danced in his head so that he could not sleep.

Stepping over the inn threshold, he saw Brian standing near the door holding Turk's reins. Had he ever been as credulous as the faithful Brian? If so, he couldn't recall it. His life had been harsh and informative, allowing him little opportunity to indulge in flights of fancy or belief in things unseen and unexplained. Yet he could spare a certain affectionate sympathy for Brian's naive beliefs without condoning them. Rhys moved forward and put a hand on Brian's slumped shoulder. Giving a start, Brian looked around, his green eyes wide and searching. "She turned you loose, milord?"

"Turned me . . . Jésu, Brian, you become more rattle-brained every day. Nay, the Elf Queen did not turn me loose. Your charm worked. I have her held captive in the pouch at my waist. D'you care to see?"

As Rhys thrust out the leather pouch at his waist, Brian took an instinctive step backward, making the sign of the cross over his chest. Rhys grinned broadly, and Brian flushed as he realized the jest.

"I only seek to protect you from harm," he muttered, and Rhys nodded agreement.

"Aye, Brian. You're a good man, I know that well. But there are some things no one can save another from." He caught up Turk's reins and gave them into the hand of his squire. "Give him an extra ration of oats, Morgan," he said, "for he performed well this day and deserves reward, as do we all."

Rhys turned back to Brian. "Come, my faeriewise friend. We'll test the inn's wine, and perhaps a trencher or two of beef. We'll all be in much better tempers after that."

Though he ate and drank with his knights, Rhys found himself glancing around the common room from time to time, and realized with a scowl that he was looking for the nameless maid of the weald. In truth, the fey maid had not been long from his thoughts. He still ached because of her, and it had left his temper raw. If he didn't know better, he'd take a vow that she had indeed spun a magic spell over him to make him think of her so often.

"Milord? D'ye not hear us, milord?" asked Sir Robert, and Rhys glanced up.

He shrugged when they all looked at him. "I wasn't paying attention, Sir Robert. Grant pardon."

Robert exchanged a glance with Brian before repeating, "We asked if you dinna wish to bide here for the night. We can still be at Glenlyon by day after the morrow if we leave at first light."

Rhys had already had the same thought. It had been a long day. And a tiring one. On the road from Coventry, they'd been set upon by a large body of mercenaries waiting around a narrow curve. The fight had been brief and vicious, and cost him two good men, but they had beaten the ruffians off. When it was over, they'd carried the bodies of their men to a village priest for burial before riding on. Dead mercenaries had been left in the road for scavengers.

With all this riding about England, his men were weary. In truth, they deserved a night spent in more pleasurable pursuits, and Glenlyon was within two days' hard ride. Rhys needed rest, as well, though he had seen little in this village that interested him. He nodded slowly.

"Aye, we'll stay the night here. The morrow will be soon enough to ride for Glenlyon, though God knows what we'll find when we arrive." Rhys frowned into his pewter cup. He could feel the glances his way and knew they wondered. Without looking up, he said, "Owain's messenger claimed he was so late meeting me because of another assault on Glenlyon. He was near caught, and had to hide for three days in the reeds before making his way to Coventry." He paused, then said flatly, " 'Tis rumored that Sir Niclas of Raglan formed the rebellion that saw my father and brothers slain. Now Niclas and his men think I'm still in Jerusalem and unlikely to return alive." He looked up with a mirthless smile. "Think of their surprise when we appear."

Rough exclamations, pounding fists, and oaths greeted his words, then turned to boasting promises of Raglan's fate. Rhys finally lifted a hand to quiet them when the innkeeper came to protest, and the uproar died down.

"This smacks of John's fine hand to me," Brian muttered with a grimace. "He's famous for stealing the lands of absent barons, then setting Welshman against Welshman."

Rhys shook his head. "Even that brash prince would not risk Richard's wrath by taking lands belonging to one of the king's loyal knights. He'd surely know that Richard would frown on any such action."

"And has that stopped John before?" Sir Robert asked gruffly. "I have not noted any reluctance in seizing lands that are not his. Even William the Marshal was not exempt from his thievery—"

"Enough." Glancing about the crowded common room,

Rhys motioned him to silence. "Best not give keen ears the chance to hear what is said."

Sir Robert looked around uneasily, then ducked his head. "Aye, lord."

Rhys leaned forward, lowering his voice to tell Sir Robert he would explain all on the journey to Wales, when something caught his eye. It was a slight motion, as if a gust of wind had caught the hem of a cloak, but it arrested him. A flash of green and purple vanished behind a curtained alcove at the rear of the common room.

Surging up from the bench, Rhys ignored the surprised faces of his men-at-arms and knights as he gave pursuit to the shadowy figure. When he reached the alcove and snatched aside the curtain, he wasn't as surprised as he might once have been to find it empty. A hint of jasmine was all that remained, invisible but distinct. She had been here. He turned around.

No sign of her was evident. The pathway behind the common room was dimly lit and smelled strongly of fish and garlic. It led to the kitchen across worn, paved stones. Rhys strode to the kitchen door. He burst inside, startling a serving wench, who dropped a basket of bread loaves with a loud squeal. Another wench studied him with a bold eye and broad smile, putting one hand on her ample hip.

" 'Tis hasty ye be, winsome knight. D'ye seek a fair maid?" She stepped closer to give him a coy, simpering smile.

He halted. Faces had turned toward him, with round eyes and open mouths, and he belatedly realized that he was still in full armor. He glanced again at the maid. She leaned toward him, giving him a generous view of her small breasts.

Rhys shook his head. "There was a maiden who came this way. Did you see her?"

The maidservant arched a brow and moved forward, hips swaying beneath the greasy, stained gown. Light brown hair hung in curling ringlets that looked as if a comb had never touched them. Though her face could have been pretty, her skin was marred with tiny scars and pits that distorted her features. Rhys took a step to the side.

"Nay, brave knight, do not flee. No other maid came this way. Yet if 'tis a maid you seek, then 'tis one ye have found," she murmured.

Rhys removed her hand from where she'd placed it on his arm. "I know she came this way. Her fragrance lingers."

Laughter greeted that comment, and the wench gave him an arch glance. "Tell me what scent ye prefer, bold sir, and I will wear it wherever ye wish me to wear it . . ." Her hand drifted to her bodice in an unmistakable gesture.

"Leave him be, Lynn," a man said sharply. Rhys glanced around to see the innkeeper at the kitchen door. His florid face was diffused with embarrassment. He moved quickly to the maid and took her by the arm. "Grant pardon, m'lord," he said ingratiatingly, "but me daughter meant naught harm."

"None has been done." Rhys felt ridiculous. He must look a cursed fool, chasing after shadows and scents. Even to these villagers he would never see again. He stepped toward the door.

"Is't there ought I can do for ye, milord?" the innkeeper asked as Rhys made for the outside door. "I would no' want ye to be taken unkind by me daughter's rudeness."

He stopped and turned back to the innkeeper. "I saw someone in the shadows of the alcove behind the curtain. They fled before I could catch them."

"Aye? 'Twas naught of me work, milord. No robbers would dare invade me inn to—"

Seeing that the conversation was about to degenerate into a lengthy defense of the virtues of the hostel, Rhys interrupted impatiently. "It was a maid." He clenched his teeth when the innkeeper's anxious expression altered to a sly smile.

"Oh, aye. A maid. Well, I did see a young maid hasten toward the stables, milord. But she warn't—"

"God's mercy." Rhys pivoted on his bootheel and left the kitchen before the innkeeper or his daughter could of-

fer further comment. His sheathed sword clanked against
the rough stones of the outer wall behind the inn. Several
long, low buildings of stone and mud flanked a courtyard
and a garden, housing horses belonging to the lodgers.
Daylight was fading.

Rhys strode swiftly across the bare ground and ducked
into the stable. Despite the mud and muck in the outer
yard, the stable itself was clean and fairly dry. The familiar, welcome scent of horses, hay, and leather greeted him.
But no jasmine. It appeared to be empty of anyone but a
dozing hosteler seated in a clump of hay just outside the
wide doorway. Hazy streamers of light filtered through
small windows and chinks in the wall. Several animals
nickered softly, and he moved through the dusty gloom
toward a familiar dark shape at the far end of a passage-
way flanked by stalls and hayricks.

When he reached Turk, the stallion nudged him, his
massive black head so steady and strong against Rhys's
shoulder that it took him an involuntary step backward.
He clubbed a gentle fist against the horse's broad neck and
murmured an affectionate greeting.

" 'Tis more than a kind word he needs, gentle knight."

Rhys whirled; one hand flashed down to grip the hilt of
his sword in reflex. "Show yourself," he commanded,
though he'd recognized the voice even as he reacted. Must
she always be hiding in the shadows?

A curve of pale light streamed through a chink in the
stable wall. Dust motes swam in the hazy shaft, growing
thicker in number as Rhys squinted into the darkness and
blinked. A teasing hint of jasmine drifted toward him.

Stepping into the thin ribbon of light, she seemed to
appear magically, as if conjured out of empty air. Rhys
grimaced at the foolish thought and released the hilt of his
sword. Jésu, Brian had him as skittish as a colt. A faint
smile plied the maiden's lips, and her dark eyes held bows
of reflected light in them. He crossed his arms over his
chest, and his mail made a faint clinking sound. He
shrugged lightly.

"He has forage and a bucket of water, and 'tis easy to

see that my squire tended him well. What more does the horse need, if not a kind word?"

She moved forward, pushing back the hood of her cloak. Dark, lustrous hair gleamed in the pale light. "He'll be lame if you don't tend his right foreleg."

"Lame?" Rhys stared at her in surprise. She gazed back calmly. Drawing his gaze from her dark eyes, he studied the stallion for a moment. Hay wisps straggled from one corner of its lips and dangled from the long, coarse mane, but the animal looked as fit as always. He looked back at her and lifted a brow. " 'Tis foolishness. He's shown no sign of being lame, nor of favoring any leg."

"Has he not?" She moved around him gracefully, her hem dragging through the straw chaff and dirt of the stable floor. "Yet he has a hurt . . . here, above the hoof."

Despite his skepticism, Rhys knelt to lift the leg she indicated. His thumb pressed into the knee, shank, and fetlock joint with no reaction. He stroked a hand downward, over smooth muscle and bone, then the curved slant of the pastern. Turk stood placidly. He glanced up at her, a quick, derisive look, and she shook her head.

"Lower."

"Any lower, and the horse will be standing on my fingers," he pointed out.

"No, I mean here." Before he could stop her, she knelt down and reached for the leg, her slender fingers moving swiftly to the pastern. Turk snorted and jerked, and he wrenched her out of harm's way before those great hooves did any damage.

A faint frown knit her brows as she pulled free of his grasp. "He won't hurt me."

"This is not a cart pony, but a war-horse trained to trample men beneath his hooves. He allows no one near him but those familiar to him, and you are not one of them."

"If that is true, how do you explain why I am so near him now?"

He had no intention of admitting that he didn't know. "If I had not pulled you from harm, you'd now be little more than a bloody bundle of rags at my feet. Step back, if you will, should he decide to attack."

A slow smile curved her mouth. She leaned against the wooden post separating two stalls. "It's an inner bruise. If not tended, it will worsen. You will be afoot by the morrow."

Turk quivered beneath the palm Rhys laid on his flank, a faint ripple of muscles. There was a possibility she was right; the battle that morning had been violent. Anything could happen in the fury of the fray, as he well knew. But how would she know?

"For a mist-maid," he mocked, "you feign remarkable knowledge of horses."

"Do I? Perhaps I'm just guessing. Or, perhaps I actually have a small knowledge of horses."

"And perhaps you have another reason for being here in the stables." He lifted his brows, smiling slightly. "Did I not just see you in the inn, fair flower? Tucked into an alcove, perhaps, to watch me in the common room?"

"What a vain creature you are. I suppose when the sun shines, you think 'tis just for you." She moved away several steps, and he settled one shoulder against the wall to watch her. She frowned. "Others are in the inn. Why wouldn't I be waiting for someone, instead of hiding to watch you?"

He smiled, a slow curve of his mouth. She was nervous. Her hands fluttered a bit, and her eyes darted toward the door at the far end of the wide corridor. And he would bet his last shilling that she'd been watching for him.

Silence spun, and he let it stretch taut before he said, "Were you waiting on me?"

Her mouth opened, closed, then opened again. "Perhaps."

He pushed away from the wall. "Nay, I think you were waiting on me. Here I am, sweet flower."

She stepped back, then paused. Her nostrils flared slightly, and her lips were parted. The tip of her tongue flicked out, darting over the curve of her upper lip, leaving it shiny and moist. "Your . . . vanity, sir, is great. Much greater than the likelihood that you are right."

He laughed softly. His gaze lingered on her mouth a moment, then lifted slowly. There was a subtle glow in her eyes that was quickly veiled by her lashes, and she tensed, poised as if for flight. He moved quickly, and caught her by one wrist, fingers circling the small bones in a light, firm grip.

"Leaving so soon, flower? Do not disappoint me again. I fain await your pleasure, now that you have me ensnared." He leaned close, felt the quiver that shook her, and smiled. His breath stirred a strand of dark hair, and it drifted across her cheek. He lifted her trapped arm and placed her palm against his chest, pressing it lightly into the mail. "Do you feel the race of my heart? See how swiftly it beats for you?"

"You dally, sir," she said faintly, not looking at him, "as if you had much experience."

Pushing back the errant strand of dark hair, he tucked it behind her ear, then traced the gentle curve with a fingertip. She shivered and strained away from him, but he still held her hand against his chest. "And you," he murmured, "dally as if you had none."

Her gaze flew to his face, eyes wide. "Would that disturb you?"

He paused in a slow exploration of the arch of her throat. With his hand resting lightly against her scented skin, he was well aware of the rapid pulse beating against the backs of his curved fingers. "Nay, it would not disturb me. Nor would it hearten me."

"I do not take your meaning."

He kissed the tip of her small, straight nose, then the tiny indentation at the corner of her mouth, and released her hand. " 'Tis simple enough—if you are virgin, sweet flower, I will leave you so. I do not deflower young maidens. Even those so impetuous as to pursue me." He smiled wryly. "Or capricious enough to invite me to a May dance in a meadow."

She stared up at him, eyes as wide and dark as glistening pieces of jet. "And if I am not virgin?"

"Ah, and if you are not virgin,'tis another matter. There is always time for negotiations, room for bargaining, terms to be arranged, prices to be set . . ." He let the final words fade slowly, so his meaning would be clear. Dalliance with a beautiful maiden was always diverting, and there had been a time he enjoyed it for its own sake. But not now. Now, there was a hard, tight ache in him that needed easing, ignited by the small girl staring up at him so intently. Most of the week in Coventry had been spent waiting in an empty church—not exactly the best place to carry on transactions of a carnal nature—as he waited for the messenger from Owain. And then, he'd been too bemused and unsettled by the message even to think of easing himself with a casual woman. Until now. Until reaching this sleepy village and once more seeing the exotic creature who'd ignited his blazing need.

"Terms?" She blinked, confusion hazing her eyes, and he gave a regretful sigh and stepped back.

"Conditions or stipulations, such as the twelve labors of Hercules," he said lightly, certain she would have no idea what he was talking about. "A reward in exchange for a gallant deed, or retrieval of something valuable. A golden apple from Hesperides."

"When I heard the myth," she said, "the reward was that the king would leave Hercules alone in exchange for his labors. Is that what you have in mind?"

Amused as well as surprised by her familiarity with the Greek legend, he reached out to cup her chin in his palm. His thumb brushed against the corner of her mouth. "I would never be so churlish as to leave you alone, were circumstances different. But like the legend, nothing is ever easy."

Unable to resist, he bent to kiss her, a regretful farewell, a final remnant of the desire that was making him so uncomfortable. Her mouth quivered beneath his lips, soft and sweet and so tempting he was constrained to pull away before he disregarded his own good intentions. The cursed thing about good intentions was how they always looked better in concept than reality. But, a momentary weakness with an untried maiden could have lasting repercussions and cause unnecessary complications in his life. He had visions of an irate village burgher pursuing him with a pitchfork, and the sheriff demanding restitution for his daughter's maidenhead.

When he pulled away, her lashes lifted, casting trembling shadows on her cheeks, and he felt a twinge of satisfaction that he wasn't the only one affected. She caught his hand before he could release her chin, and held it with a surprisingly strong grip.

"I never said," she murmured in a soft, breathless voice, "that I was a virgin."

"Nay, you didn't." He swept her with an appraising eye. Was it all a game? A masquerade to amuse her and tease him? If so, she was expert at it, for she handled herself very much like a virgin. If he hadn't been so caught up in the lingering effects of her performance in the weald, he might have noticed it that day in the meadow. But then she'd seemed age-old, timeless, as wise as the madonna. Now, she looked only very young, very nervous, and very intense.

Her fingers slipped over his hand, curled into his palm, and held tightly. She smiled up at him. "Then shall we discuss the terms, sir?"

Sasha's heart was thumping so hard, she was certain he could hear it. A bold idea had formed as he was pulling away from her with such obvious regret. She had seen not only the answer to her prophecy slipping away, but long years of tedious existence in Elspeth's village yawning before her like the shades of hell. Perhaps the idea wasn't as audacious as the twelve labors of Hercules, but it certainly was a close rival. Would he agree? Would he think acting as her champion far too great a task for what she promised in return?

The romantic tales of knightly deeds performed for a lady would have her believe that no labor was too great for love, but this was not a man who seemed to care about romance. What then, could she offer in exchange? Not even in her most fanciful thoughts did she believe he would consider a night of pleasure adequate reward for besieging a fortress. But she had taken full note of his adherence to the rules of chivalry, and knew that this was a knight who would keep his sworn word. Once he had given it, he would not default on whatever promise he made.

And therein lay the solution.

His hand closed around her fingers, holding tightly. "Yea, lady fair, name your terms."

She affected an alluring smile that felt stiff on her lips, and hid the tremor of her hand by gripping his. Not too much said, nor too little, or the ploy would be for naught.

"Twelve labors, as those performed by Hercules, would be too great a request." His amused snort was evidence that he agreed, and she ignored him as she continued with a touch of playful artifice and sidelong glances, "But perhaps a few lesser tasks would be sufficient to win my attentions for an evening, dread knight."

"A few?" His mouth twisted, and an amused gleam lit eyes the clear gray of smoke. "How great a number does 'a few' encompass, flower?"

"Perhaps . . . three?"

"Three. For a single evening. It sounds intriguing, but I'm not certain I would be able to consummate the bargain after completing three arduous labors, fair blossom."

She placed her hand lightly against his chest, fingers tracing over the metal links of his mail, then moving up to skim along the thrust of his jaw. Beard-stubble rasped beneath her fingertips. Her fingers lightly explored the hard set of his mouth, then drifted to the pale curve of scar on his high slash of cheekbone. Tension simmered in his tautly held frame, and gray eyes like smoke narrowed at her beneath the dark brush of his lashes. She rose to her toes to put her other arm around his neck. He was too tall for her to manage properly, and she settled for letting her hand rest on his broad shoulder as she gazed up at him.

"Very well, *beau sire*. I'm adept at compromise. A labor for a night."

"Ah, and what happens if I perform my labor, but you grow too shy to settle the debt, sweet lady? I caution you—I always keep my sworn word, and deal rudely with those who do not."

He was smiling, but there was a steely warning couched

in his words that left her slightly dizzy. She swallowed, keeping the smile on her lips though it felt wilted and weak. She must secure his pledge to help her, yet the resort to trickery was growing increasingly nerve-racking.

"La, sir, do you think I would play you false? First, the evening of entertainment, and then the labor performed. There, you see? You risk nothing, lose only what you will, and gain"—her fingers grazed the strands of wheat-blond hair over his ears, drifted down to toy with the thick waves that brushed the draped coif of his mail—"all that you desire to gain," she finished softly. There was a quick flash of light in his eyes, so swift it was a fleeting glimpse, then his arm coiled around her back to hold her hard against him.

" 'Tis intriguing, sweet flower. Name the labor that you wish done, and if agreed upon, our negotiation is complete."

Sasha hadn't really thought he'd be fool enough to agree blindly, and had half formed a phrase she hoped would suffice. If distracted enough, he might not see through the obscure meaning to her true purpose.

Leaning against him, pressing her breasts against his chest and hoping that his imagination could supply the details the mail obstructed, she drew one hand over his mouth in a soft, lingering glide. His lips closed on her fingertips, white teeth gently catching them in a tiny nip. Rubbing her hips in suggestive contact over the iron-muscled length of his thighs, she mimicked every woman she'd ever observed entice a man, from field whores to highborn mistresses, fabricating what she could not remember.

Apparently, it was working, for his breathing grew shallow and quick and his arm tightened convulsively behind her back, holding her harder against him. His hips thrust toward her. His hand tangled in the loose hair of her nape, pulling her head back, and his mouth came down on hers with bruising force. The kiss was hard and punishing, almost painful, but provoked the most intoxicating sensation she'd ever known. Rivulets of fire spread through her, dropping to the pit of her stomach, then pooling between her thighs, making her throb. She moaned. His hand tightened, bringing tears to her eyes. His mouth ground into hers until she couldn't breathe, couldn't think, could only hang there in his arms and try not to be swept away into the nameless sphere that loomed beyond her knowledge.

When his head lifted, they were both panting and aroused, though it was difficult for her to tell exactly who was most shaken. Her, she thought, as this was completely out of her realm of experience.

Yet, unnerved as she was, she was able to laugh softly, give him an arch glance, and say, "A victory, sir, such as those knights who wear their lady's colors at a tourney. I crave a victory."

"A victory, you say, a wearing of your colors." He grinned, a flash of white in a sun-browned face. "A unique payment, but you are a unique reward, flower. I assume there is a tournament where you wish me to ply this victory."

She smiled. "Yea, *beau sire*, of sorts. Do you swear? Do you swear to wear my colors and fight for a victory on the field of combat?"

"I would not refuse such a sweet request, for it combines two of my most cherished things, tournament games and love play. But I must leave early on the morrow." He grasped her hand, kissed her fingertips, the faint smile on his mouth doing nothing to diminish the hot glitter in his hungry gaze. "May I swear to a victory for the future, fair lady?"

"Yea, dread knight, if you will swear it to me, as I swear to come to your bed, I shall wait on my promised victory." Lightly, with teasing smile and fluttering lashes, she took his hand and placed it on the hilt of his sword. "Swear it by your knight's sword, beau sire, swear to wear my colors . . ."

She held her breath, then closed her eyes with relief and satisfaction when he said huskily, "I swear it, lady fair. On my honor as a knight, I swear to fight for victory in your name."

It was, she thought weakly, even better than she'd hoped.

CHAPTER FOUR

Lamps sputtered and hissed, and smoke filled the inn's common room in stinging drifts. Open shutters allowed in air laden with the damp promise of rain. Laughter came from a gloomy corner. Rhys glanced again at the inn door and propped his feet atop a bench opposite his. He stared at the toes of his boots. He plucked at one of the brass circles that studded the wide belt encircling his leather jerkin. Vesper bells had rung in the village church, the designated hour had come and gone, yet there was no sign of her. Impatience made him restless.

Ridiculous, the coy delay, when a swift tumble in a sweet, clean pile of stable hay would have sufficed for his pressing need. Women must have their vanities, the illusions that kept reality at bay. The reason was a mystery, as incomprehensible as her need to create a fictional quest for yielding that which she intended to yield all along. He knew full well there was no tournament to be conducted in Wytham, as she must know. There wasn't even a country fair planned, or the entire village would be abuzz. 'Twas all a ploy, a play of words meant to disguise her

desire for him. Yet if it appeased her qualms and gained
him his ends, he would not begrudge her her flights of
fancy. He glanced at the door again. It was still firmly shut,
no hint of a sloe-eyed mist-maid shadowing the portal.

Another burst of laughter from the dark corner
sounded, louder and showing evidence of ample drink. His
hand tightened around a pewter cup of wine, delivered
with a flourish by the innkeeper's daughter. If the maid
did not show soon, he might find himself reduced to re-
placing her with another, even one such as the saucy
wench bending low over a nearby table to present a tank-
ard of ale to one of his own knights. Sir Peter looked up,
slyly sticking his hand into the loose neck of the wench's
gown, fingers toying with the small breasts so boldly dis-
played. Rhys looked away, uncomfortable and unsettled.
Where the devil was the girl? Had she changed her mind,
as maids were so oft prone to do?

He took an angry gulp of wine. Time was an inconstant
thing, the shift from daylight to dark marked by a burning
candle of hours counted by the priests, but otherwise a
vague framework upon which to base events. Yet the candle must have burned to the vesper hour, for the bells had
rung clearly from the church tower, and still she had not
come.

Fire shadows danced across sooty walls, light and dark
shapes flickering against the wood grain like the gambol-
ing elves of Brian's lengthy tales, and just about as solid
as the fey creatures. Fragments of fevered dreams, half-
formed thoughts and vague ramblings, stories of elf
queens, faeries, and love spells spewed from the Irishman
most freely when the wine flowed. It had been Rhys's mis-
fortune to be treated to a prolonged story of Conle the
Red Haired, who was beguiled by a love-struck faerie and
invited to Faerie Hill, where there are no worries, no
deaths, and lasting feasts to while away eternity. Being
Irish, the tale had spun out endlessly but finished with the
ominous recital of how Conle had allowed himself to be
persuaded by the beautiful faerie's entreaties, and sailed
away in a crystal boat never to be seen again. A deaf man
could have heard the blatant warning in Brian's narra-

tion—performed with energetic gestures and pacing—but to be certain Rhys understood his meaning, the Irishman presented him with his most precious relic: the tooth of a saint.

"I sacrifice it . . . ta keep ye . . . safe from . . . her spells, m'lor'," he'd mumbled blearily, following this touching sentiment with a long, deep belch.

Appalled—not only by the separation of such a devoted believer from an object of great personal value, but the nature of the grisly relic—Rhys had politely declined to accept it. Whereupon Brian had collapsed into a blathering flood of dire predictions concerning what would befall them all if Rhys was spirited away by the Elf Queen. Thankfully, the wine soon soothed even those worries, and he'd left the Irishman snoring peacefully.

Now he was kicking his heels in a tavern, waiting for the mystical Elf Queen to grace him with her presence, he thought moodily. Curse her. He should have followed his first instinct and taken her in the mound of hay. Then he wouldn't be sitting in the common room of an inn watching his companions get drunk, but be pleasantly submerged in a much more intoxicating haze. Rarely did he imbibe too freely, disliking the inevitable problems created by careless actions. There were problems enough in his world without inviting more.

Sir Peter staggered from the table, an arm thrown around the kitchen wench, bragging about his carnal accomplishments. Rhys briefly considered escorting his obviously drunk knight to a bed of hay in the stable, then changed his mind. It appeared the wench had no objections to leading the way to a more remote location and a test of Peter's boasts.

A gust of wind pushed the door open as they reached it, and Sir Peter's drunken efforts to catch it were futile to the point of ludicrous. His clumsy fumbles sent his companions into gales of laughter and advice on how best to capture the elusive slab of oak. Rhys watched with a faint smile. There was a flurry of activity around the entrance as other knights feigned sword-play with the deeply

scarred oak door—evidently a veteran of many such en-
counters—and then a sudden shout shattered the laughter.

The difference in tone was instant, from laughing play
to shock and anger. Rhys was already on his feet and striding to the source of trouble when he heard accented tones
snarling in angry frustration. By the time he reached the
seething knot of dissension, some of his men had seen his
approach and already retreated, opening a path for him.

In the midst of the conflict stood a lean, dark young
man clutching one of the most wicked daggers Rhys had
ever seen, holding it in front of him as if he were quite
capable of using it efficiently. He barely glanced at Rhys,
even when the other men moved cautiously away with
shamefaced mutters. With his back to the scarred oak, the
youth crouched in a position of defense, ready to shift to
offense at the first sign of need.

Silent, Rhys studied him until the youth finally dared a
glance at him. He returned it coldly. The room had grown
quiet, the only sound a dull clatter coming from the back,
where the other patrons were oblivious to trouble. The
youth was breathing hard, his chest rising and falling
quickly under a torn tunic and leather jerkin. A scratch on
one cheek welled with drops of blood.

"Why stir up my men, brat?" The abrupt question
jerked the boy's head around, and dark eyes glared at Rhys
hotly.

"I have the bad habit of misliking sword cuts on my
face," he retorted. " 'Tis a failing others have tried to rem-
edy and failed."

Rhys raked him with a contemptuous stare that took in
all between his unruly thatch of black hair and laced
boots, then returned to the now reddened face. "Is that
so? Then you have come to the right place for a cure. Any
one of these men would oblige you, as they are all seasoned knights fresh from the Crusades."

"Seasoned with too much ale, it seems to me." He ges-
tured at the men with his dagger. "If these are the best of
Richard's knights, all of England will soon be speaking
Italian."

Rhys swung up his arm to halt an enraged rush from

two of his men, not taking his eyes from the wary predator against the door. "You speak boldly for a lone challenger. Do you have an army at your back?"

"If I did, would I be braced against the door like a trapped fox?" He shook his head. "Nay, signor. I am sent to deliver you a message, and would do so before yon drunken knights decide to spit me on a lance for their amusement."

Crossing his arms over his chest, Rhys nodded. "Deliver it, whelp, then begone before my men forget their manners."

After a quick, dark glance at the grumbling knights, he looked back at Rhys and said, "My lady awaits you."

Rhys stared at him. So she had not changed her mind. But how like a female to change the plans. It had been understood they were to meet here. Nothing had been said about moving the tryst to another location. He was not a man to trust sudden changes, having been nastily surprised too often.

When the silence became obvious, the boy's dark brow lifted with disdain. "I will tell her that you no longer wish to meet with her, signor."

"Hold," Rhys said when the youth half turned to move cautiously from the doorway. Curse it all, what was the maid's name? He felt a fool for not having asked. "Tell your lady that I wish to keep our meeting as arranged."

A flash of emotion crossed the youth's face, a dark flicker that was quickly gone, and he shrugged. "If you wish. I'll take you to her."

"Your lady was to come to me. I've made arrangements here. Go, and bring her back with you."

"Nay, signor. She has made her own arrangements, and bids you join her." His expression altered and he added rashly, "Unless you fear I will overpower you on the way. . . ."

It grew deathly still in the common room. Even the drunkest of his knights did not dare move or speak. Rhys merely stared at the youth until he took a tentative step backward. Then, with slow, measured words, he said, "I do not waste my time fearing the vain crowing of cockerels. Each man here now knows your face, whelp. If I am undone, there will be no place distant enough, deep enough, or high enough to hide you from them."

Angry dismay suffused the boy's features, but he gave a curt jerk of his chin in acknowledgment and stepped aside to clear the doorway for Rhys to pass. Torchlight wavered over the shallow stone stoop, and horn lamps were set atop a low wall to light the way for late travelers. Pinpricks of light glittered erratically beyond the limits of the inn's courtyard, for a deep wood stretched behind the village.

Pausing to light his lanthorn from one of the horn lamps atop the wall, the youth signaled silently for Rhys to follow. Rhys looked past him, frowning at the course the boy was taking. Erratic moonlight silvered the ground in vague, shifting shadows, but did not diminish the danger beyond the garden walls. One ambush a day was enough, and he had no desire to let his lust overrule his head.

The slick metallic whisk of Rhys's sword being drawn brought the youth around with a jerk, and the lanthorn he held high shook light over his startled face. Rhys smiled. "I've no wish to be caught unawares."

"Do you think me fool enough to come to a sword fight with only a dagger?" came the hissed question. "I may be young yet, signor, but I've enough sense to know better than that."

" 'Tis not your meager skill with a dagger that concerns me, whelp." He indicated the trees and darkness with his sword point. "An entire army could be in those trees, and I would not know it until too late."

"You flatter yourself if you think 'twould take an army to defeat one knight," he retorted.

Rhys didn't reply. After giving Rhys a scathing glare, the youth swung around and surged forward. Shadows shifted from gray to gold under the swaying lanthorn, then to deep black beyond the flame. The sharp scent of herbs filled the air, and an owl hooted softly in the nearby wood. Their footsteps crunched on rock, then grew muffled against the dirt of a wooden path. Here, the scent of whitethorn was strong and sweet.

At the edge of the wood, Rhys halted. "Does your lady lodge in a tree, whelp?"

"Nay, signor," was the muttered reply. "But we prefer more civilized lodgings than those provided by yon hostel. When possible. I've not noted a surfeit of elegant quarters for poor travelers in England, and my lady oft desires that we have more than a rude pallet."

He turned back to look at Rhys. The swaying light from the lanthorn wavered over his face in alternating shades of dark and light. There was a faint mocking smile on his mouth. "If you fear treachery, feel free to return to the inn. I will make your apologies to my lady."

"While your offer is tempting, the lady is more so." Rhys smiled at the quick darkening of the youth's face. "Lead on, brat, and remember—if there is treachery, yours will be the first throat I cut."

Silent and glowering, the youth stomped ahead, making no effort to be quiet. It grew darker in the trees where pale moonlight could not reach. Leaves crunched underfoot. In the distance, a wolf howled, the sound shivering through the night like a warning. Pitch blackness loomed ahead, unbroken by anything but the brief flicker of the lanthorn. The bob of light whisked over a shimmer of color but faded so quickly, Rhys wasn't certain he'd really seen it. When they drew several paces closer, the circle of light grew larger, and his suspicion was confirmed: A Saracen tent.

Silk walls and a pointed roof glowed with muted light, like a rare jewel in the midst of an English beech glade. A rainbow of red, blue, green, and yellow quivered at the press of wind, and the teasing fragrance of spices curled in the air. He expected at any moment to hear the liquid notes of a nightingale singing in the trees.

But the sounds he heard were from the mist-maid, who came to stand in the swagged entrance, a vision in silks and shimmering light. A changeling. No enveloping wool cloak, no rough tunic or peasant dress, but a living flame of crimson color. Dark beauty in radiant splendor. He felt, suddenly, as if a camel had kicked him in the belly.

"Good eventide, beau sire." She smiled at him warmly.

Her gaze flicked down to his drawn sword. "Has there been trouble?" She looked toward her servant, then made a small sound of dismay. "Biagio—you've been hurt. Were you set upon?"

"Yea, signorina." A darted glance toward Rhys, then a shrug, and he added, "Thugs. Ten of them. I fought free, managing to inflict great harm, but received this small cut in the battle."

Amused by the blatant lie, Rhys was not moved to challenge it. If the young Italian preferred inventions to truth, it was his business. There were other, more important, matters on his mind this night. He sheathed his sword in a rasp of steel and waited.

After a brief pause, she murmured something in Italian to the youth, and he flung Rhys a quick glance and shrugged a reply. Rhys watched them, the two dark heads so close together.

Then she was turning, a swift bright smile on her face, moving toward him as lightly as she had that day in the weald, as if on winged feet. But no mist-maid this, no faerie to carry lovers away in crystal boats, but a real woman of flesh and blood. Almost too real. Sheer silk drifted from her shoulders to her feet, skimming a slender body barely visible beneath the folds. A girdle of gold links rode her hips, and embroidered slippers fit her feet, trimmed with tiny brass bells that tinkled with every step. Silk was exotic, a luxury sparsely seen in the West, yet she slept beneath a canopy of it.

Silk and jasmine, the true Eastern version of Brian's imaginary crystal boats, a subtle allure to draw a man into the land of milk and honey for all eternity. But he was to have just one night. Having her this close, with the teasing scent of jasmine and her dark witching eyes, was enough to make him ache. And he was impatient to be alone with her. Impatient to be inside her.

"Will you come with me, Sir Rhys?" she invited. He was startled to hear his name on her lips, then chagrined that he did not know hers.

"Most assuredly, lady fair," he said, smiling, reaching out to take her hand in his.

He looked up and Biagio was staring at him narrowly, his arms crossed over his chest, brown eyes hard. Rhys held his gaze until the youth looked away, muttered something under his breath, and ducked into the tent.

The soft rustle of silk was broken by the sudden clatter of metal objects, and he felt the maid tense. She flung him a quick glance and another smile, then withdrew her hand and gestured to the tent.

"I would be honored for you to join me inside, beau sire."

Rhys followed her into the tent, ducking under a crimson flap tied back with tassels. He couldn't help a start of surprise. Thick carpets lined the silk floor. Brass lamps and braziers filled the enclosure with light and a musky fragrance. Plump cushions were scattered about the small area. His head grazed the draped ceiling as he stared at the Turkish setting.

Biagio was picking up scattered cups and a tray from the carpet with short, jerky movements. He radiated dislike and resentment in his tension and the quick, dark glances thrown like daggers at Rhys.

He smiled. Biagio dropped the tray again, and a cup rolled across the carpet to stop against the toe of Rhys's boot. He looked down, then lifted a brow at the youth. " 'Tis best for you that you are not one of my squires, brat, or you would be lessoned well in the art of serving."

Angry color flooded his face, and Biagio took an impetuous step forward, one hand clenched on the hilt of the dagger in his belt. "I would never serve as your squire, for—"

"Biagio," the maid said quickly, stepping in front of the youth with a hand against his chest, her eyes fixed on his furious face, "after you've picked this up, please help Elspeth bring the food. Then fetch your lute, for we would enjoy a melody with our meal."

It was on the tip of Rhys's tongue to say that he cared nothing for appeasing that kind of hunger, but he didn't want to appear too eager. In the wrong hands, lust could be a powerful weapon to use against a man. So he stood there, silent, his head brushing against the silk ceiling and the ache knotting inside him, waiting. All a prelude, a slow dance toward the inevitable climax of the evening that would be all the more savored for the anticipation.

"Please, beau sire," she was saying, all smiles and gracious courtesy, "be seated, and we will have some wine."

He glanced around. No chairs, nothing but plump cushions in bright colors and patterns were visible. He had a sudden vision of sitting at her feet like a love-struck swain, and shook his head.

"Nay, I will stand."

She looked dismayed. "All night?"

A slow smile curved his mouth. He looked at her upturned face and said softly, "Not all night, no."

Color flooded her exquisite features, and she gave a laugh that sounded a bit shaky. "Of course not, but—but you must sit to eat. I will have Biagio bring a chair."

The chair was brought, an odd-looking thing of sturdy material and dark wood, held together with tiny brass hinges that allowed it to fold out. He looked at it dubiously, and she laughed.

"It will hold you, beau sire, I promise. It looks fragile, but 'tis a strong chair, believe me. I got it from a man in Constantinople who was much heavier than you, and 'twas his favorite chair."

"If it was his favorite chair, why did he part with it?"

She looked up blinking, then shrugged. "He wagered on a horse race with me and lost. I won the chair, and he had to explain to his wife. It was victory twice over for me, as he was a wretched braggart of a man. Perhaps because his wife was a shrew, though he should not have suffered it so meekly."

Amused, he tested the chair's stability with one hand, then moved to sit down. Surprisingly, it felt much sturdier than it looked. His sword stuck out at an awkward angle when he was seated, and he tried unsuccessfully to adjust it. She sat down on a cushion at his feet and watched quietly for a moment before suggesting he remove the weapon.

He shook his head. "I will wear it."

"All night?" she mocked, and he looked up at her with a lifted brow.

"There are swords, sweet flower, and there are swords. You will know when I am ready to trade one for another."

She flushed, and he wondered at the feigned modesty from a girl who had apparently had much experience over a goodly portion of Europe. He leaned back to stare at her idly. There was a clatter outside the tent and he tensed, glancing quickly around the fluttering walls.

"If you feel uneasy here, beau sire," she said, "please tell me. But I would have you know, I've set no enemies lurking in the trees to fall upon you unaware."

" 'Tis part of my profession to be ever wary of trouble." He shrugged. "You chose a remote location for our tryst. Where is your home?"

She waved an arm to indicate the tent. "This is my home. I carry it with me wherever I go. Wherever the wind takes me. Or destiny."

He stared into her dark eyes. The flickering glow of an oil lamp reflected light in their depths, burnishing her face with dark gold, gleaming in the sweep of black hair. "You do not live in this village?"

She shook her head. "Nay, beau sire. Do you?"

"You must know I do not." Unsettled, he gazed at her. He'd thought her a village maid, a chance meeting on the journey home. Just a coincidence that brought them together again. Fate. But was it? The weald, the meadow, the village . . . too many coincidences. He thought of Brian's babbled warnings, his fear of elves and faeries, but knew there was a greater likelihood of human treachery than anything magical.

"Then 'tis fate that must have brought us together again," she said, a soft murmur that eerily echoed his own thoughts. "I had not thought to see you again, yet here you are." She turned gracefully to the brass tray and cups that had only recently spilled across the carpet, and took up a flagon from a carved teak table. "I have some excellent wine, sir. It was bought in a French valley before the last famine, and I have carried it with me since then. Do you care for a cup?"

"You are a woman of many surprises, fair flower. What other treasures do you hide beneath silken trappings?" Though surrounded by silk tent walls, she guessed his meaning and flushed.

The silk walls shivered, and Biagio came in, carrying a lute in one hand. Without looking at them, he sat next to the wall with the instrument in his lap, lean brown fingers strumming across the strings in a few experimental attempts before producing a pleasing but loud melody.

Rhys leaned forward, smiling at her when she looked from Biagio to him. "By all means, pour the wine." He sat back in the chair, studying her as she arranged the tray with quick, nervous movements.

"What do you do when it rains?" he asked, and when she looked up, added, "your lovely tent does well in dry lands, but I cannot see it withstanding a good English rain."

She smiled. "We stay in the wagon or an inn. I confess—I'm flaunting the few goods I have—" He opened his mouth to comment and she flung up a hand, laughing. "Nay, do not say it. I take it that you approve of my choice of garments, so you do not have to say aloud what your eyes have already said."

"Wisdom and beauty. I'm a fortunate man tonight, chérie."

A slow smile bowed her mouth. "Yea, beau sire, you most definitely are. As you will certainly agree before the night is past. . . ."

A sudden flash of heat brought him forward, one hand moving to cup her small chin in his palm: his eyes focused on her face. His thumb caressed the corner of her mouth in a leisurely glide. The heat inside him increased, coiling tightly, burning through him until even his eyes began to sting. His throat constricted, and he moved to set aside the cup.

A loud, discordant clang shattered the moment, and he looked up. "Mi scusi," Biagio muttered, untangling his fingers from the strings of the lute. "I fear it needs tuning."

She'd jerked at the jarring noise, and turned, staring hard at her servant. Rhys sat back in the chair, considering if he should demand dismissal of the insolent servant or allow the maid opportunity to send him from the tent.

But then she was turning back to him, her voice light. "Ah, here comes one of the reasons for your good fortune now, beau sire. Biagio, do help Elspeth with the tray before you leave. It looks heavy."

A delicious fragrance entered with the maidservant. After the first flash of impatience, he realized he was hungry. Truly hungry. He'd eaten only a small amount, still too tense from the day's events to do more than take a bite or two of the stringy beef and boiled turnips offered by the inn. But this—the tray placed on the small teak table bore a carved bowl with a cover shaped like the head of a rooster. The woman called Elspeth lifted the lid, and tantalizing scents wafted up in curling streamers. His stomach growled.

Leaning forward, the exotic maid pointed to the bowl. *Blanc de Syrie*. Elspeth usually does the cooking. This is the only thing I cook, so I hope it pleases you."

"What is it?" He had sudden visions of peculiar ingredients, such as those he experienced at a banquet hosted by Richard after taking Cyprus. A Syrian chef had prepared dishes of exotic foods, and when the cover of one was lifted, the English knights had been horrified to discover sheep eyeballs swimming in a thin grease. Mutton was one thing, eyeballs another entirely.

So he was relieved when she said, "Lamb in a sauce of almonds, sugar, ginger, and white wine, and garnished with pomegranate seeds. Try it. Or are you one of those rural Englishmen who won't eat anything but beef, beef, and more beef?"

"I've eaten roots and acorns when I've been hungry enough," he said, recalling a lean time in Wales, "but I've never been reluctant to try reasonable fare."

"Excellent. I've always felt the same way." She smiled at him across the small table the servant pulled between them and, while they ate, talked lightly of foods she had tried and liked and some she hadn't. He was surprised to realize he was enjoying himself. He'd thought at first he would grow quickly impatient at the obvious delay, but he found the wench amusing. As the evening's ultimate objective was a foregone conclusion, he settled back to watch the maid's performance. A definite actress, fluttering her eyelashes at him, slanting coy smiles, all the while her hands making quick nervous gestures over bowls, cups, and carved spoons.

"More wine, beau sire?"

He realized his cup was empty, and held it out. The maidservant bent quickly to refill it for him, her posture stiff, her manner silent and covertly disapproving. Apparently, the lady's servants did not care for the company she kept. He didn't know why. In honor of the evening and the lady, he'd pulled his best leather jerkin and linen tunic from the baggage. His boots, though worn, were of fine quality, as was the wide leather belt studded with brass emblems in the shape of griffyns. It was the best he could do, having moved about too often to worry about keeping a great many possessions. A few other belongings were housed in one of the many storerooms at Windsor, where he'd last stayed with Brian before joining Richard on the Crusades.

"The wine is good," he said to make idle conversation. "Though I do not usually prefer too many spices."

"My own recipe. I have a small chest of herbs and spices that I like to use, especially when I find myself in an English inn that serves foul wine."

He laughed. A spreading warmth flowed through him, pleasant and relaxing. "If you travel so extensively, what brings you to a land that serves too much beef and foul wine?"

A hesitation, then a fleeting smile, flutter of her lashes, and tilt of her head so that the fall of hair shifted, framing the thrust of her breasts beneath the thin silk. His attention wavered, then riveted on the enticing view. Impossible, but it seemed as if the material had grown thinner, the neckline lower. He barely heard her reply.

"My mother's family is from England, and I've never met them. This is a pilgrimage of sorts, I suppose."

"A pilgrimage." His gaze shifted to her face again, to the dark shine of her eyes and the elusive dimple at one corner of her mouth. It had grown warm in the tent. Very warm. He cleared his throat. "A pilgrimage is usually a quest for something, as the Holy Grail, or a religious experience. Do you think to find those in England?"

A shrug lifted her hair to her shoulder, where it curved in a silken drape down her back. "A pilgrimage can be anything the pilgrim wishes it to be, beau sire. A quest, certainly, and a religious experience as well. But there are many degrees of such endeavors, not all of them as noble."

"And yours? Is it noble?"

Her lips parted, moist and inviting, pink tongue smoothing over the tumble of her lower lip in a slow glide, then clenched between her teeth as she studied him. He took another sip of wine. She looked down at her hands, clasped before her on the small table, her half-eaten food pushed aside.

"I think it a noble quest, beau sire."

With her head bent, her hair had fallen forward again, veiling her face and her body. He wanted to lift the perfumed strands in his hand, curve his fingers at her nape again as he'd done that day in the meadow, and drag her up against him, taste the sweet arch of her throat, tease her lips open for his tongue . . . Jésu, but the thought of it was making him warm.

"More wine?" a murmur at his shoulder offered, and with a start, he realized that Elspeth was holding the flagon poised to refill his cup.

He glanced down, frowning. It was almost empty. Lamplight shimmered in the shallow dregs, catching his reflection and throwing it back. He shook his head, but Elspeth was already pouring more wine into his cup. Looking up, he saw that the fair maid was observing him with a faint frown.

"Beau sire, are you well?"

The wine cup mirrored the light, distorting the images into odd shapes. He blinked, and the wine light shifted. His limbs felt leaden, as if bearing heavy armor, and the languor in his blood increased until his eyelids felt as weighted as his body.

"Beau sire?" he heard her voice calling him as if from

a great distance, then came the strangest sound of bells and wind, and the strong, sweet scent of jasmine before the silk tent seemed to collapse atop him in a flutter of colors.

Eyes closed and breath coming deeply, Rhys slowly relaxed his arm. The wine cup tilted. Sasha snatched at it. Wine sloshed over her hand, wet and cool and smelling strongly of something besides spices. She lifted the cup to her nose.

Poppies, came the unspoken answer, drifting to her across the knight's still form, and her head jerked up. Elspeth smiled, triumph in her eyes, satisfaction in the glance she gave the long-limbed body sprawled in the chair.

"What have you done? Never mind—bring my chest of herbs. Hemp agrimony—that will purge him, I think."

"Don't take on so. He's a big man and I used only a small amount, enough to make him sleep for a time." Elspeth took a deep breath. Her voice shook slightly. "Though I would poison him if I thought you meant to keep your devil's bargain."

Already on her feet, Sasha threw the cup angrily to the floor. It bounced and rolled across the carpet, coming to rest against Biagio's left foot. He looked down at it, refusing to meet her eyes. She stared at him. "You told."

His shoulders lifted in a slight shrug and he finally looked up, defiant and challenging. "Yea. And I would tell the king himself if I thought 'twould keep you from being so foolish."

"At least I know whom I can trust now—and you," she said, rounding on Elspeth, "always preaching that I should not tell lies, should be more truthful, shouldn't be deceitful—what do you call this?"

"Saving you."

"Ah. Saving me. From what? Him?" She indicated Rhys with a flap of her arm. "What do you think he'll do when he wakes? Congratulate me on my fine food and drugged wine? Thank me for my excellent company before he strangles me? Oh no, I can see you didn't think that far."

She struck her forehead with the palm of her hand, groaning. "All for nothing, all for nothing . . ."

"Sasha." Elspeth took a step forward and put a hand on her arm, her words quavering. Tears formed in her eyes. "I could not stand idly by and watch you ruin yourself."

She sighed. She never could stand it when Elspeth got emotional. Anger was fine. Disapproval was familiar. Not tears. Not that quivering vulnerability that made her feel like the worst kind of a wretch.

"I know," she muttered, feeling ungrateful but unable to express any other reaction at the moment. "I just wish you had trusted me. Do you think me so foolish as to take too big a risk? I had a plan." She looked up fiercely, caught Biagio's shamefaced glance, and said, "You left out that part, didn't you? Aye, and now we'll have not only a disappointed knight on the morrow, but one with a raging headache. He'll be as sweet tempered as a three-legged boar."

"That," Biagio murmured, "should be a distinct improvement. Nay, don't glare at me. I knew you'd be mad. But you were in trouble with this one. This is no simpering French troubadour who doesn't know whether to kiss lads or lasses. This is a knight just back from Crusading with Richard, and you know that worthy's reputation."

"Richard doesn't like girls," she pointed out, and Biagio shrugged.

"That's not what I meant. We're discussing a man who is not accustomed to being gainsaid in his desires. You could have cooed and cuddled until pigs fly, and he still would have been mad if you had refused him in the end. It would have ended badly. Trust me."

"Never," she said coldly, "again. You betrayed me."

"Hoo, hoo, don't play the offended party with me," he retorted. "Remember Cadíz? Who left who with a drunken brute of a man just back from a year at sea? After filling him with notions of Italian romance on the high seas? He almost broke my arm before I could break a wine bottle over his head. That was not at all amusing."

She smiled tightly. "I told him you were pining for him.

You're probably the best memory he has." A soft snore came from the chair, and she looked over at Rhys. She sighed. "None of that matters now. We have to do something with him."

"I have a large sack. We could put him and a heavy stone in it, and—"

She flung Biagio a savage glance and he quieted immediately. It was Elspeth who said, "Take him back to his room at the inn. Put him in his bed, and when he wakes in the morning, he'll think he only drank too much. I've not seen an English knight yet who doesn't know how to empty too many tankards."

"No, no," Sasha fretted, "it will never work. My plan was much better." When Elspeth muttered something under her breath, she looked up at her with a faint smile . . . and lied. "I didn't mean what you're thinking."

"And what is this marvelous plan you keep waving at us?" Elspeth snapped.

Sasha stared at her. Her lips twitched, and she felt a bubble of amusement rise and lodge in her throat before finally escaping in a strangled gasp. "I was going to get him so drunk he'd think he'd seduced me," she said between snorts of laughter. It was the near truth.

Biagio hooted. "That's even worse than I thought. It's obvious that you've never . . . well, never." He shook his head. "That, bella, is one thing 'tis almost impossible to fabricate. He'd know. And he'd be mad."

They all turned to look at the knight.

"Then what do we do with him?"

CHAPTER FIVE

"If I'd known you intended to do it anyway," Biagio muttered, "I'd have given him to the fish whether you liked it or no." He dropped Rhys to the rope bed with a heave and a grunt.

"Stop complaining." Sasha closed the door, quickly and quietly, then leaned against it, blinking in the gloom that reeked of previous patrons and the next day's meals being prepared below in the tavern kitchens.

Flinging her a disgusted glance, Biagio growled something in Italian she didn't quite catch—nor did she want to—and arranged the heavy, muscled knight on the straw-stuffed mattress. Then he leaned against the wall, breathing hard from his efforts. He had borne the burden of bringing Rhys up the narrow back stairs of the inn. "Couldn't you have chosen a smaller champion? He must weigh near fifteen stone."

His complaint faded in the close gloom. A thread of moonlight came through a small window. He moved toward a tiled stove and lit a candle from the glowing coals. Cursing softly as the hot tallow dripped onto his fingers, he slowly surveyed the small room. "I note the gallant swain spared no expense in making amorous preparations."

"So I see." Sasha had already seen the earthenware flagon of wine and loaf of bread on a tray near the stove. She moved to the sagging bed and tugged at one of the knight's knee-high boots. It came free and she dropped it to the floor, reaching for the other. When she had removed it she turned her attention to his garments and hesitated. He wore a jerkin, tunic, and tight-fitting hose. She had a brief, dismaying vision of trying to undress him without actually touching him.

Looking up, she caught Biagio's faint, derisive smile and scowled. "Instead of watching, you could do this for me."

"Sì. But then you would not be able to say with all truth that 'twas you who undressed him, should he ask. Lying is a grievous sin, bella."

"I appreciate your concern for my soul," she snapped, "but 'twould be much more helpful if you were to at least lend me your aid." She jerked at the buckle of Rhys's wide leather belt, unfastened it, and slid it free. His sword twisted slowly as she held up the belt, and Biagio took it with a murmur of appreciation for a fine weapon.

"Shall I test the blade, bella? It looks sharp enough to change him from a rooster to a hen."

She flung him a scathing glance that made him grin, then turned her attention back to Rhys. The supple leather jerkin was laced over his broad chest, covering a long linen tunic beneath. Both had become twisted around his thighs, and she had to pull hard to free them.

After an irritating delay, Biagio moved to the other side of the bed to help. He didn't bother to hide his thoughts, and she quickly threw up the familiar barriers when she realized the path of his wicked reflection. He was doing it a'purpose, of course. And was highly amused by his own mischief, the cheeky devil. If she wasn't already in such confusion, she would box his ears quickly enough.

As it was, she worked swiftly to help undress the knight. She didn't know what was worse—Biagio's knavery or Elspeth's glowering disapproval. Or, she thought in the next breath as Biagio pulled away Rhys's undertunic, the turmoil inside her.

Rhys, clad only in his linen, lay sprawled in drugged slumber on the mattress. Candlelight flickered over him, revealing taut ropes of muscle on his abdomen and chest. She tried to ignore a flash of appreciation for his masculine beauty. It was too unsettling.

When she took a step back, Biagio said softly, "If 'tis dreams of love play you mean him to have,'twill be more believable if he is not still in his linen. *Capite?*"

"Of course I understand, you idiot." She flicked him an irritated glance. "And I agree. Remove them."

Biagio wisely did not say the words she knew trembled on the tip of his tongue, but obeyed silently. Sasha took a deep breath.

"Wait outside the door, Biagio. I will do what must be done and join you swiftly."

"Even asleep,'tis more than he deserves." Biagio cast a quick, dark glance at the naked knight.

She stood still in the center of the small room as Biagio let himself out the door. What to do, what to do . . . a lifetime of avoiding this very situation left her ill prepared. She approached the side of the bed again. Yet, perhaps this was the best way. She would never admit it to Elspeth or Biagio, of course, but if she'd found herself unable to bind the knight with any other method, she was fully prepared to do what must be done to achieve her goal. After all, she was well past the age when most maids were already wed, with squalling brats clinging to their skirts. The tiny membrane that signified the difference between maiden and matron had not gained her any great prizes that she'd seen, save the entertainment of watching men turn themselves inside out to be first to shatter it. And for what? The straining, grunting, and groaning that she'd observed beneath castle stairs, in shadowy corners, on silk-covered couches, and in street gutters held no allure for her. It looked to be a sweaty, messy business, not worth the efforts she'd seen others go to in order to perform such acts. Nay, she had never needed Elspeth's constant reminders that she was a princess, not needed her frequent warnings of the hazards of yielding to the persuasions of a common swain.

And yet . . . and yet, when she thought of that day in the meadow, lying under sweet-scented hawthorn flowers and the spreading branches of an alder, with the blue sky overhead and the wind blowing soft, and the knight summoning the most exquisite sensations with his mouth and hands, she could understand a small bit of what induced men and women to behave as they did. A small bit.

A thick mutter brought her attention back to the knight on the bed, and she looked down at him. She was not blind to his physical virtues. Even in the dim light of candle gloom and erratic moonlight, she could see the lure of his strong, muscled body. A beautiful male animal, a man in his prime, with the hard lean muscles of a trained knight, well accustomed to wielding heavy weapons and enduring strenuous conditions. He was a lord, a worthy champion, a man capable of achieving anything he undertook. She meant to bind him to her with wile or guile . . . or whatever it took to reclaim her legacy.

Silently, Sasha removed all her garments except for her shift, and took up the candle. She placed it nearer the bed, so that the shadows would cloak her near nudity while the glow revealed her identity. There must be no mistake, no accusation that she had not kept her word. A night of passion and heat she had promised, and a night of passion and heat he would get. Or so she intended him to remember.

A quick stoop, and she retrieved a small jar from a pouch in her garments. With her other hand, she pulled her hair forward to drape her body and hide her short silk shift. Then she moved to the bed.

Ropes creaked when she perched on the edge of the mattress and leaned over him. He smelled of wine and spices. His chest rose and fell with steady, regular rhythm, and she put a hand on the slightly furred skin between his flat brown nipples. He was warm—almost hot beneath her palm. His heartbeat strong and steady. His torso was nearly as dark as the skin browned by the sun, though faint lines marked the boundaries of his clothing. She moved her hand in light exploration. Small scars puckered his skin, raised and ridged beneath the grazing brush of her fingertips. Marks of his profession. Badges of courage. Or of being too slow to get out of the way.

Her fingers skimmed over the spaced ridge of his ribs to the hard bands of muscle on his belly. Dark whorls of hair arrowed downward from his navel. Curiosity overcame any lingering shreds of reluctance she might have felt about the invasion of privacy, and she let her gaze move slowly and with great interest over the knight's attributes. A mighty warrior indeed, in the lists of love as well as combat.

But on to business, before she grew too distracted to remember the purpose of this audacious plan. She was in his bed, as she'd said she would be. And when she was ready, she would wake him just enough so that he would have vague memories of her presence. A daring plan, a bold plan.

She braced herself as she lifted her body over his. Straddling him, one knee on each side, she rested her weight gingerly on his thighs. It took a moment of brief struggle to uncork the jar of ointment; a sharp, pungent odor filled the close air as the cork came free. She wrinkled her nose. A novel method, stopping up the necks of bottles and jars with the bark of a Mediterranean tree, and very effective. Arabs had been using *qurq* stoppers for years, though the custom was slow to the reach the West.

She clenched the cork between her teeth and dipped out a liberal portion of ointment. With the tips of her fingers, she rubbed it onto Rhys's skin, smoothing it into his chest with gentle, circular motions. The ointment of crushed eucalyptus leaves, mint, and goose fat spread easily. Her palms tingled as she smoothed it into his skin. Proof of her presence. If fortune was with her, the ointment would spread its warmth into him and penetrate his deeply drugged haze enough to leave him with lingering memories of heated embraces.

He moved restlessly beneath her hands. His long legs and arms twisted so wildly, she was almost unseated. It was like riding an untamed stallion, except that horses listened to her. Rhys was lost in a world of deep slumber and oblivious to her soothing words. Finally, he quieted, and she realized that she'd slid from his thighs up to his groin. Wearing only her shift, there was no barrier between his pressing arousal and the juncture of her thighs. It was a riveting sensation.

Frozen, she stared down at his face. Her teeth clenched tightly on the cork still in her mouth. His eyes were closed, his lips slightly parted, a pulse surging in the dip of his throat. He was asleep. Or at least, part of him was. The part of him that wasn't pushed insistently against her, moist and hot and hard, nudging at the entrance of her body with scalding determination. She moved, and it rubbed against her, a searing friction that sent exquisite shudders of pleasure through her like lightning.

She couldn't breathe. Couldn't move. She hovered over him, knees pressing into the thin mattress, thighs stretched wide over his body, caught in an agony of suspense. Any motion was likely to bring her into abrupt contact with him again, drag her into a quivering admission of his effect on her. It didn't bear thinking about to wonder what would happen if he was awake. This was bad enough.

He made a noise low in his throat. His hips moved, thrusting upward, grazing across her with arrant sensuality. She shuddered weakly. He moved again, this time with blind purpose, pushing so hard and certain the dull, clamoring throb between her thighs altered to a sharp ache of pain. Her hands flung out to stop him and the jar sailed from her fingers, clattering to the floor. The cork popped from her mouth, her teeth clamping down on the tip of her tongue so hard that she couldn't stop a wailing cry of pain.

The sound—or combination of sounds—brought his eyes open. She stared down in mute horror. The stinging pain of her tongue was forgotten as she saw the flare of candle glow in gray eyes, his smoky focus fixed on her face, and a slow smile of satisfaction curving his mouth.

"Chérie . . ."

Low, guttural, sleepy, but definitely awake. She was in terrible trouble.

Not enough poppies, not enough potion in the wine . . .
Elspeth never could get the proper amounts. Why had she
trusted to fortune? If she'd done it herself, he'd still be in
that half-dream world between slumber and awareness,
and she wouldn't be poised atop him waiting for disaster.

But there was no time to worry about that now, not
when he was reaching for her, his movements languorous
and confident. She moved at last, but she was too slow
and he was too fast, deceptively swift, treacherously bold,
his fingers hard around her wrist, his other hand tangling
in the drape of her hair between them.

Think, think, think . . .

Shaky: "Beau sire . . . again so soon?"

A husky laugh. The fingers in her hair twisted, wound
it around his fist, brought her inexorably closer, drew her
down so that she lay nearly atop him, her arms flung out
to the sides to brace herself against the mattress. Her face
was close to his now, close enough to count each long
eyelash, close enough to see the faint sun lines at the corners of his eyes and the faded white scar that stitched his
cheek. Close enough to feel the lift of his chest that grazed
against her breasts with each breath he took. She shook
inside.

He was solid muscle and determination, heat and danger
and quivering temptation, and she suddenly knew beyond
a doubt that she was not ready for this. It was more than
the physical contact. It was all that went with it, the searing reaction she hadn't expected or been able to control,
the rapid swing from euphoria to desolation. Euphoria had
come with the hope that he was the man of the prophecy;
desolation with the sinking despair that he was no more
than Elspeth insisted—a knight with little on his mind but
war and wenching.

"Chérie," he said again, soft, husky, an endearment that
drifted between them on the breath of a sigh. A casual
term, carelessly used by men, yet with this man, in this
room, at this time, it sounded like so much more than she
knew it was. And then his mouth was on hers, gentle and
tasting of wine, his tongue urging her lips apart. She
splayed her hands against his chest, helpless to resist, yield-

ing to the kiss, the touch of his tongue against her poor bruised tongue an erotic play. He dragged his tongue over the outline of her lips, a flickering stroke, then skimmed the curve of her throat when her head tilted back to escape him.

The throb was back, that dangerous pulse between her thighs that was as exhilarating as it was bewildering. Then—shocking—his head bent lower, his lips found her breast through the thin silk. Heated and damp, the strong tug of his mouth shot a spear of flame through her to fuse in the aching throb between her thighs. Her hands were on the bed, curling into the rough sheets spread over the mattress. Her back arched. Everything whirled around her in a heated haze. Coiling sensations made her writhe and moan, and a sense of urgency arose, as if there was something attainable just out of her reach, just beyond her grasp, if only she knew what it was and how to get it. . . .

She cried out softly, and there was a thump on the door and a muttered question. Biagio. He was in the dark hallway . . . waiting. . . .

"*Beau sire* . . . it's late . . . I must go. . . ." She tried to pull away but he held her, tangling the loose silk of her shift in one hand, fingers still gripping her hair in the other. His eyes were narrowed, iron gray and barely focused, fixed on her face with dreamy intensity.

Spinning thought fragments, one urgency replaced by another, and she was twisting free with a strength born of desperation, leaving him holding her silk shift in one hand. She threw herself from the bed, stumbled, caught herself, and looked up. He blinked at her. Frowning, his eyes glazed and muted with poppy glow, he blinked again, this time more slowly, and his lashes drifted down. His head slowly lowered to the mattress, and he sighed deeply.

She stood naked and trembling, poised for flight. He was asleep. Claimed by the drug again. She moved to the bed, a quick faltering step to retrieve her shift. He held it tightly in his fist. Another thump on the door sounded, this time louder and harder.

"Bella . . ."

"I'm coming." Abandoning her shift, she snatched up

her outer garments and shrugged into them, tucked her pretty embroidered slippers with the tiny bells under one arm, and flew to the door. Grateful it was so dark in the hallway, she slipped from the room and closed the door behind her.

"Is he still asleep?" Biagio asked, voice soft and curiously angry, his lean frame just a tense shadow against darker shadows.

She nodded without looking at him. "Yea, and he'll have a painful headache when he wakes."

"Good."

Noisy laughter drifted up from the common room downstairs. She smiled. "Come. We have a lot to do yet."

It was much too warm. The cloying fragrance of spice surrounded him. His head ached. Rhys lifted a hand to his eyes and was assaulted by a drift of silk and scent. Jerking his eyes open, he found a scarlet length of silk clutched tightly in his fist. A tiny prick of gray light filtered through an open window to shimmer in the sheer material. He frowned.

There were no silk walls, no cushions with gold tassels, no brass flagons or cups . . . no woman. He turned his hand, staring at the limp silk shift in his fist. Cursing, he sat up with a jerk, then swore at the stab of pain that action brought.

His eyes adjusted to the dim gloom, and he recognized his surroundings: the tavern room. It reeked of old food and lingering spice. He'd last been in a silken tent redolent with incense. He remembered being sprawled in a very comfortable chair gazing down at the maid, remembered drinking wine—so much wine he did not remember walking back to the inn. Jésu, it had been a long time since he'd been fool enough to do something like that.

But there were other memories—pleasant ones, if his head wouldn't ache so damnably bad and he could focus on them. Dark silky hair, soft skin, high breasts—he cursed softly.

Where was she? The blurred memory of her atop him—

her soft thighs on each side of his body, the taste of her in his mouth—was enough to vault him from the rough bed in search of her.

That unwise movement made his head swim, and he sank back down with a groan to rest his head in his hands. The length of silk fell free, drifting over his bare thighs. He was naked, but had only hazy memories of being un- dressed. A dull pounding made his head ache even more. It was several moments before he perceived that the sound came from the closed door.

Carefully lifting his head, he squinted at the origin of the noise and snarled a command to enter. He wasn't too surprised to see a red head thrust through the opening, quickly followed by the rest of Brian.

"My lord Rhys . . . are you well?"

Rhys gave him a sour glance. Brian looked disheveled but clear-eyed. "Nay. I am beset by a thick tongue and a thicker head. Pour me wine."

Brian blinked. "Wine. Do you think it wise for you to—"

A rough Welsh oath had the desired effect, and Brian immediately crossed to the small table that held the jug of wine and loaf of stale bread. Liquid splashed, then Brian appeared in front of him, thrusting out a battered pewter cup.

Rhys downed half in a single swallow, then wiped his mouth with the back of his hand. He peered up at Brian, squinting against the brightening light coming through the unshuttered window. "You Irish must have iron guts."

"Aye, lord." Brian glanced uneasily about the room. Si- lence fell, and he shifted from one booted foot to another, oblivious to the rumpled state of his clothes and the way his red hair stuck up from his head like broom straws. His gaze moved to the silk draping Rhys's thighs. A brow rose. "I'm relieved to find you still here."

"Where else would I be? Ah, wait. I know. Dancing in elf land, or wherever it is that faerie queens take their will- ing victims." The ache in his head had begun to dull a bit, lessened no doubt by the hair of the dog that bit him. Rhys took another gulp of wine.

"You jest about a matter you should view more seriously," Brian muttered in a wounded tone. "If she is no elf queen, explain why she was wearing a robe of purple."

Rhys eyed him darkly. "Because it's a pretty color? Jésu, Brian, but you say the most—"

"Purple is the color of royalty, you know that. Only those of royal blood are allowed to wear it, yet the . . . maid . . . flaunted it before she disappeared into the mist."

He frowned. That was true enough, but she was definitely not a maid who seemed to care about conventions. And she was discreet enough to wear the color only in wealds, it seemed, for he'd not noted it adorning her outer garments in the village. He looked hard at Brian.

"There is a difference in being reckless and being magic. The magic I've seen from her is of a more worldly nature."

Brian said nothing, but stared down at his feet. Then he bent to retrieve a small object from the floor. He held it up, squinting at it. "And this? What worldly use was this, my lord?"

Turning his head slowly so as not to unbalance himself, Rhys peered at the tiny jar Brian held. Made of thick blue glass carved with strange markings, the jar caught and held the light in muted glimmers.

Brian shook the jar, and the room was suddenly filled with a pungent odor. Dropping it as if burned, he made the sign of the cross over his chest and backed toward the window, chanting, "*Acre arcre arnem nona aernem—*"

Impatient now, Rhys moved to pick up the jar. His head swam from the effort as he held it up and looked at Brian. " 'Tis naught but a salve. From the smell of it, one much like an ointment for horses."

"And of what use was it on you?" Brian retorted. "Do you have aches you would ease with ointment instead of female attention?"

Rhys frowned. There were dim memories of the strong scent, expanding warmth, and the maid spreading her hands over him, murmuring soft words in a strange language. Enchantment, Brian claimed, but the truth was that not even a night of love play had lessened his need. He still had the tight, burning ache inside, and it made his answer sharp.

"You're the only pain I'm suffering at the moment. Pray, get you gone and stir the others to action. We'll leave within the hour."

"Sir Robert readies them, my lord," Brian said shortly. "We'll await your arrival in the front courtyard."

Rhys still held the blue jar tight in his hand, and looked up. "Pardon for my surly nature, Brian. Too much wine has shortened my temper."

"I hope 'tis only the wine that's changed your nature." Brian took a step back and said softly, "You've not been the same since the day in the weald."

It was near enough to the truth to make him irritable, so he offered no argument on his behalf. He focused instead on the more necessary action of dressing but found himself stumbling and clumsy, unable to manage even the simplest buckle and baldric. Chagrined, he suffered Brian's help. Not since he was a green lad had he required aid after a night of drinking. Worse, the memories he had of the night were hazy and unclear.

When he was ready, he turned to Brian. "Have Morgan bring Turk to the front, and I'll join you soon."

Brian held out Rhys's gauntlets. "Shall I accompany you?"

"Nay. I fear you would not like my mission." He did not miss the taut twist of Brian's mouth, nor the quick narrowing of his eyes before he turned away. "Brian—I intend to bid her farewell."

"Yea, but does she intend the same?"

"What do you mean by that?"

His fists clenched and unclenched at his side; worry and strain marked his face as Brian turned back and blurted, "She will not loose you, Rhys. I know it. Don't ask me how I know, for I swear by all the saints I could not tell you. But I know."

"Do you really think me enchanted?"

"Not, mayhaps, as you think I mean it. But yea, lord, I think you in her thrall whether you are wont to admit it or not."

His head pounded, his stomach heaved, and he didn't feel like listening to ridiculous theories. But Brian was a good friend as well as a loyal knight, and he held him in great affection. Slapping the gauntlets idly against his palm, Rhys said mildly, "If I'm enthralled by anything,'tis by a night of soft female curves, not by magic. And I am not the only man so enthralled, for even Sir Peter found his way to the hay with a kitchen wench."

"I've seen that kitchen wench, and what she spreads is her thighs, not magic. It's not the same with the other." His broad chest lifted in a heavy sigh, but there was a glint of humor in his eyes when Brian added, "If not magic, it must be powerful wine to lay you so low you must have my help to dress the next morning."

Rhys grunted. There was no escaping the truth, but it left his temper raw to admit it. Brushing past Brian, he left the room and the inn, clomping down the narrow, dank staircase and through the common room. Fresh air burst onto his senses, bright light and the sharp tang of horses and goats and chickens all mixing together in a familiar blend in the courtyard.

When Rhys stepped from the stoop, Sir Robert was striding toward him from the stables, his broad face creased in a worried scowl. "My lord, there is bad news I must give you." He halted. Sir Robert drew close, shaking his head as he said, "Most of the men have fallen sick, my lord."

"Sick. Of what malady?"

"I don't know, my lord." Sir Robert shook his head. "I thought at first it was only the scours that comes with too much drink, but some of the men who drank only a little seem to have it as well. 'Tis an affliction that has them groaning at the trenches, I fear."

"How many are ill?"

Sir Robert grimaced. " 'Tis easier to count how many are well—myself, Sir Brian, Sir Peter, your squire. . . ."

Rhys swore softly under his breath. Another delay. First Prince John, and now even nature conspired to keep him from Wales. But there was nothing he could do but yield to the unavoidable, and he gave orders for Sir Robert to see the men tended with all due care.

He switched directions, moving toward the stables to see

to the men, halting again when Morgan approached shaking his head. "I put the poultice on Turk's leg like you bid, m'lord, but it did not work. He's lame."

Rhys muttered an oath. He had a flash of memory—a slow smile and burnished skin, dark eyes staring up at him and the warning that the horse would be lame. "Are you certain?" he asked, and his brow creased at the flash of surprise and affront in Morgan's eyes. " 'Tis not what I meant to say. I know you can tell when the animal is lame. Is it only a bruise, or worse?"

"It's hard to say. But he would not bear your weight today, m'lord, even should we be able to leave. Mayhap not the morrow."

"Then it looks," Rhys said grimly, "as if we linger awhile in the village of Wytham."

CHAPTER SIX

"All of them?" Sasha pressed her lips together in a mirthful line, pretending dismay.

Biagio, however, felt no such restraint. He grinned broadly. "Yea, so the innkeeper's daughter tells me. It seems a mysterious malady felled all those knights who lingered late in the tavern last night. Even those men who did not drink too heartily are laid low, and are now groaning into trenches behind the stables."

"Then 'tis doubtful they will travel today." She nodded with satisfaction and sat down on a plump cushion beneath the tent's silk ceiling. A bit of a bellyache would be the worst of it for them. Those that drank the most would suffer the most, but other than that, there was no harm in the potion that had laced their wine.

"What was in the potion?" Biagio plopped down on a striped silk cushion and crossed his legs at the ankles, leaning back on his elbows and regarding her with a lifted brow.

"Mistletoe berries with a pinch of tansy oil. It's potent, but not harmful if used properly. Tansy in itself would

have been too strong. And bitter. There are some who
brew it in a tea to kill internal worms, and even unborn
children." She frowned. "I do not deal with those who
practice dark magic. They are dangerous people."

"Yet you have magic of your own." *Like this . . .
you know what I'm thinking . . . can hear it as if said
aloud . . . .*

"Perhaps, but I don't use it to hurt people." When he
laughed, she glared at him. "Who have I ever hurt with
my Gift?"

He rolled to one side and leaned his head on the slant
of his palm. "Where shall I start? Madríd, perhaps, when
you told that fat Spanish friar that his mistress was sleeping with the bishop—"

"He had his hand on my leg, and I would have told him
the pope was on fire if I thought it would get him away
from me."

"Oh, and the time in Rheims, when you told the buxom
wench with the busy hands that her husband Jacques knew
about her dalliance with the pretty Frankish knight named
Sir Conrad. . . ."

"The buxom wench," Sasha pointed out, "would have
gotten you killed if you'd kept listening to her blandish-
ments. I was only protecting you. She was a slut."

"And the innkeeper's daughter is not? Yet you seem to
think nothing of sending me to whisper sweet words in
her ear to find out what you want to know." He toyed
with the hilt of the dagger in his belt, eyes narrowing
slightly. "He is a lord, not just a knight. Did you know
that?"

She sighed. "Yea, I heard him called so. But whether he
is a lord of lands or air, is another matter. There are those
lords who own naught but a title and debts. I don't yet
know his situation."

A faint smile curled Biagio's mouth. "But I know."

This was a familiar game, a play of wits that all too
frequently ended in anger. She shrugged. "When I'm ready
to know, I'll find out easily enough. He must have a reason
for not flaunting his rank."

"Perhaps because he's not likely to keep his title. They
come and go, you know, rather like the wind at times."

"The winds of change alter much, but not usually the earning of a title." She frowned. Biagio had thrown up his own barriers—cleverly forming images of the kitchen wench in various stages of undress—to keep her from learning the truth. She switched tactics. "I don't care if he's a prince or a peasant. He's the knight of the prophecy, the one who will—"

Biagio made a rude sound and sat up, putting his hands on his knees as he leaned forward. "How do you know you're not interpreting it wrong? The prophecy was a long time ago, and it's not as if an actual griffyn with wings and talons rode down a shaft of sunlight to land at your feet." One hand clenched into a fist, and there was frustration in his dark eyes. "He is only a man, bella, like any other. Last night should have proved it to you."

She stared at him. Did he know what had happened in the tavern room? But he could not, for the images in his mind were of a heavy, sleeping knight oblivious to the world, with no hint of speculation about what might have happened when he left them alone. She sat back again, and shrugged.

"You're right. It's not just the prophecy." His brows flew up at her admission, and she added slyly, "It's my intuition."

Biagio groaned. "The same intuition that almost got us taken prisoner in Antioch?"

She frowned. "That was different. I felt I could trust him. Not once did Saladin think about what he planned, not once. I was as surprised as you when those men came bursting through the doors with scimitars. Good thing we were only the entertainment." She shuddered at the memory. "If we had been actual guests of Prince Bohemond, we would be dead."

"A near escape."

She looked up. "Yes."

Bella, bella, he's not the one. . . . Search your own mind and heart for the truth. . . .

Angry, she surged to her feet. "He's the answer, I tell you. Do you think I would be doing all this if I didn't really believe that?"

Biagio was on his feet as well, facing her angrily, head bent and nose almost touching hers. "No, but I think you won't look past that stupid prophecy to the truth. I'm not like Elspeth. If you want to bed the swaggering fool, be my guest, but don't hide behind some noble cause to justify it."

"If I want to bed him, I will. I'm not bound by any restraints other than my own good judgment, and certainly not by you."

"You've shown that well enough," he snapped.

His words faded, the tension between them sizzling like raindrops on a hot rock as they glared at each other.

"Children, children," came the mild reproof from the open tent flap, and Sasha and Biagio whirled at the deep, mocking voice. Rhys stood in the opening, bending slightly so his head didn't bring down the tent. A faint smile curled his mouth.

Sasha recovered first. "Beau sire . . . we didn't hear your approach."

"Obviously. Family quarrel, perhaps?" His inquiring gaze shifted from her to Biagio.

"Nay, beau sire. Not that. Our only kinship is that of long friendship. As you may have guessed, he is more like a brother to me than a servant."

"I see," he said, but it was obvious he didn't. Not the truth, anyway. How much had he heard?

Cursing the lack of her Gift with this man, she put on her brightest smile. "You are out early this morn, beau sire."

"Yea, and just in time to stop bloodshed, it seems." He looked thoughtfully from her to Biagio, the silk tent flap draping over one of his broad shoulders like a Saracen cape.

Biagio quivered beside her. His muscles were tight with the strain of anger. *Prophecy or not, he's not the one for you, bella.*

"We . . . quarrel sometimes, but never seriously," she said to Rhys, ignoring Biagio's simmering rage. "Biagio always ends up apologizing—"

Liar, liar, hair on fire. . . .

"—and then I forgive him," she continued, stepping closer to Biagio to give him a swift, surreptitious kick to the ankle, "and we are friends again."

Ouch! You go too far.

"But enough of our petty problems. We were about to break our fast, beau sire. Would you care to join us?"

I'll feed him henbane and tansy.

Rhys looked back at her. She smiled. "I'll have Elspeth prepare us a tray. And Biagio will fetch it."

Don't do it, bella . . . fool, fool if you do. . . .

A quick nudge in Biagio's ribs with her elbow spurred him forward. He jerked away, then nodded curtly at Rhys before brushing past him and out of the tent. Silk fluttered in his angry wake.

Rhys had turned to watch him and now looked back at her, a lazy smile on his mouth. "You must have left early, sweet flower. I awoke, and you were gone, leaving me only memories and this—"

He produced her scarlet shift with a flourish. Praise God he had not given it to her while Biagio was still there. He would have immediately leaped to all the right conclusions.

"Your colors," he said softly, "worn in your name. Worn in the lists of love instead of war. . . ."

She clutched at it, and the silk drifted over her palm. Rhys curled his fingers around her hand, holding it lightly. She looked up, startled and annoyed at the swift leap of her heart. He was gazing down at her, blond head brushing against the silk ceiling, his eyes as gray as smoke and as wise as time, the knowing smile on his lips making her think of things she shouldn't.

She managed a shaky smile, gently removing her hand from his grasp. "It was kind of you to bring it to me, beau sire."

"I didn't bring it to be kind." He lifted the dangling end of silk she held, wound it slowly around his fist, and drew her closer. Her hands pressed against the front of his leather jerkin, knuckles grazing the studs in his wide belt. She looked up, and he put a curled finger under her chin, thumb brushing against her lightly. "I came to see you, flower."

There was that annoying thump again. Ridiculous, that he should be able to affect her like this. Sweetly, "I'm flattered, beau sire."

She withdrew to a safer distance, putting up a barrier of coquetry and space between them, trying to think of something witty to say, something that would make him laugh and divert him from the subject of the night before. That was dangerous ground. Every time she thought of the scene in his room and she had lain awake those last few hours of darkness dwelling on every moment of it— she felt that peculiar tightness in her chest again, and the queasiness in her stomach, as if she'd eaten too many green apples.

Rhys remained in front of her, the faint smile still on his mouth and his eyes knowing. He filled up the small space of the tent. Why had she asked him to stay? But if she didn't, how would she ever bring up the bargain they had struck? There should have been more time, time to plan what she would say, to remind him of his sworn oath.

But maybe this was best. He was here, they were alone, and it would take Biagio more than a few minutes to find Elspeth and have her prepare a tray.

"Sit here, beau sire," she said, and pulled forward the folded chair he'd used the night before. It was unwieldy and stubborn, and she tugged and pushed at it unsuccessfully, cursing under her breath.

"Allow me." Rhys bent, took the chair by each side, gave it a smooth shove that spread the balky legs apart, and snapped it into place with a faint click of brass hinges and wood. " 'Tis how it's done."

"So I see." Her disgusted mutter sounded ungracious, so she flashed him a quick smile. "I'm not very good with these things."

"You have other talents," he said softly, and she looked away from the gleam in his eyes. He moved around the chair, so close he was almost atop her, and she took a step back. His hand caught the sleeve of the simple dress she wore, holding her, his voice a smooth purr almost in her ear. "Has it caused you trouble to come to my bed?"

"Trouble?"

"I heard part of your disagreement with Biagio. It seems that you've earned his disapproval."

"Yea, a bit." She looked up at him. "But it's my life and my decision. No one else's." She took a deep breath. Now or never, while he seemed to be in a pleasant mood from their tryst. "And I did what I said I would do, did I not, beau sire?"

"Yea." His finger moved to touch her left ear, circling it with light, feathery brushes that made her shiver. "You definitely did, flower. You came to my bed as promised. 'Tis a sweet memory."

She breathed deeply with relief, then spread a hand against his chest. Her fingers were dark in contrast to the pale linen of the tunic beneath his leather jerkin. "Then you are well satisfied?"

His hand moved to cover hers, large and strong, with long blunt fingers that looked capable of anything. His palm was rough and callused. "Very well satisfied, flower. A memorable night."

She toyed with the leather lace beneath her fingers. "A night in return for a labor, beau sire. My promise kept. What of yours?"

Amusement edged his voice. "My promise?"

She looked up at him. "Yea, beau sire. The victory you promised me. What of it?"

Smiling, he reached out to lift a strand of her hair, rubbing it between his fingers as he murmured, "Ah, the wearing of your colors. Was one night not enough?"

"Nay, beau sire." Her fingers tightened on the slender string lacing together the front of his jerkin. "There is more than just the night I seek." He shifted with a slight tensing of muscles, his knuckles grazing against the bare skin above the neckline of her gown.

She opened her mouth to say it quickly before she lost the courage she'd summoned, but a sudden clatter and yelp from just outside the tent drew his attention. He released her hair, and his hand went to the hilt of the sword always at his side.

The sound of quarreling split the air, Biagio's and Elspeth's voices loud with irritation as they burst into the tent. They both stopped and turned in unison, appealing to her.

"Sasha, tell this foolish boy that bread and cheese are not enough to break the fast of a hungry man—"

"Nay, 'tis what we usually have," Biagio retorted. "Why change now?"

Sasha narrowed her eyes at them. She wasn't fooled for an instant. The interruption was as carefully planned and maneuvered as a dancer's steps. "Bread and cheese are fine," she snapped. "Bring it and go."

No, my child, not and leave you alone with the hungry lion . . .

"I insist upon serving you," Elspeth said aloud, a smile on her lips and determination gleaming in her eyes. " 'Tis my duty."

"Your duty," she said shortly, "is to obey my wishes. Leave the meal here and go on with your other tasks."

"Our tasks are done, and we are at your pleasure, signorina," Biagio said, and reached outside the tent to produce his lute with a flourish. "Sweet music soothes the stomach and the air." He crossed to the side of the tent and sat down cross-legged. "You won't even know I'm here. Think of me as a little mouse in the corner."

"You mean a rat in the barrel," she muttered, and Rhys laughed.

"Lady fair, I think we are being chaperoned. Do not disappoint them." His hand moved to caress the nape of her neck, lifting her hair to allow his fingers access to her bare skin, making her shiver and Biagio glare at them. Rhys smiled and shifted his hand to rest on her shoulder, a silent statement of possession. Biagio made a choking sound, and Elspeth's face paled. Sasha stood still, at a loss. His hand fell away after a moment, and he took a step to one side. "Though I appreciate the efforts on my behalf, I must decline your offer. There are other matters that command my attention for now."

He turned, his eyes drawing her gaze so that she stared up at him. "It seems as if I will be in Wytham longer than first thought, flower. Perhaps we will meet again."

The message was quite clear. She managed a nod and a smile, a murmur of assent, and he was gone, striding past Elspeth's frozen form and ducking out the tent to disappear into the close forest.

Nothing was said for a long moment. Sasha had no intention of listening to the accusations and reproaches that she knew were imminent. Her gaze dropped, landing on the pouch she used to gather herbs. She turned with a swift shrug and muttered her intention to gather some herbs before the morning sun wilted the best flowers, then was out the open flap of the tent before Elspeth or Biagio recovered enough to stop her.

She fairly flew over dew-damp grass, bells on her feet tinkling as she ran through the trees, light filtering down through overhead branches in shifting threads. It was best anyway. She had not thought he'd shake free of the poppy haze so early, and wanted more time to plan her words. He would not take lightly her intention to hold him to his pledge, and would most likely be angry at first. But he was an honorable knight, and in the end, he would keep his oath.

Flower, he called her. Sweet flower. Fair flower. Blossom. She stopped, fingers shaking slightly as she reached out to lift the weight of a hawthorn blossom in her hand. The pale white flower cupped delicate shades of yellow in its center, tiny fragile petals in trembling shades of color, sweetly scented white against dark green leaves. Children often ate the new leaves, savoring the nutty flavor. *Flower* . . . Echoes from the past, the fading, bittersweet memory of another man calling her flower. Her father, all wise and powerful, dark and handsome and smiling at her with indulgent affection, calling her *zaharat*. Little flower.

She released the tight clump of hawthorn blossoms, careful not to touch the wicked thorns along the stalk. Enough of that. All that was left of her former life was Elspeth. And the prophecy that had promised her sweet vengeance and redemption. It burned inside her, a constant reminder, a determined objective. It would be done, and the knight of the griffyn would be her champion, as the prophecy had promised.

A fierce warrior will come upon you in a wood, a griffyn that is half eagle, half lion, and this man will restore to you that which has been lost.

Yea, he was the one. She would hold him to his oath, and it would be as prophesied.

Rhys swore softly. Was he beset with ill fortune? Nothing had gone right since he'd returned to England. Perhaps he should have stayed in Palestine with Richard, dodging Greek fire and arrows and having a generally fine time. It was certainly less dangerous. He shook his head.

"Grant pardon, m'lord," Sir Robert said with a pained glance, "but I knew you must be told."

"Yea. How many were killed or disabled?"

"A full score. The messenger awaits in the tavern, should you wish to ask him more questions. He was weary, and I bade him take meat and drink while I searched you out, m'lord."

His head still hurt. And his stomach had not yet settled from the night's abuse. Even his skin itched, and his mood was going from merely ill-tempered, to savagely uncomfortable. But it was not Sir Robert's fault that Rhys drank so much wine even his eyelashes hurt. He nodded briefly.

"I'll search him out in the tavern, Sir Robert. Go rest. You don't look well. I don't need you to come down with the same sickness as the others."

If planned by an enemy, things could not have gone much worse. If he were as Brian, fearful of elves and faeries, he'd probably be wearing the tooth of a saint and the shinbone of the pope to keep away evil spells. But the misfortunes that had befallen him were too ordinary to blame on anything but fate and villains. Mercenaries were commonplace on English roads, and the scourge that afflicted his men was found all too often in armies. And now, the men he'd hired in London to join his forces in Glenlyon courted disaster.

"M'lord," the messenger mumbled around a mouth filled with beef and bread, stumbling to his feet when Rhys approached the table. "Grant pardon . . ."

Rhys waved him back down. "Be seated. You've ridden hard and swift, and should finish your meal. There's time enough to hear the bad news." He was in no hurry. With a lame horse and sick soldiers, he'd be able to do little even if trouble rode directly into Wytham after him.

When the messenger finished, he wiped a sleeve across his mouth and swallowed a gulp of ale, then nodded grimly. " 'Tis more than just the killing of some men, m'lord. It has to do with Lord Rhys, prince of Deheubarth, and the Marcher laws. There is a dispute, m'lord, brought to the Welsh prince against the lands of Glenlyon. It has earned Prince John's attention."

The messenger paled slightly when Rhys's hand clenched into a fist atop the table. Rhys stared at the man a moment, striving for calm. "Tell me of the dispute."

Clearing his throat, the messenger looked as if he wished to be anywhere else as he said, "There is a dispute as to your right to claim your father's lands, m'lord. As you have not lived in Wales these past score years, a complaint has been brought that you are not rightful lord. . . ."

As his words trailed into dismayed silence, Rhys stared at him in the smoky gloom. He shouldn't be surprised. He'd never thought he would inherit at all, and if not for his father's and brothers' deaths, he would not have. The political climate of Wales was changing, influenced as always by the English. He was not ignorant of it, though he'd never thought to return to Wales, so had not closely studied the situation. Hadn't let himself dwell too long on things Welsh when he'd left that life behind.

Now, all was changing. In his life as in Wales. Even the names of the ruling groups had evolved, changing from the old royalty, *brenin*, to be replaced by a new set of minor rulers, *arglwydd*. Yea, he was well aware of it, well aware that the Welsh sense of unity with the Britons under King Henry II had evolved into the concept of Welsh separation of tribes, *cenedl y Cymry*. Now, Welshmen were more isolated, blending tribal and pastoral tenants under many tribal lords who fought with each other, battling over scraps of land, cattle, and possessions. But there was a new movement afoot, a move to consolidate the lords under the leadership of Gwynedd, prince of Snowdonia in north Wales—a Welshman, not an English ruler. If not for Lord Rhys of Deheubarth in the south, there would be violent civil war in the land. It was a delicate balance, and the least shift in either direction could swing England and Wales into full-scale war.

And then what side would he choose?

Rhys took a deep breath. "Sir Niclas of Raglan lays claims to my lands, I presume, but by what authority?"

Shaking his head, the messenger looked around uneasily, as if searching for an escape route. "Nay, m'lord. 'Tis not Sir Niclas."

"No? Then who? I was told Sir Niclas besieged Glenlyon—"

"Gavin, m'lord. Gavin of Glamorgan petitions for title to Glenlyon. He claims there is no lord present, and you are in default."

Gavin. *Gavin*. His mouth set in a hard line. Gavin, his own cousin, would steal Glenlyon before he could reach Wales to claim his lands.

"Is there more?" he asked after a moment, and the messenger shook his head.

"Nay, lord. Only that the prince has taken it under advisement."

Jerking up from the bench, Rhys strode from the tavern, and toward the stables. If he did not reach Glenlyon soon, it was likely to belong to another man. He had not realized until now just how much he wanted his lands.

"I heard about the hired men, my lord," Brian said when Rhys reached the stables. He gestured to the men scattered about on straw pallets and in dusty corners. "By the morrow, these should be able to ride."

"Where's Morgan? I would hate to leave Turk behind, but I will not delay past the morrow." He met Brian's gaze. "There is more to it than you know. My cousin has petitioned the Prince of Deheubarth for title to Glenlyon. If I linger too long, I may lose it by default."

Dismay clouded Brian's green eyes, and he shook his head. "Then is Gavin is league with Sir Niclas? Was it Gavin who set Raglan to besiege your keep, mayhaps attack the men you hired to meet us at Glenlyon?"

"It seems possible." His clenched fist struck hard against the post between stalls, startling the horses. He barely looked at them.

"Before God, Brian, but if Gavin thinks to steal my birthright, he will have a fight on his hands. I remember him from our childhood. A weasel face, with big eyes and sticky hands, always filching from others."

"You knew him well, Rhys?" Brian murmured, leaning close, his big shoulder against the heavy oak post.

Rhys nodded. "Yea. In those days, Welsh chieftains roamed about from summer pasture to summer pasture, living in a lightly built *hafod* that we could easily abandon. Winters, we returned to the milder valleys and *hendref*, more substantially built homes. Our cattle shared pasture land. Clan members often passed the time together."

He paused, remembering sunlight, meadows, wooden swords, and mock fights with his brothers and cousins. So long ago. Another lifetime. Another life. His life then had been a transient, pleasant time occasionally disrupted by war, but otherwise fairly tranquil. Or, those were his memories of it. A host of peaceful images, dissected by that shattering moment when his father had called him to the council fire and informed him that he had been promised to the English.

He was a chieftain's son. Even at eight he'd known better than to wail or protest. So he'd stood there, rigid and disbelieving, listening to his world fall apart around him, barely aware of his mother's soft cry of anguish or his brothers' solemn stares of sympathy. There had been no time for lengthy farewells, little time for explanation. The light of the next morning had seen him off, as he was escorted from Wales by the king's envoy. He'd not seen any of them again, his mother dead of a fever within a year, his father and brothers so recently slain.

If he'd thought leaving Wales hard, his arrival in Henry's court had been worse. Much worse. Scorned for his

Welsh ways and dress, called a savage and a barbarian, shamed for his lack of manners and his wildness, he'd reacted with defiance and hatred. He'd often wondered how he would have fared if not for a kind-hearted Englishman who'd taken him under his wing. But now Rhys knew that King Henry had directed that kindness, had foreseen the future of Wales and planned for it by turning Welsh hostages into English knights.

All he had left of Wales was his squire Morgan, and a few memories. And now Glenlyon.

He looked up. Brian was watching him, and a current of understanding flowed between them that needed no words. He smiled.

"The morrow will see us gone from here, Brian. Do you think the men will be able?"

"Yea, lord. But I'm not so certain about your horse. He favors his foreleg greatly." Brian shook his head. "We've done all we know. It will most like take time or a miracle."

"Or a maid who claims knowledge of healing horses." Rhys smiled slightly when Brian gave him a sharp glance. "Yea,'tis the dark maid I mean. I heard her called Sasha, and you will find her in a Saracen's tent a half league behind the inn. Bid her bring herbs and knowledge with her, for I favor Turk to any other mount, and would prefer riding him to take back Glenlyon."

Brian's reluctance was evident, but he nodded. "Yea, lord. I'll bring her. If she doesn't turn me into a toad first."

Rhys laughed. "Send Sir Robert in your stead. He already looks like a toad. And he has no fear of faeries or elf queens."

"Nay, and no charms to ward off evil. I'll go. I've enough chants and charms to keep her at bay. I hope," Brian said darkly.

"Be more wary of her servant than any spells," Rhys warned. "He's more likely to do you harm than she is."

"In league with her, no doubt." Brian shook his head and tightened his sword belt a notch. "I'd rather face mortal danger than magic any day."

"The chance of a sharp dagger is greater, I'd say. Watch your back."

Brian turned back to stare hard at him. "And you, Rhys, watch that you do not fall under her spell. I wish you would take the charm I bought for you to wear."

"I need no charm to protect me from enchantment. I have all I need—a strong arm, good sword, noble destrier, and wise friend—no man needs more."

"There are times nothing earthly guards against magic." Rhys stared after him, a faint smile on his mouth.

CHAPTER SEVEN

ᘒᘓ

Sunlight caught in the depths of a harebell, glowing a rich, deep blue. Sasha touched the blossom lightly, and a dewdrop trickled down a petal to land on her fingertip. A light wind sprang up, teasing blades of grass; slender poles of hazel trees with branches that rose in clusters of bony fingers from the ground clacked together. She looked up. Clouds rolled across the sky, promising rain. She'd best go back to help Elspeth and Biagio take down the tent.

By now, the worst of their anger should be faded, though she still faced certain recriminations from Elspeth. Biagio would be sulking most likely, still smarting from their argument earlier. Why did he hate Rhys so? The dislike had been almost instant. Biagio had been against him from that first moment in the weald, when they'd peered through the hawthorn branches and oak leaves and seen him riding at the head of his men, a mocking blond knight with more than enough arrogance.

Biagio's resentment was part of the reason she'd not wanted to tell them Rhys was a lord. It was distressing that he'd found out. He and Elspeth would only use that as an excuse to prove that Rhys was not the man of the prophecy, that he was just a brash English lord with no interest in becoming a powerful champion.

Sunlight faded to gloom, the threat of rain grew more imminent. She quickened her pace through the hazel coppice. The long hem of her berry red skirts caught on a branch and she paused to untangle it. She sensed the approach of a knight, the turbulence of his thoughts reaching her long before she heard him. Brian. She stopped and waited.

Sasha . . . not a likely name for a faerie queen . . . a trick, and he can't see it . . . The witch will most like kill his horse before she cures it, but would he listen if I tried to tell him of it? Nay, Rhys is too reckless for his own safety. . . .

More thoughts emanated from him, some couched in Gaelic phrases that she didn't know, all accompanied by visions of Rhys sailing away in a crystal boat, and of herself leering over him and laughing evilly. The man was truly besotted with his fears. And she didn't at all like the way he viewed her, harsh and dark and wicked—a veritable crone. Very well. If he thought her so demonic and powerful, she would be what he expected.

When he drew close, a vague shadow among the tall, slender branches of hazel coppice, she began to chant softly, lifting her voice in a meaningless patter of sounds. The hem of her gown spun around her ankles and the tiny bells on her feet tinkled as she began to swirl, dancing lightly among harebells, primroses, wood anemones, and red campions growing beneath the willowy poles of hazel.

Then she bent, swooped, plucked the fragile flower of a harebell and held it up to the thin threads of light piercing the wood. "Bluebell, bluebell, bring me some luck before tomorrow night," she chanted, loud enough for him to hear her, then knelt to tuck the blossom into her shoe.

Still crouched on the ground, she looked up at Brian where he stood, transfixed. "Greetings, fair knight. Ask me anything and I will be bound to tell the truth, for I wear the bluebell in my shoe."

It was a common enough myth that she was certain he had heard it before. He must have, for he started toward her then, his mind set on extracting the truth from her.

"You are called Sasha," he said, then cleared his throat of the rough rasp in his words. "I would know what you want with my lord."

Her brow lifted, and she curved her mouth in a faint smile. "He knows what I want from him." She reached out, fingers grazing the length of a catkin that had opened and was dangling from a slender hazel branch. "But what does he want from me?" She looked past the yellow cluster of blooms resting against her palm, eyes lingering on Brian's face. Her fingers curled around the catkin and she yanked it from the branch, holding it tightly in her hand, the faint smile still playing on her mouth. "Shall I make wreaths of hazel for us both, Sir Brian? We can wear them on our heads and none will be able to see us, 'tis said. Have you ever tried it? Have you ever danced with the faeries on Midsummer Eve? Or picked mugwort before sunrise, and said *Tollam te artemesia, ne lassus sim in via. . . . ?*"

Brian took a swift step backward, one hand fumbling at the pouch on his belt, fingers shaking as he clutched a charm. Sasha laughed. She couldn't help it. This big, stalwart knight looked absolutely ridiculous quivering with fear of faeries.

Her laughter made him halt, and he took a deep breath and glared at her. "You won't have him. I won't let you spirit Rhys away from here. He may not believe, but I know about elves and faeries, the Daoine Sidhe that think they are so clever. . . . You won't have him."

It was on the tip of her tongue to refute his vow, but she stopped herself from saying anything. To put him even more on the defensive would be foolish beyond measure, and she had already tweaked him enough. So she allowed herself a careless shrug before saying, "If you want me to heal his horse, you'd best take me there before I'm out of my charitable mood. Later, I may not feel like it."

Brian gaped at her, eyes wide. "I did not tell you why I came—"

"You didn't need to tell me. The horse was lame yesterday, but your lord did not heed my warning." She dropped the catkin and brushed the yellow dusting of pollen from her palms. "First, I must fetch my chest of herbs and salves. 'Twill do me no good to see the horse without my herbs."

When Brian remained standing as if rooted to the spot, she said impatiently, "Do you come? Or must I go by myself?"

He jerked forward, reluctance in every line of his body as he followed her through the coppice to the beech glade where the Saracen tent still stood. Wind fluttered the jewel colors, and Biagio was struggling with ropes and stakes. He paused and looked up, dark brow lowering when he saw her with Rhys's knight.

"I need my chest of herbs," she said to forestall anything he might say to Brian, "so fetch it from the cart."

There was a moment of tense silence. Sunlight flickered erratically through clouds and beech leaves, spattering on Biagio's dark hair as he glared at them. Then he shrugged and moved to the open cart, where it tilted at an awkward angle on two wheels. The broken axle was still being repaired by the village wainwright. Biagio flipped up the covering and dragged out her chest of herbs.

"You're almost out of dragon wings and unicorn hearts," he said with a bland expression, handing her the small leather cask.

Sasha glared at him, ignoring Brian's quick wheeze of horror. "Then fetch me some more from wherever it is you got the last," she snapped. "I'll be in the village should Elspeth need me."

Brian was remarkably quiet on the trek to the stables, though she had to erect her mental barriers to hold back the barrage of terrified thoughts and images that flooded his mind. Despite his distrust and fear of her, she couldn't help but admire his single-minded devotion to his lord and friend. He truly cared about Rhys, truly loved him with an emotion only one man could feel for another. It was different from that felt by women, just as strong in its way, but as different as night from day. So she could forgive him a little for wanting her far away from Rhys.

That did not mean she had any intention of abandoning her plan. On the contrary. It only strengthened her determination. For if Rhys inspired this kind of devotion from his man, he was definitely the kind of man who could regain all she had lost.

The stable was gloomy and ill lit, and filled in every corner with moaning men and the fetid stink of sickness. Appalled, Sasha paused just inside the door. She was assaulted with an overwhelming torrent of painful impressions, and quickly threw up her barriers. But it had been enough. It had not occurred to her that these men would feel quite so badly, or that the potion she had so blithely put into their wine to detain Rhys would cause this kind of suffering. No, she had envisioned only enough discomfort to keep them from riding away from Wytham just yet.

Filled with remorse, she made her way to the stall that held the huge black destrier. The horse snorted, tossing its great head and whipping the long mane into tangles. She set down her chest of herbs and opened it, channeling her energies into the horse. As she had done with Bayosha, she removed everything from her mind but the distressed animal, until she began to feel its energy and the source of its pain. Yea, as she had told Rhys, there was an inner bruise in the pastern. The unguent applied by his squire had not harmed the soreness, but neither had it helped.

The squire joined them, and moved to take hold of the steed's bridle and keep him still enough to twist a length of rope around the soft upper lip. It was a common method used to immobilize a feisty horse. Sasha glanced up and shook her head. "There is no need for that. It will only distress him more."

"If I do not," the squire muttered, "you will never be able to get close enough to apply your mixture."

She smiled. "Don't worry about that. He will not hurt me."

A flutter of skepticism mixed with Welsh phrases she did not understand flickered through the squire's mind, along with a grim relish. None of these men trusted her, and each hoped that her failure would prove to their lord that she was not worthy of his attention.

She set out to prove them wrong.

Crooning soft words in the secret language of horses that she'd learned from the desert men of Arabia—whose ways with horses were legend—she lifted the small bowl of noxious smelling salve and a length of brown cloth and approached the nervous destrier. The black hide rippled with tension, muscles sleek and shiny and powerful. Snorting, he strained against the squire's hold, eyes rolling to show the whites as Sasha drew close.

"Step back," she said softly, and the squire shook his head.

"Nay, for then it would be me who must explain to his lordship why his horse's hooves are stained with your blood."

She put a hand on the quivering flanks, and the horse snorted but did not shy away at her touch. She smiled. "See? He won't harm me, but you must move away. You make him nervous."

"I make—? Devil take it all, but you're a brash wench."

"Move away, Morgan," Brian said suddenly. "She's been warned."

Sasha's smile widened. If he thought to rid himself of her that way, he was mistaken.

Reluctantly, Morgan loosed his hold on the animal's bridle and stepped back, pressing against the stone wall.

"Move out of the stall," she said firmly. "I don't want you in the way while I tend him."

Swearing in Welsh and English, the squire moved angrily away, giving her a harsh glance as he passed. Sasha ignored him and began talking softly to the stallion, edging her way toward his head. Though nervous, he whickered, his animal mind focused on the source of his pain, the sharp, spearing thrusts in his foreleg.

When she reached his head, she ran a hand lightly over the gleaming withers and down his shoulder to his leg, then lower until she was kneeling at the huge hooves. Heavily shod and lethal, these were the same hooves that could shred a fallen man and inflict great damage on other horses. But the destrier stood still and trembling, sensing she would help him as she lifted one of the heavy hooves and propped it on her bent knee. The horse's balance shifted to three legs, and as she worked, applying salve with a light touch, she crooned softly, using the rhythmic language of horses. She praised the stallion's power and beauty, his great heart and his ancestors, likened him to the wind and the heavens. He seemed to understand and agree. As she worked, he lowered his great head and nuzzled her hair softly, blowing moist warmth gently on her neck.

She tied the length of soft brown cloth around the leg in a firm knot, then rose. Her back ached from the strain of kneeling and holding the weight of one huge leg. Pressing her hands against her spine, she bent backward to ease the cramped muscles.

"Let me do that," a deep voice said, and she looked up to see Rhys. He was watching her, a faint smile on his mouth and an amused gleam in his eyes. He indicated Brian and Morgan with a tilt of his head. "They're afraid to move, I think."

She shrugged. "They're only afraid you might replace them with someone who knows horses better."

He laughed and leaned on the top board of the stall. "There's no fear of that. I'm loyal to those who are loyal to me."

"A wise attitude. Too many men are swayed so easily."

"I'm not. Though I've no objections to asking for help from others when it's been offered." He gestured to the empty bowl on the stall floor. "What did you use on my horse?"

She glanced at Brian and smiled wickedly. "Chopped faerie wings and the heart of a unicorn. An unborn unicorn."

"No dragon teeth?"

"I used them all during the last full moon." She pressed her lips together to hold back her laughter at the expression on Brian's face. He seemed to be laboring under the suspicion that he was the butt of a jest, while still struggling with his own superstitions. The latter won.

"She did send her servant for more dragon wings, my lord," he muttered fiercely. "I heard her."

When Rhys looked at her, Sasha shrugged. " 'Twas a jest, but that pigheaded buffoon would never know it."

"Then don't torment him. It may turn out that I'm the fool for not believing in elves and faeries."

She smiled. "Yea, my lord, it may."

His brow lifted. He didn't reply to that, but held out his hand and said, "Come with me, lovely Elf Queen, and I'll pay you for your treatment of my horse."

"Do you not wish to wait and see if I've cured him?" she mocked. "What if he grows wings, or shrinks to the size of a dormouse?"

"I'll chance it."

Shrugging, she moved to her chest of herbs, then paused and looked up at him. "I've a potion that will ease your men if you wish to chance that as well."

"While I would chance it, I'm not certain my men feel quite so bold." He hesitated, then said, "But if you offer it, there may be some whose misery will overcome their fear of worse."

She picked through the dried leaves and flowers stored in neat compartments in the chest and gathered two kinds of mint, rosemary, and rue to brew into a tea. She rose and held them out to the squire. "If you doubt my intentions,'tis best to brew the potion yourself. Boil these with honey and feed the mixture to those men who wish to feel better."

After a quick glance at Rhys, Morgan took the leaves and nodded. He muttered something in Welsh and Rhys replied in the same language. The squire shrugged and backed away from them.

Rhys turned to her and held out his hand again. "Come, flower, and we'll test the tavern's hospitality. Perhaps a miracle has happened and the food is decent."

She hesitated. There was more to the genial smile than met the eye, though she didn't know what it could be. Yet, to refuse would only delay matters, and she had not broached the subject of his pledge to her. It had to be done at just the right moment, or she risked his anger outweighing his sense of honor.

So she put her hand in his, wishing she had been able

to wash away the reek of horse chestnuts and goose fat, and went with him to the tavern. She should have changed clothes. Her garment was only a simple peasant's gown, mulberry colored with long sleeves smocked at the elbows and a cloth girdle binding it at the waist; nothing pretty. A brisk wind tugged at the wide hem, flapping it around her ankles so that she had to hold it down with one hand. Clouds rolled across the sky, and a drop of rain spattered on her arm. Rhys shortened his long strides so that she didn't have to run to keep up with him, still holding her hand, occasionally smiling down at her.

The irritating thump was back, and that quiver in her stomach. She hated it. Hated the way he made her pulse race when he smiled at her like that, his eyes shadowed by those long lashes, the white gleam of his teeth so bright it made her want to smile back at him. Appalling that she couldn't help smiling, intolerable that she had to suffer an overpowering need to touch his face, drag her fingers over his jaw and mouth . . . There must be a potion to cure this. She'd research it. There had to be some herb or plant or curative that would keep her from smiling like a mindless idiot at him, looking for all the world like those women she'd always scorned.

"Mind the stoop," he murmured, and she realized with a flush of chagrin that she'd been looking up at his face and almost stumbled over the tavern's low stone threshold.

Of all the . . . gaping at him like a tavern wench, probably with the same vacuous expression . . . Lord, how low must she sink before gaining her ends?

Her face still felt hot as she allowed him to escort her to a table, ignoring the other patrons as best she could, feeling like the worst kind of fool. It was penance. Retribution for dosing his men. And for tweaking Brian . . . teasing Biagio. Her sins were many, should she care to count them. She deserved this, and should be grateful it wasn't worse.

But it was hard to be grateful when he straddled the bench beside her, a powerful leg on each side, his knee grazing against her thigh as he leaned close, so close she could see that his eyelashes were tangled. She resisted the impulse to untangle them, and folded her hands tightly in her lap. Her head bent, she stared desperately at the scarred surface of the oak table.

"Tell me," he said softly in a voice rich with humor, "how you have managed to be so wise in the ways of horses and herbs."

This was one occasion when the truth wouldn't hurt. She lifted her gaze to the bare skin of his throat above the open neck of his tunic. "There are men in the deserts of Arabia who are very wise with horses. What little I know, they taught me."

"And the salve—it wasn't faerie wings and unicorn hearts, but it would interest me to know what you used."

"Horse chestnuts." She dared lift her gaze to his face, smiling slightly. "Crushed and mixed with goose fat, it can be very effective. Nothing magical, nothing brewed in a mushroom ring on Midsummer Eve, just a simple salve."

"You enjoy posing as a mystical faerie, don't you?"

"Don't be too certain 'tis just a pose." She drew a finger down the deep crease of a dent in the oak table and said lightly, "I could be a princess in disguise, for all you know. Or the Elf Queen, come with a crystal boat to sail away with you to the land of the faeries."

He frowned. "Did Brian tell you that?"

"He doesn't need to. He's Irish. They're full of elves and goblins and faeries . . ."

Sensing the approach of the tavern wench, she paused, allowing her attention to focus on the maid. As usual, the images in the frowsy wench's mind had more to do with men than anything of real importance, and Sasha lifted her brow at some of the visions. What a busy person she must be . . . but among the images flitting through the shallow depths of the maid's mind was Biagio, his dark smiling face accompanied by a very real sigh of longing. She looked at the maid more sharply. The blue eyes were hazy and replete, the pitted face glowing. Curse him. What had he done? She hadn't meant for Biagio to plummet the depths of degradation, just lightly skim the surface. Now the maid fancied herself in love with him, and that could create problems.

The maid turned to look at Rhys, and the image of Biagio was supplanted with an appreciation of the blond knight gazing up at her with a faint smile curving the hard line of his mouth. Sasha's eyes narrowed. Viewed through the wench's eyes, he looked strong, dangerous, tempting, and very male. The maid entertained a brief, fanciful vision of him undoing her bodice laces . . . and Sasha reacted without thinking.

"Do you crave the attentions of every man you meet, slut, or will you bring us food and drink?"

Rhys turned startled eyes to her, and Sasha realized that she'd spoken aloud. She added lamely, "I'm hungry. Very hungry."

After a pause, he asked, "Shall I order you a side of beef?"

She flushed. "Nay. A small trencher will do." Glancing up at the tavern maid, she added, "And some turnips." There. That should be sufficient penance for her transgression.

But it seemed that it was not, for as the kitchen wench flounced off to the rear of the common room in high dudgeon, the front door of the inn opened and one of Rhys's knights entered, eyes scanning the room until he found him. He approached rapidly, simmering with resentment, anger, and a disturbing fear.

Rhys stiffened slightly, and she could sense his disquiet. She didn't blame him. The approaching knight was about to boil over with rage and indignation. As he drew closer, she realized with dismay that it was directed at her.

"My lord," he said stiffly, his gaze riveted on Rhys, "I would like to speak with you in private." He paused, thought briefly of betrayal and enchantment, then of Rhys's inordinate attachment to the wench with witching eyes. Sasha realized with a shock that the wench he meant was she. *Lovely enough in an odd way, but those eyes . . . see right through a man . . . Brian's right . . . not about faeries, mayhaps, but she means trouble to us all . . . those herbs . . . purple flowers . . . hemp agrimony. . . .*

Sasha blinked. Then she remembered: she'd left her chest of herbs in the stable, so flustered by Rhys that she'd not thought about leaving them behind for anyone to examine. If this man knew anything about herbs, he would recognize some of them, and then the symptoms that afflicted the men groaning in the stables would take on new meaning. Oh, what had she done, letting herself be so distracted by the smiling attention of this man?

Disaster yawned before her, dark and waiting to claim her. The end to her plans, the finish to her dreams . . . She had to think, had to have an answer ready if the worst happened.

"I tell you, m'lord," Sir Robert insisted harshly, "the symptoms are the same. I know that herb. I've used it myself on occasion, when my youngest son ate a poisonous plant by mistake. I don't know why it didn't occur to me earlier."

Rhys stared at him. "But what reason would she have for making my men sick and not me?"

"How do you know she didn't try you first?" Sir Robert glanced at the maid still sitting at the table with her head down. "I've not known you to drink so much before, m'lord, and I've known you eleven years or more. Yet this morning you were sick from it."

That much was true, though the symptoms were not the same as his men's. His mouth tightened. "How was it done, then?"

"In their food, wine—any number of ways. And you must admit, even those men who stayed late yet drank little still have some sickness on them."

Yea, that was true enough, too. Brian was not sick, but Brian had been sleeping off the effects of too much wine in a corner of the garden, before the night even began. And Sir Robert had not frequented the inn later in the night, preferring his own company to the rowdier company of drunken soldiers. Wise under any circumstances. Rhys devised and rejected several theories, but the only answer seemed to point to the maid—and he had no idea what she'd done after leaving him in his room.

He glanced toward Sasha. She still sat at the table, her

silky black hair gleaming softly in the gray light through
the window. An amusing wench. Lively and quick, saucy
and teasing—and the heated memory of her golden body
and slender thighs atop him was still arousing. He looked
back at Sir Robert. "I suggest we ask the innkeeper what
he knows before we accuse her falsely."

"I'll bring him to you," Sir Robert said grimly.

Rhys moved back to the table, idly lifting a long strand
of her loose dark hair in his palm, letting it drift free in a
silky glide. He straddled the bench again and reached for
her arm, pushing up her long sleeve to take her hand in
his and hold it.

"Tell me," he said in a pleasant tone, "what you did
after you left me last night, sweet flower."

"Did, my lord?"

He smiled. "Yea. Where did you go?"

She tried to pull her hand away, but he held it fast, and
she gave a light shrug and fleeting smile. "My servant came
to fetch me, and we carried some wine back to Elspeth.
She was feeling poorly."

"How unfortunate." He paused, letting the silence
lengthen. It stretched until she began to fidget, then he
smiled. "Is she better?"

"Who? Oh—Elspeth. Yea, my lord. Much better. It
must have been something she ate, for as you saw this
morning, she is up and about as usual."

"Yea, I remember." He rubbed his thumb over the back
of her hand in a gentle, idle circle, then turned it over to
gaze at her palm. "You still have salve on your hand. You
have a great knowledge of herbs, don't you?"

"Great enough." Her eyes narrowed. "I know what
most others know, what to eat and what not to eat, a few
simple salves and remedies." With an impatient motion of
her free hand, she said, "I'm not as hungry as I thought.
I need to collect my things and go see that Elspeth is still
well. . . . My lord, please release my hand."

Half-standing, poised for flight like a skittish mare, she
stared at him with huge dark eyes and a questioning lift
of her brows. He shook his head. "In a moment, fair lady.

116 J U L I A N A G A R N E T T

I've a notion to have some questions answered first, and I know you will oblige me."

"Truly, I would be most happy to answer any questions you wish to ask, my lord, but a sudden apprehension has seized me that my servants may need me. As you know, we are close, and there are times I can just sense their—"

His fingers tightened, not savagely, but enough to warn her of his mood. "Gladly. After my questions have been answered."

She stared down at him, dark eyes reflecting the rich glow of the lamp and pale light from the window, her lips parted, the breath coming in quick, shallow gasps. There was a deep color to her cheeks, like the dusky rose in late summer, beautiful and enticing, but hiding sharp thorns beneath fragile petals. A lovely flower. And like the flowers of the Deadly Nightshade—called Fair Lady by some— beguiling and deceptively fatal. Her face told the tale, gave the lie to her words, and he did not really need confirmation by the innkeeper to know the truth. It was staring down at him from her eyes.

Sir Robert arrived with the innkeeper and his daughter in tow. "Tell him what you've told me, Master Howard." Sir Robert nudged the innkeeper forward a step. "Tell him."

Master Howard bobbed his head, looking uneasily from the maid to Rhys. "She were 'ere, m'lord. Last night late. 'Er and 'er servant, that dark lad wi' th' wolf's face. I saw 'em in th' back, near my wine pitchers, but they said they only needed a bit of wine ta taik back ta summat who was sick."

"See," Sasha said, breathless and bold, tossing her hair from her face with an indignant gesture. "I told you El-speth was ill."

Rhys let his gaze rest on her face a moment, the faint smile still on his mouth though it felt frozen there. "Yea, so you did."

Then the kitchen wench pushed forward, brazen and angry, her small breasts pushed out as she put both hands on her wide hips. "I saw w'at you done, I did, but didn't know 'til now w'at 'twas."

"Hush, Lynn," her father said, reaching a hand out to draw her back. But she shook loose, tossing her head impatiently.

"Nay, I won't hush. It were 'er that done it. She poured sumthin' in some o' th' pitchers, but I didn' know at th' time w'at she was doin'." She snorted. "And now she's tryin' ta blame it on 'er servant, w'en 'twas 'er all th' time."

Sasha gave a low hoot of scorn. "You're just angry with me because I caught you making sheep's eyes at Biagio and ran you away from him. You still had the stink of another man on you, and I didn't want my innocent young servant caught up with the likes of you." She turned to Rhys. "It's true. I did tell her to go away last night and leave Biagio alone."

"I've no doubt of that, flower. 'Tis only your reason for it that is in doubt." He stood up, towering over her, not releasing her hand. "I find that I've a great curiosity about you, and who you know and what you're doing here, and why you seem to turn up near me at the most surprising times." He held tight when she tried to twist away, and looked over her head to the innkeeper and Sir Robert. "I'm going to have a long discussion with my fascinating young guest, and would appreciate it if you would not allow anyone to interrupt us. Ah ah, flower. Not here. We'll go to my room where we can be alone."

When she resisted, leaning against his grip and protesting that she had no intention of being alone with him in his room, he scooped her up and flung her over his shoulder. No one tried to stop him as he moved to the narrow staircase leading to the second floor.

CHAPTER EIGHT

E choes of the slammed door vibrated in the dim closeness of the room. Rhys stalked across the floor and flung her to the bed in a smooth motion that made her bounce on the mattress like a child's cloth doll. The hem of her skirts flew up and draped over her knees. She clutched at the sides of the bed with both hands, staring up at him as he stood over her. A fleeting glance toward the closed door only earned her a chiding murmur. He didn't move, staring down at her until she looked away.

He smiled. "Come, flower. You've more spine than that. Tell me why you poisoned my men's wine to make them sick, and perhaps I'll just scold you and let you go."

Sasha glared up at him with eyes spitting fury. "I'm not that big a fool. If you thought I'd put something in their wine—"

"I know you put something in their wine. What we're discussing now is why." He took a step toward the bed and she scuttled backward on the mattress like a mouse scurrying out of harm's way, until her spine was pressed against the wall. Her chest rose and fell with quick, panting breaths. He wondered what she saw in his face to make her so afraid; she must see the rage he felt at being betrayed. Again. It wasn't a new emotion but still held far too much power over him. Would he ever learn to accept a betrayal without this deep, churning sense of futility and frustration? Nay, he doubted it. If he'd not learned to by now, 'twas unlikely that he ever would learn to just shake his head and go on.

He leaned over her, fists pressing into the mattress on each side of her small form, his face a handbreadth from hers. "Tell me, flower . . . why?"

"I—" She looked away, tongue flicking out to wet her lips, eyes darting about the room as if searching for the answer. "I don't know. No—wait." She took in a deep breath, one hand up to halt his instinctive move forward. "It was to keep you here. Truly."

"Ah. To keep me here." He nodded thoughtfully. "I can believe that. It has the ring of truth. But tell me, flower, who wanted you to keep me here? Who sent you to delay me?"

"Who?" She licked her lips again, shaking her head in an excellent imitation of confusion. "No one sent me, my lord. I—I just wanted you to stay here another day."

He smiled. "Sweet child. Of course you did." Reaching out, he drew a finger lightly along the curve of her cheek, then over the tumble of her lower lip and down to her chin to grip it firmly between his thumb and fingers, holding her head still when she tried to twist away. "Now, tell me the truth. No maid would go to such lengths to keep me here unless sent to do so. I want to know who sent you. Was it an Englishman?" His grip tightened as she shrank away, "Or was it a Welshman?"

Her eyes widened. She shook her head as violently as was possible while he still held her so tightly. "I don't know what you mean. . . ."

Swearing, he moved to kneel over her on the hard mattress, his hands crushing her shoulders against the wall, his expression fierce as he could make it without actually scaring her to death. She looked terrified already; but apparently not enough, for even when he threatened terrible things, drawing on imaginary and not so imaginary terrors, she only shook her head and gasped out that no one had told her to keep him there.

"It was . . . my idea . . ." she said in a half sob, shaking with fear and rage, her glances like poisoned arrows but her tears real enough, "my idea. I told you . . . why I did it . . . to keep you . . . here. . . ."

Releasing her with another oath, he sat back on his heels, staring at her in frustration. Whoever had sent her, had chosen well. She did not budge from her tale, from the ridiculous insistence that she'd wanted him to stay and fight for her victory. He couldn't make out all the foolish story, for between her sobs and his shaking of her, it was hard to hear and harder to understand. Something about a prophecy and long quest—and him, of course. A griffyn. Brian must have told her who he was. He couldn't recall giving her his name, just as he couldn't recall her ever giving him hers. He'd had to overhear her servant call her by name just to discover it. And of course, it was probably not even her real name.

He stared at her thoughtfully. Short of torture, he couldn't think of another way to make her tell him what he wanted to know. Unless . . .

He smiled, and her wet eyes narrowed with immediate suspicion. She'd already learned that particular smile, it seemed, for she stared at him warily as he caressed her face again.

"I wonder, would your servants tell me what I want to know, flower?" He caught her when she tried to twist from the bed, setting her back against the wall firmly. "Nay, do not try that again. My patience nears its limits. I've asked pleasantly and not so pleasantly. You've not given me the answer I want. So now I must use other methods to gain the proper reply. Perhaps you won't answer to save your skin, but you might to save theirs."

As he pushed away from her, moving to stand beside the bed, she threw herself forward and caught him by the hand, holding as tightly as a tenacious animal. "Nay, lord. Don't do anything to them, I beg of you."

She paused, quivering, and pressed her wet face against

his hand. He felt a distinct self-disgust at the moment but reasoned that she had brought this upon herself. He laid his other hand atop her head, patting it as he would a small child's. "Tell me what I need to know, flower. It's not just for me, you understand. There are other lives in the balance, and I must know who betrays me."

Looking up with drowned eyes, she sniffed. "I—I don't know his name. No, wait, my lord—truly, he never told me. And I don't know English from Welsh. You all look alike to me. But he was dark. With a thin face like—like a weasel. And huge, dark eyes like black flames . . . all burning and hot and terrifying. . . . He said if I didn't keep you here, he'd kill us all. Boil us in oil. Skin us first, and use our hides as shoes." She drew in a deep, hiccoughing breath. "And if I fail, he'll hunt us down with dogs, find us wherever we go, then feed us to them in pieces. We'll be hung from trees along the roads as a warning. Shot full of arrows as targets and—"

"Did it never occur to you," Rhys interrupted dryly, "that there is only one time you can die? Never mind, flower. Whatever he said, it was obviously enough to convince you. Would you recognize him if you saw him again?"

She nodded, hair flying into her eyes in silky wisps. "Oh yes, my lord, for he looks like the devil. I expect that if you took off his boots, he'd have cloven hooves and a tail beneath his cape and horns beneath his helmet—"

"Cease. I take your meaning. Your imagination is vivid, flower. Let's hope your memory is as excellent."

He stepped away from her and moved to the small table beneath the window. He lifted the flagon of wine, sniffed at it cautiously, then poured some into a cup. After considering it a moment, he took it to Sasha. "Here. Taste this."

She gave him a wary look, and he shrugged. "I've put nothing in it. If you haven't either, then you'll drink."

She drained the cup and handed it back, wiped her mouth with her hand and gazed up at him defiantly. Amused, he shook his head. "It's either pure, or you've chosen the coward's way out, flower."

"Are you quite through with me now, my lord? Have I satisfied your questions?" She crossed her arms over her chest, some of her former defiance and arrogance returning.

He poured another cup of wine, looking over at her to smile. "For the moment, I'm quite satisfied. I'll be even more satisfied when we reach Wales and you identify the man who sent you to delay me. Or to slay me with poison, whichever it was."

She'd been smoothing her gown over her legs, but now her head jerked up and she stared at him with wide, dark eyes. "What do you mean? Wales? Identify who?"

He walked over to her again, tracing a still-damp tear track over the slope of her cheek with his finger. "We leave in the morning for Wales, sweet flower, and you will be accompanying us."

Wales. Wasn't that somewhere at the edge of the earth? At the edge of an ocean that dropped off into the kingdom of dragons? Wales. Blinking blearily, Sasha flung a glance of acute loathing in Rhys's direction. He ignored her. If he even noticed. Early morning mist surrounded them in eerie shreds, muffling forest noises, muffling even the thud of hooves on soft, muddy ground. The sound of her cart's wheels was only a distant rattle somewhere far behind them.

At least Elspeth and Biagio had not been left behind, though they traveled at the tail end of the caravan, trailing so far back they would soon be out of sight. But it was a hard-won concession, purchased with pleading and groveling. She still wasn't quite certain why Rhys had agreed but was relieved that he had.

Too bad she hadn't seen either Elspeth or Biagio except at a distance, for Rhys had kept her away from them. If only they could hear her thoughts as she could hear theirs. She knew how worried they were, and knew that they'd heard enough of the story to understand they were being taken to Wales.

No doubt, that wretched tavern wench had run straight

to Biagio with some pitiful excuse for her lies. Well, not exactly lies, but untimely truths. Lynn had seen them at the wine casks, and it was true enough they had put something in them. But she hadn't really seen them do it. Stupid wench. If not for her—Sasha blew out a sigh. It didn't matter. All that mattered now was the future, not the past.

While she was with Rhys—and likely to be with him for some time to come—it was not as she had envisioned. Not only had he not believed the prophecy, but he'd dismissed the entire thing as an invented excuse. Who knew if she'd ever be able to convince him now? And she'd had to make up that wild tale about some dark man with big, burning eyes and impossible threats just to keep him from doing something terrible to all of them. What would he do when they got to Wales and she couldn't point out the man who had supposedly frightened her into keeping Rhys in England?

It didn't matter. She'd worry with that when it happened. There were other, more pressing matters to worry about. She flung Rhys another glance. He rode ahead of her, mounted on his destrier—who was no longer limping—and not even looking at her. She was flanked by two hard-faced men with cold eyes and the bad habit of lewd thoughts. She shuddered and huddled deeper into her cloak.

It had rained most of the night. A hard rain, rattling shutters and beating against the inn's roof, making her shiver and shake in her hard pallet on the floor. Apparently, Rhys was so angry he didn't even want to bed her again. Not that she was complaining. But he'd tied her to his wrist with a length of thick rope, and every time she moved in the night, he'd lifted up from his bed to stare at her, eyes glistening in the faint candle glow. She hadn't slept much.

Just knowing he was there, only a short distance away, had kept her very much awake. She'd tossed and turned until he snarled at her to be still before he wrapped her neck with the rope, and then she lay so stiff that her muscles still ached from the strain. Her only consolation was that Brian was almost as appalled as she by the circumstances.

"Take her with us," he'd exploded in horror. "But my lord, we can't."

There had been a short, low discussion, ending with Brian slamming angrily from the room, leaving her smiling with grim satisfaction. It had felt better then than it did now. Now, it had begun to rain again, a steady patter that made her miserable and didn't seem to affect the mailed knights slogging through mud up to their horses' hocks. She thought of the little wooden cart, and how it had a canopy over the back, and how Biagio would drive it until they found a spot under some trees to wait out a storm all cozy and dry. It was a nice cart, a sturdy cart, for all that the broken axle had caused them such a delay in Wytham.

That had been repaired very swiftly under Rhys's orders, she'd learned, another lesson in how villagers were quite capable of taking advantage of travelers. She couldn't imagine a wainwright telling Rhys it would take several days to repair. Her one glimpse of the cart had been evidence enough that it was repaired swiftly and efficiently. Biagio had been leaning against it, arms crossed over his chest, his face sullen. When he saw her, he'd glared, his mental direction so angry that she quickly threw up her barriers against him.

But not Elspeth. She'd waved, a brief flap of one hand and the mental assurance that they were fine and wouldn't leave her. It had almost brought tears to her eyes. Not that she would be able to produce any more for weeks. Her entire supply had been spent on stammering denials and then pleading excuses. She flushed with shame to remember it.

Rhys had terrified her. There had been a ferocity in his expression and actions that had swept her from denials to mindless fear before she could blink. None of his usual humor and mockery had surfaced to replace the cold determination. Not until she'd said something that satisfied him, and that had been such a wild, improbable tale she still couldn't believe that he'd accepted it.

Her horse stumbled, and she grabbed at the high pommel in front of her, holding tightly to the saddle as the animal regained its balance. Not a noble beast such as a destrier or her own sweet mare, but a baggage horse had been given her to ride. Still, it was a gentle-natured animal, with no malice and an accepting disposition. Duller than most, just as some people were slower of wit than others.

Looking up, she saw one of her guards watching her, his eyes narrowed and thoughtful. She didn't like the direction of his thoughts, and said casually, "Your nose will turn black and drop off if you even try it."

He stared at her, startled, and she smiled. It was enough to make him view her more carefully, and she settled back into the grueling pace with a sigh. Not even rain seemed to slow Rhys in his momentum. Before she knew it, they would be in Wales.

Slanting cloud-shadows crossed the deep green of fields on each side of the winding road that led into the Welsh vale. It was near the midday hour. Peasants tilling a field looked up, some of them leaning on their hoe handles to watch the band of armed men pass down the road.

From his vantage point atop the hilly crest, Rhys had an expansive view of the valley and rough hills beyond. A winding band of water, sun chipped and glittering bright enough to sting his eyes, cut across the vale. He blinked against the glare and glanced up at the sky. It was a vibrant blue, a huge bowl tufted with scudding white clouds that drifted lazily, like the windblown seeds of a thistle.

"The River Wye," Brian commented, and Rhys nodded.

"*Ydi,*" he said, the slip back into Welsh easier than he'd thought it would be. The closer they drew to Glenlyon, the sharper the memories were. Yellow charlock mantled the dipping ground, catching sunlight in the tiny golden blooms. Butter-colored blossoms of bird's-foot clover dotted tall grasses. Since reaching the banks of the Wye, he'd begun to remember: Twilight games played among the willows crowding the green banks of the river, practicing with small blunt-tipped arrows and his bow, cracking a flimsy wooden sword against his eldest brother's head and being soundly trounced for it—so long ago, as if it had been another life, another lad who had laughed and romped and lived among the beautiful Welsh valley and hills.

But there were other memories as well, less peaceful and infinitely more grim. Armed warriors streaming over these same placid hills, brandishing swords and spears and screaming for blood as they stormed fortified walls. Welsh against Welsh, English against Welsh, there had always been enemies waiting like vultures to seize the rich lands of Wales. And it was no different now, only the names of the enemies had changed.

Halting only one league from Glenlyon, Rhys signaled a rest. They would wait for the scouts he'd sent ahead to return and report. He dismounted beneath the spreading shade of a birch tree. A sparrow perching in the branches above twittered and hopped, erratic and noisy.

Rhys looked down the line of mounted men and saw Sasha dismount with a sprightly bounce. She'd kept up with them, enduring the grueling pace with only a few complaints, and most of those directed at the men and not the hard ride. He smiled faintly. She was as noisy as a sparrow, chittering protests at everything but what should matter most. Despite his anger at her faithless trick, he couldn't help an odd twinge of occasional sentiment that was certainly misplaced. It was his own fault for being witless enough to allow himself to be charmed by her. He should have listened to Brian, though not for the reasons he'd given.

But Rhys had had no trouble keeping his distance from her, even if the memory of that first night was still an annoying distraction at times. The images would come to him at the most inconvenient moments, vague memories of her golden body and the curtain of silky black hair, the feel of her soft thighs around him . . . it was enough to arouse him if he let it. But he was a grown man and not a youth incapable of harnessing his passions, and he had no intention of allowing her to incite him to more foolishness. Nay, he would keep her at a distance. There were other, more important matters to capture his attention.

Sasha looked up suddenly, a quick flash of dark eyes and red mouth beneath a cloud of loose hair, staring at him; Rhys was arrested by the swift change of her expression, the softening that looked almost like vulnerability. But he knew better. She was a changeling, melding from woman to child to sorceress like the shift of the wind. He deliberately turned away.

As the day wore on and the scouts did not return, Rhys grew impatient with the delay. "We ride for Glenlyon," he said, slapping his gauntlets across an open palm. He stood on a high crest, staring toward the keep that was still hidden from sight. "Choose twenty men to go with us."

"Should we not wait on the scouts to return?" Sir Robert asked hesitantly, and Rhys shook his head.

"Our previous scouts reported none of Raglan's men in the area, nor other enemies. No troops sighted, nor siege engines hidden in the woods."

"I don't like it that the men we sent out this morning have not come back," Brian muttered. "Nor have we seen the messenger we sent to Glenlyon to tell Owain of your arrival. Your father's steward should have replied. I don't like this."

"Brian, I don't intend to attempt an assault on the keep now. It was in Owain's hands a week ago. I want to know if it still is. We are enough men to resist any attack by a small band. If there was a large Raglan force we'd have heard reports of them by now. It's not easy to hide a vast body of troops for long." Reaching for his reins, he vaulted into Turk's saddle and pulled on his gauntlets. "We ride for Glenlyon."

Glenlyon itself he remembered as a rough motte-and-bailey structure mostly of wood and half-hidden by surrounding forest. Time had changed it. For leagues around, trees had been felled to provide timber for construction, leaving the hills strewn with stumps. When they rode around a sharp bend in the road, high stone towers soared upward like dragon's teeth, seeming to graze the clouds. A banner fluttered from atop a tower, waving scarlet and gold against the rose and purple sky. A familiar standard. The griffyn still flew.

Glenlyon.

It was so different, yet somehow unchanged, grander than his memories, but unmistakable: The glitter of the river, the green hills and the impressive high spur on the riverbanks still commanded an ancient crossing over the river. It was the structure that had changed most; the steep stone walls and towers that overlooked the village had been built since last he played here as a child. But it was still home. . . .

The village of Cwnllew huddled not far from the foot of the high spur on the banks of the Wye. The streets were empty save for an occasional dog or chicken, doors and windows shut tight. Cottages were strung out along the twisting band of water, but no kine or sheep could be seen in fields or behind fences. A warning of imminent invasion must have been sounded sending the people running to hide themselves and their goods. Cwnllew was deserted. Their approach had been duly noted.

It was quiet as they drew nearer the keep, with no sign of struggle or siege, no mark of recent battle or indication of what they would find inside the stones looming high against the Welsh sky above the village. "I cannot like this, milord," Brian muttered uneasily. " 'Tis too calm. No one is about."

"It's obvious our messenger delivered his message," Rhys said wryly, "for the peasants have fled. You know the saying—when two noblemen quarrel, 'tis the peasant's roof that burns."

Echoes of hoofbeats on empty streets were strangely loud. Brian gripped his sword hilt tightly. "Do you think the keep has been taken?"

Rhys frowned. "The griffyn flies, not Raglan's banner. Owain might just be cautious, as Sir Niclas already attempted an assault. And Owain must know by now of Gavin's petition to take Glenlyon by legal means. With all that, he may not trust my banner until he sees proof. Whatever, I'll have an answer before long."

The winding street led up from the village, skirting a

deep ditch that curved around the base of the keep, ending at a drawbridge and the tower gates. Rhys rode to the closed gates and demanded entry.

"*Pwy dod?*" came the sentry's challenge in thick English-accented Welsh.

Unaccustomed as he was to the Welsh tongue, even Rhys could detect the English accent. He exchanged a wary glance with Brian, then shrugged.

"*Fy enw yw Rhys ap Griffyn,*" he shouted up, "Lord of Glenlyon. Grant entry."

"Lord of Glenlyon?" A broad, flat-featured face appeared in the lancet window, then withdrew. After a time, the sentry reappeared to announce, "The old lord of Glenlyon is dead."

Rhys swept his helmet off so that the fading sunlight would shine on his face and hair, and summoned his standard bearer. As the pennon shook free, the gold griffyn on scarlet unfurled, glittering in the afternoon sun. Rhys looked up at the sentry. "As you can see, I am the new lord of Glenlyon. Open the gates."

"I've had no orders to open for a new lord. Now go, before I summon archers to drive you away."

So that was the way it was to be. Rhys curbed his anger with an effort, and demanded an audience with the bailiff. There was another brief discussion before the sentry returned to the slotted window to say that the bailiff would speak with him if he entered the keep alone.

"Nay. Send the bailiff out." Rhys waited, his shield reflecting sunlight, his patience waning, then finally agreed to meet the bailiff in the middle of the drawbridge.

Brian's protest was alarmed. "My lord, do not go in—"

"Do you think me fool enough to ride into the keep alone?" Rhys retorted. "I go as far as the bridge unless I am convinced otherwise."

With his destrier snorting restlessly, Rhys waited on the banks of the moat, staring across shallow green water at the stone walls of Glenlyon. Frogs croaked a gruff melody. In the lengthening shadows cast by high stone walls, insects emerged to bite and sting, buzzing around him as he waited. The sun was still in the sky, yet it was growing dark where he stood in the shadow of the keep. It was an impressive fortress, and one that would not fall easily to assault.

When the signal was given to lower the drawbridge, Brian fretted that it was a trap. "You're being reckless, Rhys. I fear dishonesty."

"Yea, as do I. Put a few of our good Welsh bowmen behind me. And make them visible, so those inside will know we're not completely trusting fools."

"Let me pretend to be you," Brian broke in quickly. "An entire army could be in that keep. If I'm taken, 'tis no great loss."

"It would be to me." Rhys met Brian's eyes and smiled. "We don't know for certain this is a trap. We're here now. If Owain no longer holds the keep for me, I need to know." He glanced toward the lowering drawbridge, listened to grating chains haul the iron gate slowly upward. Every instinct screamed a warning. Any cautious steward would meet him at the postern gate, thus guarding castle defenses while still allowing him in. Why lower the bridge for only one man and risk an assault?

Brian was right, of course. Despite the bailiff's promise of a safe conduct, there was the real possibility of mounted knights waiting inside to surge across the bridge toward him. But there was no reason for such an event save one. He'd brought no huge force with him, posed no serious threat to a well-fortified keep. So there was no swifter way to find out if there was treachery afoot than this.

Brian was of the same mind. "I'll watch the walls," he muttered as Rhys donned his helmet and made ready, "but at first sign of treachery, I'll be at your back."

Rhys looked up and grinned. "That I know well enough. Never have you failed me." Reining his mount around, he waited while Turk pranced impatiently, huge hooves churning up well-traveled dirt and mud.

The bridge lowered with a final solid crack against the ground, and Rhys swung his shield to the front, firmly gripping the leather strap that secured it. His sword was at the ready, his blood running hot. There was always this familiar surge of eager anticipation before a battle. Despite the fact that it was to be only a meeting, his instincts prepared for a fight.

Inside the gates a man rode to the edge of the drawbridge, pausing beneath dark shadows. Rhys could not see him clearly. He wore mail and helmet, but at a distance, his face was only a blur. Would he even recognize Owain? It had been so long, and he only a lad when last he'd seen his father's steward. All Rhys had known of him through the years was sprawling penmanship and the familiar signet on sealed letters, for Lord Griffyn had no lettering skills and Owain had penned the infrequent letters.

Rhys kneed Turk forward at a steady pace, keeping his gaze trained on the approaching man. He heard the loud pop of his pennon in the wind, the jangle of curb chain and bridle bits, his destrier's rasping breath, and the creak of saddle leather. Hooves sounded loud on the thick boards of the bridge. When they neared the middle, Turk began to toss his head and snort. Rhys turned his attention to the agitated animal, and a motion just above and behind the bailiff caught his eye. It was only a tiny flicker, not much more than the briefest flutter of a sleeve and glint of fading light on metal, but enough to give him warning.

He leaned to one side, and heard the whistling sound of an arrow pass by. A knot of armed men appeared behind the bailiff, who was now pounding across the bridge at a run. There was no going back. He dug his spurs into Turk, though there was no need. The uneasy war-horse had sensed the danger long before him and had already braced for action.

Rhys bent over the horse's neck, and swung his sword up and out as he clashed with the bailiff. Armed knights rushed across the drawbridge toward him in an effort to surround him. The jarring shocks of sword meeting sword sent a jolt through his arm and fierce pleasure coursing through his veins. This was familiar, reflexive: thrust and parry and turn, using knees to guide Turk and at the same time choosing his next opening in the flashing glitter of lethal blades. In front of him, an arrow sank deep into a man's chest, driving him backward from his mount. There was a scream, then a splash as the man fell into the moat.

His bowmen. They were among the best, and Rhys was glad to have them at his back.

Brian's familiar whoop sounded at his elbow. They were outnumbered, but the space on the bridge was limited. The clash of blades was loud, mingling with grunts of pain and the screams of horses, the sound of hooves clattering on the wood, and the angry shouts of his men at such treachery.

In a short time, the skirmish was over. The surviving attackers retreated across the drawbridge and under the safety of the *porte coleïce*. The heavy gate was already being lowered, chains shrieking with strain. Wheeling his mount, Rhys ordered his men from the drawbridge as it began to shudder and creak beneath them. They barely made it onto firm soil before the planks lifted clear of the ground.

"I'd like to go after them," Brian growled as they trotted out of arrow range. Rhys shook his head.

"Now who's being reckless? There will be another time. For now, we'll wait." He turned to look at his friend. "At least we have an answer."

It was full dark by the time they made it back to the camp tucked deep into the thick Welsh woods. Rhys was quiet. He'd half expected such a reception. But he'd recognized the colors worn by those on the bridge as belonging to Sir Niclas. Raglan was formidable, with a strong fortress to the southwest. It would take a long, hard struggle to wrest his lands from that worthy lord.

Moving to the fire, he stared into the orange and yellow blaze as he peeled off his gauntlets. The leather beneath the mail was wet, and there was a sharp stinging on his palm that he knew must be a sword cut. He rubbed at it absently until Brian noticed.

"I'll tend it," he said, frowning, "or you risk losing the hand."

A faint smile curled Rhys's mouth. It was obvious Brian preferred his own ministrations to those of the faerie queen's. He looked up at him. "You've become as protective as a woman, Brian."

"Devil take you, Rhys. Lose the cursed hand then. A lot

of good you'll be as a one-armed knight. Will you like sitting at the castle walls begging for bread?"

"I may be doing that anyway if I don't drive Sir Niclas from my keep." Rhys shook his head, weary, angry, and puzzled. "Never did my father suffer assault from Raglan. They were once friends. It was even suggested that one day his daughter would wed my brother. Now my father is hardly cold in his grave and Raglan seeks to destroy the house of Glenlyon. What makes a man turn so quickly?"

Brian shrugged. "Greed, mayhaps. I don't know. It's a bad business, Rhys. Bad business."

"Yea, it is that. So now I am caught between two forces, one ranging the countryside, the other secure in my keep." He frowned, deliberating.

"My lord, perhaps we should rid ourselves of Raglan at his source—his own keep. If his forces are divided, they won't be as strong. We can besiege Raglan instead of Glenlyon, so he'll be forced to return to defend his castle and we can—"

"Brian, you're brilliant." He smiled when Brian looked surprised and pleased. "That's just what Raglan wants us to do. Divide our forces between his keep and mine. He must know I don't have enough men to take a keep as strong as Glenlyon, but don't dare leave it. Yea, I see it better now."

"I'm glad you do." Brian shook his head. "Intrigues make my head hurt. I like a good, honest fight, not all this yea and nay and mayhaps. If Raglan wants your keep, he should have challenged you directly, not sent men to occupy it and harry us when we get here. A bold challenge, yea, that's what I like."

"Odd, once I thought Raglan of the same mind. From all I heard, he wasn't a man to lend himself to sly methods, but spoke his mind forthright. It never occurred to me he would be so devious."

"You can't trust some people, my lord. Let me see your hand. The cut is deep. I'll need to sear it with my knife. . . . After all this time and trouble, now we get here and find Glenlyon occupied. Mayhaps it's not meant to be. I think it's a curse. It's the only thing that makes sense. We've been cursed . . ."

Despair filled Brian's voice, a melancholy that could infect the others and doom their morale. Rhys didn't want this. Discouraged men were never at their best when fighting.

He laughed softly. "Your thoughts usually stray more in the direction of willing village maids than the bloody business of assaulting unwary keeps, Brian. Do they not?"

Brian had knelt by the fire to heat the blade of his dagger, and he looked up now with a smile. "Whenever possible. I do my best to brighten the lonely hours of winsome maidens everywhere. In Coventry, while you were sitting in a church and watching candles burn, I met a wee kitchen lass with bonny brown hair and a sweet smile, and—"

A shout rang out from one of the posted guards, and both men turned. Idle conversation was forgotten as a rider approached through the dark night. "Make way, make way! 'Tis Sir Wallis!" Exhausted and bloody, the returning scout slid from his lathered mount to his feet, then sprawled on the ground near the fire.

Gasping for breath, Sir Wallis panted out, "Glenlyon . . . is held . . . by an enemy. . . ."

"Yea," Rhys said grimly, "we learned that earlier. Easy now, man, and take another sip of wine before you try to say more. That's right." He began giving orders. "Morgan, fetch salves and bandages for his wounds. Brian, clear the area. What he will say should be for our ears alone." He looked back down at the scout. "Now, Sir Wallis, can you go on?"

"Yea . . . lord . . . Glenlyon was taken . . . near four month ago . . ."

"Four months," Brian exclaimed. "Impossible. Did you not just meet with Owain's messenger in Coventry, Rhys?"

"Yea, let him speak, Brian. Go on, Sir Wallis, tell me what you've learned."

As he listened, confusion was slowly replaced by a deep, burning rage. Rhys curled his hand into such a tight fist that blood spurted anew from the sword cut. Wallis finished his story. Rhys gave orders for him to be cared for, then straightened slowly and turned to Brian.

When they were alone by the fire, Brian gestured at his hand. "I'll reheat my dagger. The hot blade should seal it. So now we know it's not Sir Niclas who assaulted the keep."

"Nay." Rhys shook his head. He stared down at his hand without really seeing it. Blood dripped to the ground. "My own cousin. 'Tis my own cousin who has stolen my lands and my name."

Brian was silent for a moment. "Do you think 'twas your cousin that killed your father?"

"God help him if he is." Rhys looked up at Brian, surprised at the cold certainty in his own tone. "He'll wish for death long before it comes if he's the man responsible for the deaths of my father and brothers."

CHAPTER NINE

ॐ

Sasha stood in the shadows and clutched her hooded cloak more tightly around her. Too bad she couldn't make herself invisible and get closer. In the excitement created by the injured scout's arrival, no one had noticed her stealthy approach to the center of activity. But Rhys and Brian were talking so low she couldn't hear them, and Brian's thoughts were mostly in Gaelic instead of a language she readily understood.

Yet the little she did understand was enough. Rhys's cousin? How intriguing. Cousins seemed to be adept at treachery. Al-Hamin had certainly managed to do a lot of damage in her family. If she could—

"There you are," a voice growled, and she squeaked with alarm. Her guard's hand descended on her shoulder, gripping tightly as he dragged her forward. "Don't you be stealing away from me like that, wench. You know you're not supposed to talk to anyone. And it'll go badly for you when I tell his lordship you were eavesdropping on him again."

Sasha looked up with a scowl. She'd been so busy trying

to find out the cause of the excitement, she hadn't even heard this crude ape sneak up on her. Her eyes narrowed. She snatched at a scrap of information she'd gleaned from his teeming brain earlier. "If you tell him, Vachel, I'll make certain everyone knows that your sister married the village idiot instead of the mayor's son like you've been boasting. Not that they believed you anyway, but you'll look a fool for saying what isn't true."

He gaped at her, his face a dull red that had nothing to do with reflected firelight. "Curse you for a witch and a fiend," he finally choked out. "How did you know that?"

"How doesn't matter. I do know. And by now, even you dull-witted men have learned that I seem to find out unpleasant little truths."

"Yea, 'tis true."

His hand dropped away from her shoulder and she brushed away the imaginary hand print. "Very wise of you, Vachel. Tonight, I would like some extra cheese with my bread. Be certain I get it."

"Sir Brian's right," he said hoarsely. "You're a witch. You should be burned at the stake or drowned in the river."

"Don't be starting rumors. It would look bad if his lord-ship were to find the extra coins you've hidden in your pouch. You know the one—with the secret lining on the bottom? Where you put things you just happen to find lying around in other men's baggage?"

He backed away a step, his eyes narrowing. "You're just guessing."

She smiled. "Am I? Or do I really know? Mayhap 'tis as Brian says, and I'm a witch with the powers to be invisible. But then, if I were, would I still be sharing a disagreeable meal with you every night? Take a chance, Vachel."

He stared at her, then shook his head. "Nay. But don't get me in trouble with Lord Rhys. I'll keep your secret if you'll keep mine."

She laughed scornfully. "You're a fool if you think I'd ever trust you. And I'll keep your secret as long as it's convenient. Betray me, and you'll find yourself explaining

your thievery to the lord in a trice." When he glanced
around, she added softly, "And if you think a sharp knife
in the night would end your troubles, I promise you,
'twould only be the beginning of them."

Apparently, he believed her. He took another backward
step, making the sign of the cross over his chest but promising to keep her secret. She watched him flee to his own
campfire. It was getting dangerous. She couldn't keep making invalid threats for long, for sooner or later, one of the
men would call her bluff. And then she would have to
either do what she'd threatened or try to turn someone
into a toad.

And turning a man into a toad would be easier than
telling Rhys bad things about his own men. He wasn't
likely to believe anything she said. But as long as these
men didn't know that, she could bully them into small
favors. Nothing big. Not even the prospect of eating flies
and crouching on a lily pad outweighed the more certain
danger of incurring the lord's wrath.

A squabble sprang up around the campfire among some
of the men. She listened idly for a moment. All this turmoil—wait. Perhaps she could take advantage of it and
find Elspeth and Biagio. It had been three days since she
last spoke with them alone. The cart and donkey were too
slow, and trailed far behind. But she had seen them arrive
just before dark that evening, while Rhys and some of his
men were gone. Now might be the only opportunity she
would have.

Several fires dotted the camp at intervals. She slipped
from shadow to shadow, ever wary that one of her guards
would come after her, until she was within sight of the
familiar cart. The donkey and their horse were tethered
nearby. Socrates brayed softly in the night, head coming
up and ears pricked forward when he sensed her. His action alerted Bayosha, and the horse whinnied shrilly. Sasha
tensed.

One of the soldiers growled a rough oath and got up
from his place near the fire. He checked around the animals and gave a cursory glance into the trees before de-
ciding that there was nothing there. He went back to sit

by the fire, ruminating over the ill fortune that had seen him stuck as guard for an old woman and an insolent wolf cub.

Sasha smiled. Biagio wasn't nearly as complacent as the soldier, nor as weary. Within a few moments, he muttered something about relieving himself in the bushes, and walked toward the line of trees. She waited until he was near, then hissed to gain his attention.

"Psst. Psst. . . ."

I hear you, bella. Stop hissing or you'll have them all over here looking for you. It's about time you showed up.

He was still irritable. She'd expected it. And she couldn't really blame him. He had warned her what might happen. She just hadn't listened. He edged closer, fumbling at the tapes holding up his linen chausses, his back still to the men at the fire.

What happened? It's as I warned you. . . . Some of the men say he's furious, but they don't know the details. . . . Now there's this trouble with a fight. We're in the middle of something very nasty, and—say something!

"You're so busy complaining, who has time?" she hissed, crouching in the bushes and glaring up at him. "Don't you dare do what it looks like you're about to do. . . . I'm still wet from all that rain. How's Elspeth?"

Worried, how do you think she is? How do we get away from here? Are you ready to give up yet? What else do you need to convince you that—

"Not yet. He'll get over being angry, and once he's gotten back his keep, he'll be agreeable. I don't have a choice now anyway, so don't start berating me. . . . He keeps two guards on me most of the time. I need to get back before they come looking for me. . . . Biagio, don't do anything foolish. Stay with me. Please?"

I'll stay a while longer bella, but I warn you, I don't like these men. Or Wales.

Then he was gone, turning on his heel and stalking back to the fire, making a sharp retort to one of the men who glanced up and said something. Sasha waited a moment, looking for Elspeth. She must be in the cart asleep. It had been a rigorous journey over rough ground.

Pausing only to murmur reassurance to Socrates and Bayosha, she slipped back into the darker shadows of the trees. Leaves crackled underfoot and a branch snapped loudly. She stopped. Nothing. Only her imagination.

Keeping to the shadows and using the fires as a guide, she moved through the trees again. Now where was that guard? He should be nearby, ill tempered and testy, and full of resentment and fear. Ah, that must be Vachel she heard grumbling not far away, worried about stolen coins and retribution, for—

"Not so fast, flower."

She jerked to a stop. Even without the heavy hand that reached out for her, she knew her captor. The bright, brittle silence that surrounded him was as distinguishing as Vachel's evasive worries.

She turned, tossing her head in the gesture that she knew irritated him, pasting an innocent smile on her face. "May I not even tend to private needs in solitude, my lord? Am I to bring my fierce guard with me even into the bushes to—"

"Enough." His fingers tightened on her arm. "Your needs must not have been too pressing, or you wouldn't have gone so far to tend them. Come into the light."

Not that she had a choice. His grip was hard enough to peel away her skin if she was foolish enough to resist. And here she'd made a recent vow to be charming and sweet to him when next they spoke.

Hauling her around roughly, Rhys put a hand beneath her chin to tilt her face. He had his back to the fire. His eyes bore into her steadily, and though it was too dark to see their color, she was well aware of the angry shadows that must cloud them. His mouth was a taut slash and his voice was cool, though his words were calm.

"Where have you been, flower?"

"You must already know. I went to see Biagio and Elspeth." Her voice quivered slightly with strain, and she cleared her throat. "I have not seen them since Wytham."

"There's a reason for that." His hand fell away from her face, though he kept his grip on her arm. "And did you see them?"

She hesitated, then shrugged. "I saw Biagio. Elspeth must have been asleep. She's not young anymore, and I fear this journey is too hard on her."

"Perhaps you should have thought of that before you begged for their company."

She glared at him. "Perhaps you should have left me in England, and I would not have had to beg for their company."

"If we're going to get into the 'should haves,' flower, I'm afraid you have a few more to your credit than I do." He pulled her forward, closer to the fire, and the light spreading outward flickered over them. "Where are your guards?"

Oh, it wouldn't do for him to reprimand Vachel, for that coward was likely to tell him all. She gave a careless wave of one hand. "They have more courtesy for a lady than you, my lord. I left them waiting at a clump of bushes, so do not blame them for my excursion."

"I accept no excuses," he said abruptly. "Your privacy means nothing to me. Nor will it to them in the future, I assure you."

Alarmed, she opened her mouth to plead Vachel's case, galling as it would be, but the guard chose that moment to come running up, breathless and agitated, one hand holding his sword to keep it from flapping against his leg. His spurs jangled as he came to a stop.

"My lord . . . grant pardon, but she—she must have slipped away when I turned my back for only a moment. . . ."

Rhys gave him a cold glance and jerked his head toward the fire. "See Sir Brian. He'll give you your new assignment. One more suited to a man incapable of guarding even a small female. Tending baggage, perhaps."

Dismay was evident in Vachel's face, and she didn't need to hear the direction of his thoughts to know how he would defend himself. She'd best tell the truth before he did. She turned abruptly to Rhys. "I have a confession to make. Now. Right now. But we have to be alone. I don't want every man here to hear me admit this."

"My lord," Vachel protested, "the maid—"

She gripped Rhys's arm, squeezing hard. "All right, I'll tell you. I've been eavesdropping on you. I heard about the keep, and your cousin. I hid in the bushes and listened."

Vachel's breath blew out in a wheezing gasp. *Now what'll I do? Th' crazy bitch. . . . he'll skin us both. . . .*

Sasha imagined having to train a new guard; it took time to properly terrify a man. She took a deep breath and, before Rhys could speak, blurted, "It wasn't Vachel's fault, my lord. He was going to make me tell you, but I managed to get away first."

Vachel looked startled, then nodded vigorously and grasped at the chance. "That's right, my lord. I was looking for her to bring to you."

Rhys shook his head impatiently. "Go, Vachel. You're relieved of guard duty. I'll replace you in the morning."

Backing away uncertainly, Vachel flashed her a resentful glance, then left swiftly before Rhys could change his mind. Sasha looked up at Rhys and lifted her brow.

"So now I know. Do you think I stole away to whisper the information to some mysterious allies?"

"Something like that." A faint smile pressed at the corner of his mouth, and she saw for the first time the weariness that weighed on him. It was evident in the slight slump of his shoulders, in the fatigue etched into his features. "But you seem to have a way of confounding me, flower. I should have known better."

Pulling her with him, he moved toward the campfire. She fell silent, not daring to be too bold, afraid that he would retaliate harshly.

But when they reached his campfire, only Brian gave her harsh glances from across the flames. Rhys just swung her around and seated her on a fallen log. Then he held out his other hand so that the light flickered over it. "If I asked you to treat my hand, as you did my horse, do you think you could manage to do it without grave harm?"

Startled, she looked up at him. "Yea, my lord. I could tend it. That looks to be a nasty cut."

"It is. But I may need my sword hand on the morrow,

and prefer not to have it seared with a hot blade. That leaves it stiff and sore. Do you know another method?"

She smiled. "Yea, my lord. I do. And it will not leave your hand too stiff to use. May I send for my chest of herbs?"

He nodded, but added, "I intend to watch you closely, and Sir Robert will verify that you don't use anything harmful."

"I may be a bit rash at times, my lord," she said indignantly, "but not even I am fool enough to dare anything that would see me slain. There's not one of your men that would mind killing the woman who dared harm you."

"Keep that in mind, flower."

When he looked up, he was smiling, but there was no sign of humor in his eyes. She was not fooled for an instant.

"My lord," she murmured, "it's not been out of my mind for the past three days." And she meant it.

Rhys studied the top of her head as she bent over his hand, fussing with herbs and salves, clucking to herself about the vagaries that led men to inflict such injuries. Then she looked up, the dimple at the corner of her mouth deepening with a smile.

"You're a cautious man, my lord."

"Yea," he agreed easily. "I am. What of it?"

"You could have left my chest of leaves and herbs with Biagio. He has knowledge of potions and such, and he would not be as terrified as your men were to be holding such powerful magic."

"They survived it."

She laughed softly. "Barely. I thought poor Brian was nigh to collapse when he handed me the chest."

"As did I." Rhys grinned and looked up at Brian glowering across the campfire. "But as you can see, he is a stalwart knight, and made of sterner stuff."

"So he would have me believe. . . . Hold still. I cannot tend your hand with you jerking about. I know it must hurt, but all the dirt and bits of leather and metal should be removed before I apply the salve."

" 'Tis no great pain to bear, only confining to have my hand held so tightly."

She looked up at him, a wise smile, knowing how greatly it hurt. But all she said was a soft, "Yea, lord. I'll be swift."

It seemed to take forever, and he couldn't stop a sigh of relief when at last she released his hand and sat back. He tested it, frowning at the strip of cloth binding his palm.

"It will aid the healing," she said, correctly interpreting his frown. "And cushion it when you don your gauntlets again. Leave it on three days. When removed, you will be surprised by how much improved it is."

"I'm counting on that." He flexed his fingers again, then looked up at her. There was a faint, satisfied smile curving her mouth. His brow rose. "Do you think yourself saved from careful observation because of your help? You're not. You are still under close guard, flower, so do not think to slip away from me."

She blinked, a dark flutter of her lashes as if amazed that he would even suggest such a thing. "I've told you, my lord, that I don't want to slip away from you. Don't you recall? I searched for you. It took me years to find you, and—"

"Ah yes. The prophecy." He stood up. Firelight gleamed in her eyes and on the sweet curve of her cheek. Lovely dark rose, soft and tempting and without a shred of truth in her. False flower. He smiled. "I'll make a prophecy of my own, flower. What is mine, I keep. I will take back my lands from the man who has taken them. When they are in my hands again, I'll decide your fate. Until then, you will remain at my pleasure."

Stepping closer, he leaned down and trailed a fingertip over the slope of her cheek in a light caress. Her bottom lip trembled slightly, and she gripped it between small white teeth to still the quiver. Yea, bold and defiant, faithless and treacherous, she was as enigmatic and mysterious as the pattern of the heavens. And as easy to read. He could set his course by her, as mariners plotted sea courses by the stars.

Bending lower, he brushed his mouth across her parted lips, and she sighed softly, yielding to the kiss. He deepened it, a testing of her and of his own resolve, a sweet trial of the senses to strengthen his resistance. Yet despite his will, he found himself aroused by the feel of her mouth under his, the taste of her on his lips and the heady pressure of her answering kiss. It wasn't at all what he'd expected. Or wanted.

He straightened and abruptly turned. "Brian, see that she's made comfortable for the night. I must meet with Sir Robert and plan our strategy, and when you've seen to her security, please join us."

Sasha made a small sound in the back of her throat, chin lifting, gaze knowing and infuriating. He spared her a brief glance, then pivoted on his heel and stalked away to find Sir Robert. She may be predictably false, but it seemed his own body betrayed him of late. It was as if he'd not been with a woman in months instead of only a few days.

Sir Robert sat before the fire with a comrade and rose to his feet when he saw Rhys approaching. "My lord, we were just discussing the best method to assault the keep. Sir Peter suggests siege engines until the rest of your troops arrive. A steady barrage should at least harass Sir Niclas and keep him well-occupied until we can form an effective assault, and free other men to harry any troops in the area."

It was a tried and true method of warfare. Rhys had applied it with Richard at Acre, and then Jerusalem. One had been much more effective than the other, and he was well aware of how long such a strategy could take, as well as the variable factors that could mean success or defeat. And meanwhile, Gavin was busily deploying men and forwarding petitions to the Prince of Deheubarth and Prince John in England.

" 'Tis a good suggestion, Sir Robert, but there are other facts you should know. Sir Niclas is not in command of Glenlyon. 'Tis my cousin, Gavin of Glamorgan. So now we must worry about an enemy at our backs as well as before us. But I have an idea that may gain us much swifter entry into the keep than a long siege." He smiled. "It's a bold plan, and daring. If we succeed, we win all. If we fail . . . if we fail, we lose all."

There was a moment of silence. A burning limb snapped in two in the flames, and Sir Robert turned to look at it. He didn't speak until Brian reached them, then he said, "I'm with you, my lord. In whatever you undertake, I'm with you."

"So am I," Brian said immediately, and looked from one man to the other. "What is it we're going to do?"

"Assault the keep," Rhys replied softly.

Brian stared at him with wide eyes. "Assault the—are you mad? We're only two score men. . . . You do mean wait until the others arrive, don't you? You can't intend for us to try anything so—why, we'd have to be magic to succeed. Rhys, why don't you say something?"

"Because you've already said it all, Brian. We'll use magic to defeat them." He smiled when Brian staggered back a step. "Think of it—our own men were laid low by a maid only a few days ago, too sick to think of anything but their own bellies. Does that give you any ideas, Sir Brian?"

After a moment of tense, stunned silence, Brian smiled. "Yea, lord, I believe it does." He looked around, then laughed. "But how are we to manage it?"

"I think I know a way. . . ."

CHAPTER TEN

Faint curls of smoke drifted up from the fire, barely visible in the first gray light before sunrise. Rhys blinked sleepily, frowning. Something had penetrated his haze of slumber to jerk him from sleep. He looked around. Pelt-shrouded forms of men spread out in all directions like the spokes of a cart's wheel; nearby there was the muffled stamping of horses's hooves in the soft dirt. Quiet, familiar sounds. But something was wrong.

He sat up, frowning. His gaze moved over the camp and he raked his bandaged hand through his hair. Nothing was awry that he could see. Wait—Sasha. Her pallet was empty. The rope that had bound her to a tree lay limp, snaking along the ground.

Rhys surged to his feet, cursing loud enough to wake the men nearest him. "Get up," he snarled at them as he bent to grab his sword, clad only in his linen tunic and chausses. He traversed the distance between his pallet and the cart in quick, determined steps, but found Biagio still asleep. The young Italian was securely fastened to the wheel of their own cart by a length of sturdy hemp.

Brian ranged behind him, kicking awake more men as Rhys moved along the line of trees edging the camp. The camp stirred to life. Men grumbled sleepy questions, then grew quiet upon hearing the reply. Rhys bent to study the ground. Scuffed footprints led into the trees here, with the dry sides of the leaves in the new depressions turned upward. Curse her. She'd escaped. To meet with the enemy? To warn them?

He stood up and turned to a perplexed, sleepy-eyed knight staggering toward him. "Go that way, Peter, and pray that you do not let her slip by you again."

"My lord," came the protest, "I was not on duty. Sir Brian set four guards on the wench, so if she fled, it must have been with the use of magic."

"Aye," muttered Sir Clyde, hitching up his chausses. He buckled on his sword and looked up at Rhys. "I know not how else it may have been done. It had to have been magic, my lord."

Sir Clyde's broad, flat-featured face registered wary indignation at the suggestion a mere woman had managed to slip past them by mortal means. Rhys stifled a curse. He certainly didn't need men befuddled by tales of magic or enchantment. They needed to keep their wits about them.

He fixed Sir Clyde with a cold stare. "If the maid has fled, 'twas not by magic. I'll warrant it has more to do with sleeping sentries. Now spread out and search. The next man who mentions magic will feel the flat of my sword against his thick head."

His harsh words and tone did more to reassure the uneasy men than anything else he could have said or done. They swiftly ranged into the trees to look for the missing maid.

"Well done, mighty warrior," came a softly mocking voice. He turned to stare coolly at Biagio. The youth was awake now, leaning back against the hard wooden spokes of the cart's wheel, secured by ropes. A taunting smile curled his mouth; dark humor lit his eyes. "How is it that you've managed to misplace one small maid?"

Rhys strode to him. "Where is she?"

Biagio shrugged. "How should I know? I was asleep and bound."

"But you would know where she went. Tell me." Rhys nudged him with the flat of his drawn sword. "Danger thrives in the forest. I would see her safe."

"Some would say it's more dangerous here than in the forest, where the wild beasts are of a more predictable nature." Biagio bent one leg, the faint smile still curling his mouth. "You Welsh are a savage lot—"

Rhys's sword flashed up. The tip pressed against Biagio's chest in a silent warning that choked off the rest of his comment. "I think," he said softly, "that you will swiftly see how savage we Welsh can be if you do not tell me what I want to know. Where is she?"

After a moment of thick silence, Biagio indicated a line of trees with a jerk of his head. "She went in that direction." When Rhys lifted his sword and turned away, Biagio leaned forward with another taunt. "Beware she does not turn you into a toad, Welshman."

Rhys flashed him a harsh glance over one shoulder. Mocking laughter followed him into the trees. He was getting tired of being confronted with that wild tale. If she was such an enchantress, why hadn't she escaped? He scowled and swung at a low-hanging limb with his sword. It dropped with a shiver to the ground. He made his way deeper into the trees.

Silver-gray beech branches soared upward to blot out early light; only thready streamers pierced the dense, silver-haired leaves and golden tassels of flowers growing overhead. Little grew on the forest floor here, for the sunlight was too meager. It was easy to track the maid's progress through the wood, slapping aside the occasional straggling limb and new growth. Cursing her with every step, he followed the trail as it climbed upward, where the ground grew rocky. How had she come so far so quickly?

He came upon Sasha in a rowan grove. Here, early sunlight penetrated lacy, white-flowering branches in a wide, diffused band that danced over the dark ribbon of her hair. She was kneeling on thick, springy moss by the edge of a small stream. Birds gathered noisily in the treetops. He halted at the clearing's edge, watching her.

She was wearing the purple cloak, absorbed with a clump of flowering plants. A long-legged hare emerged from beneath thick bushes, creeping close to her with nose and whiskers twitching; it sat up, front paws dangling and the furry ears erect. Sasha spoke softly, and the small animal approached her outstretched hand. It nibbled daintily from her palm, ears jerking back and forth. A swallow landed impudently on a fallen branch, twittering excitedly.

He stared at her. Brian's warnings haunted him. Despite the early morning chill in the air, beads of sweat dampened his skin. Caused by the long walk, of course. Not from anything she might be doing, no matter how odd it seemed at the moment. She was only feeding a rabbit. She was a willful maid, not an elf queen or faerie. And she was a maid who had managed to escape his camp when he'd warned her not to try it.

He straightened. He'd taken only a single step when Sasha rose to her feet and held out her arms, palms upward over the running water of the tiny stream. Murmuring words he didn't recognize, she uncurled her fingers. Pale white flowers fluttered from her palms, twisting, turning, landing lightly on the water's surface, spiraling in the currents.

Intent upon the maid, he did not hear Brian behind him until his friend spoke. "Do you think she's casting a spell on us, Rhys?"

He stiffened but didn't turn. "Don't sneak up on me like that."

"Aye, lord. I understand. She frightens me as well."

Brian's shaky voice was ample evidence of fear, even if Rhys hadn't felt his slight shudder. He shook his head. "It's not the maid that sets me on edge, Brian. She's wandered too far. Gavin could have his men all around us."

"I hadn't thought of that."

"I have." He looked back at Sasha. She still faced the stream, kneeling at the edge, oblivious to anything around her. Mushroom caps grew in decaying leaves near her feet, and a rough circle of stones surrounded several white-flowered rowan trees. She scattered more flowers on the water.

Enough. He strode from the brush toward her. Still she did not turn around. She must have heard them. They'd made no effort to be quiet, and the crunch of leaves and limbs underfoot should have warned her they were there.

Sunlight glinted in her dark hair, and the strong, sweet scent of jasmine drifted toward him. He bent to lay a hand on her shoulder, and she said evenly, "You took much longer to find me than I thought you would, my lord."

His hand jerked back. She rose to her feet and turned, a move as light and graceful as a dancer. A slight, knowing smile curved her lips.

His eyes narrowed. "If you knew we were here, why didn't you acknowledge us?"

"And spoil your valiant efforts at skulking?" Her mocking smile widened. "I couldn't disappoint you."

"You didn't." He grasped her arm, holding fast. "I expected you to try to flee me. 'Twas why I set guards on you."

"Guards?" Her eyes widened with fraudulent surprise. "I don't see any guards near me, my lord. Are they with me now?"

"You know they're not." His fingers tightened on her wrist. "How did you get past them?"

Looking toward Brian, she smiled again. "Hazel wreaths. If the twigs are woven into a crown, one can be invisible. Is that not so, Sir Brian?"

Busily digging into the pouch at his waist, Brian muttered an agreement as he fished out a charm of twigs and red thread. He held it up. His swift glance toward Rhys was half-defiant, half-afraid. "She tried to coax me into it before, my lord. When you sent me for her to heal your horse. I found her in a hazel coppice, gathering magic and herbs to be invisible."

It would do no good at this point to remind Brian that if the wench were truly magic, she wouldn't be his prisoner. He shook his head. "Go back and tell Sir Robert and the others that we've found her. And we may need magical herbs, so don't be so quick to condemn them."

Sasha's wrist turned slightly in his grasp, and he looked down at her. She was staring at Brian, her dark eyes so wide the thick brush of her lashes was quivering. Her nostrils flared slightly, and her lips were parted and moist. Then a faint smile curved her mouth, and she glanced up at him before looking back at Brian.

"Will you need my talents then, my lord? Perhaps I won't feel so generous as to share what I know. If I'm a witch and a wicked faerie, perhaps I'll just turn you all into toads or weasels instead."

Brian's face was a pasty white beneath the splash of freckles, and his hand shook as he held up the charm. "*Acre arcre arnem nona aernem*—"

"Enough, Brian." Rhys pushed her behind him, impatient with Brian's superstitions and her flagrant taunting. "Can't you see she enjoys goading you?"

Sasha laughed softly. "He makes it so easy. . . . Here, Irishman—catch!"

Rhys grabbed her other arm as her hand flashed up, and a shower of white flowers flew through the air. Brian bellowed in alarm, staggering backward and tumbling over a fallen log to sprawl on the ground. Rhys brought her arm up swiftly between them. Her fingers were curled tightly into her palm, holding something. Keeping his eyes locked with hers, he pried open her fingers. Pale white blossoms fluttered from her palm, drifting in the air, some landing lightly on the water, the others scattering over the thick moss.

She smiled. "Rowan flowers for a magic spell." Her words were soft, almost a whisper drowned out by the sound of rushing water. "I can summon the wind or the rain, make the sun set, and pigs fly. Watch me, my lord, and p'raps I'll show you how to make your enemies disappear."

"Enough." His fingers dug harshly into her wrist to hold her fast. "I'm not a child to be impressed with vain boasts."

"Are you not?" Shaking back the hair from her face, she stared up at him. "Yet you want me to help you. I know what you want from me. But what will you promise to gain my help? What could I possibly want from you, save that which you've already promised me?"

He stared down at her. There was more than just mischief in her eyes. There was a gleam of determination. He looked over at Brian, who had lurched to his feet and was brushing damp leaves from his chest.

"Leave us, Brian. I would speak with our unpredictable guest alone."

Brian scowled. "Are you certain 'tis wise, Rhys? I mean, to be alone with her now."

"I'll be fine, Brian. Just go."

He waited until Brian was gone from the clearing before he swung Sasha around by her arm. He kept a firm grip on her wrist as he seated her atop a fallen log. She sat quietly, gazing serenely up at him. He smiled slightly.

"How did you get past my sentries?"

"It's not difficult to slip by sleeping men." Her brow rose. "You'd best hope to make Glenlyon's invaders sleep as deeply as your posted guards."

"How did you know about that plan?"

She shrugged, a light lifting of her shoulders, careless and infuriating. He pulled her toward him with a swift, angry tug. He tangled his hand in the wealth of dark hair at her nape, tilting her head back and startling a gasp from her throat.

"It seems to me you eavesdrop too much, flower. And I can't help but wonder what you intend to do with all the information you learn by lurking in shadows."

"I didn't mean . . . I don't intend to do anything with it. What could I do?"

"That," he muttered, dragging her up hard against him with his arm behind her back, "is what I mean to find out. Tell me. Are you supposed to meet someone? Get a message to someone?"

She pushed at his chest, a gesture that even she seemed to recognize as futile. Her eyes flashed angrily. "I tried to tell you all I want from you is your help. You swore an oath. On your sword, to keep the pro—"

"Not that cursed prophecy madness again. I've heard enough of it." His arm tightened. "If you value your pretty neck, flower, you won't mention it to me again. I want the truth."

"No, it's not the truth you want. You won't listen when you hear it." She glared up at him, frustration in the straight slash of her brows and the tight set of her mouth. "All you wanted was to bed me, and you said anything I wanted to hear. I kept my word, didn't I? Now you want to pretend you never swore—"

"Yea, you kept your word." Catching her thick hair in his fist, he drew his spread fingers through the silky strands in a lingering glide. He frowned. The memory of that night was so vague, so wine fogged. He shook his head slowly. "A labor for a night, but now you claim a war. A ridiculous request to rival the labors of Hercules. A distraction from the truth, and no more."

"But . . . you agreed."

"Don't change the subject. You know I did not. I would never have sworn to wage war for a warm tumble, not even with so fair a flower."

The motion of her body against his as she struggled to get free was arousing. His body reacted instantly, and there was a subtle change in the way he held her. She grew still, staring up at him with wide dark eyes, and he knew she was aware of the difference. Slowly, with a soft, lingering stroke, he drew his hand down her back, fingers grazing the gentle curve hiding beneath the weight of her cloak. She shivered.

The small tremor conveyed a searing message to him, and despite the barriers he'd erected, he began to burn. Inconvenient, unwanted lust. Curse her. He ached, the dull throb growing higher and harder, focusing all his attention on the pressure of her breasts against him. The front of her cloak had parted, and there was nothing between them but the thin materials of her gown and his tunic. It was arousing, tempting, inflaming.

His entire body burned. The memory of her soft skin and bare thighs around him returned with sharper focus, and he saw no need to deny himself. She was warm, willing, available.

Sasha grabbed his arms as he bent her back toward the ground. White rowan flowers lay strewn on the bright green moss like snow. The rush of water was loud. Her dark eyes were wide beneath the fringe of her lashes, soft and exotic, drawing him into their depths. Her fingers dug into his arms, muffled by layers of linen tunic as she clung to him. "Lord Rhys, wait—"

"Nay, flower. It's been three days since I bedded you, and I see no reason not to ease myself again now." He kissed her fiercely, until he felt her resistance fade. "Truce, flower. Truce."

She made a faint sound in her throat, wordless and dismayed. He laid her gently but firmly on the ground, cushioning her on the thick moss and her wool cape. He knelt, unfastened the small clasp that held her cloak, and spread it to the sides. Then he bent to kiss her brow, cheek, closed eyes, the arch of her throat as her head fell back with a soft moan.

He lifted his head. Her breath came swiftly, lips parted and lashes quivering slightly with each indrawn breath. He smiled. He pulled his tunic over his head and tossed it aside. Her gown was a simple garment, gathered at the waist with a cloth girdle and laces. He wanted to see her in the light of day instead of the shrouding shadows of candle glow and gloom. He reached for the laces.

"Yield to me, flower," he murmured as he loosened her gown, "yield all . . ."

Breathing warmth along the curve of her throat, then lower, he slipped his hand beneath the soft wool gown to cup her bare breast. His fingers found the tight bud of her nipple, and she gasped when he teased the rigid peak. Shoving aside the wool, he replaced his hand with his mouth. She arched upward with a wordless cry; her hands moved to his shoulders to pull herself against him.

He reached up and caught her hands, pressed them back into the cushion of her cloak as he slid his body atop hers. He rested his weight on their clasped hands, and bent again. His mouth returned to that sweet bud and lingered. His bare chest scraped against her soft skin in a smooth, arousing glide. She was silky softness and exotic fragrance,

warmth and shadows, turning beneath him, her cries floating up through the pounding haze around him in soft entreaties.

She turned again, twisting, a slow curve of golden skin
and high, bare breasts, teasing his body into hardening
purpose. He wedged between her thighs and pressed hard
against her, shuddering at the exquisite sensation. With
one hand, he reached down to unbind the ties to his linen
chainse, to remove the last barrier.

Sasha wrenched free, put out a hand, fingers stilling his
short jerks at the tapes. "My lord," she choked out, "do
not. I cannot allow you to continue this when—"

"When what?" he demanded when her words faltered.
He stared down at her through narrowed eyes. His body
throbbed, straining against the confinement of his garments and the arousing pressure of her hand against him.
"When what?" he repeated.

She held tightly to the tapes of his trousers, not quite
meeting his eyes as she tried to twist away from him. He
let her sit up. Her reply was a mutter. "When . . . it's not
the right time."

"Not the right time." He took a deep breath. "Is the
moon in the wrong quarter of the heavens? Is it on the
cusp or the wane, or whatever else you can think of?"

She released his partially untied tapes, her words sharp.
"It's not that at all. It's . . . you know."

He stared at her, at the high flush staining her cheeks
and the slight quiver of her lips, and shook his head. "You
could have told me that before you let me go so far. But
I suppose you enjoy tormenting me."

She smiled slightly. "Yea, lord, I admit I do. But it
wasn't for that reason, I swear it."

He studied her, cursing the throb in his loins and the
heat she'd ignited that didn't seem likely to fade quickly.
Vague memories returned, images of a stuffy room and
this exotic maid, of her soft thighs and heated scent, and
he frowned. There were memories aplenty of being
aroused; none of reaching fulfillment. Scarlet silk and
burning skin, the erotic glide of his body against hers—

but no memory of the exquisite penetration that should have followed.

Reaching out, he circled her wrist lightly with his bandaged hand, fingers caressing her smooth skin. "Tell me again, flower, of our night together. My memory is hazy. Since I must wait, I would hear how satisfying it was for both of us."

She stared at him, a quick flutter of her lashes, then a shrug and a smile. "You were a stallion. Over and over. I was exhausted, and you were so fatigued you fell asleep. I left. Regretfully, of course."

"Of course." He smiled faintly. "You left to go downstairs and poison my men. But how did you know I would sleep so soundly? How did you know I would not wake and want more from you?"

Her hand fluttered impatiently. "Like all men, you sleep soundly after love play."

"Yea, I most likely do, flower." He drew her closer, a gentle but steady pull on her arm that brought her face close to his. He reached out to fondle a loose strand of her hair, twisting it around one finger. "But I don't think you know that. I don't think you stayed long enough to test my . . . prowess."

Her laugh was light and scornful. "If you must know the truth, my lord, you were quick. Very quick. A rabbit. Fffft! Over with before it had really begun. Too swift to remember, I imagine. Please release my arm. You're hurting me."

"Am I?" He smiled but did not lessen his grip. "Such a facile liar you are, flower. I stand amazed."

"You're sitting down." She tugged a little, then leaned forward. "I am weary of you calling me a liar."

"Poor flower. The truth is not always palatable."

She stared at him. "No. It's not. As you should know."

He frowned. A brisk breeze blew over his bare chest, chilling him. When she pulled away this time, he let her go. She stood, reaching down to tug at her cloak until he got up. She flung it around her shoulders in a quick swirl, then held it under her chin with a fist, staring up at him. He shook his head.

"You know, of course, that I'm going to have to put you in chains when we get back to camp. It's the only way I can be certain you won't give warning of our plans."

"Who would I warn? The birds? Your dull-witted soldiers? You give me far too much credit, my lord."

"No," he said, and reached out for her again, "I don't think I've given you enough. Perhaps I should do more than just chain you."

Sasha stared at him for a moment before yielding to panic at the sudden fierce glitter in his iron-hard eyes. Wrenching free of his loose grasp, she bunched the hem of her cloak in both hands and whirled away. But Rhys was too quick, and he was on her in an instant.

When he spun her around, her reaction was swift and instinctive. Her foot shot up, catching him squarely in the groin. The effect was immediate. Doubling over, he dropped to his knees on the moss, and she fled.

Hems lifted high, she leaped over fallen logs and ducked around thick clumps of bushes, running like a hare, blindly panicked, not pausing until she was certain she'd left him far behind. Only then did she stop to lean against a thick-trunked oak and catch her breath. Her lungs ached for air and her side hurt. She was shaking so badly she could scarcely stand, even using the tree as a support.

Now what? She'd ruined everything. He'd guessed the truth. Despite her blithe assurances to Elspeth that she had the situation well in hand things had somehow escaped her control. Curse him. It was bad enough that she'd almost allowed him to take her on a bed of moss like a whore. Worse, she had wanted him to. Yea, she had found herself sinking into the giddy whirl of passion like a stone, not caring for anything but the touch of his hand or his mouth, the searing caresses and sweet words he whispered in her ear. For a brief span of time, she'd lost her senses and it had been as bright and glorious as she'd heard women say it was. Where was that familiar smug superiority to those weak, fragile females who allowed a man to rule them? Gone like yesterday's sunlight.

Still shaking, she gave her cloak an irritated flounce to dislodge dead leaves. Her fingers shook when she reached down to smooth the wool folds. Her hand grazed the pouch of herbs she'd gathered, dangling from a frayed length of cord inside her cloak. The pouch was open and limp, and she peered inside. She'd managed to lose most of the flowers she'd spent an hour gathering that morning. Her pouch had been full when Rhys came upon her.

By all the saints, it was the final affront. Rowan flowers blossomed only in May; they had to be gathered when in bloom to be effective. She'd had an abundance. Now she'd have to find another tree, and try again to gather enough blossoms. There were different purposes for all parts of the rowan, and her supply was growing scarce. When the flowers turned into orange-red berries, she'd gather them to use in healing sachets and mixtures. Two twigs tied together with a length of red thread to form a cross could be used as an amulet for protection, such as the one Brian wore. She smiled. Yea, the foolish knight wore it as protection against her, fearing that she would turn him into a toad. It would hardly be much of a transformation, in her opinion, but she wished she knew how to do it. It would have saved her much annoyance.

Now her precious flowers were gone. Rowan trees growing near stone circles had the most potent powers of protection. It might be a long time before she found more such trees again.

"Things could hardly be worse," she muttered. An oak leaf fluttered down from overhead, skimming past her cheek. She put out a hand to catch it in her palm. Suddenly, she stiffened as she felt a barrage of impressions descend on her like a shower of leaves. Words in French and English whirled in a deafening tide of overpowering, dangerous intentions, threatening to drown her. Dazed, she looked up.

Nay, she'd been wrong. Things had just gotten much worse than she could have imagined.

Forming a half circle, a dozen armed soldiers stood a short distance away, staring at her with satisfaction. It would have been bad enough were they Rhys's men, but from the direction of their thoughts, she knew that these men were his enemies.

These were the men who held Glenlyon.

CHAPTER ELEVEN

❧

"What did you do to her?" Biagio strained against the ropes binding him to the cart. "You must have done something. Sasha wouldn't have fled you like that otherwise."

Rhys shot him a narrow glance but didn't reply. He turned back to Brian. It didn't help that Brian was staring at him with fear and dismay. He asked again, "Did you find any sign of her?"

Brian shook his head. "No sign. But if she didn't want to be found, I doubt any mortal man could find her." He glanced around them, then said softly so only Rhys could hear, "I even checked a circle of stones, and one of mushrooms, but saw no evidence that she'd been there. Often, there's some sign—trampled grasses, or cowslip blossoms, or the faerie triad—I found nothing." Lowering his voice even more, he leaned close. "Tell me true, Rhys—did she turn into a puff of smoke and vanish? Or enchant you in some way? Were you turned to stone, or into an animal, or even—"

"Enough." Rhys was furious with himself for allowing

a mere slip of a maid to outwit him. And he was chagrined that she'd done it without any magic at all. It was embarrassing. It was infuriating. And it was intriguing. Few men had gotten the best of him so easily. Never a woman. She was beginning to earn his grudging respect.

"But how then did she escape you?" Brian was asking plaintively, "if not for magic?"

Rhys looked at him, considering the truth, but Biagio chose that moment to call out, "Yea, tell them of her escape, Welshman. Or do you dare?"

Turning toward him, Rhys gave the Italian youth a hard look no man could have failed to understand. "How she fled is no matter. She's managed to escape. She's meeting whoever sent her to delay me, I suspect."

Biagio laughed scornfully. "Yea, fool that you are, believe that. But it's not true, though I wish it was. She's alone out there, and likely to be in danger."

"The only danger she's in is of me finding her before she gets far enough away."

"I admit there's not much worse than being held captive by a ruthless band of Welsh knights just back from plundering Cyprus with Richard Coeur de Lion," Biagio snarled, "but aren't you overlooking the obvious?"

Rhys walked to the cart and stared down at him narrowly. "The obvious what, whelp?"

"That she might really be in trouble. She ran from you, no doubt. I don't know the details, but I can imagine them clearly enough." Biagio took a deep breath. "If she doesn't return soon, I'm afraid she might be in real danger." He shifted against the hard spokes of the cart and strained against the ropes binding him. "Release me, and I'll help you search for her, my lord. I swear she's not in league with your enemies. I don't know where she is, but you can trust me to find her."

"Don't do it, Rhys." Brian stepped forward, his sword slapping against his thigh with a harsh metallic clink. "He's in league with her."

Rhys studied the dark-eyed youth for a long moment. Then he shook his head. "Nay, Brian, I think he means it. And if he betrays us, I'll personally slit his throat." He slipped his dagger from the sheath. Bending, he sliced through the thick ropes binding Biagio. Then he held his dagger tip against the youth's throat and added softly, "You can depend upon that."

Rubbing at his wrists, the youth looked at Rhys with darkly glittering eyes. "I give you my word that I'll not betray you as long as she's in danger. After that, you must know that my first loyalty lies with her."

"I expect nothing else." He moved the dagger and rose to his feet, pulling Biagio up with him. He held the young Italian's arm. "Truce, until she is found."

"Yea, lord. Truce until she is found."

Biagio took a step away, shaking loose Rhys's grip on his arm. "I'll need my dagger. And some men, on the chance that your enemies already have her."

Beckoning a scowling Brian close, he said, "Give him what he needs, Sir Brian. And go with him. Just to keep him honest."

Brian nodded jerkily. His eyes narrowed. "I'll keep a close watch on him, my lord."

Rhys smiled faintly. "I know that you will. Take Sir Clyde with you, and two others of your choosing. Sir Robert and I will make for Glenlyon to begin building our war engines."

Startled, Brian looked at him. "Do you still intend an assault then?"

"Eventually. We don't know if they have the maid with them yet, but we do know Gavin has Glenlyon. Our other plan will have to wait, but I don't intend to wait idly for his next move."

Brian grinned. "Nay, lord, you never have. This is much better than waiting."

"Better for Sasha as well?" Elspeth demanded. She stepped from the shadow of the cart, her voice quavering slightly. Pointing a bony finger at Rhys, she shrilled, " 'Tis your fault she's in danger, and woe be unto you if she's harmed."

"Cease your prattle, old woman," Brian said harshly. "Can you not see that my lord is doing all he can to find the troublesome wench?" He made as if to shove her aside, but Rhys held out a hand to stop him.

"Leave her be. She's worried about her mistress. Under the circumstances, I cannot blame her."

"It's not your fault the wench is willful," Brian protested. "If she had listened, she'd be here now, safe and protected."

Rhys looked at Elspeth. Most likely, the old woman was well aware of all that had happened. Sasha's servants would know of her trickery. When she was with him again, he'd see that she paid well for that ruse, but now there were more pressing things to think about.

To Elspeth he said shortly, "I'll do my best to recover her unharmed, old woman."

Shakily, she muttered, "See that you do. She's worth more than this entire country to me."

Rhys could understand that. He nodded curtly before turning away. Morgan had cleaned his harness and weapons, and Turk was saddled and waiting. He donned his mail, stepped into the saddle, and urged the prancing stallion forward. Men were ready and waiting, helms glittering in the morning sunlight, bright rays bouncing off their shields.

Those left behind with Elspeth, the extra horses, and the baggage, watched silently as they rode past. If fortune was with him, Sasha had not yet made it to Glenlyon. If it was against him and she'd already betrayed him, his first plan would have to be discarded. It would put his men in too much peril. There were other ways to regain Glenlyon, though they would take longer.

While time might be on Rhys's side, it would also be to Gavin's advantage. His cousin could summon more men to his standard, while Rhys had been gone too long from Wales to readily call men to his banner. Was he still Welsh? There were times he didn't know, couldn't recall how it had been. Then there were the times, he remembered sitting at his father's feet during councils, clad in rough pelts and skins, happily squatting in the dirt and smoke of a crowded room. Politics had always been the most frequent topic, then had come Rhys's favorite—tales of battles fought both recently and long ago, recounted over and over, with each telling emphasizing the bravery and courage of his ancestors.

Such were the stories he'd been reared with. He'd always known what was expected of him. He'd been born to fight. Even being wrenched from his family had not diminished that knowledge. Floundering in an unfamiliar land in an unfamiliar court peopled with strangers speaking an unfamiliar tongue had not lessened that certainty. And then Richard had sent him back to hold his lands for England.

For England.

Not Wales. Not for his homeland, the country of his birth, but for his adopted land. Never mind that it had been unwillingly adopted, that he'd been a hostage most of his life—he was expected to ignore the past and secure Glenlyon as an English stronghold.

There was much he loved about England. And God help him, he loved Richard as only a comrade-in-arms could love him. He'd fought at his side, recovered from wounds at his side, and admired the man as a brilliant soldier. But he could not admire him as a king. Richard might have majesty, but he was no English monarch. England was unimportant to Richard. Yea, Rhys thought more of England than did its king. And now his father's dying had brought him back to Wales, to his true homeland.

"My lord," Sir Robert said, bringing his horse alongside Rhys's, "do we ride to the gates of Glenlyon as we did before?"

"No, not to the gates but in sight of the keep. I want them to know we're there, to watch us build siege engines to assault the walls." He thought a moment. With the maid gone, any chance of surprise had vanished. But he'd not left himself with only one option, and he looked at Sir Robert with a faint smile. "I have another idea, something to try while they're busy watching us construct war machines and toss stones at the walls."

Sir Robert nodded and grinned. "I thought you might, m'lord." He hesitated, then said, "And the woman? If they have her?"

Rhys's hands tightened on his looped reins as he said grimly, "I pray they do not."

That prayer was doomed, he discovered, when Brian and Biagio caught up with him on a hill overlooking Glenlyon.

"My lord," Brian wheezed, reining in his mount in a cloud of dust, "she's been taken."

He looked from Brian to Biagio. The truth was in the youth's dark, anguished eyes. He exhaled slowly. "Are you certain?"

In reply, Biagio held up a small pouch. It dangled from his hand by a length of frayed cord, twisting slightly in the breeze. " 'Tis hers. I would know it anywhere."

Rhys was silent. He remembered the pouch, and the white rowan blossoms that had been scattered on the moss. And the dark eyes and mocking smile . . . curse her. Curse her for fleeing him, for being faithless. He shook his head. "Where did you find it?"

"Two leagues from where we saw her this morn," Brian replied. " 'Twas Biagio who spied it on the ground, trampled by hooves. The marks were distinct. There had been men and horses there. The ground was cut up, and not yet dry."

"If your cousin is as harsh a man as you," Biagio snapped, "we waste time standing here bemoaning her fate. We need to rescue her."

Rhys stared at him coldly. "Don't presume to tell me my business, whelp. Don't you think I know what should be done?"

"Yea, but how long will you delay?" Biagio shot back. "We should already be at the castle gates demanding her release."

Silence fell. Rhys leaned on the high pommel of his saddle. "If she has been taken against her will, they would not yield her up should we be so naive as to ask, whelp."

"You don't even want to ask. You don't care if they kill her." Biagio's face was taut, his eyes black pits in his uncharacteristically pale face.

Rhys straightened, uttered a crude oath, and started to turn away.

Biagio nudged his horse forward, and the bay pranced in a nervous half circle to block Rhys's movement. Fixing him with a dark glare, the youth snarled, "I don't propose asking anything. I propose that we take her from them whether they're willing to let her go or no."

Rhys leaned on the saddle pommel again, returning Biagio's angry glare. "And if she isn't already in league with them, it's the swiftest way I know to get her killed. If Gavin learns that we value her, he'll be certain to dangle her before us as a carrot before a cart horse. There would be no guarantee of her safety."

"Afraid to try, Welshman?" Biagio said softly. "I'm not. Let me go. I can get into the castle and free her while you're still out here thinking about it."

"Can you?" Rhys's irritation was tempered with grim amusement.

Brian guffawed loudly. "You'd last as long as a rabbit in a wolves' den."

"I don't think so. I've spent time in enough castles to know my way around." Biagio calmed his mount with a steady hand, still staring hard at Rhys. "Italians are expert at adapting to murderous situations, my lord. We get so much practice at home. Give me a chance. I know a way."

Rhys grinned. "I'm intrigued, whelp. Tell me more . . ."

"Welcome to Glenlyon, demoiselle." The fluent French phrase came from a man seated in a high-backed chair on the dais at the far end of the great hall. He beckoned her closer. "Come forward, so I may see you better. 'Tis no use hanging back like a frightened child."

A guard took her arm and urged her forward. Sasha curled her fingers into tight fists at her sides, ignoring the curious gazes directed at her as she was escorted to the dais. The tiny bells on her shoes tinkled with every step, muffled slightly by foul-smelling rushes on the hall floor. She came to a halt at the foot of the dais and tossed back her head to stare up at the man in the chair. Heavy tapestries hung on the walls, fluttering in numerous drafts. Armed guards ranged the sides of the hall.

She forced herself to remain calm. "This is a poor welcome to my way of thinking. Why was I brought here?"

"Are you not enjoying your stay? Have you not been treated well?" came the mocking reply.

"If you consider being dragged from my own interests and forced to comply being treated well, then yea—I've been treated quite well."

"Excellent." A faint smile curled his mouth. He leaned forward to gaze at her. "I assure you more such considerate treatment in the near future, lest you feel cheated of my assiduous attention."

"How kind." His identity still eluded her. Those in his employ thought of him either in Welsh or in general epithets instead of by name. But she guessed that, this must be Rhys's cousin, the man who had stolen Glenlyon.

He wasn't an ill-favored man. He had dark hair, piercing black eyes, and high-cut cheekbones above a square jaw and firm mouth. Yet his eyes were just a whit too close together, and the lips a bit too petulant. Petulant and curling into a cruel smile that didn't do a thing to reassure her of a long and happy future. He looked like a weasel. She took a deep breath. This was certainly a man whose face betrayed his character.

She focused on him, narrowing her gaze. It was at times like these that she was most grateful for her Gift. It could pierce the clouds of whirling impressions surrounding him to rivet on his true intentions. She was met with a barrage of half-formed thoughts, darting this way and that like hawks seizing on hapless prey. A sense of pervading evil was staggering, and she held tightly to her focus, suddenly assailed by blackness and a fetid sense of malevolence that was almost overpowering.

Snatches of thoughts formed fragmented sentences. Desperation, jealousy, hatred—*All the waiting and worry . . . naught, all for naught if I do not kill him as well . . . I'll see the skin flayed from his bones and his heart taken still beating . . . plague take the king . . . even gone he always had the best . . . now it's my turn, my turn . . . vengeance will be sweet . . .*

Instead of answering her questions, his disjointed

thoughts only increased her confusion twofold. She reeled slightly when the man's attention shifted and she saw herself as he saw her, garbed in a ragged purple cloak and loose gown, hair floating about her shoulders in wild tangles.

Abruptly, his regard of her took on a more sinister view. A sweeping view of torn cloak and dirt-streaked skin, the thrust of her breasts against the unlaced gown that made her want to reach up and cover herself with her arms . . . He jerked his attention to one of the men at his side. "Tell me again where you found this unkempt creature, Bowen."

It was Bowen who supplied the man's name, both in thought and word as he inclined his head, speaking gravely in English, "We came across her deep in the wood nearby, Lord Gavin. She's a stranger to the area. As her cloak is purple and of fine wool, we assumed her to have come with your cousin. I thought it best to bring her to you for questioning." *My father would be ashamed . . . but what else can I do?*

That unexpected thought was quickly followed by a glancing perusal of her, and she saw herself through Bowen's troubled eyes—tousled hair, unlaced gown, and enveloping cloak. A spurt of pity for her was tempered by the despairing thought that he'd had little choice but to do everything possible to ingratiate himself to Gavin.

That was the trouble with this Gift. It had no definite guidelines, no guarantee that knowing someone's deepest thoughts would always help. Though perplexed by his exact meaning, she understood that Bowen wasn't a cruel man, just one caught in a precarious situation. Something to do with his father and Gavin.

"You did the right thing by bringing her here, Bowen." Lord Gavin again fixed her with a sharp stare. *A casual whore, most like . . . stolen cloak . . . not at all what I would have thought my cousin's style. . . .*

Sasha flushed at his silent assessment. Her chin lifted slightly. She should be accustomed to such appraisals; she'd heard similar thoughts as long as she could remember. The favored ideal of womanhood was of fair-haired,

ivory-skinned females, and she'd long been aware that her
dusky skin and dark hair were not in fashion. It had never
mattered before. Now, she wondered briefly if Rhys held
the same sentiment.

"So who are you?" Gavin leaned forward. "You're not
Welsh. What were you doing wandering about the forest
alone so early of a morn?"

She lowered her eyes, feigning timidity and fear. That
should appeal to a man who craved power. "I was lost,
my lord. And frightened. I've been wandering about alone
for so long I have no idea where my companions could be,
or even where I am." She managed a decent quiver—not
completely pretense—and lifted her gaze to stare up at him
through teary lashes. "I was . . . gathering plants . . . to
eat."

Gavin stroked one hand over the small dark beard on
his chin in a thoughtful gesture. His eyes narrowed
slightly. *Spreading your thighs most likely. . . .* "With your
garments all awry? I find that difficult to believe."

"I fled when I heard something in the wood. I thought
perhaps it was a wolf or bear . . ." Letting her voice trail
into shuddering silence, she did her best to appear terrified.
In truth, she wasn't that far from the emotion. If this man
suspected that she was close to Rhys in any way, she was
doomed. He'd use her in any manner he could to best his
cousin.

"Did you see anyone in the forest?" Gavin demanded.
"Armed men, perhaps, or even peasants?"

She shook her head. Her hair fell in front of her to
screen her face as she kept her eyes downcast. "I saw no
one, my lord. Not until your men came upon me."

"I think you are lying to me," he said in a soft, chilling
voice. *Curse her, I know the bitch must have seen him,
must know something . . . He's out there waiting, plot-
ting . . . I've done everything to get Glenlyon and I won't
stop now . . .*

She didn't reply, but kept her head down, shaking it
vigorously. If he thought her scared speechless—A brief,
vivid vision of a disrobed woman startled her, and her

head jerked up to stare at the Welsh lord. A crafty smile curled his thin lips upward, and his eyes slitted.

After a lengthy silence filled with chaotic thoughts and impressions, some believing, most distrustful, Gavin motioned for one of his men to take her away. He met her gaze with a thin smile. "We'll speak more later. I'll give you the opportunity to reflect and remember what you saw."

Sasha made no protest, not even when she was taken deep into the bowels of the keep where there was no light other than that of sputtering, hissing torches. Footsteps were loud and echoing in the narrow stone corridors. There was the dank odor of decay and death. The guard finally stopped at a narrow wooden door and slid a huge key into a metal lock. It turned with a loud, grating sound. The hinges creaked protests as the door was swung open. A fetid odor wafted out, striking her cruelly in the face. When she took an involuntary step backward, the guard caught her by the arm, his grip firm but not too harsh.

"*Mynd*," the man said shortly, and gave her a rough push that sent her stumbling into the dark cell.

She turned to gaze at him. His eyes met hers, and she held his gaze until he backed away. His thoughts were in Welsh and indecipherable to her, but she could sense his fear, the dread that filled him when she did not cower or shrink away.

"*Tylwyth teg,*" he mumbled, "*rydych chi'n tylwyth teg. . . .*"

Stumbling backward, he fumbled at the door, slamming it shut and turning the key with a metallic scrape that betrayed his panic. She watched quietly. She may not know the meaning of the Welsh words he'd used, but she was fully aware of a powerful wash of emotion, assaulting her repeatedly, as if it bounced off the dank stone walls.

It was dark. The only light came through bars over a small opening in the door. She listened to the guard fleeing down the corridor with heavy, booted steps. Then, slowly, she became aware of another presence. There was someone else in her cell. . . .

"*Bore da,*" came a pleasant voice in Welsh, and she

turned slightly toward the sound. *"Rydw i'n siarad Cym-raeg—"*

She interrupted in English, "I do not speak Welsh."

"Ah." There was a scuffling sound, then the shifting of shadows in a dark corner. A man stepped into the faint torchlight threading through the bars. "Grant pardon."

Relieved, she said, "You speak English."

"And French," he said in that language, and she felt rather than saw his smile in the shadows. "I've found knowing several languages to be a great help in these times."

As her eyes grew accustomed to the dim light, she saw that her companion was of medium height and older, with gray streaking the temples of his unkempt brown hair. Beneath a ragged beard he had a kindly face, and his clothes were of good quality, though soiled and torn in places. Because his inner thoughts were couched in Welsh, she had to draw on her intuition as to his character.

"Welsh is not a language familiar to me," she admitted, "and I'm beginning to feel my lack most sharply."

"Natural enough." He indicated the upper heights of the keep with a jerk of his head. "How goes it above the bowels of hell?"

She smiled faintly. "Not having any former experience to draw upon, I'd hazard a guess that things are as usual. Lord Gavin is an overbearing weasel, and most of his men are terrified."

"Ah. Yea, that is as usual. Unfortunately. He seems to have that effect on some men."

"More than some. I've seen more bravery in a barrel of trapped rats."

"An interesting comparison, and quite accurate, if my memory serves me," the man replied with an amused twist of his mouth.

"I hope not, or we may end our days here." She glanced about her. "Surely there are more comfortable places in Wales."

"I'd offer you a seat if there were one, so I'm left to prove myself a gentleman by more simple means." With a flourish of one hand, he brought up a thick crust of bread.

"I've been saving it for a special occasion, and I think your arrival is more than adequate. Shall we?"

Until that moment, she'd not realized she was hungry. Now, her missed morning meal made her stomach ache, and she nodded. "I'd be most honored to break bread with you, sir."

"Owain," he said. "And you are—?"

She hesitated. This was always the difficult moment, the giving of a name. "I am called Sasha."

"Sasha. 'Tis Russian, is it not?"

"Yea." She took the hunk of bread he held out and nibbled at the edge. Maybe it was the dark shadows, or her circumstances, or the tension that gripped her, but she found herself telling him the truth without knowing why she did so. "In my childhood, I traveled with a band of Russian wanderers. They called me Sasha. I've been called that since."

"But Sasha is a masculine name. You're definitely not a lad. Here. I also have a wedge of cheese, if one doesn't mind a bit of mold." As he scraped away the growth with his fingernail, Owain glanced up at her with a keen appraisal. "You're not Russian. Were you in disguise, perhaps?"

She smiled. "You're very astute, Master Owain."

"Yea, so I've been told. Come, child, and let us sit on a pile of straw and reminisce. I'd be fascinated to learn what folly you have committed to earn entrance to Gavin's dungeon—and if you are truly one of the faerie folk, as yon guard seemed to think."

CHAPTER TWELVE

✥

"It won't work."

Brian's gloomy announcement earned him an amused glance from Biagio. "It wouldn't work if you attempted it, clumsy Celt, but I can perform such a miracle."

Rhys was only half-listening. He looked up and frowned as the Italian youth brandished a flaming torch in a sizzling arc. "Be 'ware lest you set fire to the trees around us, whelp. It would certainly alert our enemies to our stupidity if not our ability to perform miracles."

Biagio doused the torch in a bucket of water. "I'm ready. I've passed ready. This delay may have already seen my mistress come to grief."

Rhys still had his private theories about that, but didn't intend to argue the point again. He shrugged. "It couldn't be helped. To attempt a stronghold like Glenlyon without proper preparation would be fatal as well as foolish. We'll have only one chance. We don't need to fail."

"Have the new men been given their orders?"

He smiled. "Yea. Such as they are. It all hinges on you,

brat. You'll have only until the vesper bells have rung seven days hence to accomplish your goal. Remember what I said—do nothing once you've found her. Leave the rest up to us."

"Don't be late," Biagio said, "for you'll doom us if you are."

Rising from where he straddled a fallen oak, Rhys tested his sword hand. The sword flashed. A severed tree limb fell with a faint thump to the ground, cut cleanly. "I'm not in the habit of failing, whelp. Be certain you don't."

Dark eyes glistened slightly as the youth gave a short jerk of his head. "If I do, they'll kill me before you can."

Because it was so true, Rhys didn't bother with a reply. They both knew the risks involved in their desperate plan. If it succeeded, it would be both a miracle and a blessing. And if it failed, few of them would survive to be hung on Glenlyon's walls.

Elspeth approached, surveying Biagio with a critical eye. "You look more the fool than a mummer," she observed harshly. "Where did you find that costume?"

"In the cart. I improvised a bit. Do you not like it?" Turning on the heel of his soft leather boot, Biagio preened, his hand skimming over the bright varicolored hose hugging his legs. A cap perched rakishly atop his dark head, the long tip folded over and jangling with bells sewn along its length. His jerkin was a blazing scarlet, belted with a brilliant yellow sash, boasting brass studs along the dagged hem. His cloak was bright blue.

Looking askance, Elspeth shook her head. "You're blinding. It looks as if you fell into a vat of dye. Can you not be less conspicuous?"

"Ah, but that's the secret." Biagio grasped her hands and forced her into a hopping dance with him until she managed to jerk free. Dodging Elspeth's blow, he skipped away, crowing, "Look at me, look at me, notice only me, my lords and ladies. . . . Watch my right hand—no, my left, and I will show you magical feats seen nowhere else in the world."

Elspeth crossed her arms over her chest and glared at him. "Beware you're not skewered for a peacock, young fool. Don't you recall what happened when Sasha wore that in Toulouse? You'd have been skinned by that fat butcher if not for—" her hands rose to cover her mouth; her fingers trembled, "if not for Sasha. Be wary of those who would harm you and my lady."

Sobering, Biagio crossed to her and murmured in her ear until the old woman slowly nodded. Then he smiled down at her and gave her a comforting pat before turning back. He looked at Rhys.

"I'm ready to play my part, milord."

Intrigued by the notion that Sasha had worn the tight-fitting hose and short jerkin, Rhys found himself smiling. "Then it's time to begin." He beckoned Sir Robert to him and gave orders to range the men along the bare crest overlooking Glenlyon. "Make a great show of it, so that those in the keep will be aware you're there. If we can keep their attention trained on what they think are our entire forces, mayhaps they won't notice the thin ranks and similar men."

"Mind," Biagio interrupted, "I must have a good start on you. And make the chase convincing, Welshman."

Rhys grinned. He hefted his sword with an agility that gave evidence of his healed hand. "It will be my greatest pleasure, whelp."

Biagio's glance was startled, and his grin slightly weak. "Not too convincing. I've no desire to sport holes in my skin."

"Then you'd best ride that nag as swiftly as you can, for I'll be close behind you." Rhys slid a glance toward the saddled bay mare. It was a small horse, but sturdy, with the wide chest and strong legs of the desert horses he'd seen Saracens ride. Much too small to hold heavily armed and mailed Englishmen, the animals yet seemed perfectly suited for the burning sands of Arabia and their lighter riders. Even while under attack, he'd admired them as they darted confidently about the desert.

Following Rhys's gaze, Biagio said, "My lady claims this mare can run like the wind. 'Tis certain her moods are as changing."

"It's a female prerogative. Go. I'll be behind you, and

Brian will be behind me." He met the youth's eyes steadily. "May God grant you success, whelp."

Grinning, Biagio nodded. He strode to the skittish horse, and took up the reins. Then he looked back at Rhys. "I'll meet you in Glenlyon's hall, Welshman."

After vaulting into the saddle, Biagio reined the horse around and spurred her down the hill. Rhys mounted more leisurely, donning his helmet and hefting his sword. Turk pranced impatiently at being tightly reined, and Rhys held him back until he could see Biagio barreling through the village streets. Villagers scattered from his path, jerking children from harm's way and flinging curses at him. Rhys smiled. Then he pressed his knees into the destrier's sides. Turk leaped forward and broke into a dead run.

Thundering down the steep slope, he concentrated on Biagio. Turk's powerful muscles worked in perfect rhythm, churning up the earth. The wind whistled around them, and he could hear the sound of horses in pursuit. Brian. And Sir Clyde. Turk would outdistance them, of course, but the small bay horse ahead was as swift as the wind. Sasha was right. He urged Turk faster, and the destrier's longer reach finally began to tell.

He gauged the distance and gained on Biagio as he urged his mount up the winding road to the keep. When he was close, he rose in his stirrups and swung his sword. It descended in a singing arc that sliced away a large portion of billowing blue cloak.

Biagio flung him an alarmed glance. Urging the mare faster, he leaned over the horse's neck, mane whipping at his face. Rhys's next swing lopped off a portion of the cap. It flew through the air with a mad jangling of bells. Almost imperceptibly, Rhys slowed Turk from the pursuit. Any closer, and the next strike would remove a generous portion of Biagio's scalp. The trained warhorse resisted Rhys's efforts to slow him, his nature demanding that he overtake the smaller horse and rider. It took all of his skill to hold his steed back without making it too noticeable to those men watching them from the castle gates. He could hear their laughter, and from experience, knew they were most likely making wagers on who would win the pursuit.

Ahead, Biagio lifted his voice in a demand for entrance as he crossed the lowered bridge, but the sentries had already begun to close the gates. For a moment, Rhys thought they would deny him. Then Biagio was under the falling iron teeth of the *porte coleïce* and inside before the gate slammed shut.

Rhys rode to the very edge of the drawbridge and stopped his mount in a sliding halt. Hurling curses and threats at the sentries, he demanded the surrender of the escaped felon. Hoots of laughter greeted his demands. Insults were flung down. When a shower of arrows rained out from the lancet window, he retreated.

He met Brian and Sir Clyde just out of arrow range. Brian stared past Rhys to the castle. "Do you think they'll believe him?"

"God only knows. I hope so." Rhys spurred Turk forward. Foam flecks spattered the ground beneath the lathered destrier. It had been a rousing race.

He glanced up as they rode back through the village at a more sedate pace. Sir Robert was forming a line of men atop the ridge above Glenlyon. The timing was perfect. During the past few days, war machines had been built. Now they were being dragged up into view. Sir Robert would parade men back and forth across the crest, up and down the slopes, mounted and unmounted, using the same men to make it seem as if their number were ten times as many. Rumors had been planted in the village that the old lord's son had returned with a great force to take back his keep; such gossip was certain to reach the castle. And to the observers within, it would appear as if Rhys's vast army was at last ready to lay siege to Glenlyon.

"Ride toward our men as if we are to join them until we reach the bottom of the hill, then follow me into the trees," Rhys said over his shoulder.

Once swallowed by the thick forest beyond the Wye, he slowed his mount to a walk. It was quiet here, and shadowed. Leaves muffled the sound of hoofbeats. When Brian coughed, the sound was intrusive and loud. They wound through the trees slowly. Birds rustled in the branches. Bridle bits and curb chains rattled, and one of the horses snorted at the sudden flush of a bird. When they reached a familiar clearing, Rhys reined in. The others halted, waiting.

It had taken him two days to find this clearing. But he'd known it was here, though hidden by time and the wild tangle of brush and trees. As a boy, he'd played here. Now he searched until he spied the branch he'd broken a few days before. The limb dangled downward like a spiny finger, pointing to a pile of stones. The ancient cairn had stood on Glenlyon land for longer than time. Yea, he'd been most relieved to find it still here after so long. It was the answer to everything.

He turned in his saddle and smiled grimly at Brian and Sir Clyde. "Now, 'tis our turn for treachery."

Narrow tunnel walls and a low stone ceiling seemed to close in around him. Rhys stooped, sword in one hand, his other hand holding a sputtering torch. Tiny sparks singed his hair and clothes with annoying frequency. Behind him were forty men, all that could be spared from those manning the war machines and being marched back and forth atop the ridge opposite Glenlyon. He had not been idle during the past week of chafing delay. It had taken that long to clear the accumulated rubble of years from the tunnel, working as quietly and surreptitiously as possible so as not to alert the keep to their activities. Biagio should have accomplished his goal by now.

"Milord . . ." Brian's rasping breath was swift and harsh in the dank air of the tunnel. "Are we there yet?"

Rhys glanced back at him over his shoulder. Sweat was beading on Brian's face and dripping from his chin. "Are you unwell?"

Brian's normally ruddy complexion had paled until the freckles stood out like painted spots on his cheeks. There were white lines bracketing his mouth. " 'Tis the closeness . . . I cannot abide close quarters," was the croaking reply. "There . . . is . . . no air."

"The torch still burns, so there's air aplenty, Brian. We'll reach the end soon." Rhys glanced down the length of the tunnel. "The distance from the cairn entrance to the wine cellar is great, but we've traveled most of it already. Can you go on?"

Brian nodded grimly. "Aye m'lord. 'Tis better . . . than being left."

By the time they reached the hidden door to the castle wine cellar, Brian was stumbling badly. Rhys ordered him to sit down and wait while he opened the door. It took several fumbling tries to find the latch that would release the cellar door. Finally his hand grazed the iron clasp tucked beneath a projecting stone, but the door was so heavy it took three men to heave it open. With a final shove, it gave in a grating creak of rusty hinges, and Rhys stepped out cautiously.

A quick glance around showed nothing but rows of heavy oaken wine casks and barrels. It was chill and dark in the cavern, much like the tunnel. At least this room had not been changed in his long absence. Perhaps Gavin didn't know of its existence. He went back for Brian and hefted his friend to his shoulder. "The cellar is not much improvement over the tunnel, Brian, but it's at least more spacious."

He leaned Brian against a huge wooden cask, and motioned for Sir Clyde to fetch wine. The strong spirits soon fortified the knight, infusing Brian's face with much-needed color.

Brian managed a weak grin. "This happened once before . . . a long time ago. I thought perchance it was only that once."

"You just like the attention."

The jest widened Brian's grin. "Nay, lord. 'Tis the wine I like."

After a moment, Rhys stood up. He glanced at the other men. "There are forty of us. Though it may sound like few, if Biagio has done his work, we will be able to take the keep easily."

"How will we know if he's succeeded?" Sir Clyde glanced around the dark, shadowed cellar uneasily. The only light was their torch, and it wouldn't last much longer.

Rhys heaved the door closed. On the inside, it was disguised by a rack of barrels and he leaned against it. "We'll know. He'll find a way to alert us."

"You put much faith in that Italian brigand," Brian said darkly. "I don't trust him."

"Nay, nor he you. If it was for any other cause but his lady's, I'm not certain I'd chance him. But he wouldn't betray her, so our causes meet."

Resting his head against the wine cask, Brian studied Rhys for a moment. "I thought retaking Glenlyon was of the most importance."

"And so it is." Rhys turned to meet his gaze. "Is there a question about that?"

"Nay, lord. Not from me."

"Good." He paused. He could feel the men watching him, knew they wondered if that was the truth. He didn't like feeling as if he should explain, but hated more that they may think him weak. He bunched a fist and pushed idly against a wine cask. "When I happen upon the wench again, I intend to discover the truth. If she betrayed us, I'll settle the score."

There was such steely softness in his tone and words, no man could mistake him. It grew so quiet, water could be heard trickling down the dank stone walls.

It was Brian who broke the sudden, heavy silence, turning his eyes away to mutter, "The wench should have turned Gavin and his men to stone by now. 'Tis the least she could do to help us."

"She's not Medusa."

Brian said nothing to that, and Rhys let his irritation fade. Might as well try to convince the stone walls as a hard-headed Irishman. But for all his superstition, Brian was a good friend. None better. He'd not let a woman come between them.

Time passed slowly while they waited. When a distant clang echoed through the vaulted stone cavern, Rhys jerked to attention. He silently motioned his men back into the deepest shadows as a wavering pool of light approached. One of Gavin's servants? Or Biagio?

"Signor?" The single hissed word echoed eerily from the

high curved walls and ceiling, sounding as if it came from several directions at once.

But it was in Italian. Rhys stepped out from behind a wine cask. "Here, whelp."

The pool of brightness halted, then swerved toward him. Flickering candlelight cast harsh shadows over the youth's face, giving him an even more sinister appearance than he normally bore. He grinned.

"Ah, so there you cower. How like a Welshman to be found hiding in a deep hole."

"Do we feint and thrust, or will you tell me if you've been successful?" Rhys snapped.

Biagio shrugged. "Successful, of course. Used as they are to crude entertainments, my wonderful performances have them all awed."

"No doubt." Rhys's dry tone conveyed his opinion of Biagio's talents but did not affect the youth, who swept him a low bow. "So tell me, how many are they?"

"Two hundred or more in the bailey," Biagio said promptly, straightening, "and likely a score or two in the hall. A great many, my lord."

Pondering, Rhys shook his head. "Do they suspect you?"

"Not at all, though there were questions aplenty at first." He grinned. "I told them I became separated from my companions, and that you captured me. Naturally, I was clever enough to escape you, though your army is so vast."

"Naturally." Rhys gave a derisive snort. "Are you certain you can manage to deaden them all?"

"Enough. Those not deep in slumber, will either be too groggy or too few to hinder fierce fighters such as you and your men," Biagio replied lightly. When Rhys scowled, he stepped close and said more softly, "I've put enough sleeping potion in the kitchen wine casks to send all of Wales into sweet slumber. When compline bells ring—strike hard and swift."

"But are you certain the potion will work?" Brian interrupted. "What if it's useless?"

"Nay, 'tis the best mixture my mistress knows. It will work." Biagio regarded Rhys with a wicked grin.

He didn't need reminders of the night the maid had put potion in the wine. Rhys stared at him coldly. "It had better. Your own life depends on the result."

Biagio whirled, a gay clash of colorful garments spinning with the sound of tinkling bells. He bent low, then swept out one arm, producing a cluster of flowers in his hand. When Brian made a strangled sound, he glanced up, a wide grin creasing his face as he gave a flourish and the flowers vanished. As he straightened to meet Rhys's gaze, his grin vanished as swiftly as the flowers.

"It will work, my lord. On my lady's life, it will work."

"Where is she?"

"In the east dungeon."

It was not the answer he'd expected, and he saw that Biagio knew it. Why would Gavin imprison his own spy? Rhys scowled. "There was no east dungeon when I was a lad and Glenlyon was my father's. Where is it?"

"Ah . . . below the storerooms, but toward the river more. Do you think you can find it?"

Rhys nodded grimly. "Aye, after I've taken care of Gavin, I'll find it."

"I'll warn her you're coming, so she can be ready," Biagio said, and Rhys grabbed his arm when he turned to go.

"No. If you're seen, Gavin may guess our intent. Sir Robert can only fool them with his ghostly parade for so long before a spy informs Gavin of the truth. If she's truly a prisoner, don't risk her, whelp."

"My lord, can it be that you care?" Biagio mocked, but when Rhys took a threatening step forward, he shook his head. "I can warn her without going near, my lord. She'll be waiting."

"Plague take you, brat, if you ruin this . . ."

Dancing just out of his reach, Biagio said coolly, "Don't be so nervous, Welshman. I'm doing my part. You just do the killing."

With that, he was gone, turning to disappear behind a stone wall. Rhys stared after him, scowling.

"They're all bewitched," Brian muttered and Rhys swore so harshly, no man dared speak for some time.

An oppressive tension settled over them, so that when the compline bells began to toll, their nerves were stretched taut and ready. Rhys rose, and the men filed silently behind him up the wide, shadowed stairs. Only sparse lamps of fish oil and reed pith were set at odd intervals in the stairwell, tucked into stone niches carved for that purpose, shedding pale light that was barely enough to save missteps. Biagio's doing, no doubt. Rhys smiled grimly. Not even a lord who had stolen the keep would squander his goods so carelessly.

Opening the cellar door with the abrasive creak of unoiled hinges, he paused a moment before stepping out. Beyond a faint rustling no sound could be heard. He felt Brian nudging at his back, his breath harsh and rasping with strain. They all felt it, the daring of what they attempted, the dire risks they were undertaking.

Rhys swung the door wide and stepped out, glancing around him. No one waited in the small alcove, in the kitchens beyond. Motioning the others with him, he moved silently along the walls and out into the courtyard, keeping to the darkest shadows and avoiding torchlight. He jerked to a halt when he spied a huddled form just ahead. Drawing nearer, he saw that it was a snoring servant slumped against the wall. He grinned. Here was proof of his long-held suspicion that most servants stole from the wine casks. At least none would be awake to sound the alarm.

Fickle moonlight filtered through the clouds above them as they moved through the bailey toward the massive stone structure housing the great hall and its private chambers. As silent as fog on the moors, they passed men slouched against walls or crumpled into snoring forms on paving stones. Evidence of preparations to withstand a siege cluttered the bailey. Vats to hold boiling water and hot pitch were scattered on the ground in the shadows of the walls; pikes to push away ladders leaned against the stones.

As arranged, they separated. Sir Clyde took twenty men toward the gates to open them for Sir Robert and the rest

of the men. Rhys, Brian, and the others made their way to
the entrance of the large building housing the great hall.
Once inside, they found sleeping men blocking doorways,
some on stools while others lay flat on the stone floor. It
was eerie, the silence that pervaded the keep, when any
fortress was customarily filled with noise and talk, as so
many inhabited it. Not even a child's cry broke this still-
ness. Yea, this was unearthly and unnatural indeed.

A sudden noise clattered around a bend in the corridor.
Rhys put up a hand to halt. It grew silent again, but there
was a difference. This silence was thick with tension, an
almost palpable wave of tautness that emanated from the
darkness.

Tightly gripping his sword and shield, Rhys stepped
around the stone wall and was met with a mighty blow.
If he'd not been prepared, it would have felled him. Yet
he was able to parry it, leaping back so that it fell short
of the mark and only grazed the surface of the shield he
quickly threw up. The clang of striking metal reverberated
from the walls. Turning, he swept his sword in a level arc.
It caught his assailant before he could parry it with his
own weapon, and the man went down with a cry of pain
that ended in a gasping rattle as he died.

Rhys stepped over him and moved swiftly along the corridor wall. The few men they met were easily overcome,
and Rhys was soon at the entrance to the great hall. The
doors hung open. A fire blazed brightly, and there was an
occasional yelp or bark from a hound, but none of the
usual clatter. Rhys exchanged glances with Brian, then
stepped through the open doors.

He was startled to see the tables filled with snoring
knights, men-at-arms, and women. Overturned flagons
and cups bore silent testimony to the potency of the
drugged wine, some of it dripping from tables to the
rushes. A branch of candles had been overturned and set
fire to the straw, and Brian moved to stomp out the small
blaze.

Rhys removed his helmet and tucked it under one arm.
He ranged among the tables and benches, barely glancing
at the slumbering diners as his attention moved ahead to

the table on the dais. It, too, bore sleeping revelers. His lips drew back in a tight smile when he recognized his cousin slumped in a high-backed chair. At his side was a fair-haired woman who looked to be no more than ten and five years of age, still awake, sitting stiffly in her chair and staring at him with horrified eyes.

He ignored her to stare at Gavin, sprawled in his chair. He'd have preferred him awake, awake and aware of his mortal danger. But not even a swift kick roused his cousin; Gavin only slid deeper into the chair. Frustrated, Rhys gestured to him with his sword point and looked hard at the girl. "He is my prisoner, as are all who swore to him. Yield, demoiselle, or it will go hard with you."

Wide-eyed, she swallowed and nodded. "Yea, seignior. I yield."

Rhys turned and beckoned Brian to him. "Are Sir Robert and the rest of our men through the gates?"

"Yea, lord. The gates are open and our men inside. Little or no resistance." He grinned. " 'Twas as easy as taking milk from a cow."

He nodded in satisfaction. It had been almost too easy. He should have trusted the Italian puppy more. He turned to catch Brian before he left the hall again. "Have you seen Biagio?"

"Nay, lord, but Sir Vychan said he saw him going toward the storerooms as we were entering the hall."

Startled and inexplicably alarmed, Rhys swung around and stepped from the dais. "Toward the storerooms?"

"Yea, lord—is something wrong?"

"Secure the prisoners. Put Gavin in chains." Anxious fury speared him as he strode toward the hall doors. If Biagio had managed to alert the soldiers that were certain to be guarding the dungeons below the storerooms, he would slit his throat from ear to ear for endangering Sasha.

It had been two weeks in this dingy cell, two weeks with little food, no privacy, and too much time to think. Sasha stirred restlessly, tilting her head back against the cold damp stone wall. If not for her companion, it would have been much worse. Owain had proved to be a pleasant, informative fellow prisoner, and she was grateful for his presence.

Grateful despite the fact that somehow he knew of her Gift and had tried questioning her both bluntly and delicately about it until she flatly denied knowing what he was talking about. Then he'd subsided, but mental messages appeared every now and then that she found difficult to pretend she didn't hear.

Now he was sleeping, his breath a steady, gentle rasp in the dense gloom. She lifted a hand to peer at her fingers. Sometimes the light was a bit brighter as it threaded through the bars, providing enough illumination to actually see how filthy she'd become. But it was welcome, even for that. She hated being in the dark. Hated the furtive, rustling sounds in the filthy straw covering the floor, hated the not so furtive and more terrifying sounds coming from other cells when guards would arrive to drag away a prisoner to some unknown fate. At those times, she flung up her barriers quickly, for the fear and desperation she sensed from the doomed prisoner were too horrifying to endure.

It seemed that she was one of the forgotten. Food was scarce, smuggled to them by a friendly guard. Owain always gallantly and insistently shared the meager chunks of bread and molded cheese. This was not the first time she'd found herself in a prison—there had been that harrowing time in Tunisia that Biagio still reminded her of on occasion—but at least that had been quick and she'd been able to talk their way out of it before it became too desperate. Unlike this.

Did anyone intend to get her out of here? She'd thought at first that someone would—Elspeth and Biagio, certainly, and . . . and Rhys. She didn't know why, but she'd confidently assumed that he would come after her, even if 'twas only to harshly berate her for monumental stupidity.

But nothing. Not a word. No sign that he even cared if she was condemned to the pits of hell. She sighed. Owain had known Rhys since he was only a small boy, and seemed to think that if the man was anything like his father, he would stubbornly come to retrieve his possessions. The little news the guard whispered to them was not at all comforting. Glenlyon was under siege. As yet, there was no sign of crumbling, for the fortress was strong and self-contained. It could hold out for years.

Years. She was doomed. Already, itchy things infested her clothes and tormented her, and she'd almost grown accustomed to continual scratching. She would give up one of her father's palaces to be clean again. If she had the choice. If Rhys would only say he'd take them back, if he would only come for her . . . he was so strong, capable, handsome, even if irritating beyond measure—she missed him.

That brought her upright against the straw. Could it be? She missed him. Missed his blinding smile, the way his gray eyes crinkled slightly at the corners when he gave her that infuriatingly mocking grin, missed the way sunlight gleamed in the wheat blond of his hair. She hated this. It couldn't be. No man had ever mattered to her. Not this way.

Burying her face in her palms, she groaned.

"Are you all right?" Owain's voice jerked her head up, and she saw in the dim light that he was looking at her. She nodded.

"Just thinking about . . . fleas. They itch terribly."

Owain nodded wisely, an amused smile pressing at the corners of his mouth. "Fleas. Pesky creatures. A blight on humanity."

"Definitely. I've been thinking about blights on humanity." She scratched idly at a bite on her arm. "Do you think he'll come?"

Owain laughed softly, and when she frowned at him, said, "If you mean Lord Rhys, most definitely. If he's anything like the man his father was, he'll come. This keep may tumble down around our ears, but he won't yield it up to the likes of Gavin."

"I still don't see how Gavin managed to get the keep if Rhys's father was such a good warrior."

"You can guard against assault more easily than treachery. Lord Griffyn made the mistake of trusting his nephew to keep his word. A fatal mistake, as it turned out." Owain took in a deep, shuddering breath. "Like a weasel skulking in the night, he rose up from the bed Griffyn graciously lent him, and slew father and sons, taking by trick and treason that which he could not get by force and courage. A weasel."

She frowned. "He does resemble a weasel. I thought so myself when I saw him. I wonder why he's not sent for me again? He's certain that I know something."

Owain shrugged. "It's easier to let time take care of the problem of certain prisoners."

"I suppose that's why you're here. To let time rid him of you."

"Exactly. It wouldn't do to actually execute a man in King Richard's high regard, but if that man were to accidentally die while in custody, it would be a tragedy more easily explained." He snorted. "Gavin favors the prince with his devious ways."

"Prince John? You keep talking about him as if he and Gavin are in league together."

"They are. I'm convinced of it. If they weren't, there would be no explanation for John's troops to be at Glenlyon. And I know they're here, because the guard has told me. It's only logical that John and Gavin have concocted some scheme, for John hates his brother Richard, and would like nothing better than to be king himself."

She shuddered. "If John becomes king, what will Rhys do?"

Owain shifted position, and there was another vague rustling in the straw as some elusive creature scuttled away. "Whatever he has to do, I imagine. He's familiar with English ways, so he would know how to deal with John, just as he's always dealt with Richard, and before him, King Henry."

"It still doesn't make sense, sending an eight-year-old boy to live in a foreign land away from his home and family. I don't know what Rhys's father thought it would prove."

A sudden, soft silence fell around them. Then Owain

said heavily, "Lord Griffyn didn't have much of a choice. If he did not yield up his youngest son as hostage, the chances of the entire clan perishing were great. Henry was strong, and our forces at the time were depleted from sickness and famine. So he gave in to Henry's demand, and sent Rhys away. It was not the best of situations."

"And now Rhys has come home."

Shakily, Owain said, "Yea, now after twenty-one years of silence and contempt, he has come home."

"Contempt?"

"Aye. Lord Rhys did not kindly accept the situation. He was so young, and he did not fully understand. We wrote, Lord Griffyn and I, but he never answered our letters. Never forgave us for giving him to the enemy. We heard that he became one of them, that now he's more English than he is Welsh."

After a moment, she said, "I don't think so. I can't read him well, for he defies my efforts, but I think that Rhys is fiercely glad to be home. Perhaps he should have come home long ago."

"Perhaps."

In the gathering silence, she could feel Owain's gaze on her, and knew from the direction of his thoughts that he was studying her curiously. Most of the time, his thoughts were in Welsh. Now he deliberately wondered in English about her Gift, wondered if she truly were one of the Tylwyth Teg, or faerie folk. She had no intention of setting his mind at ease on that score. Let him think what he liked. Further denial would only draw them into a discussion that she did not want.

Sasha. . . .

Her name drifted to her in a familiar, silent cadence and she sat up, straining to hear.

"What is it?" Owain asked softly from his corner of the cell. "What do you hear?"

"I—I'm not certain." Muffled groans from the dungeon's other occupants were accompanied by the faint clank of chains. She glanced at Owain. His eyes glistened faintly in the gloom. "Perhaps it was just my imagination."

Bella . . . are you here . . . ? Do you hear me . . . ? Which door?

Not her imagination. "Biagio—it's Biagio. I can hear him . . . calling me. God above, how do I let him know where I am?" She leaped to her feet and looked wildly for something to shove through the barred grating or bang against the door.

Owain was thoughtful. "Biagio is Italian, so call to him in that language. Few here would understand, and those that do will only think you are in despair. 'Tis worth a try."

Turning back to the door, she waited until she heard his mental summons again, then called, "Diritto! Aiuto! Sette porta!" over and over until she was hoarse. As her voice faded, she strained to hear his reply. There was only silence, stretching out longer and longer, until she began to think he hadn't heard her.

Then, louder this time, and closer: *I heard you. Seven doors . . . It won't be long, bella, so—Dio, get away from me, you drunken fool! Oh, not you, bella. 'Tis this idiot who has drank too much—or not enough . . . Be patient, and when—get away, you babbling sot! Be ready, bella. . . .*

He faded into silence again. But she'd heard him. They were here. A satisfied smile curved her mouth when she turned to Owain. "Didn't you hear? He answered me. We're saved."

Surging to his feet, the older man joined her at the door. "My hearing isn't as sharp as yours, it seems. Ah, if only I had my sword. I feel helpless without it." His voice grew hard. "I'd like nothing more than to have Gavin at the end of my blade."

"I doubt Lord Rhys would relinquish that pleasure."

Several minutes passed. A rattle came from the far end of the corridor. The torch outside their cell flickered. A metal gate slammed, ringing loudly in the damp gloom. Shouts were heard, and the clang of steel against steel.

"They come." Owain flexed his arms and took a deep breath. "I pray that if I am to die, 'tis with a sword in my hand."

"Pray for success instead," she said tartly. "Don't waste prayers. We may need them later if we're to get out of here."

Whatever Owain might have replied was lost in the sudden tumult that burst through the far door and raged down the corridor—men's curses, the clash of swords, grunts of pain and bodies slamming against stone, all creating a chaotic din. Sasha stepped away from the door, not knowing if they were saved . . . or lost.

The incredible confusion was too much to absorb; she threw up her barriers before the onslaught of unspoken words and desperation could crush her. Not even daring to open her mind to search for Biagio, she kept them all at bay with so great an effort that it made her weak. She swayed, leaning against the wall to keep her balance, fighting the overpowering turbulence that threatened to consume her.

Through a haze of blurred images, she watched as the cell door swung open. Owain surged forward; a knot of tangled men flowed into the cell like a gigantic, misshapen creature. Clinging to the wall, her fingers dug into stone to gain purchase, desperately trying to keep herself upright.

As the struggle swarmed toward her, a seething mass of arms and legs and metallic glitters, she picked out a recognizable figure—Rhys. Towering over the others, his tawny mane was a bright banner among darker heads. He fought with savage fury and he wore no helmet, the fool—a chilling dread skipped down her spine, catapulting her from the wall as a man slashed at Rhys's unprotected head.

With all her strength, she seized the man by the back of his tunic, tugging at him to keep him from reentering the fray. He barely noticed. Shrugging free, he stepped toward Rhys and swung, his sword lifted high. She leaped up and grabbed his wrist. Her momentum carried them both several steps before the man shook loose and knocked her away with a powerful swing of one arm. She sprawled in the dirt and straw of the cell, looking up to see him standing over her.

He might have finished it, but a thrust from behind caught him unaware. He stumbled with a surprised grunt, then pitched forward in a lifeless heap, draped half over her. She made no sound but pushed his still body away as quickly as she could. Death everywhere, blood streaming, men screaming, the deafening clang of weapons . . . and fear, tearing at her with sharp talons, lending her sudden strength. She leaped to her feet and struck out at the nearest man. Panic drowned out common sense. She used her bare fist as a frail weapon against leather, hard muscle, and steel. Then a hand descended, catching her by the upper arm and hauling her roughly from her feet, dragging her through the straw.

She struggled, pushing and kicking, but could not free herself. She slid along on one knee, scrambling for purchase, but found the floor too slick with blood-drenched straw to do more than keep her face from being dragged over the stones. Her fingers curled around the edge of the doorframe and clung desperately. A harsh yank dislodged her. There was a whirl of color, harsh words, rasping breaths, and her hair in her eyes, and she was in the corridor being hauled up by a strong hand on the back of her tunic. The material pulled tight around her neck, cutting off her air. She tore at it with her free hand.

"Be still," came the grating command. Her head snapped up at the familiar voice.

"Rhys," she croaked, "Rhys." She almost wept with relief, but he gave her a slight shake that rattled her frame.

"You cost me dear with your folly," he snarled, "now be still so you don't hang yourself in your own clothes."

It was not the most gracious reunion. Her eyes widened with hurt and shock. As he disentangled her from the cords of her gown, she jerked free and regained her balance. With a toss of her head to clear the hair from her face, she looked up at him. There was no welcome in his eyes, no look of love that had compelled him to come to her rescue. Only a cold glitter lit the steel-gray orbs, and his lashes were lowered to reveal only frowning slits. Pride came to her rescue, overpowering her first flush of elation. Her chin lifted with a jerk. "Oh my. You're still mad about that little disagreement in the forest, aren't you? I see that you're walking well enough now, however."

Without replying, he reached for her, grasping handfuls of her gown to pull her with him.

It was too much. After all she'd gone through, she had no intention of letting him drag her along behind him like a whipped puppy. Her temper snapped. One hand curled into a fist and she surged to her toes. Drawing back her arm, she struck her fist hard against the side of his head.

He grunted, then gave his head a slight shake. His eyes narrowed, and he bent to catch her behind the knees, and heaved her up and over his shoulder. She slammed against him with jarring force, knocking the wind from her lungs. His shield was slung across his back by a leather strap, and she grabbed at it for stability. The corridor swung by in a dizzying blur of torchlit stone. When she levered herself up to look behind, she saw that the fighting had ended.

Men wearing Rhys's colors were victorious and breathless, herding captives into one cell, dragging bodies to another. Owain stood amidst them, a sword finally in his hand, a bemused expression on his face as he watched her being borne away over Rhys's shoulder.

"Owain—don't just stand there," she managed to gasp out, "make him stop."

'Tis not right for me to interfere came the mental reply, *but you will be safer with him than with any other man.* . . .

Glaring at the older man, she had the sinking feeling that she had misjudged not only Owain, but Rhys. What did he mean to do with her?

The answer came swiftly.

CHAPTER THIRTEEN

❧

Fury born of fear had seized Rhys when he saw Sasha clinging like an enraged cat to the soldier's arm. For a brief, heart-stopping moment, he'd thought he would not reach her in time, would not be able to halt the downward swing of the man's sword. Time had crystallized into one frozen moment as he forced himself through the knot of fighting men, feeling as if he were running against the ocean's tide, desperate to keep her safe.

But when he succeeded in reaching her, did she wisely seize the moment to ensure her own safety? No, she sprang into attack. It was too much. Now that the brief, vicious battle was won, he was removing her from danger. And for what reward? A blow to his face hard enough to rattle his teeth. She was damned fortunate that he did not retaliate in kind.

He ignored her sputtering anger and strident demands. When she got too loud and unruly and her thrashing feet threatened to unman him again, he slapped a warning hand against her backside to remind her that she was hardly in a position to be giving orders and making demands.

That shocked her into sudden silence and blessed immobility.

He carried her past the entrance to the great hall, where his men had routed the remaining pockets of resistance. Most of the older guards still awake had thrown down their weapons upon recognizing Rhys's coat of arms; only Gavin and John's men had continued to fight hard, knowing there would be little mercy for them.

As he passed through the hallway to the curving staircase, a voice called out peremptorily: "Lord Rhys! Where do you take my lady?"

Rhys halted and swung around. When he saw Biagio, he lowered Sasha to her feet, keeping her at his side with his left arm. His other hand still held his sword, poised and ready. Sasha tried to steady herself, flinging a hand out to snatch at his arm, but he caught her fingers in his fist, gripping them tightly to keep her still.

Biagio's garments were rent and bloodied, a dagger jutting from one hand and a scowl marring his face. When he reached them he paused. His gaze slid over Sasha and then moved to Rhys, darkening.

Before he could speak, Rhys said harshly, "You disobeyed my command by going to the dungeon."

"Yea, I did. Yet if not for me, there would have been even more guards wide awake and in a fighting mood." His brow arched. "Who do you think was kind enough to bring the thirsty men flagons of wine?"

"That's not the point. You disobeyed an order and endangered her."

"Nay, lord, that is the point—I did not endanger my lady, but found where she'd been placed."

"It's true." Sasha tugged at her trapped hand, snorting in frustration when he didn't yield. "I was in no greater danger for his warning. And he did find out where I was, so that you—"

"Enough. You were safe in the dungeon, though perhaps not comfortable. Safe until this whelp routed the guards to action, that is."

"Not true," Biagio snarled. "I fed them enough wine to

dull their senses, so that your puny men could take them easily."

He smiled faintly. "Listen to the wolf cub howl boasts, yet I did not see you among the fighting men."

"Then you did not look." Biagio held up his bloodied dagger. "I was there."

"Please," Sasha interrupted, "you sound like crowing cocks instead of men. It would be best if—"

When Rhys tightened his grip, she quieted. He looked down at her. She was staring hard at Biagio.

After a moment, the young Italian shook his head. "Where do you take her now?"

"To my chamber." His reply made Biagio stiffen, and Sasha tried to jerk away. He held her more tightly, and when Biagio took a step forward, he lifted up his sword. "Hold. She's not your responsibility. She is mine."

Biagio's dark eyes glittered. "Why do you think matters have changed so? Did I not tell you that my loyalty was yours until it differed from my lady's best interests?"

"So you did." He smiled. His hand shifted to the nape of Sasha's neck, fingers holding her in an iron caress. "What would make you think I mean her harm? Has she done something so dreadful? Something that would anger me if I discovered it now? Did I hack my way through Gavin's men to find her, only to do her harm?"

"*I* found her." Biagio took another step, his eyes narrowed in frustration. His gaze flicked to the sword poised so menacingly in front of him. "In spite of your orders to the contrary, 'twas my efforts that discovered which cell held her. I provided the distraction necessary for you and your men to creep like thieves into Glenlyon. And I did not do it for you to harm her now." His gaze slid to Sasha and lingered. Their eyes met, and after a moment she gave a violent shake of her head.

"Nay," she said, "do nothing, Biagio. He won't harm me."

"I've no great assurance of that." He looked narrowly at Rhys, then back at her. "He looks none too cordial at the moment."

She smiled. "Neither do you." When she turned, Rhys

let go of her neck. His hand rested at his side, still close enough to grab her quickly should there be the need. Her gaze shot from him to Biagio. "Both of you reek with blood and sweat. You smell like you've been slaughtering hogs."

"Is that an example of your gratitude for risking my life to save you from a lingering death?" Rhys mocked. "You've an odd notion of appreciation, flower."

"I'd be much more appreciative if you'd both stop quarreling over me like dogs over a bone," she said sharply. "And if you think—"

"Enough, flower." He lifted his hand in a warning, and she subsided, though not without a brief, furious glare. He smiled slightly. Some of his tension eased at her swift submission. Then he turned to eye Biagio. The whelp's glowering stare meant trouble, and there had been enough of that for the day.

"It's late, and I'm too weary and short of temper to endure your yowlings any longer, cub. There's still a lot to do yet. Since you seem to have so much enthusiasm left tonight, go to Sir Robert and help him find shelter and food for our men. We'll speak more on the morrow."

Though the youth's eyes narrowed, he gave a short jerk of his head. "Yea, I'll go—though not to run this fool's errand you think will distract me, but because my lady wishes it."

Without another word, he spun on his heel and stalked away.

"You didn't have to shame him," Sasha muttered, and he shook his head.

"It was the kindest way, flower, believe me." He escorted her up the close, winding staircase and down a corridor, passing men sprawled on the stones. Torches sputtered in holders, casting flickering light over the bodies. She shuddered. "Some of these men look as if they're sleeping rather than dead."

"They are." He felt her start of surprise.

"What do you mean?"

"I mean that young Biagio is apparently a most apt pupil of yours." He gave her a meaningful look, but she only stared up at him with wide, innocent eyes that didn't fool him for a moment. He smiled wryly. "Sleeping potion, flower. Enough in the wine casks to render the entire garrison senseless. The only men awake enough to fight were those who either didn't drink, or didn't drink enough."

She nodded approval. "Very clever of him. I wonder how he managed it."

"Biagio seems to have many talents." He paused in the dimly lit hallway to swing open a door and peer inside the chamber. Two elderly matrons cowered in a corner, whimpering when they saw him. He pulled the door shut. "Too small anyway." He pulled her along the hallway, and tried several more rooms. At last, one suitable for the lord of the castle. He pushed the door wide.

The main room beyond the antechamber was spacious, with a massive bed against one wall and a deep brazier filled with burning coals in the middle. Woven wall hangings shifted slightly in a draft, and candles burned in branched holders around the room, some on tall stands, others set on tables scattered about. It looked as if the chamber had been hurriedly vacated, with stools turned over and bed hangings awry.

"This looks promising. No, don't hang back, flower. I'm in no mood to chase you." Pulling her inside, he slammed the door shut behind them and lowered the huge bar. It fell into the bracket with a solid crack of wood against wood, and he saw her wince.

Sheathing his sword at last, he shrugged his shield from his back and leaned it against the wall. Then he crossed his arms over his chest and gazed at Sasha. Her hair was hanging about her head and shoulders in wild, dark tangles. The cloak was gone, ripped away, no doubt, in the tumult. Her gown was torn and loose, and she wore only one shoe. But despite the dirt streaking her face and a few scratches on her bare arms, she looked whole and unharmed—and beautiful enough to make him ache. It wasn't the most gratifying emotion, to realize that she had this alarming effect on him. Until seeing her almost slain in the dungeon, he hadn't known that he even cared enough to save her from impending doom. It was a new—and disturbing—realization. Especially in light of the almost certain discovery that she had betrayed him.

He should be elated—triumphant. Instead, he was courting black doubts and suspicions, diluting his feeling of victory at the retaking of Glenlyon.

"Do you care to explain your actions?" he asked finally, when it seemed as if she had no intention of offering any comments. "You're quite silent for a woman who had so much to say earlier."

"You're weary. I'll wait."

A faint smile pressed against the corner of his mouth. "Ah no, you won't escape quite so easily this time. I want an explanation for your betrayal."

Tossing back the hair from her eyes, she tilted up her chin in a gesture he'd come to recognize as defiant pride. "And if I choose not to give you one?"

"I would not recommend that course of action. I'm not in the temper to suffer it gladly."

Silence spun and stretched between them, growing taut. Her lips pressed tightly together, and there was a mutinous gleam in her eyes that boded ill. "If you refer to my escape in the weald, I simply did not wish to bed you."

"I'd like to go back even further. Let's begin with the first time. Or have you forgotten such an ancient event?" He pushed away from the door, walking past her, aware of her strained composure. A flagon of wine sat on a table, and he lifted it, raising his eyes to hers. "Surely you recall that night."

"Yea." It was a faint whisper, hoarse and rasping, and he smiled.

"Odd, but I recall little, and I'm not a man who drowns himself too often in a surplus of wine. Yet I did that night. Too much wine, too much food—but apparently little else." He poured wine into a cup and lifted it to his lips, sniffing at it. When he looked up at her over the rim of the cup, she flushed. "It smells remarkably similar to the wine I drank that night, flower. This wine has been diluted with a sleeping potion. And so was my wine the night I spent with you."

She lowered her gaze and clasped her hands in front of

her. Her mouth was set in a straight line, but her voice was loud and clear. "Yea, so it was."

"Why?" He kept his temper with an effort. Up came her chin again, and her eyes were cautious. Curse her for a clever little liar. She'd drugged him insensible to keep him from Glenlyon, and he intended to know why she'd cast her lot with Gavin. His hand tightened around the wine cup. "You didn't have to bed me at all. There are other ways to delay a man. You've already admitted you were sent to delay me. It must have been Gavin who sent you, for here you are. What did he promise you to deceive me?"

"Nothing. I had my own reasons."

"Apparently. I want to hear them."

She waved a hand impatiently. "One doesn't always get what they want."

He stared at her. "I do."

She flung him a wary glance. "Very well, since you insist. I'm not supposed to mention the prophecy again, so I'll just say that you don't interest me. I was playing a game, and you took it seriously. You wouldn't take no for an answer. I had no other choice but to pretend an interest I don't feel, and drug you."

His anger battled with disbelief and won.

Slowly setting down the wine cup, he unbuckled the baldric that held his sword and scabbard, then removed it and leaned the weapon against the table. He walked toward her with slow, measured steps, watching her closely. The straight slash of her dark brows drew together in a frown over her eyes. She took a step back. He smiled, his mouth stretched thin in a grim parody of humor as he stalked her, advancing faster with her every retreat until she was against the far wall. Behind her, the tapestry fluttered with her nervous agitated movements.

Turning her face away from him, she closed her eyes.

"What," he mocked softly. "Do you fear me?"

"Yea." The single word was a faint whisper from lips that were pale and bloodless. "But not for the reason you might think."

His hands moved to cup her shoulders, feeling bare skin beneath one palm where the gown had slipped low. Raking his thumb leisurely over the smooth slope of her shoulder, he felt her quiver beneath the caress.

"Why," he murmured, bending his head to graze her skin with his mouth, "do you fear me?"

She didn't answer but stood stiff and silent. Her lashes lowered and cast long shadows on her cheeks; her lips pressed tightly together. Challenged, Rhys slid his hands down the length of her arms to catch her wrists and bring her hands up between their bodies. He held them there, lightly, but firmly enough to let her know he would not release her. Slowly, he pulled her toward the huge bed, his boots scraping loudly on the bare stones.

When he turned her back to the bed, he gave her a gentle push to lay her down. Kneeling with one knee on the bed, he bent over her, still holding her wrists, watching her closely. Only the flutter of her lashes betrayed her, and a tiny quiver of her lower lip relayed the answer that he sought—it was all a lie.

He should have known. She'd teased and flattered, flirted and flaunted herself, and he'd thought she wanted him. But she wanted only to deceive him. It would be interesting to learn what reward she earned for going to such lengths to betray him. Gavin would promise her anything, he was certain. Yet the men he'd seen tonight had worn colors belonging to John.

Was she sent by Prince John? The whole affair smacked of the masquerade the prince enjoyed, sending a damsel to lure knights to him for whatever purpose he might have. It was certain John had his eyes on Glenlyon. Yea, he must have lent aid to Gavin to take the keep. Not quite daring to murder one of Richard's favorite knights, it would be so like John to send a pretty maid to try and avert Rhys from his purpose. A marvelous plot. Devious and complex, just like John.

But this time, the prince had misjudged his man. Rhys intended to win. And he would back Richard, as he always had.

"Come," he said softly, " 'tis time to tell me."

A wild banging rattled the chamber door in its sturdy frame. Rhys looked over his shoulder with a scowl. Brian, of course. It had to be. No other man had such horrible timing.

Then a woman's voice raised in distress, her cry wild and keening, grating on his nerves. Cursing, he jerked himself up from the bed and stalked to the door. He yanked up the bar and slammed it back. A slender maid with fair hair and a vaguely familiar face catapulted into him, sobbing uncontrollably.

Catching her in a reflexive action, he stared down at the top of her head in surprise. She clung to him, wetting the front of his mail with her tears, babbling incoherently in Welsh. Curse it all, but what Welsh he recalled was spoken slowly, not rattled off like a chattering squirrel.

"Silence," he thundered, losing patience. He set her firmly back and away from him. "I can't understand you, and even if I could, it doesn't matter tonight. Go to your pallet. Air your grievances with my steward on the morrow."

Snatching loose, she glared up at him through wet, matted hair in her eyes. " 'Tis not a matter for your steward," she spat, then scowled at Sasha across the chamber. Tossing back her hair, she set her chin firmly. "Send your whore away. This is a family matter that must be resolved."

She'd spoken in slow, clear Welsh that even he could understand, and he shook his head. "She's not my whore and you're not my family. Now—"

"Ah, but you are wrong," the girl said softly. "You may not know me, but I know you. I'd know you anywhere. You're just like them. Tall, blond, and arrogant. You're just like our brothers, save that you are alive and they are not."

He blinked. "My brothers?"

"Nay, *our* brothers." She took a step away, then said, "I am your half-sister, Rhys ap Griffyn, born after you were in England. My mother was no more than is yon wench on your bed, but our father brought me into his house and I am his heir just as you are . . . and I am wed to Gavin of Glamorgan."

Still sitting on the edge of the bed, Sasha stared at the

girl. Beneath her outer defiance whirled a barrage of pain and uncertainty . . . though she hadn't understood their Welsh, she did understand the seething emotions churning inside the maid. Her eyes flew to Rhys's face.

Disbelief and shock were mirrored on his features. Then anger lit his eyes as he snarled something at the young woman.

Replying in kind, she stared up at him, hands on hips, eyes locked with his in a battle of wills. And, as she gazed at them, Sasha suddenly had the horrified thought that this must be his wife. She should have guessed he'd have a wife, but it had never occurred to her. Not that it mattered. All she wanted was her legacy, for the prophecy to be fulfilled.

Yet, she was aware of a keen disappointment raking sharply at her. There was an annoying lump in her throat, and no matter how hard she tried to swallow it, it remained. *Wife* . . . The knowledge settled like a huge stone in the pit of her stomach. Her hands shook, and she linked her fingers together in a fierce grip. It didn't matter. It just didn't matter. What did she care if he was wed? That wouldn't affect her, only the prophecy. Curse him. There had been no hints . . . the knave. He was as bad as all the English knights she'd heard of, but his wife was beautiful. The kind of pale beauty that was fashionable: slender form, with gold hair and creamy skin, light-colored eyes, and elegant garments. Yea, very beautiful.

She slipped from the bed. She'd leave the chamber and the pair to their own ends. She'd gone no more than a few steps when Rhys barked a command at her to remain. Jerking to a halt, she turned and looked at him. She was tempted to tell him what she thought of him.

"Don't think our dispute is done," he growled, "for it's not. I must first make sense of—of this." He indicated the girl with a contemptuous sweep of one hand, which had the effect of launching her at him with hisses of fury.

Rhys caught her easily, pinning her wrists in one hand. He dragged her toward the open chamber door and bellowed for Brian. As usual, he was not far from his lord, and came running. When Brian halted, eyes wide and heaving for breath, Rhys slung the girl toward him.

"Get her out of here," he said in English, "and put her where she cannot flee."

"Whoreson!" The girl's English was swift and furious as she struggled against Brian's efforts to hold her. "Do you think I'll be put aside? Nay, I will not. Our father thought me fit to acknowledge, and I'll not tolerate less from you—a brother who is more English than Welsh."

Sasha watched with increasing interest. Brother? His sister? Yea, she could see it now. It was striking—the same coloring of hair and tall build, features mirroring Rhys's in a feminine cast. She should have seen it at once. Satisfaction tinged the sweep of relief that flooded her. This could prove quite interesting.

When she looked past them, she saw shock in Brian's face. Apparently, this was news to him. She frowned. Just what was going on?

The answer came from the girl in fragmented thoughts in English and Welsh, scattered words and phrases that explained much: *I may be bastard but I am kin* . . . Rydw i trist, trist . . . Rwyt ti ffwl . . . Brodyr . . . *What can I do to save myself* . . . ?

Sasha turned her attention to Brian, hoping to glean some information that wasn't in Welsh. But he was staring at the girl with obvious dismay. He saw her the same way Sasha did, the strong similarities in features and coloring, and the fleeting thought that the maid even had the same wild temper as Rhys flashed through his mind, along with Gaelic phrases that she couldn't understand. Then he glanced at Sasha, and she had a sudden, dizzying view of herself as he saw her, disheveled and staring, wide-eyed and intent. Smoothing back her hair with one hand, she reached to tie the loose laces of her gown with the other.

Brian jerked his gaze back to Rhys and said, "Where shall I take her, my lord?"

Rhys hesitated. The fierce scowl on his face altered slightly, and he finally gave a shake of his head. "To her own chamber, though I want guards set on her. If she's wed to Gavin, she must be watched closely."

Straightening, the young woman gave Rhys a scornful look before turning to Brian. "This was my chamber.

Now, it appears to have been taken. Lead me to a dark and dreary cell, then. But treat me kindly, for I am still your lady twice over—as heir to Glenlyon and wed to the lord bold enough to capture it."

"And incapable of holding it." Rhys stepped forward, fixing her with a cold stare. "I remember you now. You were beside Gavin in the hall. Glenlyon is mine, and no matter your birth, I am the lord here. On the morrow, I'll decide as to your position in the household. Gavin is imprisoned. Even if I let him live, he'll never be lord of Glenlyon. That makes your position very unstable, so don't speak unwisely."

That speech brought a short jerk of acknowledgment from her. Rhys pushed her toward Brian with a growled command to see to her. As she turned, her gaze chanced to meet Sasha's before wrenching away.

Sasha sensed the young woman's effort to hold back tears of anger and fear, the waves of emotion emanating from the small quivering frame as she desperately defied Rhys. Sasha could understand. At the moment, she wasn't exactly in his high regard either.

Brian flung Sasha a quick glance before taking Rhys's sister by the arm. "As you will, milord."

"Send Owain to me. I'll not put off until the morrow what should be done this eve." Rhys raked a hand through the thick mane of his hair. "And send up a flagon of wine—untouched wine. I'll need no help sleeping this night."

"Yea, lord." Brian gave the angry young woman a dubious look as he took her gingerly by the arm. "Come, milady. Don't be giving me those looks, for I'm only obeying my lord's command. Go gently now, and all will be well."

Whatever she replied was in a tart tone, though Sasha did not understand the content. Apparently Rhys did, for he gave a sardonic bark of laughter that sounded strained.

"I can well believe that the wench is my father's spawn, for she has the devil's own temper," he muttered as he turned around. His gaze fell on Sasha, and his brow lowered even more. "Did you enjoy the play, flower?"

"Yea, lord. 'Twas most enlightening."

"No doubt." Rhys stalked past her, jerking at the thick leather laces binding his harness. A knot was stuck in one of the metal grommets, keeping it from sliding free. He swore horribly as he tried to unfasten the tangled traces.

She watched quietly for a moment before moving to him. "Let me, my lord. You'll only tangle them worse."

"I didn't know you had experience as a squire," he snapped, but stood still to allow her to attempt it.

"It shouldn't take much experience to untie tangled laces and listen to you rail." She frowned at the knotted leather. "I pity your poor squire."

"Morgan is used to it. And I don't rail at him, for he gives me no cause."

"Is that so? I've not noted that you need cause to vent your temper on those around you."

When he started to turn angrily, she gave him a sharp nudge with her elbow. "I've almost got it undone. Don't move or you'll tangle it worse."

In a moment she had it loose, and held the heavy chain mail while he slid his arms and torso free. He gave a grunt of relief. "It grows heavy at times."

Watching as he draped the mail over a stool and shrugged free of his leather tunic, she was slightly annoyed by a detached admiration for him. The harness of chain mail was heavy indeed, wrought of tiny metal links closely bound so as to resist the thrust of a sword or lance. These links formed a garment that covered the knight's body from the top of his head to below his knees. The thick leather gambeson worn beneath was heavy enough even without the mail, able to repel arrows or check their force enough to keep them from penetrating anything but leather. His sword would have been beyond her meager strength, for the huge weapon was over four feet long. It rose almost to her chin, and would have been too unwieldy for her to manage. Yet Rhys managed it with ease.

"You stare at my sword as if longing to use it," he remarked caustically. "I would not suggest you attempt it."

A scornful smile curved her lips. "Nay, lord. I doubt I

could lift it high enough to do much damage. A dagger would be much more practical."

"As I recall, you have a weapon just as practical beneath your skirts." When her head jerked up and she stared at him, he lifted a brow. "The knee you drove into my belly."

She snorted. "It was my foot, not my knee, and it wasn't your belly that I struck."

"So your aim was true. I wondered."

She could cheerfully have bitten her own tongue. Better to have pretended otherwise, but now he knew the truth. She shrugged carelessly and turned away, examining a streak of dirt on the back of one hand. It was safer to look at her hand. He was steadily disrobing, and she had a queasy feeling he meant to finish what he'd started earlier. What had been started in a meadow weeks before. . . .

"Bring me some heated water."

She shut her eyes and pretended not to hear. When he repeated his command, this time in a snarl, she moved to the small metal pot near the brazier. It was hot, and she burned her fingers, muttering an Arabian curse, then lifted it carefully with a cloth. An empty bowl stood on the table, and she poured water into it, then draped the cloth over the side.

"Your water," she said shortly, still not looking at him.

"Do you intend that I scald myself? Pour some cold in with it, or have you never had any kind of a bath before?"

Angry, she flashed him a scathing glance, then wished she hadn't. Garbed in just his linen chainse, he looked less the savage warrior and more the handsome man that he was. Weariness was etched into his features, and the scar on his cheek was more evident than usual. A faint stubble of beard darkened his jaw, and there were deep circles beneath his eyes. Inexplicably, she smiled. Obviously surprised by her response, he smiled as well, a genuine reaction that made him look even younger. They stared at each other in silence. She thought of that day in the meadow, when he'd been teasing and playful, a delightful companion. He'd taken away her breath with his sweet words and kisses, and she'd thought of that day too often and too wistfully of late.

The silence was broken by a solid rap upon the chamber door. As it was ajar, it swung slowly open. "My lord Rhys? I was told that you wished to speak with me."

Stirring, Rhys swung his gaze from her toward the door. "Owain. Enter, and close the door behind you. I need to know what's happened here since the last message I received from you in London."

Owain turned from closing the door, a puzzled look on his face. "My last message, milord?"

"It was waiting on me when my ship docked in London, yet I arrive here to find you imprisoned. Events must have moved swiftly."

Shaking his head, Owain said, "I sent you no message in London. I've been sitting in the dungeon for three months or more."

"No?" Rhys pulled out a chair and indicated that Owain should be seated. Then he looked at Sasha with a faint frown. "See Sir Clyde outside the door and have him hunt you a meal. A hot meal. When you've eaten, return here."

Owain's gaze rested on her curiously, and she stuck her chin in the air. She hadn't forgotten how he'd abandoned her in the dungeons, leaving her to Rhys's uncertain mercy. Humph. There was as much mercy in Rhys ap Griffyn as there was milk in a male tiger. Now it was obvious they wanted to be rid of her. Nay, she'd not quickly forgive either of them.

"Aye, my lord," she said sweetly as she moved to the door, and Rhys gave her a hard stare.

"Wait. I'll tell Sir Clyde myself."

Feigning amazement, she shook her head slowly. "What could I do even if I did wander Glenlyon alone? It's filled with your men, and all the gates are shut tight as a water drum. Do you think I'd summon the wind to carry me away? Perhaps grow wings and fly over the walls? Are you that afraid I'll escape your loving arms, my lord?"

Owain laughed softly, and Rhys's mouth tightened. "I don't think you'd like the consequences if you did, flower. Not that you've proven very successful at escape."

"You're right. I'll stay here. I'll be a mouse in the corner, so pay no attention to me. Go right on with anything you wish to discuss, my lord. I won't listen."

A faint smile curled Rhys's mouth, and he glanced at Owain and said something in Welsh. Owain replied, but there was the barest hint of a smile tugging at his mouth when he focused on Rhys.

To her surprise, thoughts in English were scattered through Owain's replies. *Oh, child, you've got a bull by the horns and don't know what you're doing . . . I can't imagine Rhys suffering it long . . . Curse John for making deals with Gavin and risking us all . . .*

As the direction of his thoughts drifted to other matters, Sasha made a decision. She cleared her throat, and Rhys looked up at her. She smiled. "I've changed my mind, my lord. I've not eaten in some time, as I'm certain Sir Owain can tell you. May I go?"

Frowning, he lifted his head and bellowed a command for Sir Clyde, but she was already at the door. She peered out but saw only shadows and wavering torch light. No guard was visible. Her heart thumped at the sudden possibilities. As distracted as he was, Rhys did not know that.

"There you are, Sir Clyde," she said to the empty corridor, "Lord Rhys wants you to see that I'm fed. You must stay with me every moment, for he fears that such a dangerous felon as myself will escape, but I can see that you're not the kind of man to allow that." She glanced behind her, and Rhys was still at the table with Owain. "Is there anything you wish to add to that, my lord?"

He looked up, frowning. "Nothing but that the man who allows you to escape again will not live long enough to regret it."

She glanced into the empty hallway again and shrugged. "So there you have it. No, don't look at me that way, Sir Clyde. It's not my fondest desire to be with you either. . . . I'll be back soon, my lord."

Slipping into the empty hallway, she waited a moment to be certain Rhys wouldn't check on the guard, and then fled.

She found Biagio in the stables. He was brushing Bay-osha with quick, hard strokes that the horse found enjoyable, and did not see her at first. Men milled in the huge stables, feeding animals, currying them, tending to the mundane tasks required as if nothing had happened. A few glanced her way, and she knew they recognized her. None tried to stop her, nor even asked if she was supposed to be there. She smiled. They preferred pretending she was invisible, and it certainly suited her for them to do so.

The mare alerted Biagio to her presence, looking up and tossing her head, neighing at her down the long, wide hall-way that ran the length of the stable. He turned. His eyes lit when he saw her. "Bella—"

"You don't see me. I'm invisible," she said with a faint smile, and he shook his head at the vague warning.

"I thought you'd be closeted with yon grim knight for the remainder of the evening," he said when she reached him. "Blood lust takes time to fade in a man, often turning to another kind of lust."

"As it might have done with Rhys, had not a problem come banging on the chamber door." She caressed the mare's soft nose, reflected briefly on the recent events, and decided not to say anything. With a shrug, she said, "He's conducting business and doesn't trust me to remain. I think he believes me a traitor."

"No!" Biagio's eyes widened ludicrously, and he laughed when she aimed a blow at his ears. "Easy, bella. I'm amazed that he trusted you to leave his sight."

"He didn't." She smiled when he stared behind her. "Not alone, anyway. He thinks I have a guard with me. But, as you can see, I don't."

"Then your head will likely adorn a pike at the gate before long." Biagio shook his head. "Come. We'll slip out before he finds you. It's still so confused no one would notice. We can be back in England before you know it."

She considered it. Then she shook her head. "Nay, Bia-gio. If I fled now, all I've gone through would be in vain."

"Bella, have you not noticed that he has no intention of leading an army to the Euphrates to regain your legacy?" He dragged the brush angrily over the mare's hide, and the animal shuddered.

"You're hurting my horse," she said tartly. "You know I don't tolerate that."

Biagio tossed the brush aside and turned, slamming his fist hard against a wooden post. The startled mare snorted and danced. Her hooves struck the side of the stall, and Biagio turned back and murmured soft words of apology. He looked at Sasha over the mare's gleaming rump. "I knew this would happen."

"I don't know what you're talking about."

"You don't want to leave him. It has nothing to do with the prophecy, stupid as that is. It has to do with that Welshman."

Angrily, she glared at him. "Did you receive a blow to the head in the struggle?"

"Would you care if I did?" He returned her glare, hotly. "Do you have any idea how worried we were about you? Any idea how Elspeth has been making herself sick because of this?"

"I didn't plan to be taken captive, it just happened." She paused. "I'll explain it to Elspeth when she arrives. She should understand."

"She won't. Neither of us do." He turned to study the horse closely, not looking at her. "Something's happened, bella. You're different."

"Different? Me?" She hooted softly. "I'm not different, unless you think being determined is so different than what I've always been."

"Before, it was different. You spoke of the prophecy, but it was vague. Like a dream you had, or a wish. It was even fun to imagine how it would be once you regained your father's land, and how we would sit on silk cushions and eat grapes and figs all day, while slaves fanned us with gold-tipped feathers." He turned back to her, dark eyes troubled. "Now, all I hear from you is the bargain you made with the Welsh devil, and how he'll get it all back for you."

"What's so different about that? We'll still sit on silk cushions and stuff ourselves with figs and grapes. I'll order a dozen gold-tipped fans. We'll have every fat merchant from Venice to Constantinople thronging our gates."

"And the Welshman? Even if he does agree to—"

"He agreed. I told you that. He swore a knight's oath on his sword hilt."

Biagio's gaze didn't waver. "I don't think he knows that. I'm not saying he didn't agree, but I know how you word things at times."

"There will be no mistake. When he finally believes me, he'll have to do it." She felt suddenly sick. What if he didn't? Despite what she was saying to Biagio, she'd begun to see that manipulating this knight was not going to be as easy as she'd once thought. The past few weeks had been ample evidence that he didn't kindly tolerate manipulation. But she'd just have to change her tactics. She couldn't quit now. She just couldn't. She blinked. "He'll do it. I know he will."

"You don't even believe that yourself, do you?" Biagio asked softly, and she stared at him helplessly. He shook his head. "Bella, I think that you've misjudged your own motives. I think you need to examine your heart. At least be honest with yourself."

"I don't have to listen to this." She turned away, stopping when he put a hand on her arm.

"Nay, bella, you don't have to listen to me. You've never listened to anyone. But listen to yourself. You can at least do that."

She hated it when he was so intuitive. And right. He knew her too well. Perhaps better than she did herself. She turned and looked at him. "You can be very annoying."

He grinned. "I know."

She sighed. "What do you think I should do?"

"You can't mean you'd actually take my advice."

"I can at least listen."

"That's an improvement." Biagio frowned thoughtfully. "If you won't abandon the idea of the prophecy—you needn't look at me that way—you can bring it up with him again. Get a definite answer from him. Then you'll know what to do. If he agrees, then you'll reclaim your legacy. Providing he's capable of taking it back for you."

"He took Glenlyon, didn't he? And with only a handful of men compared to the troops inside."

Biagio smiled. "Yea, and it took trickery and guile to do it. He may have managed it this time, bella, but he doesn't strike me as a man with much patience for scheming. He's more like a lion, roaring with defiance and attacking anyone foolish enough to oppose him. Remember that."

"You've grown so wise in your dotage," she mocked. "And you're all of what—sixteen now?"

Shrugging, he said, "Old enough to have learned a great deal in the past few years. And almost as old as you, bella."

"I've got years on you."

"Not that many."

"I'd traveled over all of Arabia and half of Italy by the time you were born, boy child." Though she meant it jestingly, she found herself thinking of those times, of those long-ago days before the prophecy. She'd been as a windflower, blown hither and yon by the winds with no sense of time or place. And then had come the prophecy. It had given her a goal, a star to reach for. A purpose in life. A means to achieve victory. Honesty compelled her to examine her motives, but she saw only the one answer— Rhys ap Griffyn, Lord of Glenlyon.

CHAPTER FOURTEEN

"I t's true, my lord." Owain looked down at the flagstone floor. His throat worked. "My son turned traitor. After Gavin slew your father and brothers, Bowen must have copied my signature and written the letters for him. Understand, it was a terrible time. There weren't many choices left—yield or die. So he joined Gavin. I chose prison and death rather than cast my lot with Gavin, but I'm older and past my prime. Though I cannot say I like Bowen's choice, I can understand it." He looked up. "But I ask of you, don't slay him for it. He's all I have."

Rhys looked up and past him. He knew all about being faced with desperate choices. There had been a few of those in his life. He sighed. "Bowen fought against us, so I can't excuse him completely. I'll ask his reasons before I make a decision. If he didn't cast his lot with Gavin willingly, I won't fault a man for doing what he must under dire circumstances."

Owain nodded. "Yea, he's young yet, and doesn't understand that there are things worse than death for a man.

Living as a coward's tool would be intolerable. I'm certain he soon found out that truth."

"Truth is the reason I summoned you to my chamber tonight instead of waiting till the morrow, when matters are calmer." He frowned down at his closed hand, opening his fingers and studying his palm before looking up again. "Tell me of Gavin's wife."

Silence fell. Owain looked uncomfortable, then gave a shake of his head. "So you've already learned of her. 'Tis not unexpected, I suppose. You would have found out about her eventually."

"Is the wench my father's bastard daughter as she claims?"

Owain met his gaze. "Yes. Cailin was born several years after you were sent to Henry's court in England."

"And her mother? Who was her mother?"

Broad shoulders lifted in a faint shrug. "A village woman who took Lord Griffyn's fancy. Your mother had been dead awhile, my lord. And your father was still a young man."

"Is it true? Did my father recognize her as one of his heirs?"

Owain hesitated. "He did recognize her. She lived under his roof, was educated and cared for as natural children are. It's a common enough matter to mention such a child as receiving a legacy, but I cannot say that Lord Griffyn intended her to inherit Glenlyon."

"And her marriage to Gavin? Did my father arrange that?"

"Nay, lord. He did not. It was mentioned several times but always by Gavin, who sought a hold on Glenlyon. Lord Griffyn was willing to accept Gavin's oath of fealty, but not close ties that might one day conflict with his legal heirs. He meant for Davyyd to inherit, and then Wynn, should Davyyd die."

Rhys looked down at his palm again. The cut was healed. It was still a faint red mark against his skin, but that was all. He looked back up at Owain. "And me? Did my father not consider me as heir?"

Owain looked startled. "He never thought both his

older sons would die as they did. He spoke of you frequently, but I cannot say that he thought you would ever come back to Wales, my lord."

"Did he not." Rhys curled his hand into a fist and dragged it over the edge of the table in a slow sweep. "I suppose that's true enough. I was the expendable son. An extra, should there be a need for collateral. And as it turned out, there was."

He hadn't meant to say it so bitterly, but the words had flowed out before he could check them. There was an appalled silence. He looked up after a moment. "Now I'm back. If you wish to remain as steward, I'll respect your advice on matters unfamiliar to me."

After a moment, Owain nodded. "I would be honored to remain as your steward. Since Gavin had me imprisoned, I'll need to find out what has been done in my absence. Or not done." He smiled slightly. "I know there was no great expenditure on food for prisoners. One of the guards was still loyal to your father, and if not for his generosity in getting scraps of food to me, I would have starved to death three months ago."

"There were many here still loyal to my father." Rhys drew his thumb along the edge of the table, smiling slightly. "Some of those still awake enough bluntly refused to fight, and yielded up their swords with no struggle. Others swore to me immediately. If we had not won, they would have been killed for it."

"Mercy was never one of Gavin's strong points. He emulates John, in allowing death to overtake his enemies instead of killing them outright. Starvation is the weapon of choice, slow but effective eventually."

"John." Rhys frowned. "Now I know that Gavin sent the message that caught up with me on the road back from completing John's errand. Another delay, of course, with the hope that I might never make it back to Wales. Did Gavin stir up Sir Niclas against me?"

"Sir Niclas? Do you mean of Raglan?"

His eyes narrowed. "Yea. Did not you write me of Raglan's assault on Glenlyon?"

"Nay, lord." Owain paused, then shook his head. "Another forgery, I suspect. As far as I know, Sir Niclas was your father's friend. He would not assault Glenlyon unless Gavin pushed him to it. But I think I see a reason for leading you to believe he might—if you had divided your forces and your attention between Raglan and Glenlyon, then you would be much weaker and more likely to fail at both."

"As I might have done." He frowned. "Gavin's purpose in refusing me entry to Glenlyon then eludes me. It would have been easier for him to attempt treachery if I was allowed inside at once instead of barred entry."

"I see John's fine hand in this. Could he explain to King Richard that the man he appointed as steward of your lands lured you into your own keep for the purpose of murder? Nay, Richard would retaliate most swiftly and harshly. But if you had formed an assault . . . why, any man would defend himself. With all the rumors about Raglan wanting the keep, it would be natural to defend it fiercely. And of course, it would be such a pity to see the true lord slain by tragic mistake at his own gates."

"There's sense in that explanation. And it does indeed smack of John's liking for devious plots." He rubbed a fist over his chest in an absent, back and forth motion. "It also explains why he sent me off on a foolish errand when I unexpectedly returned to England. It gave him time to form other plots—such as the mercenaries who fell upon us on the road from Coventry, and the long delay in a church for what I thought was your messenger, and even the damsel sent to distract me from Wales with false seduction. Who knows what else she's been told to do."

"That sounds like John. Better than a poisoned egg, perhaps, but just as treacherous."

He smiled slightly. "Don't rule out poison. That's been tried. Or a form of it, anyway. First on me, then on my men." He stood up and raked a hand through his hair. "Next time, she's likely to have me convulsing on the garderobe floor."

"My lord," Owain exclaimed with obvious alarm, "you don't mean to keep this treacherous woman near?"

"Why not?" He eyed Owain for a moment, still smiling

slightly. "Why should I rid myself of an enemy I know, only to worry about one I don't? Sasha certainly hasn't succeeded, and—"

"Sasha?" Owain looked startled. "You cannot mean the dark lass who just left—the one Gavin's men took from the wood."

"That's the one." He curled his hand into a fist and studied his knuckles for a moment, then looked up. "She shared your cell. Tell me what you think of her."

Obviously dismayed, Owain opened his mouth and shut it again, then shook his head. "I confess I don't know all the details, but it's my opinion that the maid would never willingly do you harm."

"No? And what brings you to that conclusion?"

"Forgive me, my lord, but I think she admires you greatly. She spoke most highly of you."

"She's adept at deceit. I've seen her shift from teasing temptress to raging virago in less time than it takes a man to blink. She's as constant as the wind, and less predictable." He shrugged, clenching his jaw. "And she will soon learn the folly of her ways."

Owain fell silent. When next he spoke, it was of neighboring barons, and the Marcher lords' strength. They talked of the Crusades and Richard, and England's slow decline in his absence, and how the king was needed at home to curb his brother's villainy.

"And now," Owain muttered with a sigh, "brigands roam all of England and Wales, taking what they will and killing those who oppose them. If Richard was to return, perhaps his presence would discourage the lawless men who abuse the land."

"Richard is more concerned with glory these days than ruling." Rhys shrugged at Owain's frown. "But the people adore him. He's all that a king should be—tall and magnificent, a mighty warrior and expert at gallantry."

"But not a ruler, you think?"

Rhys didn't reply. Owain had been his father's steward for years. He remembered the older man from the days when Rhys was still a young lad running half-naked over Welsh hills. But he'd made the mistake of trusting too

freely before, and it had cost him dear. It was hard over-
coming an old habit.

Rising from his chair, Owain smiled sadly. "Lord Rhys,
I've known you since you were a squalling brat toddling
about a dirt yard and soiling your trews. I never betrayed
your father, even upon pain of imminent death at Gavin's
hands, and I would not betray you. You're so like Lord
Griffyn in ways, it's like having him here with me now.
I'm grateful that you grew into the man you are. But if
you don't feel easy with me as adviser and confidant, I'll
depart your company for wherever you wish to send me."

There was honesty in Owain's gaze, and a clear steadi-
ness. Rhys was almost ashamed of his brief suspicion, and
shook his head. "It's not always easy to trust when there
are so many waiting to see me laid low."

"Command is always more a burden than a privilege."
Owain smiled. "I've seen it destroy weak men. Gavin
would have brought his own destruction on his head soon
enough, even had you not come back from the Crusades
to take up the reins of power." He put a hand on Rhys's
shoulder. "But I'm most grateful you came to hasten his
demise. How do you intend to deal with him?"

"I haven't yet decided. If I kill him as he deserves, I'll
have John at my door. I'm not ready to invite more trouble. To free Gavin would be foolish. He'd soon be at my
gates with an army. I think I'll cavil a bit should John
demand his release, until I see how many men will come
to my banner."

"Once the barons learn of your return, you'll see many
flock to your standard, my lord. It was a dark day when
your father was so foully slain. There are many who remember him most kindly. If not for John's troops, Gavin
of Glamorgan might have been dragged from Glenlyon
and torn to pieces by Griffyn's defenders. Lord Griffyn's
loyal men will certainly want his son to carry on his banner."

"Perhaps." His memories were so faded now, with only
brief flashes of his father. Yet he had kept the few letters
he received through the years, some full of admonitions
about reported misdeeds, others giving advice to the son

so far away. Perhaps he would read them again. He looked up at Owain. "On the morrow, we'll send out summons to those men who would answer my call. By the replies, we'll know my strength."

Owain nodded. "Yea, lord. I'll draw up the list for you to see. And I'll be glad to write those summons myself."

"There's much to do, for taking Glenlyon was only the beginning, as I knew it would be." He raked a hand through his hair, his attention shifting to another, more immediate problem. Sasha had not returned. There had been more than enough time for her to eat a hot meal. He reached for his sword and buckled it on.

"Owain, where are the stables? I have a notion I may find my pretty prisoner attempting escape from Sir Clyde."

"Not far from where the old stables once were. I'll take you there before I seek my former chamber." Owain hesitated. "With your leave, I'll repossess my chamber, unless you prefer another to have it, my lord."

He looked up at him. Many things went through his mind, from childhood memories to the carefully written letters. He took a deep breath and smiled. "I can think of no other man so worthy to be steward or have the accoutrements that go with the office, Owain. Whatever my father bestowed upon you, I return with gratitude and confidence."

Smiling, Owain clasped Rhys's offered hand in a bond to seal their renewed goodwill. "We will avenge your father's murder, my lord, and see those responsible punished."

He nodded. "I intend to do just that."

It was quiet and gloomy in the kitchens. The only light came from an oven and a few candles. Sasha rummaged through bins and baskets, searching for bread, cheese, something to eat other than green apples. Perhaps they should have gone to the storerooms, for the larder was almost empty. Occasionally she lifted her head to peer about cautiously. A few servants had wakened. One of them staggered dazedly through the kitchen.

She turned to look at Biagio, perched atop a barrel eat-

ing one of the unripe apples. "You certainly did well. I'm
amazed that you didn't slay them outright with the
strength of the potion."

He shrugged. "I calculated the size of the wine casks
with the amount of the potion and divided it by the number of idiots certain to drink. I think I may have misjudged
the last, however. Don't look at me like that. It was dev-
ilish difficult to manage. I used all your herbs, and had to
wheedle more out of a comely village wench just to have
enough."

"I'm certain that was unpleasant for you. Where's the
wench now?"

Biagio grinned. "Pining for me. If she'd guessed my true
purpose in sampling her wares, I might be swinging from
a village gibbet right now."

"Do you think this turnip still good?" she muttered,
peering at a dried, wrinkled root she'd found in a basket.
"Never mind. I'm hungry enough to eat it anyway. So, tell
me all the details of how you concocted this mad scheme,
and what potion you fed Lord Rhys to get him to agree."

"Ah, he was most agreeable to any suggestion that
would secure him the castle. Almost pleasant, actually. I'm
certain it won't last. Now that he has what he wants, he
can revert to his normal surly disposition." He took another bite of apple, crunching it noisily. *Beware of him,
bella, for he will give you no quarter. . . .*

Frowning at Biagio's silent warning, she looked up to
ask him what he meant, when she heard the slamming of
the kitchen door behind her. She turned. Rhys leaned
against the wall, his arms folded over his broad, bare chest
and his brows drawn down. He looked ominous.

Biagio slid from the barrel and waved an arm in greeting. "The dread lord arrives. Do we bow and kiss your
ring, or just prostrate ourselves on the floor?"

Rhys gave him a hard stare. "If you wish to please me,
whelp, you'll vanish. Swiftly."

"From the kitchen, the keep, or all of Wales?"

" 'Tis your choice."

Biagio bowed low with a flourish, then straightened.

"We shall be delighted to accept your invitation to depart, my benevolent lord."

"Nay, whelp. 'Tis only you that has been extended that invitation. The lady stays."

I told you, I told you, bella, he is not a man to yield keep or chattel or belief, and he thinks you guilty of treason. . . .

Aloud, Biagio mocked, "Forsooth, I sense my presence is no longer wanted. I'm grieved to hear it."

"You'll bear up under the weight of sorrow." Rhys pushed away from the wall, leonine and menacing.

Sasha took an involuntary step back. Her grip loosened, and she dropped the turnip so that it struck the floor and rolled crookedly over the stones. Rhys kicked it aside and reached for her.

"I'm disappointed, flower. Your other methods of resistance have been much more effective. And painful. Can it be that you're growing enamored of me?"

Position him so that his back is to me, bella, and I will slide my dagger between his ribs. . . .

"No!" Her frantic outburst had the undesired effect of making Rhys stiffen warily. She drew in a deep breath and tried to remain calm. "I mean . . . if I were so foolish as to be enamored of you, I'd drown myself."

His brow lifted. Amusement danced in his clear gray eyes and curved his mouth. "You couldn't have chosen a more convenient method. The River Wye runs alongside Glenlyon. But it's only fair to warn you—this keep commands the crossing. And I command the keep. If you want access, you have to ask me."

She tried to keep Biagio in her line of vision without alerting Rhys to his intent. There was no predicting what he might do if he thought Biagio foolish enough to attack him.

"As I'm not enamored of you the least bit"—she angled to keep Biagio well in sight, flashing Rhys a quick glance to be certain he still hadn't seen the young Italian—"there's no danger of me flinging myself from the ramparts into the river. Not that I'd ask you for anything anyway."

Oh, that certainly put him in his place, bella. . . . He'll

never release you willingly. . . . All it would take is a quick
thrust and we could all be free. . . .

The idiot. Did he think himself able to catch a trained
knight off guard with only a dagger and desperation? She
flung a glance at Rhys, and made a swift decision. With
an agile twist, she wrenched her arm from his light hold
and bolted toward Biagio. It had the desired effect of
swinging Rhys around to catch her, thus bringing Biagio
into his line of vision and aborting a move that was far
too foolish.

Rhys caught her with an arm around her middle, lifting
her easily from her feet so that she was dangling above the
stone floor. His voice was heavy with irony and irritation.

"Not again, flower. You've escaped me once too often,
and I've no intention of allowing you a reprieve. We've
unfinished matters to discuss."

"I really—put me down—have nothing I wish to speak
with you about."

He set her on her feet and stared down at her with sus-
picious eyes. "You've played your innocent part too well.
And too long."

She'd been glaring at Biagio as he toyed with the hilt of
his dagger, but Rhys's words jerked her gaze to him instead. Her alarm shifted focus. The implied threat in his
words had not gone unnoticed by Biagio.

He took an angry step forward. "What do you mean by
that?"

"Are you still here, whelp?" Rhys's gaze shifted to him.
"Whatever I mean is for her ears alone. If you're still here
when my sword clears the sheath, neither of you will like
the outcome."

Frustration and fury flared in Biagio's eyes, but as
Rhys's hand dropped to the hilt of his sword, he moved
swiftly backward. "I take your meaning, my lord." *I cannot fight a sword with a dagger, bella, but there are ways
to rid ourselves of him. . . . Do not despair. . . .*

Helpless to offer denial or reassurance, especially when
she felt the same frustration, Sasha watched silently as Biagio slammed the kitchen door. The sound of its closing

reverberated from the high walls and vaulted ceiling. She winced.

"Frightened?" he mocked.

"Of a knight who bullies a beardless youth trying to protect his mistress? Why would I be frightened of such a man?"

A slow smile curved his mouth. "Any other man worthy of the name would have slain him long ago for his insolence. Or at the least, let him wear a striped back to teach him the folly of his ways. 'Tis my thought that he needs to be lessoned well in the behavior of servants."

"Biagio is not your servant. He is mine."

"Yea, but you are mine, so what does that make him?"

A chill shivered down her spine at the implications of that statement. Surely, he didn't mean—but no, he must, for there was a heavy darkness in his eyes like thunder, and no mercy on his face. She wished he'd put some clothes on. He looked much too formidable with his broad chest, hard stomach, and taut-muscled arms.

She swallowed the sudden surge of irritating fear that made her knees weak. Her chin lifted, and her voice was remarkably steady under the circumstances. "I'm not your servant. You are mistaken."

He shrugged. "Perhaps not a servant, no. But you are mine, indeed. I seem to recall a pledge, flower. It was your suggestion, was it not?"

"I would never suggest that I be your servant." She took a backward step but he reached out to stop her. She hadn't really expected him to release her until he was ready. And apparently, he wasn't ready.

"Ah flower, it was your suggestion that you come to my bed—"

"Which I did." She stared up at him. "I just didn't do what you wanted me to do when I got there."

"Don't split hairs. We both know what was intended. You had your reasons for wanting it and I had mine, but the bargain was struck. You betrayed me. That releases me from keeping my sworn word, but you—ah, that's another matter."

Sasha stared at him. Her head hurt. Her stomach was

empty, her feet were sore, and she was thirsty. She shouldn't have to parry his verbal thrusts when she was so vulnerable. Why wouldn't her Gift work with this infuriating knight? She wanted a bath, rest, and food, not necessarily in that order. And being so afraid put her in a dreadful temper.

Switching tactics, she put one hand to her head and moaned.

Rhys moved his hand to her wrist, and his fingers closed around it in a firm grip. "That won't work. This is not the place to finish our discussion, but I find myself impatient to hear some answers with the ring of truth in them. Come along, flower."

He pulled her forward, and she stumbled slightly, stubbing her bare toe on the corner of a stone. When she gave a soft cry of pain, he swore as he glanced down at her feet. "God's blood, where are your shoes?"

Hopping on one foot, she clutched at her toe with her free hand. "Lost. One of them, anyway. I took the other off, preferring my feet to at least be in matching shades of Welsh muck." She lifted the hem of her gown and showed him her feet and the dark brown film that crusted them well above her ankles.

Rhys grunted irritably and swung her from her feet in an unexpected motion that made her gasp and clutch at him. She had a swift, blurred view of the huge stone ovens and hanging pots as he crossed the kitchens and strode out into the darkness. Moonlight spattered across a bailey littered with the remnants of war and recent strife, and occasional torches flickered over knots of men bedding down for the night. A soft wind blew, and in the distance, a dog barked.

He shifted her in his arms, holding her more tightly against his bare chest as he traversed the bailey. His heart beat swift and steady beneath her palm. Her throat ached suddenly. She thought of the meadow on May Day, when they had danced and laughed, enjoyed a flirtatious romp and breathless kisses. She'd thought she could control events, could toy with fire and not be burned: a chaste dalliance and harmless flirtation with a rogue knight be-

fore bending him to her will, using him to win back her
lands for her. But it hadn't turned out that way.

Curse him. She hated feeling vulnerable and helpless.
And she hated admitting to herself that somehow she'd
come to feel something more for him than just tolerance
and a need for his strength. All that time languishing in
the hungry darkness of Gavin's dungeon was to blame.
She'd had too much time to think, too much time to examine her own motives. Maybe Biagio was right.

God help her, what if he was? What if she truly cared
for this grim, arrogant man? She wasn't as good as she
should be at pretense, not when it really mattered. Playing
a part was amusing and entertaining when the stakes were
minor, when she didn't really care if anyone believed her.
What was so devastating about an empty purse or a lost
wager? Nothing. But this was different.

*Fool, fool, to yield your heart to a man who does not
care. . . .*

Disaster. She was doomed if she didn't do something.
All her plans, her hopes—everything would be ashes if she
didn't think of a way to set things right.

Torchlight grew bright, casting a brilliant glow over the
ground as they neared the great hall. Men milled about
the bailey near the hall, and one of them stopped Rhys to
ask him a question. She could feel the curious glances,
knew they wondered and conjectured, even mocked the
fact that she was barefoot, bedraggled, and powerless.
Their lord had won. The elf queen's magic was useless
against him. Her chin came up though her cheeks were
hot with shame and humiliation.

With all her inner turmoil, she was barely aware of the
conversation, dismissing everything from her mind, keeping her barriers up to stave off the barrage of chaotic
thoughts. She said nothing, offered no protest or even
question as Rhys bore her up the winding staircase to the
long, dimly lit corridor. But even as he carried her to his
chamber, grim purpose etched on his features, it occurred
to her that there was always one way to deal with such a
man. . . .

When they reached the chamber, Rhys kicked open the

door and lowered Sasha to her feet. In their absence, someone had come to straighten the room, rearranging bed curtains and clearing away tainted wine to replace it with new flagons and clean cups. The filthy harness of mail was gone, and overturned stools and tables were set aright. Chests had been brought in and put in place. The fire had been stoked in the huge brazier in the center of the room, blazing a beckoning warmth.

Rhys recognized Morgan's fine hand in the changes. An efficient, able squire, as always. He released Sasha, and she moved away from him with so much haste he was certain she'd finally realized the depth of his anger. He lifted a brow.

"It's well past the hour for you to recognize your danger, flower. You should have thought of it when you were spinning your lies so unwisely. Now it's too late to offer defense, when before I might have been willing to listen."

Silent, she stared at him. Her wide dark eyes reflected the fire's glow. She was rigid, chin lifted at a defiant angle, hands curled into fists at her sides. Any other woman might have appeared ridiculous, clad in a ragged gown with bare feet covered in muck, affecting a regal air as if he should pay homage. Yet, oddly, Sasha did not. He didn't know what it was—her spirit, perhaps, or her brazen defiance. He had to admit a grudging respect for her refusal to cower in the face of greater force. But it was the unwilling affection he felt for her that annoyed him most.

She may not cower, but she would yield to him. She would yield all, reason and rhyme and whatever else he demanded of her. She would yield all or he would find a way to make her.

A hesitant thud sounded on the chamber door, and it creaked open a bit on its hinges. He turned, and Morgan stood in the opening holding a tray. Behind him stood several servants.

"I thought you would want food and a bath, milord," Morgan said.

Trust his squire to arrive at an inconvenient moment. Rhys nodded. "Yea, it would be welcome."

Morgan swung the door wider to admit the servants,

and in a few moments, a bath had been set up and heated water was being poured. A tray was placed on the table and covers removed. The smell of hot meat and bread made his stomach growl, reminding him he hadn't eaten all day.

He looked at Sasha. Her nostrils flared slightly, but when she saw him watching her, she turned her head away. He moved to the table and cut large chunks of meat with his dagger, then ate some bread. After a few moments, he looked up at her and smiled.

"Sit and eat, flower. You'll need your strength for the night to come."

A high flush rode her cheekbones, and she gave him a dark stare but moved to the table with feline grace. And disdain. As if she was doing him a favor, she relented enough to eat, her attitude obvious. She picked delicately at the bread and meat, sipped daintily at the wine. A marvelous performance. He had to admire it, even when he intended to swiftly shatter her pretenses once they were alone.

But he allowed her the moment, indulging her fantasy of being in control as Morgan silently and efficiently readied everything for his bath. When it was prepared, he dismissed him and the other servants, and closed and barred the door after them.

He turned. Sasha was watching him with an air of expectant wariness. He would not disappoint her. He removed his sword and baldric, then unlaced the waist ties of his chausses. After dragging a stool close to the huge wooden tub, he sat down and began to unlace his boots. She was watching every move, as poised and alert as a cat. He removed his boots and tossed them aside, then stood and looked at her.

"You first, flower."

She took a step back. "I don't know what you're talking about."

He gestured to the tub. "Hot water and a pot of soap. Clean towels. It may be a bit audacious of me to suggest it, but I think a bath would do you a world of good. It would certainly make you smell better."

She glared at him. It was obvious she wanted to refute his words, but there was no way she could. Two weeks in the dungeons had removed all traces of the tantalizing jasmine scent she usually wore, and applied several layers of dirt and grime in its stead.

After a moment, she shrugged. "I have no intention of disrobing for your amusement."

"It was your choice, flower." He strode swiftly to her before she guessed his intentions, and in one motion swung her into his arms. While she squealed alarm, he held her over the water, then released her. She dropped like a stone. Geysers of water spewed up into the air and sloshed over the wooden sides of the tub to wet the stone floor.

He smiled when she glared up at him, sputtering and gasping, water dripping into her eyes and from the end of her nose. Placing both his hands on the edge of the tub, he leaned over her. "Will you bathe yourself, or shall I help?"

Her reply was a quick slice of her hand through the water, sending out a small tide to drench him. He didn't move, even when she lavished colorful names on him along with the water. The air was thick with curses and verbal abuse, and he listened to it for several moments. When he'd heard enough, he cupped her chin in his palm, holding tight.

"Enough, flower. I've reached the end of my patience."

She stared up at him, dark eyes still furious, her lips drawn back from her small white teeth in a feral snarl. Then she seemed to give herself a mental shake. She exhaled sharply. Her lashes fluttered. Her lips eased into a faint semblance of a smile. And she nodded.

"You're right. I do need a bath. I would have preferred privacy and a few maids, but I suppose that's too much to ask."

The last word ended on a questioning lilt. Amused, he released her chin. "Yes. That's too much to ask."

"Too bad. Very well. Please hand me the soap and a cloth, and I will bathe."

To his surprise, she stood up, uncurling her slender body, and with a few tugs, removed the gown and tossed it aside. It fell in a sodden lump on the stones, and she added her undertunic to the heap. She stood there, bare and golden, her high, firm breasts just as he remembered them. His gaze drifted helplessly over her graceful form, from breasts to the flat plane of her belly, halting at the dark triangle at the juncture of her smooth, rounded thighs. Despite the cool air in the chamber, he felt suddenly much too warm.

Curse her. How had she gotten the upper hand again? Was he so callow that just the sight of her nude form rendered him speechless and as awkward as a youth again? He turned away and soaped a cloth for her, then gave it to her silently.

Regal and gracious, she took the cloth and sat back down in the tub. Ignoring him, she soaped her arms, her breasts, her neck, with slow, leisurely circles of the cloth, eyes half-closed, and a dreamy smile on her face. She sighed softly. Then she lifted a leg, bending it to pay particular attention to her feet and toes. Soapy water lapped about her rib cage just below her breasts. Her uptilted brown nipples were laced with bubbles. He watched silently.

Heat churned in his belly, radiating outward in spreading waves that made his fists clench at his sides. When she tilted back her head to gaze up at him with a bright smile and ask if he would hand her more soap, he did so, still silent. Then she slid slowly, down into the water until only her hair was left floating on the surface, an ebony drift of seaweed and silk.

Sitting up again, she scraped water from her eyes with the flat of one hand, her wet hair draped in a dark cape over her bare shoulders. She pulled it forward and began to rub soap into it, working up a brisk lather as if he was not standing there watching.

Another pain like a kick in the belly. Breathless and heated, the ache returned to torment him. He took a step back. Best to put distance between them, for only a glance would reveal how aroused he was. He didn't need to see another one of her secretive feline, smiles that could be so infuriating.

She bent forward to rinse her hair, dragging her fingers through the long, glossy strands. Soap bubbles floated on the water's surface and skimmed her arms, clinging like sea-foam to her golden skin. With a lithe flip of her hair behind her, she rose to stand in the middle of the tub, one of her straight black brows lifted inquiringly.

"Is that to your satisfaction, my lord?"

He nodded, a short jerk of his chin that was all he could manage. Jésu, but he burned. How humiliating.

She stepped from the tub, and he handed her a dry towel that she wrapped around herself, unabashed. Then she looked up at him with that small, secret smile that he resented. "Your turn, my lord."

He looked at the tub, then back at her. Still silent, he untied the last cord of his chausses and peeled them away, turning toward the tub. Pride would not allow him to let her know she'd affected him with her obvious play. He stepped over the wooden sides and into the tub, sinking down and stretching out his legs as far as they would go. Most of his body was under water, but his knees protruded from the soap bubbles. He scooped two handfuls of water and splashed his face, then looked up at her through wet, clogged eyelashes.

"Wash my back," he said shortly.

There was silence but no movement, then she muttered something he couldn't understand and picked up the pot of soap. With the towel still swathing her body, she paused at the tub's side and held out the pot of soap. He shook his head.

"I said wash my back, not bring me the soap."

"Did I ask you to wash my back?"

He looked up at her. "No. But you will wash mine."

There was another sizzling silence, then she knelt at the tub's side and dipped out a generous portion of soap, slapping it against his back in a stinging whack. He turned his head, narrowing his eyes, but she only smiled sweetly.

"Is that enough, do you think?"

He caught her hand, holding fast. His eyes met hers, and he said softly, "Beware how harshly you tread, flower. I always retaliate."

When he released her arm, she silently and diligently applied herself to washing his back, using a cloth and scrubbing his skin clean. Without being asked, she washed his hair, his chest, and even his arms. Then she stopped. Relaxed, he lifted his head from where he'd leaned it against the back of the tub and opened his eyes to look at her.

"Is that all, flower?"

"All I intend to do." She held out the soapy cloth. "I know it's done, but I've never bathed a man before."

He smiled. "Never?"

"There's no tub hidden in my cart. My baths are usually taken in a running stream or public baths. Not like this."

"Poor flower." He reached out to stroke the side of her face. Tiny beads dotted her cheeks and forehead, and damp hair clung to her skin in delicate silken threads. She was flushed with steam heat, and the towel around her had slipped lower so that he could see the high, rounded tops of her breasts. A darker shadow separated them, and he couldn't resist sliding a finger into the tempting hollow. She didn't move, but he felt her quiver.

"Lovely flower," he murmured, leaning forward with a splash. Water washed up against the sides of the tub and over when he drew her closer with a hand behind her head, his body pressed against the wooden lip. The edge of the tub was hard against his ribs as he held her still, putting out his tongue to trace her lips in a light flicker. She shuddered, and with his other hand, he gently pulled away her towel.

Her head tilted back, wet hair tangling around his hand; he dragged his tongue over the arch of her throat and down, down to the sweet tempting rise of her breasts. The smell of the soap was arousing. She was honey and silk, sweet and soft, fire and ice, all blended together in a tantalizing prize. It was a wonder the water didn't boil around him.

He stood up, dragging her with him. At this moment, he didn't care if she knew how she affected him, didn't care about her betrayal, didn't care about anything but the driving need to put himself inside her. His time of waiting was at an end.

CHAPTER FIFTEEN

❧

She looked up into his eyes and knew he would wait no longer. Wet, naked, cool and yet on fire, she said nothing as he carried her across the stone floor to the high, wide bed against the wall. The bed hangings shifted in a slight draft, and the ropes creaked when he lay her on the mattress and leaned over her. The musky smell of soap surrounded them. There was heat in his eyes and his touch, in the very air between them.

It was over. All the coy pretense, the delay and resistance, didn't matter now. There would be no more reprieves, only the inevitable moment of truth. Nothing she said or did would stay him, and in truth she did not want to prevent him. Not any more. This was—for all that he thought the victory his—her moment of triumph.

Never had she felt this way before, this swelling anticipation, the breathless rush of excitement and need that swept her at such swift pace from a trembling maiden toward the promised fulfillment. It had been there since that first moment in the weald, when she'd looked up at the bright, golden knight mounted on a fierce destrier and seen her own destiny looking back at her.

Rhys slid his long body up over hers, bending to lavish kisses and caresses on her damp skin along the way, his hair still dark with water, his eyes like twin flames. She smiled.

Her arms came up to curve around his back in an embrace, and he nudged her thighs apart with his knee. He moved up, sliding between her legs, bare skin against bare skin, breathtaking and erotic, a sensual prelude of what was to come. His head bent and he kissed her. Her mouth, her closed eyes, her brow, and then her ear, breathing heat against her skin until she shuddered. Then he kissed her lips again, lingering, tantalizing and sweet. He tasted of wine and soap.

And all the while he was kissing her, that hard, heated length between her legs nudged at the throbbing center of her, fierce and insistent. He pulled her beneath him, slid inside her the tiniest bit, then stopped. When he finally lifted his head to stare down at her through steely eyes the color of flint, she found it hard to breathe and impossible to talk. Rhys watched her, and there was an odd expression on his face, almost angry. She moved blindly, urgently. He trapped her hands at her sides with a low growl, and his head bent again to capture her mouth.

Even while he kissed her harshly, his hands were skimming her sides, fingers trailing over her arms and then her rib cage, cupping her to pull her up and into him so that she could feel every inch of him against her. Darkness and sun sparks lurked at the back of her eyes, flashing. It was as if she'd drunk too much wine. Or as if she'd balanced precariously on the high, high edge of a precipice, lightheaded with her own daring, afraid and yet exhilarated with the danger of it all.

Daring, oh so very daring, she pressed a kiss against the hard line of his jaw, then his throat, savoring the heady taste of him, the masculine smell and strength that was so rousing. Her hands drifted over him, over the broad width of his shoulders and down, fingertips tangling in the light mat of curls on his chest. She grazed the hard ridge of muscles banding his chest and belly in gentle exploration. No lower, for his body was wedged against hers, the solid pressure that was hot and hard and soft all at the same time. His hands had shifted somehow, and his palms were pressed deep into the mattress on each side of her as she investigated him, his weight balanced over her. He made a low, guttural sound when her hand moved low into the heat between their bodies, and closed his eyes.

It wasn't as if she hadn't seen him before, hadn't made these same explorations, but this time was different. This time, there would be a different ending, a yielding to his will instead of what she'd wanted. Or thought she'd wanted. She ached for him. Her thighs were spread wide, cradling him intimately. Her skin tingled with expectation and a reaching for something just beyond her grasp, and she knew he held the answer.

His head bent. He found the sensitive peak of her breast and his lips closed around it, tugging. Fire blossomed in the pit of her stomach and between her legs. His hand moved, fingers seeking, stroking her, making the throbbing ache worse. She couldn't breathe, could only arch upward, wordless and dazed, whimpering softly.

Fiercely, he kissed her again. This time his hands weren't soft and gentle as he pulled her up against him, his hips driving into her until the firm pressure altered swiftly to a sharper one. She twisted, gasped, and arched upward, seeking the end his body promised. He shifted slightly, and the sharp ache inflamed into a hot, searing stab as he thrust forward with a swiftness she had not anticipated.

It caught her off guard and she cried out, fingers digging into the bare skin of his back and shoulder, raking his flesh. Impaled and anxious, with the needy frenzy still working inside her, she pushed at him with the heels of her hands, a hard shove that did nothing to budge his heavy weight.

He lifted his head, a frown on his face, his eyes hazy and his breath coming raggedly. He pressed forward again, the slight movement dragging a gasp and groan from her. She shivered. He stared down at her, but she could tell nothing from his expression. The heavy pressure of his body inside hers dispelled all else but that—and the promise of pleasure that hovered so close. She lifted a hand to touch the damp strands of hair brushing his shoulder, dark gold and soft. His hands shifted to curl behind her, gripping her shoulders and holding her still as he eased more deeply into her, a wide, stretching burn that took away breath and thought and logic, leaving her floundering helplessly. She couldn't help a small, soft cry.

"Curse you," he muttered, hoarse and thick, inexplicable. "Curse you for a liar. . . ."

It didn't make sense, but it didn't matter. She arched upward, seeking an end to the teasing torment. Her hands fluttered over his back, his sides, slid between them, then moved again.

When he withdrew, then rammed into her again, the thrusts deep and short, she whimpered at the mix of pleasure and pain. It was like riding an ocean wave, up and up and up, reaching for the elusive pinnacle, hopeful and breathless, not knowing what would happen.

But suddenly, as he moved inside her in a hard, erotic rhythm she felt the swelling like a tidal wave begin, rolling up and over and consuming her, a shattering, drowning surge that swept her with it. She shuddered, clutched at him, heard wild, keening cries like seabirds, dimly realized they were her own but didn't care. Nothing mattered but this—this rushing eclipse of quivering emotion that was an explosion of light and sound and splintering release.

Fire and ice, heat and frost, and he was holding her as she clung to him with half sobs, breathless and shaking. She blinked, and the haze around her shifted. The blur of firelight and candlelight seemed to grow sharper. They were both still damp. She vaguely remembered his long, low groan, sounding as if it had been torn from him, then his deep shudder. He lay atop her, his weight half on her, half on his side, his arms still around her and his body still inside her. His face rested close to hers. His eyes were shut, his lips parted, his chest heaving.

She blinked again, and his long eyelashes lifted. He held her gaze for a moment, looking sleepy and satisfied. "Sweet flower," he murmured, and she smiled. His hand moved to tangle in a length of her hair spread on the pillow. As his fingers curled among the strands he held her gaze with strange intensity. "You are mine, flower. Only mine."

"Yea, lord," she agreed softly, inexplicably filled with an odd emotion that left her close to tears, "I am yours."

She woke first the next morning. Gray light filtered in through an open shutter over the high window. It was still shadowed in the bed, and the candles had long since guttered. The fire, too, had gone out, and the air was cool. But Rhys was warm, his body a solid, heated length close against her, one leg thrown across her as if to hold her. She ached, but only a little.

Her hair was caught beneath him, and his hand was still wrapped in its length. In recent times she'd thought of shearing her hair level with her ears, wearing it like a lad again, but Elspeth had always convinced her otherwise. Now, she was glad she hadn't. Rhys seemed to like it, even if it wasn't the color of ripe wheat or gold coins.

While he slept, she studied him. There was an innocence in his face that wasn't apparent when he was awake, a sweet quality of vulnerability that made her sigh. Why did he feel he must roar and bluster all the time? Life could be so much less complicated if only he would recognize that he wasn't infallible. She had no problem admitting mistakes—well, most of the time. And she'd been gracious enough to yield herself to him without a struggle, though if the truth were told, she'd be forced to admit that she'd wanted him as well.

For the first time, she understood some of what Biagio had tried to tell her. There was a magic of sorts between a man and a woman, a coming together of more than just flesh and bone, a blending of the senses in the most intimate manner imaginable. It had been wonderful. It was probably a very good thing she hadn't known before how wonderful it was. Elspeth's frequent admonishments and warnings of the dangers of yielding to a commoner still rang in her ears, but Rhys was hardly that. Nay, he was

a lord of his own demesne, brave and strong—a fit mate
for a princess. Even Elspeth would see that now.

Surprising, how peaceful and content she felt. She
couldn't recall the last time she'd felt this secure. Had she
ever? Oh yes, she remembered. But that had been so long
ago. She'd been a child, loved by her parents and secure
in that knowledge, playing happily in a world free from
dangerous shadows. Warm sunshine and cool mosaic
floors, lush greenery and laughing children, love freely lavished by adults who always had enough time to spare for
a small child. She'd been happy then. Too happy. Too
content. The shock of losing it all had almost destroyed
her.

But it had not. Somehow, she'd survived those dark
days. But for so long she'd thought peace and happiness
were gone forever, never to be found again. Until the
prophecy. Until the Russian gypsy Rina had taken an
eight-year-old child aside and whispered to her of her future, and the champion who could reclaim all she'd lost.
The mythical griffyn, the magical beast capable of taking
back her legacy, was promised to her. Finally there had
been hope, after years of being mired in dismal despair
that not even Elspeth's efforts had banished. Then he had
come at last. Rhys. And though elusive, the promise of that
sweet contentment hovered closer than it had ever been
since those bright days.

Shifting slightly, she let her gaze roam over him. Sleek,
muscled, golden, as fit and powerful as a lion, he sprawled
in the bed shadows like one of the giant cats. She wouldn't
be surprised if he threw back his tawny mane and let out
an animal roar. Unable to resist, she put out a hand and
trailed her fingers over the taut band of muscles on his
upper abdomen. It was just a light touch, curious and admiring, compelled by a force stronger than herself. She'd
been right that first night—he was a most dangerous male.
And a most beguiling one.

Curiosity—or something close to it—drew her hand
lower. A mighty knight, indeed. She was not completely
ignorant of the workings of a male body, for her life had
not been as sheltered as Elspeth would have liked, but she

found herself slightly amazed that it could change so rapidly and drastically. How fascinating that the powerful male weapon of the previous night should now seem so innocent in slumber.

It was exciting. Dangerous. A compelling lure, and she couldn't resist touching him. Her fingers explored lightly and tentatively, gently gliding over his length.

Her heart gave a sudden lurch when his hand closed around hers, and her eyes flew up to see him watching her. A faint smile curved the hard line of his mouth. "Greedy flower."

She flushed. How like him to say just the wrong thing. She managed a shrug of indifference. "Curious, not yearning. Don't be so vain, my lord. It ill becomes you."

His laugh was soft. Beneath her palm, his body began to stir. She tried to pull away her hand, but his fingers tightened around her wrist. "Now that you have it, shall I show you what to do with it, flower?"

"I'm not certain you'd like my notion of what to do with it," she said tartly. "You may be dismayed at my suggestion."

"I find myself dismayed every time you open your mouth to speak," he said but did not release her hand. "Perhaps we should find something else to do with that busy tongue of yours."

She succeeded in snatching her hand away. Not daring to look anywhere but at his face, she saw the amusement in his eyes. He was laughing at her! How dare he mock her like this?

She sat up, jerking her hair from his other hand, ignoring the sharp sting that motion brought to her scalp. "I have no intention of allowing you to speak to me so vulgarly and crudely. Just because I allowed you to bed me, doesn't mean you have the right to—"

"Allowed me?" His brows lowered. "You allowed me because I gave you no choice. Though if I'd known you were lying again, I might not have taken you so quickly."

She stared at him. Was he sorry for it? It had not occurred to her that she'd displeased him. She'd been so caught up in the unfamiliar haze of passion that she'd not even noticed his reaction. But now she recalled his frowning stare, the way he'd paused.

"What does lying have to do with anything?"

He reached for her, dragging her down and beneath him, his arousal pressing against her thigh. He kissed her. "Nothing. Everything. You should have told me and I would have been more gentle."

His hands moved over her, reaching lower, stroking her and making her shiver so that she clutched at him and the sense of their conversation drifted away. Before she lost control completely, she grasped at the place where they'd left off. "Told you what?"

"That you lied. That you were a virgin." His tongue trailed a wet fire between her breasts, then paused to lavish attention on the beaded nipple. A low, heated pulse began between her thighs and in her belly, and after a few moments, she sighed softly and reached for him.

"Oh. That. It doesn't matter now."

"No," he agreed, nipping lightly at her breast with his lips, "it doesn't matter now. Now, flower, you are mine. Only mine." He moved up and over her, his body a hard, exciting promise. He surged forward, making her gasp softly at the slight ache as he filled her, his eyes holding hers as he repeated, "Only mine."

Yes, yes. She was his. Only his. Oh, God help her, she couldn't think when he was with her like this, could only feel, only react, as if she were swept away by a whirlwind. And the aching emptiness inside her, that small secret hope that she'd thought long dead, slowly began to come to life. Like a flower that had withered from neglect, shriveled and stiff, the hope lifted tiny, trusting shoots toward his warmth.

She answered his thrusts with her own, fierce and wild, not a battle but a contested surrender, a yielding without concession. Hot, sweet, a meeting of more than flesh— something else, something elusive, hovering just out of reach, an intangible emotion that she could glimpse but not catch.

And then it was gone, that fleeting glimpse, fading into the pounding reality of Rhys's body, his eyes holding hers,

clear gray and light tricked, mocking and proud and hopeful. And with a swiftness that was frightening, she suddenly knew what Elspeth had meant: There was much
more involved in yielding her body than just the obvious.
He had a hold on her now that was much stronger than
any magic.

A rattling knock on the chamber door woke him. Rhys
opened his eyes and frowned. Sasha muttered a sleepy protest, and he looked down at her. Surprising. A virgin after
all, against all odds. He wasn't sorry for taking her, but
resented her lie. A foolish lie. One more proof of her du-
plicity. She'd obviously never meant to yield all to him
willingly.

The knock sounded again, and he growled a reply that
woke Sasha. She rolled over and looked up at him with a
dreamy smile. Her long, thick lashes fluttered slightly. She
drew a finger along the line of his jaw. He smiled a grudging reply and caught her hand in a light clasp.

"If I don't answer the door, Brian will most likely break
it down. He'll think you've taken me to faerie hill."

"An enticing notion, my lord. Perhaps I will."

He slanted her a glance as he lifted himself off the bed.
The bar holding the door slid back with a solid thud, and
he wrenched it open. Brian blinked twice, then reddened
as he realized the situation.

Amused, Rhys held the door wider. "Come in, Brian."

Sidling along the wall, Brian managed to avoid looking
toward the bed. He cleared his throat once, then twice,
and fixed his gaze on the wooden tub. "Lady Cailin ex-
pressed a desire to meet with you at once, my lord. She
insists that she is innocent of treachery."

"Yea, I can imagine that she would hope so." Rhys
crossed to the chest Morgan had brought in the night before, and flung open the top. He pulled out clean garments,
shut and locked the chest, and began dressing. "Were you
able to discover any important facts?"

"A few." Brian coughed slightly. "It seems that her marriage was not one of choice, but thrust upon her after the

death of your father. Gavin wed her before the bodies were cold, is what I understand."

"Yet she seemed so defensive of him last night." He pulled a fine linen tunic over his head and laced it at the throat, then reached for a leather jerkin. "Now she claims it was no love match."

Brian shrugged. "I think she's being truthful about that. She's caught in a threatening situation, and is trying to think of the best way out."

He pulled on his jerkin and reached for his belt. "And you believe her."

Another shrug lifted Brian's shoulders. "It seems logical. And anyway, easy to prove or disprove once we're able to question other prisoners and some of the soldiers that swore to you. It would be foolish for her to claim otherwise."

"Yet females rarely see beyond the moment of the lie to the eventual discovery," he muttered, thinking of the girl in his bed. "They think only of what they want, not what is best." He half turned to look at her. She met his gaze coolly, small chin lifted in that familiar gesture of defiance that never failed to rally his temper. Brazen wench. She hadn't even the decency to properly cover herself, but sat as proud and bold as if she were fully clothed. Her bare shoulders gleamed in the shadowed light beneath the bed hangings, and though her knees were drawn up to her chest and the coverlet draped over her, she revealed far more than she should have.

For reasons he couldn't explain even to himself, Rhys snarled a demand that she close the bed-curtains and stop displaying herself. There was a moment of silence, a flash of her eyes, then a sweet smile that should have been warning enough. Still, he wasn't quite prepared when she shoved aside the coverlet and rose to her knees in the bed, bare breasts thrust out impudently as she reached for the hangings in all her exposed beauty.

Brian wheezed. Rhys stood still, immobilized by her blatant insolence as she slowly drew the curtains closed, taking much too long. Finally heavy cloth concealed her. The bed ropes squeaked as she settled herself into the mattress. Soft laughter sounded from the enclosure.

After a moment of appalled silence, Brian said, "There is meat and bread below in the hall. I'll go down and wait on you. We can finish our discussion later."

"No," he said, so angry he could scarcely think, "we'll finish it now. I'll go to the hall with you." If he stayed, he'd likely do damage to the wench, and he didn't need to begin his first morning at Glenlyon with a murder.

He buckled his belt and grabbed his sword, slamming the door as he left the chamber. A guard snapped to attention, and Rhys gave him terse orders to make certain the lady did not leave that room. Fixing the man with a harsh stare, he repeated, "She is not to leave for any man but me, do you understand?"

"Yea, my lord," the poor guard replied, "I understand full well."

"Be certain you do. If she escapes,'twill be your head as well as hers."

Brian was quiet as they passed down the corridor to the stairwell, and kept his silence until they reached the great hall. All traces of the previous night's events had been removed. Clean rushes had been strewn on the floor, new candles placed in the holders, and rushlights in the outer hallway. Servants moved quietly and efficiently about their business, setting up the long tables and benches that ran diagonally to the high table on the dais. The smell of food was enticing, and trenchers of bread already adorned some of the tables. A silver nef sat atop the high table, but salt and spices were set out in more humble containers on the lower tables.

"Owain has been up since well before first light," Brian said as they moved toward the dais, "seeing to all the necessary details. Fortunately, Gavin didn't have enough time to do too much damage to keep or supplies."

Rhys nodded approval. His anger cooled as he looked around. It was an odd feeling, coming back to a well-known place to find everything so familiar, yet so different. The location he remembered well, and the village and surrounding landscape were almost the same. But this—gone was the rough wooden keep, though some of the buildings bore close resemblance to the old ones. He tried to envision his father at the head of the hall, sitting in the high-backed chair that awaited the lord of Glenlyon, but found it too difficult.

Griffyn ap Griffyd he better remembered as a burly, gruff man clad in rough garments and pelts, his face weather-beaten and commanding, his domain as wild and savage as all their Welsh ancestors. It was hard relating that man to the man that must have inhabited this dwelling.

"I feel like a stranger," he muttered, and Brian nodded. "But you are true lord here, Rhys. None can deny that." He smiled. "No, they can't."

He began to feel more comfortable when he finally sat in the high-backed chair with griffyns embroidered on the bolsters. He looked down the tables at the familiar faces of his knights and soldiers, gathering to break their night-long fast. Most were men he'd fought with, some he'd known before accompanying Richard to Jerusalem, others he'd met in that distant place and since. All were sworn to him. And once matters were settled, with his place as lord secure, there would be oaths of fealty to accept. Yea, it began to feel right.

After the morning meal, while servants were clearing trenchers and cups and feeding the noisy pack of hounds the scraps, Owain came to him with the day's business. First in importance was the disposition of prisoners and the summons to be sent out. Rhys decided to save the question of Gavin and Cailin and deal with the other prisoners first.

Bowen ap Owain was brought before him, and he eyed Owain's son with a narrow stare. The young man was nervous but met Rhys's gaze steadily.

"You know the charges," Rhys said when they'd been read aloud, "and I've heard your witnesses."

Bowen nodded. "Yea, lord."

"How do you plead?"

"Guilty with reason."

Rhys studied him. "State your reasons."

Chains clanked as Bowen shifted from one foot to the other. His father stood nearby, silent and tense, waiting. Clearing his throat, Bowen said evenly, "I was given the choice of taking up my father's duties or watching him die. I chose the first, my lord, despite my loathing for it."

"Yet your father languished in prison to be starved to death. What did you accomplish?"

"I could not prevent that, but by my efforts, he was taken enough food to keep him alive."

Someone coughed, and a quarrel broke out between two dogs that was quickly silenced by one of the guards. Rhys said nothing. The story had the ring of truth in it, for certain, and the very fact that Owain was still alive and in reasonable health despite his ordeal was proof that he'd received enough sustenance. He was inclined to acquit Bowen of any blame.

Looking up, he saw other prisoners watching and listening. There were others who might also plead fear as an excuse, when they'd had no threats but their own cowardice. If he showed any sign of weakness to the men who'd served his father, he would lose respect. No man wanted to serve a weak leader. But if he was too harsh, he'd be held in contempt and fear. The fear he didn't mind, but he would not risk the contempt.

"Bowen ap Owain," he said, "I believe that you were forced to submit under pain of your father's unjust punishment, but that does not completely absolve you. Because you had no hand in the rebellion that saw my father and brothers slain, I grant you your life. Nor will I maim you for taking up arms against me, but you shall not go unpunished. I sentence you to receive fifteen lashes on the day after the morrow, after which you shall be freed."

Bowen paled slightly but did not quiver. He nodded. "Aye, lord, I accept your judgment."

Rhys met Owain's eyes. A faint smile pressed the corners of the steward's mouth; he nodded slightly and held up a scroll.

"The next prisoner to be brought up on charges is Arnallt of Cwnllew, who has no witnesses to swear for him . . ."

It was midday before the prisoners' judgments were given. There were no death sentences, for those who fought for Gavin had fought to the death. John's men he dared not hang, though he wouldn't have minded it. Prison sentences were meted out, and judgments pronounced. Only two prisoners remained—Gavin and his wife.

Gavin, he dealt with first.

A faint sneer curled his cousin's mouth as he was brought in, his limbs hung with heavy chains. His feet dragged over the floor with loud clanks of metal, and he was forced to his knees in front of Rhys. His eyes burned with hatred, and he refused to bend his head.

"So, cousin, you return to Wales," Gavin said harshly. "Not as I would have once thought, however."

"You chose the circumstances." Rhys slapped the hilt of his dagger into his open palm, idly, as if bored. In truth, it was all he could do not to step down from the dais and slit his cousin's throat. "If I had made the choice, I would never have returned to Wales had it meant my father's death."

Gavin snorted disbelief. "I find that difficult to believe. A rogue knight with no lands and no title, a hostage more English than Welsh? And you say you prefer it? I've done you a favor, cousin."

Rhys leaned forward. "You've chosen your own death, cousin."

"Kill me and Prince John will have you in chains for the executioner before you can blink," Gavin snarled. "I have his protection and his sanction."

"And I have Richard's."

Gavin laughed. "Richard is in Jerusalem and has no thought of England or Wales, save how much money he can wring from the treasuries. Would he leave his precious Crusades to come to your aid?"

"Do you really think Richard's arm so short he cannot affect matters of state?" Rhys smiled. "He has a long reach, cousin, even from Jerusalem. And if he thinks John is set for betrayal, it will go badly with that prince, I can assure you. There's little enough love between them as it is, with all that bad business about John's attempts on William the Marshal still so fresh in Richard's mind. William was King Henry's favorite, and Richard trusts him."

Drawing in a deep breath, Gavin blew it out again slowly. "Then I am at your mercy for the moment, but do not think John will swallow this bitter news without retaliation. I pity the man who incurs his enmity."

"Between the two, I would choose John's enmity over Richard's." Rhys smiled. "Even John quails before Richard, as he has proved over and over again by fleeing after yet another of his treacherous schemes has failed. When Richard returns from Jerusalem, John will be boxed in again."

"I am wed to your sister," Gavin said then, "and am rightful heir when Glenlyon is left untended."

Rhys stood up, tightly gripping his dagger in one hand. "It was not left untended until you murdered the rightful lord. Be grateful that John stands between you and a slow death at this moment. It will give you time to reflect on your sins until Richard returns. When he is back, I intend to have you hung on Glenlyon's walls as an example for any other man foolish enough to consider murder."

As Gavin made an incoherent noise low in his throat, Rhys signaled the guards to drag him away. It was deathly quiet in the great hall, save for the rattle of Gavin's chains and his gabbling protests as he was removed. Then silence fell again, and Rhys slowly realized that he was still standing and gripping his dagger. He looked down, not surprised to see a bright line of blood where the blade had cut into his skin. It seemed that he was his own worst enemy at times, and he allowed Brian to come and bandage it before he faced the problem of his half-sister.

Apparently, she had witnessed his confrontation with her husband, for she was pale and defiant, her eyes wide and frightened despite her air of bravado. He took a deep breath and sip of wine, then set down the cup and looked at her.

For some reason, Cailin reminded him of Sasha. Perhaps

it was her defiance and the way her chin jutted out so pugnaciously. Or it could have been her tart tongue.

"As John is not my protector, I suppose I'm to be killed now," she snapped. A slight quiver in her voice betrayed her fear.

"Who are your witnesses that you wed Gavin under duress?" he asked mildly, and was surprised when Brian stepped forward.

Flushing slightly at Rhys's amazed regard, the Irishman said loudly, "I was not here of course, but I can produce several witnesses to state that she was forced into the marriage, my lord."

Recovering from his surprise, Rhys nodded. "Produce them, Sir Brian."

Brian hesitated. "One of them is Bowen ap Owain, and since he was not convicted of treason, his word should be good."

Another surprise. He scowled. Apparently, Brian's regard of the maid had grown. He shifted and nodded. "Very well. Bring him back to testify for her, and any others you think can bear witness."

Testimony on Cailin's behalf was short. Exonerating. With her father and brothers dead, she'd found herself heir and wed to Gavin within the day. It had not been her choice, but her fate. And now he must decide what to do with her.

He stared at her. This was different than the others, for not only was she female, she was young and helpless. There had been no one to keep her from Gavin, and Rhys could not render harsh judgment on the innocent. Yet she was no longer a maid, and still wed to his cousin and enemy. He rubbed at his eyes.

"The marriage will be annulled and you will be found another husband," he said after a moment. His gaze rested on her flushed face. "One more to your liking, perhaps."

"That man does not live," she retorted. "I refuse to wed."

He frowned. An unwed maid of marriageable age and with a sizable dowry would be more trouble than he cared to contemplate on top of everything else. Weariness made his temper short. "You'll do what you're told."

"You'll have to kill me first."

"In my present mood," he snarled, "that might be your next choice."

"My lord," Brian protested in alarm, "the lady is over-wrought. Give me leave to see her taken back to her chamber for now."

He stood up. "You have my leave, Sir Brian, but watch your back. She seems the type for sharp daggers."

When they'd left, Brian dragging Cailin from the hall, Rhys turned to Owain. "See that her marriage is annulled as quickly as possible. I need to find her a husband who will take her off my hands."

"Yea, my lord." Owain scrawled an entry on the parchment he held and looked up. "It will be done."

There was a faint gleam of sympathy in the steward's eyes that made Rhys hesitate. He met his gaze. "I gave the best judgments I could under the given circumstances, Owain."

"Yea, my lord, I agree. They were fair judgments. All of them."

It was the closest he could come to asking for approval, and Owain's answer was enough. Rhys smiled slightly and nodded. Then he left the dais and moved to the curve of stairs that led up to his own chamber. As long as he was in this mood, he might as well deal with the naked, rebellious wench he'd left in his bed.

CHAPTER SIXTEEN

᷒ᲛᲘᲝᲒ

The gown was almost dry. Sasha felt along the seams, where it was still slightly wet, then decided to wear it anyway. It had grown late, and she didn't want to chance meeting Rhys again without being clothed. A faint smile curved her mouth. What a sight he had been, staring at her with fury in his eyes, speechless for once. It was almost worth the scene she knew was imminent.

And Brian . . . Laughing softly, she slipped her clean, ragged gown over her head, shivering slightly at the dampness of the seams. Brian had been the most entertaining, with his wheezing rattle and bulging eyes. And the thoughts he'd held . . . yea, it was his dark regard that had first prompted her to mischief, and she couldn't say she was sorry. But the knight had been so dismayed at the indisputable evidence before him, he'd not taken care to guard his thoughts or reaction to her. Faced with evidence of Rhys's bedding her, he'd come to the immediate conclusion that she had bewitched his lord.

He still considered her a veritable crone, until she had risen from the mound of coverlet and leisurely drawn closed the bed-curtains at Rhys's arrogant command. That should teach both of them a lesson. Brian, she knew, already viewed her differently. And Rhys? It should be interesting to see if she had taught him anything.

Pushing back a strand of hair from her eyes, she crossed to the table and reached for a chunk of bread. It was hard now, and the meat had grown cold and congealed in its own grease, but no one had brought her anything else to eat. Save for the guard at the door, she'd spoken with no one. And the guard had informed her that none was allowed into the chamber and she was not allowed out. That had been that. He'd obstinately refused her request for a maidservant. Nothing she said could convince him differently.

Piqued, she'd barred the door, though it had taken a struggle to lift the heavy bar and wedge it into the hasp. Then she'd bathed, washed her clothes in the cold, soapy water of the tub, and explored what interested her. She'd felt no compunction about going through his chest, but found mostly clothes. It had been locked, but that was no problem. Most locks were simple matters, easily picked open. A man in Seville had taught her the art, but he'd been hung for it, and so she'd never felt easy about using the talent.

Until now. Circumstances were too unreliable to rule out anything that might help her situation. Perhaps Elspeth had arrived at Glenlyon by now. Once she had, there would have to be a way to arrange a meeting with her and Biagio. She missed Elspeth. For all her fussing and protective warnings, Elspeth was a sane and guiding light in her life.

Sasha sighed. She'd know, of course. As soon as Elspeth saw her, she'd know what had happened with Rhys. There was no way to hide things from her, for Elspeth seemed to see inside Sasha's soul with a remarkable keenness. The older woman just didn't say it as bluntly as Biagio did.

Biagio. He'd been right. But how had he known when she hadn't, when she thought more of the prophecy than she did of Rhys? And now—now it was all mixed up, the prophecy and her legacy and Rhys. But she had to be right about that. What else had she lost that was so important to her? Her home, her childhood. And the last no one could restore.

Frowning, she perched on the stool and nibbled at the bread, contemplating all the ways and days that had brought her to this moment.

Afternoon light streamed through the unshuttered window before Rhys returned. She lifted her head, smiling slightly when she heard him in the hallway. Placid and waiting, she heard him speak with the guard, then heard him try the door. It was barred on the inside, and he rattled it so hard the frame shook. Her smile widened.

Rising slowly, she crossed to the door and struggled with the bar for a moment, sliding it across the hasp to land with a clatter on the floor. The door swung open immediately, banging loudly against the frame. Rhys stood in the opening, his eyes as dark as storm clouds.

"What the devil do you mean barring me from this chamber?" His voice was much cooler than his eyes and somehow, infinitely more threatening. She took a step back.

"I did not bar you, my lord. If I'd meant to keep you out, you would not now be standing here."

The subtle warning seemed to miss its mark. He slammed the door shut and turned to lean against it. She began to think she'd misjudged the effect of her strategy. The barred door was meant to symbolize her ability to shut him out of her life should he be foolish enough to risk it. Perhaps she'd been too subtle. When he left earlier, she'd known he would think of how last he'd seen her, naked and in his bed. As she'd meant him to. To return and find the door barred against him had seemed the perfect way to remind him that she might not always be at his disposal.

Now it didn't seem like such a good plan. In fact, she may have erred grievously.

His gaze flicked around the room, came to rest on her, then shifted again. At the exact moment he saw it, she remembered that she'd forgotten to close his carved wood and leather chest. Another step back seemed expedient for survival. His gaze returned to her, ice cold and piercing.

"Were you looking for something in particular, flower?"

"No." A quick breath for courage. "Nothing in particular. Just . . . just curious."

"Ah. And I thought it was locked."

"It was." Might as well confess. A simple glance at the lock would be enough to reveal the truth. "I—I unlocked it."

"Without a key? Or did you use magic?"

She winced a little. "Neither. It's an easy lock to open if one knows how."

"Suppose you show me." His voice was still soft, not exactly the enraged roar she'd expected. She shifted uneasily.

"I'd rather not."

He moved toward her then, and even though she wanted to flee, she knew it was useless. There was nowhere to go. So she stood her ground, chin lifted to meet whatever he might say or do, hands clasped behind her to hide their trembling.

Taking her by the arm, he moved her to sit on a stool next to the table, then leaned over her, bracing his lean frame with one hand on each side of her. His face was close, and it was easy to see the pinpoint flames of fury in storm gray eyes as he held her gaze.

He smiled, a lion closing in on its prey, and she went cold. There was banked fury in his eyes and purring voice, a warning that she could not miss. "Tell me, flower, what you seek. Perhaps I can help you find it."

"I told you . . . nothing. I'm just . . . curious. It's a bad habit of mine, and one I should really break." She took a shuddering breath. "Really."

"Another lie? If lies were stones, you'd have a formidable fortress built by now, flower." He straightened. "Or a crypt."

She winced. The imagery was obvious. She looked up at him. "All right, I'll tell you what I was looking for—the truth."

"And how would you recognize truth when you're so

unfamiliar with it?" He shook his head, the look he gave her cool and dangerous. "Try again, flower."

How could she explain that she'd been looking for a piece of him? Something to hold and cherish, a piece of his past or his present that would lend her insight into what made him who he was. She knew some things, small facts gleaned from his men, but there was so much she didn't know. So much she wanted to know. And he'd have to use torture to wring *that* truth from her.

Angry more at herself than him, she shrugged her shoulders. "I have no defense. Anything I say you'll just use against me or ignore, so why should I bother? Think what you want to. You will anyway."

He stepped to the side, lifted the wine flagon and a cup, then hesitated. It was obvious he was wondering if she'd had access to her herbs, but she refused to give him the satisfaction of knowing. After a moment, he set down the wine and turned back to her.

"Gavin is imprisoned. My steward is writing the letter that asks permission for his trial and execution for the deaths of my father and brothers."

A warning, apparently, but not one that bothered her. She shrugged. "I hope you get permission if that's what you want."

"It's what I want. And you? What do you want?"

She lifted her gaze from his belt buckle to his face. "You know what I want. I've told you enough times."

"No, you've told me what you think would satisfy me. Or some ridiculous tale of prophecy and vengeance."

"Ridiculous?" She shook her head, anger making her voice tight. "No more ridiculous than petitioning the king to exact vengeance on your cousin. It was my father's cousin who betrayed him. Why should my desire for vengeance be any less?"

"Is that what you're after? Did you think if you helped Gavin win that he'd fulfill some foolish prophecy for you?"

She shot to her feet like a bolt from a crossbow, forgetting caution in her frustration and rage. "Gavin, Gavin, I'm sick of hearing about your stupid cousin. I'm talking about my father's cousin, about Al-Hamin. I never met Gavin until his men brought me here, and I didn't betray you to him."

"Another lie." He caught her by the arm when she threw up her hands in disgust and whirled to stalk away. Spinning her back around, he gripped her tightly by her upper arms, fingers digging painfully into her flesh. "You knew him before, because you described him perfectly to me in Wytham. Have you forgotten that?"

She stared at him. Then the memory returned, of her stammering fear and description of a weasel face and dark burning eyes—and cloven hooves and horns. How was she to know it resembled Gavin? She shook her head. "I made it up. I would have said anything then. You were so angry and I was so nervous. It was just coincidence—"

"A coincidence such as your meeting me in the weald? in the meadow? and again in Wytham?" His grip tightened. "A few too many coincidences, I think."

Belatedly, she saw the awful net of her lies and half-truths close in around her. Doom. There was nothing she could say now that wouldn't sound like another lie, and the new truth was so silly and half-formed that she wasn't even certain of it herself.

All she could manage was a weak "But it's true, my lord."

That didn't satisfy him. She saw it in his face, in the terrible truth of his eyes. Disaster. Nothing she said would convince him that she'd never meant harm to him, only wanted him to help her. And if she was honest with herself, she had to admit that it did sound ridiculous, for all that it was the truth.

Yet she felt compelled to try again. She put her hands on his forearms where the muscles bunched beneath the fine linen of his tunic. With his grip on her so tight, it was all she could do. "You may believe me, Lord Rhys. I never betrayed you. I never meant you harm."

A tremor went through his taut muscles, and there was a sudden flash in his eyes. It was quickly gone, and his long lashes lowered to hide himself from her.

Deliberately, coldly, he said, "You are made of lies. There's no reason for me to believe you now."

And he stepped away from her, releasing her, moving away into the shaft of light that came through the window and tangled in the sun gold of his hair, and she felt an awful, aching emptiness again. A teasing move, a barred door, and he was lost to her. What had she done? How had she erred so gravely? The small flower of trust and hope that had slowly lifted its head to the sunlight shriveled again, plunging her back into the cold, barren winter that had been inside her so long.

Cartwheels rattled on the stones of the inner bailey, and the donkey brayed softly as it came to a stop. Rhys turned, eying the old woman guiding the cart. Elspeth. She looked up and saw him, and her gaze sharpened.

He turned away. His reserve of patience for Sasha and her servants was nearly depleted. He had no desire to be confronted with another scene such as the one he'd barely tolerated earlier from the Italian whelp. Amazing that such a treacherous wench could inspire such devotion and loyalty. How on earth did she manage it?

Deliberately putting her from his mind, he focused again on the problem at hand, discussing with Sir Peter the housing of troops and animals. But, when he turned to leave, he wasn't surprised to find Elspeth waiting for him.

"My lord," she said, and he stopped to look at her. Her eyes were worried but steady, her face creased with concern. "Is my lady well?"

"Better than she should be." His cool words did nothing to alleviate the distress in her eyes, and he silently cursed. He looked past Elspeth to the storerooms, where men were busily sorting and recording supplies. Kegs of salted meat were being counted, stores of wheat and corn being figured, and barrels of ale and wine casks tallied. It was a long and arduous task, but necessary. He looked back at Elspeth. "She is in a comfortable chamber under guard. Not mistreated, but neither is she trusted."

Elspeth nodded. She didn't seem very surprised by that last. "May I see her?"

He studied her for a moment. Sunlight was bright in the bailey, picking out the gray hair peeking from beneath Elspeth's head covering, showing the faint lines that fanned from the corners of her eyes, and the steady glow of honesty that even he could recognize.

"If you will tell me," he said abruptly, "why she followed me."

Elspeth hesitated. Her fingers smoothed an invisible wrinkle from her gown, brows lowering as she considered his request. Then she said, "It will sound foolish."

"No more foolish than what I've already heard," he retorted. "Tell me."

A faint smile curved her mouth, and she nodded. "I can imagine what she told you. Yet I have a feeling that what I'll say will sound just as foolish." She took a deep breath. "She told you of the prophecy."

"Jésu, not that again—"

"Hear me out, my lord, please." She put up a hand when he would have turned away. "It's true enough, though not, perhaps, as she told you. Or even as she knows herself. It's rather a long story, should you care to hear it."

A loud clatter of wagons rumbled over the stones, and men cursed and strained at heavy burdens, almost drowning out Elspeth's words. Rhys took her by the arm. "Come inside. We'll discuss it in the hall. I have a feeling I might want to hear this after all."

The great hall was empty of people. Only dogs roved the floor among the rushes, wandering, sniffing, roaming as castle dogs did, intent upon their own business and oblivious of human presence until meal time. Clean rushes lent a gentle fragrance to air spiced with the scent of candles and burning wood. Rhys seated Elspeth on a wooden bench near the open fire.

She looked up at him, spreading her hands on her knees. He noted that her fingers shook slightly. She took a deep breath, managed a wavering smile, and said, "I don't know how much she's told you, but she has the memories of a child, seen from a child's perspective. And because it was the kindest thing, I've allowed her to hold to those memories."

When she paused, he frowned. "All I know from her is that she claims I'm the answer to some vague prophecy. I'm supposed to claim her legacy for her. A hilly patch of sand and some goats, or something like that."

Elspeth smiled faintly. "Not quite. It's a beautiful spot, actually, a garden on the Euphrates River. Cool water, green trees, and white-washed towers and minarets ... lovely. My lady—Sasha's mother—came to appreciate the beauty, though she longed for home and England. We both did. It was not our choice to be there, you understand."

A delicate pause lengthened, and he nodded. "Arranged marriages are often hard for a woman."

"It wasn't even that, my lord." Elspeth sighed. "Sasha does not know, but her parents were not wed. Ben Al-Farouk was a sultan, a caliph, if you will, with many wives and concubines. It was accepted. Natural. He had wives and children and relatives everywhere. Then the Crusaders came to Arabia, men such as yourself. They brought women with them, not all of them willing. Some were captives, stolen from ships bound for foreign ports. Such was the fate of my lady, Elfreda. Sasha's mother. She was to wed a wealthy Spanish nobleman, but our ship was attacked and the women taken. Ben Al-Farouk purchased Elfreda in a slave mart, and because she was so beautiful and clever, he allowed himself to be persuaded to buy me as well." Her voice shook slightly at the memory, and faded.

Rhys beckoned to a passing servant and had wine brought for Elspeth. She gratefully sipped from a cup, gathering her composure. He knew of such things, of course. Captured women were a common enough occurrence. His brow lifted, and Elspeth met his inquiring gaze with a slight nod.

"Sasha thinks they were wed, my lord. I've not had the heart to tell her differently. She remembers an adoring mother and affectionate father, and I cannot tarnish that memory."

"Then this legacy she claims—"

"Is not hers. If she had been a mature male, strong and warlike, she might have rallied men and reclaimed the lands stolen by Al-Hamin. But of course, she is not. Yet to a child, the hope that one day she would return to the place where she'd known such happiness and peace was all she had. Everyone was gone. Everyone. Her father and mother slaughtered, the wives and concubines and any child that could possibly grow up one day with a valid claim—slain in that terrible massacre."

"If Al-Hamin slaughtered everyone, why not her as well?" Another silence fell, and he could see that she was measuring him as if to gauge how much could be told and believed. He frowned. "The truth."

"Lady Elfreda knew of Al-Hamin's treachery but could not convince Ben Al-Farouk. He would not believe her, a mere woman, over the smooth speech and promises of Al-Hamin. And so she made her preparations. It would be impossible for her to escape, for eunuchs closely guarded all the women. But her child . . . I did as I was told, though it broke my heart . . . I left my beautiful Elfreda early one morning . . . I can still see her face, those eyes . . . and the knowing and love in them . . ." She sobbed suddenly, one hand curling to press against her mouth, tears wetting her own eyes. "We did," she said after a moment, "as she wanted, though Sasha did not know the truth. She was only five. We went to the marketplace, and there met the caravan that had been arranged. I gave them the promised payment of jewelry, and they took us with them, out of the marketplace and across the sands. I looked back only once, and saw the smoke rising into the sky, and knew that Elfreda had not been wrong. I made her a promise, my lord, that I would always watch over her beloved daughter. And so I have. And so I will, though it may cost me everything." She took a shuddering breath. "I love her. Because I love her, I cannot hurt her. She thinks she's a princess, and in truth, she is. But she has no legacy. Nothing but memories and hope to take her through the days, and I do not want those taken away."

Silence fell again. A burning log popped in the fire pit. He turned to gaze at the flames. It explained much. He kicked idly at a tangle of rushes beneath his feet, then looked up. "And the prophecy?"

"That once puzzled me. We had to hide at first, you see, for I was not certain if Al-Hamin would miss a little princess. We stayed with the caravan of Russians for some time. There was an old Russian woman who had the sight. Rina could foretell the future. She gave Sasha her new name; and it was Rina who promised that one day a griffyn would appear to her and return to her all that she had lost. Sasha immediately decided that meant she would reclaim her lands one day." She smiled slightly. "I think I know the true meaning now, though for a long time, I thought it only a kindly meant attempt to comfort a grieving child."

He could understand what Sasha must have felt, understand the confusion and bewilderment, the pain at losing those she loved. It explained a lot but still did not excuse her lies. Hadn't he felt the same? Hadn't he been betrayed by those he loved when still a child? Yet he held his sworn word dear and would not break an oath. He looked up at Elspeth, and she returned his gaze steadily.

"My lord, I know that you must think her a liar, a fraud, or a cheat. But listen—she has always had to play a part. Since the day we left her home behind, she has masqueraded as what she is not. First, she was a boy, to hide her identity. When she grew old enough and her body made that lie impossible, she became what every stranger needed her to be—a poet, a magician, a dancer, or whatever was required at the moment for survival. It wasn't always easy, but it required great talent and resilience. Never has anyone allowed her to be herself. I'm not certain *she* even knows herself anymore."

"Why do you tell me all this? She won't thank you for it."

"Nay." Elspeth drew in another deep breath. "She

wouldn't thank me for it at all. Yet I feel that you must know, though I cannot say why."

He didn't know why either. It told him nothing, beyond the fact that her childhood had been as uncertain as his. He stared into the fire with a frown. It occurred to him that his childhood had been composed of harsh truths, while hers had been made of airy lies. Two entirely different forms of betrayal, but painful for both of them. He looked back at Elspeth.

"I'm glad you told me the truth about her. It doesn't excuse her lies, but it explains them."

"That's all that matters, my lord." Elspeth stood up, her hands smoothing her skirts. "Now that I'm here, may I see her?"

"I'd better take you. Her guard has strict orders not to allow in anyone but myself." He smiled wryly. "She's adept at trickery."

"Yea, lord, I know that. She learned early and well. 'Tis a skill that rarely fails her."

They were almost to the chamber when he paused and turned to look down at her. "Tell me one more thing— what is that whelp to her?"

Elspeth blinked. Then her brows lifted. "Do you mean Biagio?"

"Yea. That's who I mean." His mouth tightened. "He's always near her, always protecting her. While I know they were not lovers, I would know the truth of their friendship."

"It is just that, my lord—friendship. Biagio came to us near five years ago, a frightened orphan boy, belligerent and cocky, and all alone in the world. He's been a blessing. There have been times neither Sasha nor I could have managed without him." She smiled slightly, and he didn't like the way her eyes took on a knowing gleam. "But that is all they are, my lord. Friends of the heart."

He didn't reply to that but walked her to the door and instructed the guard to allow her in. When the door opened, he heard Sasha's glad cry of greeting, and stepped back into the corridor. He exchanged a glance with the guard, then went back down to the hall.

It was just his bad fortune that the first person he chanced upon was Biagio. The youth was sitting on a stool near the fire, scowling. He looked up and saw Rhys, and slowly rose to his feet.

"I've been waiting for you, my lord."

Rhys just lifted a brow and shrugged, walking past him to the wine. Biagio followed him, as Rhys had somehow known he would, and hovered at his elbow as he poured wine into a cup. Irritable, he turned to rake the youth with a hard stare. "If you've come to plead her cause, let me give you a word of warning—don't."

"If you're talking about my lady—"

"I'm talking about Sasha." He took an angry sip of wine. "I still haven't made up my mind what to do about her, so anything you say will be for naught."

Biagio stared at him. "Haven't you already done it?"

His fingers tightened around the stem of the cup, and his temper rose. "Already done what, whelp?"

"Made her your whore. Isn't that enough?"

Before he thought about it, his arm moved in a reflexive action. The back of his hand caught Biagio across the face and knocked him backward to sprawl on the floor. Standing over him, he said softly, "She is no whore. Mind your tongue, or you're not likely to keep it much longer."

A small trickle of blood seeped from one corner of his mouth and his eyes were filled with rage, but Biagio nodded curtly. He stared up in silent defiance.

Rhys had seen the same expression aplenty, in keeps everywhere. It was the numb patience of an animal that has been beaten too often, yet refuses to cower. He'd seen wives and daughters with that look in their eyes, as well, and men so craven they had to beat the weaker to feel powerful. Never had he thought it would be turned on him.

He took a step back and held out his palm. "Get up, whelp. I've not harmed your lady."

Ignoring his hand, Biagio rolled to his feet and stood, brushing rushes and dirt from his jerkin. "Haven't you?" His head lifted, eyes boldly meeting Rhys's gaze. "Do you

think I don't know what you had in mind when you took
her from the kitchen last night?"

"It's none of your business what I had in mind. I didn't
harm her. She's well and as reckless as always. Never fear
about that."

"I'd have to hear her say that before I'd believe it."

Rhys held his temper with an effort. He couldn't blame
him for wanting to see her safe. "Elspeth is with her now.
I just left them together, and I doubt they need you there.
Have some wine. Sit down. When you're calm, I'll take
you to see her."

"Is she your prisoner?"

"Yes. Of a sort. Not as you might think. There are no
chains, no bars on the windows. But neither do I want her
fleeing just yet."

Biagio's eyes narrowed slightly. "Why not? Are you
afraid she'll betray you? I thought Gavin was already in
chains and you are lord here. Why would you fear what
she might do?"

"I don't fear what she might do. But neither do I relish
the idea of having to chase her across half of Wales and
all of England should she decide she's not happy here."

Biagio smiled. "And her happiness is important to you,
my lord?"

"Not in the least. My peace is important to me. And
when I'm ready to release her, I will." He set down the
cup and wiped his hand where some of the wine had
spilled on the table, then looked up at Biagio again.
"Gavin may be in chains, but Richard is still in Jerusalem.
I have no intention of loosing my cousin or your lady until
I hear from the king. Is that plain enough?"

Shrugging, Biagio said, "More plain than you know, my
lord. I can understand keeping Gavin under chains. Sasha
is an entirely different matter. She's no threat to you."

"She's a threat to anyone she chances to meet." He
picked up his wine again. "She has more lies than an oak
tree has leaves, and she sheds them just as easily."

"Not unless she's forced to lie. There are those men who
will not listen to or accept the truth." Biagio turned as if
to go, then looked back at him. "Not everyone has been

fortunate enough to know who they are, my lord. Some of us must invent ourselves every day, or we would not survive. Just because you've not been put in that position, don't think it doesn't exist. It's real. Very real."

"Don't presume to tell me how harsh life can be, whelp. I've lived it much longer than you, and know full well the cruel realities. But it's not made me a liar. I can still recognize the truth. And tell it."

A faint sneer curled Biagio's lips. "Is that right? But are you so honest with yourself, my lord? I think not. If you were, you would admit why you insist upon holding so tightly to my lady."

Furious, Rhys took a step forward, but the youth retreated. Biagio's swift backward step brought him up flush with the edge of the fire pit, and he glanced at Rhys, then the flames. "One fire for another—but which flames burn hottest, my lord? The flames of love or the flames of fury?"

Rhys reached for him, but with an agile twist, Biagio leaped over the fire pit and landed in a half crouch on the opposite side. The light of flames playing over his face gave it a hellish cast, and he laughed softly. "With your leave, my lord, I depart."

Rhys didn't bother to reply. Nor would he give the whelp the satisfaction of chasing him. He had no desire to look a fool. So he let him go, and stood still by the fire as Biagio disappeared from the hall. Curse him for a wagging tongue and vast imagination. Love? Nay, no such tender emotions for him. He'd learned of the folly of love years before, and knew it caused more pain than the sharpest sword.

He may feel something for Sasha, but it was lust, not love. Never love. Never.

CHAPTER SEVENTEEN

❧❧

A tear trembled on her lashes, then slid down her cheek, and Sasha wiped it away angrily. "You needn't look at me like that. It wasn't as if I had a choice, Elspeth."

"Child, child, I never said that. And don't think I'm condemning you. I'm not. I'm just concerned. Now tell me, have you taken any precautions against a babe?"

"No. I don't have my herbs with me, as you must know." She took in another deep breath, surprised at how shaky she felt. After the first glad reunion, Elspeth's concerned, gentle questions struck deeply. She was ashamed to admit she hadn't even progressed to the practical concern of a possible child. All her focus had been on Rhys, not the consequences of what they'd done. Now she felt foolish and very young for not having immediately considered the potential results.

Elspeth tapped a finger thoughtfully against her chin, musing aloud, "It may be too late for prevention. Perhaps Lord Rhys will let you have your herbs for the next time."

Sasha gave her a look of disbelief. "He doesn't trust me

enough to turn his back on me. I hardly think he'd allow me access to my herbs and potions."

"True, but he may allow me to mix you a potion. For your health, of course. I might convince him that your recent stay in the dungeon has weakened your stamina so that you require healthy potions."

"Oh yes, and while you're at it, offer him some." She snorted. "I think he too well remembers the last time we offered him food and drink. He doesn't forget anything, even chance remarks about weasels." It was obvious Elspeth had no idea what she was talking about, and she didn't feel like explaining, so she waved a weary hand and muttered, "Never mind. What are the symptoms?"

"Symptoms?"

"Of a child. How will I know if he . . . if I'm . . . if there is . . . you know."

"Yes. I know." Elspeth sighed. "Nausea, particularly in the mornings. Tender breasts. Sleepiness. What are you doing?"

Sasha was moving a hand over her stomach. Her eyes widened with horror. "I feel sick. And I'm sore. Oh, and I can't get enough sleep . . . What if I'm with child already?"

Shaking her head, Elspeth said shortly. "From the looks of that hunk of meat on the table, that's why you're sick. If you're sore, it's most like because of other things. You're always sleepy. It's too early yet, Sasha. Unless you lay with Lord Rhys that day in the meadow, you wouldn't have any symptoms yet." Her gaze sharpened. "Did you?"

"Not like last night." She met the older woman's eyes defiantly. "I do know the difference between the two. Kissing is not at all the same as what he did last night."

"Praise God." Elspeth looked down at her hands for a moment. When she looked up again, there was a faint, misty sheen in her eyes. "I've cared for you since the day you were born, Sasha. I've loved you always. Never doubt it."

Alarmed by the tone and words, Sasha put a trembling hand out. "What . . . what is the matter? You're not leaving? He hasn't banished you or sent you away, or—"

"No, no, nothing like that. But I've finally realized that you're a woman, though still so like my child at times. Natural enough, I suppose, since the truth has been so hard to face, and I've shielded you from it. I did you a disservice, perhaps. I've not forced you to grow up." She leaned forward and placed a gentle hand against her cheek, and Sasha put hers over it, holding the caress. Elspeth smiled. "You may want to know, that I believe you were right about the prophecy. This is the man that was sent to you."

Sasha stared at her, hardly able to believe what she'd heard. "Do you really think so, Elspeth?"

"Yes. I do. Beneath that rough exterior, lies a good man. Just as you always said. I should have trusted your instincts."

She frowned. "I'm not so certain I was right. He hasn't been very nice at times." Caught by the naïveté of that remark, she smiled ruefully. "He thinks I'm a terrible liar, and has been quite nasty about it."

"Yes. I can imagine." Elspeth sat back and smiled at her. "You'll just have to apologize."

"Apologize . . ."

"If you want to smooth things over, yes. Think about it. You'll find a way, I'm certain." She paused, frowned down at her hands, then looked up again. "About the prophecy—"

"Oh, I know what you'll say. But I'm certain that he'll agree one day."

Elspeth smiled. "That's not quite what I was going to say. Repeat it for me, Sasha. Repeat the prophecy for me."

Slowly, her eyes half-closed, she echoed the words from so long ago, rote melding with remembrance: "*A fierce warrior will come upon you in a wood, a griffyn that is half eagle, half lion, and this man will restore to you that which has been lost.*" Opening her eyes wide, she looked at Elspeth.

"Think about it, child. The prophecy promises that that which has been lost will be restored. What have you lost?"

"My home. My parents. My childhood."

Shaking her head, Elspeth said softly, "Your parents are

forever gone from this world, and your childhood cannot be relived. What else is there that you've lost?"

"My legacy. My father's palaces, the security I had there . . ."

"Yea, the security you once had is gone. Peace. Happiness. All gone. Like the wind across the sands, they flew from your grasp. But other winds blow, and not always across sand and minarets. Winds blow across barren rocks and bend tall trees . . . more was lost than your legacy. Even your name was taken from you. Think of your true name, child. Remember it. Remember its meaning. Then I think you'll find the truth as well."

Sasha stared at her blindly. Not even her Gift would come to her at this moment, only a crushing sense of sadness and despair, the wail of orphaned children and lost souls . . . she tore her mind from it, unable to bear the pervading sadness and sense of loss, the desperation of a lost child. She couldn't recall. Didn't want to recall. To remember would bring back all those overwhelming emotions.

"I don't remember my name," she said stubbornly, and Elspeth sighed.

Standing, Elspeth bent to caress her cheek, then stood back. "You will. When it's time. Now, I think I'll find Lord Rhys and ask if I can mix a healthy potion for you. Or would you rather I mix another kind?"

She stared down at her hands for a moment. She didn't want a child, of course, for that would only complicate things terribly. And she'd seen enough to know that it was often the swiftest way to send a man in the opposite direction. But neither did she want to destroy any part of what had gone between them. After a long silence, she looked up at Elspeth.

"I'll not do anything that would cause harm. What's been done is done, and I cannot change it now. I'll trust to God and fate for my future." She paused, then added softly. "I'll just have to prevent another risk."

Elspeth took both her hands and gave them a squeeze. "I knew you'd make the right choice. As to the future, you may not always have control over it, but keep your faith that matters will be resolved."

"That's what I'm afraid of." Sasha sighed. "Things are always getting resolved, and I always seem to be in the middle of the wrong resolution. When I first met Rhys, I had no notion that I'd end up in Wales instead of Arabia."

"The winds of fate are always shifting."

Sasha smiled. "You're beginning to sound remarkably like Biagio. I think you two spend entirely too much time together."

"Not of late. I need to find him, and be certain he's not managed to cause trouble for himself. He's reckless and brash, and never stops to think before he speaks. So much to do, but it contents me."

When Elspeth had gone, Sasha moved to the wide bed against the far wall and crawled into the middle. She sat there with her knees hugged against her chest. So much to think about, so much to worry about. Never had she thought that one small act between a man and a woman could so irrevocably change everything in her life. And now there was the possibility of another life to worry about, the chance that between them, they'd created a miracle. It was a frightening thought. And yet it was exciting as well.

She was still sitting in the middle of the bed when Rhys returned, though the light coming through the window had dimmed and faded into nothing but a thin gray sliver. She heard him at the door, heard a brief exchange with the guard, then the door swung open and he stepped inside.

"Sitting in the dark, flower?" The door slammed shut. His boots scraped across the floor, and after a moment, a bright ellipse of light flared. He held up a candle and looked toward her. Shadowed, with pale light and dark shades playing over his face, he made her think of that first day she'd seen him in the weald. He lit several more candles, until a soft glow held the dark shadows at bay. She sat still and silent, content to watch him, afraid that anything she said would be wrong. It usually was. Was

Elspeth right? Should she apologize? Make the first move toward conciliation?

He approached the bed. Candlelight behind him left his face too dark to read his expression, but it was easy enough to see the tension vibrating in his lean frame. Even without the bulk of mail, he was a big man, broad of shoulder, with thick sinews and strong, well-shaped legs. His black jerkin was of fine leather, and his tunic of good quality white linen. Dark hose ended in knee-high leather boots, and his broad leather belt was studded with gold emblems in the shapes of griffyns. A jewel-studded dagger jutted from his belt. Impressive. Aristocratic. And arrogant beyond belief. How like him. She was amazed he hadn't donned a golden crown and made himself king of Wales.

Her pique must have shown somehow. When he reached the bedside, he bent down to lift her up, his hands under her elbows. She put both hands against his chest, leaning back to stare at him dubiously. He wasn't harsh, but neither was he gentle. He grinned mockingly.

"Poor flower. Did you miss me so much?"

"Incredibly. I languished for hours. Did you bring something to eat? I think the meat has gone bad, and the bread is hard as paving stones."

He laughed softly. It wasn't one of those laughs that made her spine tingle with apprehension, but a real one, soft and amused. "No, I didn't bring food. It will be served below in the hall."

His hands traveled from her elbows up her arms to her shoulders, then moved to brush the hair back from her face. Hair clung to his fingers in silky strands that crackled slightly, like faraway lightning. She held her breath at the intensity in his eyes as he observed her from beneath the thick brush of his lashes. There was something different in his regard of her, a subtle change that hadn't been there earlier.

Twisting uneasily, she removed herself from his grip with little trouble. He let her go, though he did not move away from the bed. For several heartbeats he stared down at her, as if seeing her for the first time, a slow, raking stare that took in her shabby garments and bare legs and feet. She flushed with embarrassment. How like him to come to her in finery while she had nothing but rags to wear. Wasn't she a princess? Royalty, not just a belated lord of rocks.

She opened her mouth to deliver a scathing appraisal, when he reached out to cup her chin in his palm. His thumb dragged across her lower lip leisurely. "You're too lovely a flower to be in these rent garments. I should have seen to it before now. Is there anything in particular you would like from your trunks?"

She stared at him, momentarily too shocked to reply. She recovered quickly enough, however, and nodded. "Yes. I have several very pretty gowns that will do. Just send up my trunks from the cart, and I'll choose one."

Rhys smiled slightly, and released her chin. "I'll have Elspeth choose one for you. Forgive me, flower, but I'm not certain I trust you to have access to your trunks until I've had them inspected."

"What do you think I have in there? Never mind—very well. Bring me the red silk." When he lifted a brow and frowned, she said hesitantly, "Is that not an appropriate choice?"

"For seduction. Not for dinner in my hall."

Surprised, she just stared at him. He stepped back from the bed and ran a hand through his hair, leaving darker streaks among the pale. His brows were lowered, and his mouth set in a taut line.

"Choose another," he said shortly. "One that's not so . . . sheer."

So that was it. It was as earlier. Brian had known, and been shocked. *He's jealous, by God,* had flashed through the Irishman's mind, accompanied by a sense of vague apprehension. All that had been wiped out, of course, once she accepted Rhys's challenge and drew shut the curtains as he'd so arrogantly commanded her to do. Blank astonishment had been Brian's reaction, and she'd had an instant of seeing herself as he saw her before she found Rhys's white fury a more interesting reaction. It had been one of her better moments of triumph, for all that it may have cost her so dear.

A smile tugged hard at her mouth and she bent her head so he wouldn't see. Studying her fingers, she nodded. "Very well. I have another gown that will do. It's blue. High at the neck, with long sleeves and an undertunic. Does that sound more appropriate?"

"Much more. I'll see that she brings it to you." He moved to the door, then paused and looked back at her. "Is there anything else you require?"

She considered, then shook her head. "Only shoes. Elspeth will know what is to be brought. Let her take care of it."

When he'd spoken to the guard, Rhys lowered the bar over the door. His gaze moved around the room, from cluttered table to stools, to brazier and candles, then the tub still sitting on the floor in a puddle of cold water. He looked at her again, a faint smile on his mouth.

"I should have allowed my squire in to clean, I suppose."

She shrugged. "If you want it tidy. I'm not a scrubwoman."

"No," he said, the smile still on his lips as he moved toward her, "you're not a scrubwoman. But what are you, flower? Sometimes I think I know, then you change right before my eyes. You've been an elf queen, a fey mist-maid, a sultry temptress, then a thorn in my side. At times, you're more thorn than rose." He reached the bed again and put out a hand to draw a finger lightly over her cheek. She shivered at the soft caress, and at the glitter in his eyes. "Sweet," he murmured, bending his head, "and dangerous." His finger curled under her chin and lifted her mouth to his, and she did not resist.

In truth, she wanted this. She wanted him to kiss her, to reassure her with his touch that he wanted her. Something must have happened after he left earlier, because the icy anger in his eyes was gone. It had been replaced with another familiar light, and one she welcomed.

Which was a good thing. All purpose wavered and faded under his touch, under this new, exhilarating magic she'd discovered with him. It was hard to think clearly when he was kissing her, when he was caressing her face or her

throat, or her breasts . . . letting his fingers trail down to
cup them in his palms, thumbs dragging slowly over peaks
that grew hard beneath the attention. She shuddered. The
strange heartbeat was back, a steady, aching throb low in
the pit of her stomach, between her thighs, a curling white
fire that flared hot and high.

Still kissing her, he pressed her backward on the bed,
his body weighing her down, heavy pressure and heady
comfort, the long length of him atop her, smelling of wind
and leather. Familiar now, with the power to set her heart
fluttering, dispel all rational thought, and scatter any good
intentions like the wind. Vaguely, she remembered that
there was something she was supposed to do—or was that
not do? It didn't matter. Nothing mattered but the man
removing her gown and his own garments, the hot light
of desire in his eyes and the aching need in her own . . .

She lifted her arms to him and he came to her, bare and
powerful and oh so beautiful to her . . . his mouth and
weight left her breathless. The light behind him eclipsed
his face, so that she could see only the outline of him and
the gleam of his eyes, the way light caught in his hair to
make it shine dark gold. And then he looked up, and in a
strange twist of light and shadow and shape, she saw a
hunger in him she'd not seen before, a need that overtook
any other emotion. It was more than physical hunger,
more than the urges of the body, but a famine of the soul.
And she understood it. She knew it intimately, because the
same privation had haunted her all her life, this terrible
aching need that never quite went away, was never quite
appeased no matter how much was given to sate it. It
waited, a hungry gnawing beast inside, waited for the right
word, the right touch, the right gift.

And so she gave him all she could, recognizing a fellow
sufferer, wanting to ease him as best she could, because it
would ease her as well. She reached out silently, yielding
heart and mind and body to this arrogant—often insen-
sitive but always certain—man who had spun her world
into chaos from that first sight in the weald.

At that moment, she gave him her heart, the best of her
gifts, the most precious she could give. It was the most

dangerous thing she had ever done in her life. Nothing else came close. There was no reason to it, no logic, but that had never mattered much anyway. Now there was only instinct and intuition, and the knowledge that perhaps she had made wrong choices at times, but they were always honest ones.

It was all mixed up, this wild feeling inside her and the whirlwind outside, the way he made her feel and the way she responded. . . . He was kissing her breasts, her stomach, and lower, silky fire, melting words and heated breath, drawing trembling responses from her body. She cried out, hands tangling in his hair, his tongue a writhing flame that shocked and pleasured her as she'd never dreamed . . . and then she couldn't think, could only feel, could only cry out his name and hold him as a great shuddering washed over her and took her on a high, impossible wave and left her there, suspended for a moment, until the breathtaking drop into dark currents that gently drifted her back to time and place.

Rhys was lifting himself over her, murmuring her name, his voice ragged and hoarse and husky as he slid inside her, another vibration of shock that made her moan and hold to him. A long, shivering stroke, a quiver as he held there, then dragged away, then thrust again, slow and luxurious pleasure, aching need and hovering promise, faster and faster until she was caught up in it again and answering his thrusts with her own, legs wrapping around him and clinging, head thrown back, hearing his wonderful husky groans in her ear as time shattered and careened around them in a spinning arc.

And then there was peace. Peace and contentment, a blissful rest. A promise.

It was noisy in the hall. As normal. Noisy with knights and soldiers and servants and yapping dogs. Dinner was the main meal of the day, eaten early. Supper was lighter, with minstrelsy and sport. The gathering was informal and relaxed in most keeps, and so it was here.

But when Rhys appeared in the open doorway of the

hall with Sasha, it grew quiet. Laughter faded into whispers and coughs, and only the dogs remained noisy and congenial.

Rhys smiled slightly. His first evening meal in his own keep. And they all waited to see what he would do, if the new lord would be as relaxed as his father had been, or if there would be the constraint that he'd heard attended Gavin's household.

Without speaking, he escorted Sasha down the length of the hall, past the tables set at angles to the dais, skirting rowdy dogs and subdued diners, around the central fire and up to the high table. Tiny brass bells sewn onto her shoes tinkled lightly, a brittle accompaniment to their progress. Blue silk swished softly around her legs as she walked beside him, and there was the tantalizing, familiar fragrance of jasmine that teased, tormented, and reassured him. All eyes were on them as they reached the dais, and Sasha stepped up with a lithe grace and tinkle of bells.

Brian already sat at the table, and next to him sat Cailin. She watched curiously with pale eyes that reminded him of his father and brothers, a kinship he couldn't deny. He should have been the one to think of seating her at the high table, a concession, a peace offering, but it had been Brian.

Chair legs scraped against stone and rushes as Brian rose to his feet, awkward and faintly shamefaced, as if he'd been caught in an error. "We did not think you were joining us, my lord."

Rhys lifted a brow. "As you can see, I am." He seated Sasha in the place next to the lord's high, bolstered chair. She sat quickly, as if relieved, and folded her hands in her lap, head held high. No cowering flower, but a brave blossom, facing the curious, daring them to say anything. Royal and arrogant, as always.

Still standing, he glanced toward Cailin, and then Sasha. Light and dark, so different and so alike. Two women caught in the middle of a struggle for Glenlyon. He wondered if Sasha would have allowed herself to be wed to a man she hated. No, she would never have submitted. But then, she had not been faced with that choice.

When Brian cleared his throat, Rhys looked up at him and smiled. "Take your seat, Sir Brian. The servants wait."

Brian sat down, still awkward and uneasy, and pages and squires came into the hall bearing platters of food. After being brought from the kitchens and across the bailey, food was rarely hot, but steam rose in tempting curls from some of the dishes as covers were removed. Dropping clumsy curtsies, pages placed their burdens on the high table, while squires came immediately behind them to carve meats that had not already been cut up or minced fine. A thick stew was ladled onto large slices of bread in wooden trenchers, a single trencher to every pair of diners along the lower tables. Flagons of wine sat on each table, and cups were often shared although each diner had their own knife and spoons were provided.

Leaning close to Sasha, Rhys murmured, "No *blanc de Syrie* such as you prepare, perhaps, but edible I hope."

Her lashes quivered, lips trembling into a slight smile. "I have a confession to make."

"Not another lie."

Mirth glittered in the quick flash of her dark eyes and she nodded. "Yea, lord. I'm afraid so. I don't cook at all. Elspeth made the meal that night. I make potions. She prepares food."

He shook his head. "I'm not in the least surprised by that confession. Is everything you say a lie?"

Her gaze held his, and her voice was a husky whisper. "Not everything. There are times I tell the truth. When it's important."

"It would be interesting to know when you think it's important." He toyed with his spoon, looking away from her. She created a strange yearning in him, an uneasy feeling. There had been a moment in his bed when he felt suddenly at peace, even with the wild need that she sparked in him. Like a homecoming. He didn't understand it. There was absolutely nothing about this woman that should appeal to him. He appreciated honesty and candor, loyalty and honor, not a maid more given to wild caprices and wilder lies. She was moonlight and stardust, vague and elusive, as nebulous as both. And yet he wanted her.

He craved order in his life. A certainty of place and time. He liked knowing that there were definite boundaries, definite loyalties. He didn't want it all changed. It was too disruptive.

She was too disruptive. And yet—he wanted her.

He looked up, and his gaze chanced upon a pair of dark eyes at the lower table. Biagio was watching them intently, his gaze resting on Sasha with such intensity that Rhys frowned. When he glanced at her, she was looking back at Biagio with the same intensity.

He leaned forward. Sensing his stare, Biagio's eyes moved to him and a dark brow lifted, mocking and certain, but not foolish. There was a shrug, a twist of his mouth, and then he turned to his neighbor at the table.

Ryhs sat back in his chair, and Sasha laughed. He glanced at her quickly, frowning. "What do you find amusing, flower?"

"You." It was said serenely, softly. Confidently. She leaned close to him, and there was something in her dark gaze that was different. A dimple flashed at the corner of her mouth and was quickly gone. "I find myself intrigued, my lord."

He held her gaze a moment, toying with the carved handle of his spoon. He had no idea what she was talking about, which didn't come as a big surprise. He usually had no idea what she was talking about. It was mostly nonsensical chatter. He shrugged. "Good."

"Yea," she said, the dimple still deep and flirting, "it's very good indeed. I like interesting people."

Now he was amused, and shook his head. "Then you must be in ecstasy here, for there are many interesting people. Brian. Sir Peter. Sir Robert. Owain. Sir Clyde. Even my half-sister. All interesting people."

Waving a hand in blithe dismissal, she shook her head. "I don't find myself sufficiently interested in them. You, however, are different. I've recently discovered a deep curiosity about you."

"That," he said shortly, "could be unwise. It's best not to be curious about me."

"Not just you, but this—" She waved a hand at the room, smiling faintly. "It's a grand hall, yes?"

"Great hall, but yes, grand as well."

"Yet I see no marble. No fountains. No mosaic tiles or rich carpets, no silk hangings. There are no gilded carvings, or delicate scrollwork, or even elegant doorways. There is stone, grass on the floor, and a few heavy hangings. The food is dry, the wine strong. It's damp and cold, even in the master's chamber." She rested her chin on her curled hand, staring up at him. "But I know a place where the sun shines constantly, the wind brings sweet breezes, and fountains splash cool water in open terraces. It is green and beautiful, with painted tiles and the delicate scent of oranges and lemons, with grapes and stuffed figs to be eaten on plush silk cushions, while slaves fan gold-tipped feathers to keep away insects. Does that not sound better?"

He stared at her. He'd seen palaces such as she described, and had thought them beautiful and exotic. But they weren't Wales. They weren't home, and though he admired them, there had always been a sense of displacement. He'd felt it for years, ever since he first left Wales, but had not really known what it was until he returned. Now he knew. There was a feeling of homecoming here, of being where he belonged. After all the years away, years of restless longing when he didn't even know what he longed for, he'd found it again. A peace. A return. And though it might not be palatial and exotic, it was home.

Shaking his head, he smiled slightly. "It sounds beautiful, flower, but unsuited to Welsh climate. Here is where I belong."

There was a quick flash of something like dismay in her eyes, and then she turned away, staring down at her wine cup. "It's not where I belong," she said softly, and looked up at him again. "Wouldn't you rather be a prince than a baron?"

"I didn't know I had that choice."

"You do." She took a deep breath, glanced around the hall, then back at him. The blue silk of her gown shimmered under the glow of torchlight, and her eyes reflected flames in their depths as she held his gaze. "You could be prince of much more than a stone hall, my lord. For a brave warrior like yourself, it would be easy to take what you wanted."

He looked around the hall and saw it through her eyes: the cold stone instead of warm tile, the absence of bright colors and open windows and doors, with no warm breezes or intricately worked carpets. It must all seem shabby to her. Even the food, spiced but not exotic, plain minced meat and boiled vegetables, hard bread and dried fruit—yea, he could understand that she found it sadly lacking when he knew where she'd once lived. But none of that was important to him.

"I've taken what is mine, flower. I have it now. Everything I want is here."

"Everything?"

"Everything important." He looked away, unsettled by the grave intensity in her, disliking the turn of conversation. Deliberately, because he felt he'd lost control somehow, he turned to Brian on his other side. A dismissal. And an end to the discussion that she could not misunderstand. And she didn't, because as he spoke with Brian about the summoning of loyal barons, she settled back into her chair with a soft sigh.

He'd half expected more argument. But Sasha was quiet. Unusually quiet. The main courses were served. Game birds, venison, beef, and lamb, fish stew and boiled eel, seasonings of garlic, pepper, and mustard, trays of fine white breads, honeyed fruits, and pastries, colored sugars from Alexandria and shimmering jellies—all adorned the lord's table. Gavin had not stinted on supplies, it seemed, for there was much more than just salted meats and boiled turnips to eat.

A minstrel began to play, strumming a popular ballad on his lute. Rhys pushed tempting morsels toward Sasha with the tip of his dining knife, a silent offering and a question. She smiled, nibbled daintily at a rose-and-violet-colored sugar wafer, and looked away. Question answered. Rebuffed, he frowned and took a sip of wine. There had been a quivering eagerness about her earlier.

Now it was gone, replaced by this distant, almost regal, reservation.

But he remembered her with no reservations, with her arms around him and her body melting under his, her cries soft and eager and rich in his ear as she clung to him. His and only his.

Determined that she would not change again, would not meld into some other form that wasn't nearly as pleasing as the one he'd so recently enjoyed, he leaned forward and held out his wine cup. "A sip, flower."

Dark eyes slid to him and she shook her head. "I do not care for wine, my lord."

"Wine at all, or just from my cup?"

Long lashes lifted and she shrugged. She shredded a tiny piece of wafer between her fingers, crumbling it into shards of rose and violet sugar. "Wine tonight."

Frustrated, seeing the chasm between them widening and not knowing how to halt it or even if he should, he studied her. It was the prophecy again. She wanted him to claim her legacy. Or what she thought was her legacy. He was tempted to tell her, brutally and honestly, that she had nothing to claim. But even as he thought it, the fleeting temptation swift and fierce, he knew he couldn't. As Elspeth had said, it would hurt her. And there was no point in it. The truth had always saved him, but it had been her lies that saved her. He saw that now. And he couldn't take away the fiction she had woven, the fantasy that had kept her forging ahead, kept her from giving up and becoming as so many others would have become, a fading nonentity, a flashing presence in time. Instead, her fiction had given her purpose and substance, and she had become a fugitive princess waiting to reclaim her palaces.

Though removed by time and circumstance, he'd always known who he was. She had not. And though his life may not have been as peaceful as he would have liked, neither had he been forced to wake up every day and wonder who he would be when the night came. Beneath all her lies, that carefully structured but fragile web she'd woven around herself, was honesty and truth and all that was good in life. Not, perhaps, as he would once have defined it, but there in all its many nuances.

Compelled to try again, he leaned close, breathing jasmine and silk, his voice soft. "We cried truce, remember?"

A flash of dark eyes, a smile, and another shrug, silk and scent and beauty, and she said, "Am I quarreling with you?"

"No. That's what worries me."

Bells tinkled as she shifted in her seat to stare at him, head turned so that a dark fall of hair cascaded down her arm to brush against the sugar crumbs on the table. "Did it ever occur to you that you can't be happy with yea or nay? Do you want peace or war, my lord?"

"Honesty."

"Ah. That's not as easy to accept. I've given you honesty before. You didn't like it."

Because she was right, and because his own honesty compelled him to admit that to himself, it made his temper rise. "Your form of honesty is not quite acceptable."

"Is it not?" The straight slash of her brow lifted. "But it's all I have to give." Her arms spread out to the sides, and silk shifted across her shoulders and breasts in a soft hiss as her long sleeves drifted downward. "See? No magic here. No illusions. No flowers up my sleeve, or mirrors to reflect distorted images. Just me. I'm what I've always been, what you wanted me to be or thought I was or feared I was—I haven't really changed. I still want what I always wanted."

"That cursed prophecy."

"Yes." She smiled slightly. "That cursed prophecy. It's been my dream since I was eight years old. I held to it at night when we didn't know if we'd wake the next day, and brushed it off and kept it bright when everything around me was black and gloomy. You're the answer to my prophecy, Rhys ap Griffyn."

"I'm not the answer." Aware that Brian was listening, that even Cailin was leaning forward to stare at them curiously, and somewhere down the line of tables Biagio watched, he kept his voice soft and even. "You don't know what the answer is, flower. We all have dreams that don't come true. Sometimes they're meant to be just dreams."

"This isn't a dream. It's a promise."

"It's a damned lie." His words were louder, harsher, and he felt Brian stiffen and heard Cailin's inquiring whisper. But Sasha just stared at him, her eyes wide and dark, reflecting candlelight. He took a deep breath and shook his head. "We'll talk more of this later. This isn't the time or the place for this discussion."

He sat back, the mood and evening ruined, the food tasteless and the music a little too loud and clamoring. Even her damned tiny bells irritated him when she moved, turning to stare straight ahead again, her back a rigid line and her posture radiating hurt and disapproval. Curse her. He'd tried. Despite his best judgment, he'd let Elspeth's story affect him and he'd offered the olive branch of peace. He should have known she'd reject it. He wasn't surprised at all. Not really.

Lost in thought, he looked up with a frown when Sir Robert approached the high table. "Yes, Sir Robert?"

With only a brief hesitation, Sir Robert smiled. "It has been suggested, my lord, that we have a celebration now that Glenlyon is occupied by its rightful lord again. Both a welcoming home and a statement at once, a pledge to your arms of all neighboring barons and your own villeins. Perhaps even a tournament."

Brian sat up straight, his voice eager. "A tournament?"

Rhys considered a moment. It would be the perfect opportunity to determine who would pledge to his standard, and a tourney always drew a crowd. Yea, the idea had merit. If the prince of Deheubarth could be persuaded to come, it would also solidify his position in Wales as a Marcher lord. And a tournament would accomplish something else as well—a wearing of colors for a lady. A statement. A declaration without words or commitment, but a promise of sorts.

Clearing his throat, he nodded. "I'll discuss this with Owain. A celebration would be welcome after all that's happened."

"Yea, lord. Welcome indeed."

When he looked at Sasha, she was staring at him, wide-eyed and mysterious, a faint smile curving her mouth. He smiled.

"Does the thought of a tournament please you, flower?"

"I've always loved pageantry and gaiety. Noise and music, jugglers and tumblers, acrobats and the excitement of armed men in mock combat. It pleases me well, my lord."

"Then on Midsummer Day, we shall have a tournament." He looked back at Sir Robert. "Does that give us enough time?"

Sir Robert looked slightly startled, but nodded. "It's just as well that it will be done soon, my lord, for the people need reassurance that all will be well. Midsummer Day."

Tiny bells rang softly, and Sasha laughed. "A most fitting date, my lord. Most fitting."

CHAPTER EIGHTEEN

Preparations had reached a fever pitch. Sasha watched idly from the window that looked out over the inner bailey. She could see down into the village from this vantage point, and out over rolling hills and the bright, glittering ribbon of the River Wye. It appeared and disappeared from sight, a sun-chipped serpent winding through trees and thatched roof huts, winking in the afternoon sunshine.

"My lady?"

Sasha turned, unable to halt a smile. *My lady.* A title meant for the lady of the manor, not her. *Your Highness* would have been acceptable, but of course, no one here would call her that. She was only the lord's mistress, no one important. She smoothed her blue skirts and shrugged.

"Yes, Sir Bowen?"

Owain's son smiled back at her, and she knew from the direction of his thoughts that he found her fascinating. He was a handsome young man and bore no grudges against Rhys, though it had been the lord's arm that had levied the punishment of fifteen strokes of a whip for the involvement with Gavin. Easy-going, witty, and smitten with her, Bowen had become a constant shadow of late. Now he looked up at her, blue eyes shining and full of humor and admiration, a not unpleasant reaction to bear.

He cleared his throat. "All the arrangements are made. Are you certain you have Lord Rhys's permission to do this?"

"I told you, Sir Bowen. It's a surprise for him. He's not expecting it, but he'll enjoy it. Don't you recall how Biagio performed so well? This is the same thing. We've done it hundreds of times all over Europe. Once, there was this Austrian duke, and we—well, never mind. That's an old tale that's best not relived now." She smiled. Her brightest smile. Her most captivating smile. "Remember—it's a secret."

"A secret." He looked dubious, but when she assured him that it was all quite safe, he reluctantly agreed not to reveal it to anyone.

"Biagio knows, of course, as he is to assist me, and Elspeth. I've even told Lady Cailin of it, but not Sir Brian, for he gets too nervous and worrisome."

"Oh. If the lord's sister knows of it—"

"She does. Now remember, there will be smoke, but no fire. And do not rush forward too quickly, or you'll spoil it all."

"Yea, my lady. I'll see to it that everything is prepared just as you said."

"Very good. Biagio will assist you in any way possible." She frowned slightly. "When he's not too busy playing at being a knight, that is."

Bowen took a step forward. Sunlight from the open window slanted over his fair hair and into his blue eyes, and he squinted. "He's learning quickly, my lady. Sir Peter says that Biagio is most agile and quick, especially for a man not trained up to the quintain as so many are."

"Yes, yes, so I've heard from Biagio." A thousand times at least. It was ridiculous, how delighted he'd been to take up a wooden sword and staff and run a horse at some small ring dangling from a crossbeam. More than once, the weighted quintain had swung back around and caught him in the back to knock him from his horse, a most amusing sight that still had not dampened his enthusiasm for the ordeal. Idiot. All this planning and practicing for a tournament made normal adult males degenerate into little boys again. She was sick of it.

And sick of all the precautions being taken, as if an entire army would be able to sneak into the keep under pretense of attending the festivities. Councils and more councils, discussions and disagreements, arguments over whether to disguise men to mingle among the revelers or just hold the entire tournament outside the village as originally planned, went long into the night.

Piqued at the focus of attention swinging from her to the tournament, she'd found herself unwillingly doing silly things to gain Rhys's notice. She felt foolish, felt the need to puncture his silly conceits with sharp words, and all the while this odd restless yearning inside grew stronger and stronger. At least that was the only thing growing inside her; she wasn't with child. A happy discovery. A disappointing moment, though she had no idea why. Rhys had been indifferent to her state, shrugging his shoulders and refraining from comment. Infuriating.

"Then by your leave, my lady, I shall see to all the details." Sir Bowen knelt on one knee, a habit he had formed when coming into her presence or leaving it, as if giving her the adulation she was due. She rather liked it, and smiled down at him.

"Your efforts are most appreciated, Sir Bowen. I cannot imagine what I would do without your help." She meant it, for he'd been invaluable in assisting her without asking too many annoying questions.

He looked up at her, still on one knee, his eyes blue adoration. "If I might ask . . . 'tis a daring request, and I am too bold, but—I would like a favor to wear in the tourney, my lady."

"My favor?" She was intrigued. No one had ever asked to wear her favors before. Except Rhys, and he hadn't asked, he'd been requested to do so, and he still hadn't obliged. He wouldn't even discuss the prophecy at all anymore. She was flattered and pleased, and began to feel like one of those silly, virtuous heroines in a poetic romance the jongleurs told to entertain an appreciative audience. "Would a silk scarf do, Sir Bowen?"

"I would cherish it, and will bring it to you in victory when I've won the lists," he promised.

She fetched a length of red silk. It was shot through with tiny gold threads and was inundated with the scent of jasmine. One of her favorites, and fit to be worn in her honor.

As she bestowed it on him with her most madonnalike smile, he grasped her hand and pressed a kiss against the back of it. Still kneeling before her, he held her fingers in his grip, and murmured, "For your honor, my most gracious and beautiful lady. . . ."

"Well, how tender," a low voice purred from the doorway, and Sasha looked up to see Rhys leaning against the doorframe, one arm above his head, his hand curled into a fist against the thick wood. He was smiling, but it was one of his smiles that always made her think twice about being reckless. She stared at him, not moving as he uncoiled from the doorway and walked toward them in a lithe stroll.

How like him, to look more menacing in a jerkin and tunic than he did in a full suit of mail. He still wore a sword, though a light one instead of the wicked battle sword he usually carried, and his step was easy and controlled, like a large cat stalking his prey. She snatched her hand from Sir Bowen's without thinking how guilty that might look. Rhys noticed. His eyes narrowed at her, gray smoke and dangerous glitter, but the smile still slanted his mouth.

Sir Bowen was panicked. He remained on one knee, the red silk draped in his fist, his thoughts frantic. *Mary and Joseph . . . I know how jealous he is about her . . . I didn't think . . . He'll kill me for even being near his woman . . . He doesn't think I would actually . . . I should never have been so foolish . . . Oh God, oh God . . . I knew better than to touch what is his. . . .*

It wasn't pleasant to have such easy access to a man's mental hysteria, and she wished she hadn't let down her barriers. On the other hand, it was quite pleasant to hear that Rhys was jealous. Gratifying. If it wasn't just because she was a possession, that is. Was that it? Did he consider her chattel, as Biagio said? Just another asset, like Glenlyon, or even his trusty horse?

Her eyes narrowed slightly in return, and she spared Sir Bowen a brief glance. "Get up, sir. I'm certain my lord is well aware that it is normal for a knight to carry a lady's colors into the lists." Her gaze lifted to Rhys's face, and she smiled sweetly. "Why, once, he even said he'd carry my colors. Didn't you, my lord?"

"Yea." He'd reached them, and lifted a brow as Sir Bowen stumbled clumsily to his feet and lurched backward a step. "And if I remember aright, I did carry them. Though not as you thought I would."

His silky voice and dangerous smile was wearing greatly on Sir Bowen's nerves, and the poor man mumbled something that was indistinguishable from the gurgle of water through a pipe. Rhys studied him for a moment, eyes thinning at the length of red silk still clutched in Sir Bowen's fist.

Not about to allow Sir Bowen even the opportunity to return it to her, Sasha stomped right over his mental anguish with blind determination. "If Sir Bowen were not so gallant a knight, my lord, he would not have offered to carry my colors in your honor. Would you, Sir Bowen?"

Trapped, blue eyes darted between the two, and then lowered in numb defeat as he nodded. "Not . . . that you cannot . . . are not fully capable of carrying them, my lord. But I only thought—"

"How pleased you would be that he was so thoughtful," Sasha put in with another sweet smile. "And look—you are pleased. I knew you would be." She ignored Bowen's anguished groan.

"My lord, 'tis growing late. . . . There is still so much to do. . . ."

"You may leave," Rhys said shortly. It wasn't so much an agreement as an order. Bowen left rapidly. Rhys moved to shut the door behind him, then turned.

She was reminded of how many times he'd done just that—shut the door and stared at her in an attempt to intimidate her. The last few weeks had been outwardly calm. She'd come to enjoy being near him, despite those inner qualms that occasionally shook her soul. It was easier to shut her eyes and yield herself to the present than to look beneath the surface. But now, in the flash of a moment, she saw what she feared most—he cared for her only as property, not for herself. The sweet words and tender caresses, the heated love play in the wide, shadowed bed, had lulled her into dreaming that he cared, though he'd never said he did. Now she wanted to know.

It would be useless to ask him directly. He'd shrug aside the question or avoid it deftly, as he normally did. But there were ways to find out the truth, if she could manage it. So she gave a little shrug of her shoulders and turned away from him, walking to the window and gazing out at the busy work in the bailey and beyond.

For a few moments, Rhys was quiet. He moved to his clothes chest and rifled through the contents, then slammed the lid shut with a loud bang. She curled her fingers into the stone ledge to keep from jumping and kept her gaze trained on the stand that carpenters were building to hold spectators for the lists.

"Do you think it's high enough?" she asked after a moment when the silence stretched too long. "It seems like we'll only be able to see the jousters' knees as they pass by at that level. . . ."

"What is he to you?"

She turned, feigning surprise. "What is who to me, my lord?"

"Don't play this game, flower. You're too obvious." He walked toward her, and there was a pinched look around his nose and mouth that didn't look promising. She frowned.

"If you're talking about Sir Bowen, I—"

"We both know who I'm talking about. He was kissing your hand, and you gave him your red silk."

"Ah, then it is Sir Bowen we're discussing." She nodded. "Yes, I think he will make a most competent champion in the lists."

He stopped in front of her. She wouldn't have been surprised to see him breathing flame and smoke like a dragon. His eyes were hot and furious, that banked disaster that always made her take a mental step back. When she wasn't feeling so reckless and unloved, that is.

Now, she stepped off the high cliff of common sense into empty space and smiled sweetly again, her voice a sultry murmur. "You can't be jealous, my lord."

"Don't," he said softly, "tell me what I can and can't be." He smelled of wind and leather as he put a hand on her shoulder. His fingers curled into blue silk and skin. "I won't share you, flower. Not even whispers and glances across a room. Don't think it for a moment."

"Really, my lord, and you accuse me of having an imagination. Just because you introduced me to the pleasures of love play, why do you think I'd want to test my appeal elsewhere? Don't you think you're enough for me?" She smiled when his fingers tightened. "Why, Lord Rhys, you're holding me far too tightly. . . ."

She let her words trail into silence, and saw from the sudden flare in his eyes that he'd caught the double meaning. As she had meant him to. The white fury was back, evident in the glitter of his eyes and the way the scar on his cheek paled against his face, stretched taut against his harsh features.

"I always hold tightly to what is mine," he said softly. "I told you that."

"Yea, but there's a difference in possessions and people. Or weren't you ever taught that? You can't deal in people as you do in rugs or barrels of wine."

"On the contrary—I learned at an early age how dispensable people are, even sons. It was the first big lesson I was taught. And I've never forgotten it."

Fool, fool, to have forgotten that. . . . She stared at him, silent and floundering, recognizing the gravity of her error but unable to retract it now. And she had started this, albeit by chance. A testing. An answer to the aching need inside her that yearned to hear words of love. She closed her eyes.

"Ah no, flower, open your eyes. Look at me. Don't think it's that easy to escape." His words were a soft purr, low and growling, an enticement to disaster. "I've seen it all before, you know. Since I was a boy. It was easy to be a hostage then, to be largely ignored. So I sat in corners aplenty and saw this same game played, over and over— the whispers and glances, the innuendos and then the quick, furtive couplings in the dark beneath the stairs, or in alcoves, and on occasion, just plain rutting where it didn't matter who saw. Yea, I watched and listened, and I learned. And I won't allow you to play that game with me."

Her eyes had opened at his command, and she stared at him helplessly. And as always in moments of stress, she blurted the truth. "It wasn't a game, my lord, I wasn't playing. . . ."

His hand moved to tighten cruelly in the loose hair at the nape of her neck, pulling her head back, his mouth coming down on hers to crush and punish and ravage. Gone was the gentleness she'd known from him, the teasing, arousing caresses and heartstopping kisses . . . this was different. As different as night from day. This was a taking, a marking of her as his, an obvious warning to her and any other man that she belonged to him.

No words of love. No sweet endearments, or even soft whispers. Just this—the strong sweep of his hands over her body, the pulling away of her gown without regard to seams or laces, and the hard, driving kisses that he forced her to accept.

And yet, in the midst of the fierce anger, she heard a note of despair as he held her against him, lifting her and carrying her across the room to the bed, putting her down and bending over her. She looked up. His eyes were storm clouds, dark and thunderous, his mouth twisted in such an expression of pain, she did not fight. He didn't take her forcefully, though she half expected it. Instead, he applied searing caresses and scorching kisses, holding her when she would have twisted away, pushing her legs apart with his knees, touching her with such arrant sexuality that she found herself responding. He smiled then, a satisfied, savage smile, and his hands moved on her again until she was panting and moaning and clutching at him with both hands.

Ruthless and tender, a hot-cold combination of fire and ice, he touched her everywhere, her breasts, the throbbing ache between her legs, fingers drawing shuddering responses that took away her breath and left her weak. She shifted once, a slight pushing away, and he put his palms against her shoulders and held her.

"Nay, flower . . . don't think to fight me. You'll only lose."

And then his hands were moving down her arms to her wrists, clasping lightly, pulling them over her head to push them down into the mattress. A pressing weight of his body on hers, his mouth taking hers as she lay helpless beneath him, then a brief lifting as he moved one hand to the waist cord of his linen chausses. Then he lowered himself again, and this time, in the embrace, there was a lessening of the violence, a tender touch, a groaning slide of his body into hers, his breath fanning her cheek. With her free arm, she reached up to lay her palm against his face. Her fingers grazed the curve of the scar on his cheek in a light caress. His head lifted, a blur of his features and the gleam of his eyes, shuttered as his lashes drifted down.

She pressed her face into the curve of his throat and shoulder, teeth scoring his skin, and he answered with a sound of excitement. A groan, a dragging of his body inside her, another luxurious glide that made her shiver and cling to him. Her legs wrapped around him, feet sliding down the length of his thighs, bunching the linen with her toes. There was something wickedly erotic about being totally naked when he was fully dressed, something arousing and dangerous and seductive.

Rhys levered his body halfway up, resting his weight on his palms, looking down at her with a strange half smile slanting his mouth. "You're mine, flower."

A question, not a statement for all that it was said so strongly. She smiled back at him, and circled the curve of his ear with her fingertip until he shuddered. "Yea, lord. I've always been yours."

It must have been the right response. The half smile dissolved into satisfaction, and his mouth came down on hers, and now there were the soft, heated whispers, the endearments, the teasing caresses that made her arch up to him with answering passion. It was a combat, a tournament, a jousting that neither would win but both would treasure. And if it wasn't the definite answer that she'd wanted, it was an answer.

The fire had burned low in the central pit of the great hall when Rhys entered. He paused in the doorway, aware of the soft snores of men and women sleeping on straw pallets and in alcoves ranging along the walls. It was quiet. Only a few dogs were awake, and those drowsy and lethargic. Not even a decent bark greeted him. Perfect. He needed solitude. There was little enough of it to be found in most keeps, but he'd not wanted to ride from Glenlyon in the dark. Not when he still wasn't certain of the temper of his barons.

Most had sent acknowledgment of his invitation to the tournament, and announced that they were coming. Only a few had not answered the gentle summons. Would they come? Would they rally to his standard? He'd know soon enough, for the first guests had begun arriving. The keep would soon be packed with barons and retainers.

In two days' time, the tournament would be held. A list. A rousing joust between knights and lords, a contest of arms. He anticipated it eagerly. With all the waiting, the worry, the wondering, he needed a release of the tension that had built up inside him.

Word had come that Richard would soon leave Jerusalem. When the king returned, he would deal with the problem of Gavin. And then he would have to make a decision about Sasha. He'd given his word, and he could not break it. Curse her. Brian still muttered about enchantment and witches and faeries, and there were moments when he thought it might be true. She'd certainly managed to bewitch him. Never had a woman occupied his thoughts as she did. Never had a woman had the power to drive him to such ridiculous extremes.

As earlier. Jésu, when he'd seen Bowen on one knee in front of her, gazing up at her with obvious adoration and her smiling down at him as if she were a queen bestowing favors, he'd felt like crushing the man. And he knew— somewhere deep inside—that Bowen was not the man to do more than sigh with longing over her. He was little more than a half-grown youth, for all that he'd managed to survive Gavin's schemes. But Rhys hadn't been able to keep from reacting, had felt an overpowering need to hear her deny the betrayal. Always, the pain of betrayal haunted him. Would he ever forget it?

He kicked at a clump of matted rushes, and a spray of chaff and dust rose into the air. He moved to the fire and gazed into the flames as if an answer burned there.

"Did the Elf Queen throw you out of your own chamber?" came a soft, mocking question, and he whirled.

Cailin stepped from the shadows, a faint smile on her lips, her eyes a steady gleam. He frowned. He still felt uneasy with his half-sister, though Brian was more than taken with her. He managed a shrug.

"You've been listening to Sir Brian. She's no Elf Queen."

"No?" Cailin's shrug matched his own for indifference. "But there is something about her. It's her eyes. They're so deep and dark, full of mysteries and knowledge. Some whisper that she's one of the Tylwyth Teg."

He smiled slightly. "And you? You don't think so?"

Moving gracefully to a small stool near the fire, she sat down, clasping her hands around one knee as she gazed up at him. The half smile still played on her mouth, and the firelight made her pale hair glow in shades of red and gold. "I like her. She's different. No pallid, weak-kneed twit as I'd always imagined you would choose."

He shoved at the edge of the fire pit with the toe of his boot. "And why would you even think about the woman I'd choose?"

"Because I knew you'd come back some day. Davyyd said you would. He believed, though our father had given up hope. Wynn thought you preferred the English now, and maybe he was right after all." She studied him when he remained silent, her blue eyes silently appraising. Then she nodded. "Yea, Davydd was right. It's too bad you didn't care enough to come back before they died."

Stunned by the cruelty of her words, he could only stare at her. A log popped in the fire and collapsed in a shower of sparks and smoke. His eyes stung, and he blinked, raking a hand across them.

"What would you know of it?"

Her head tilted. "What, do you think we never talked? Do you think that just because I'm a bastard I wasn't part of the family? I was. Our father loved me, and I heard the talk at night, heard his pain because you had forgotten him."

"Forgotten—you don't know what you're talking about. You're just a child. You weren't even here when I left."

Mocking, clear, her eyes held his, the blue-gray glint in them so like his brothers' that he could almost see them in her soft features. "I know all about it, Lord Rhys."

The last was said softly, sneering, a challenge that brought him upright and tense. "Don't mock me, girl. You know nothing. Do you think I left willingly? I was eight when I was sold to the English king, eight when I saw my father and mother for the last time in my life." He hated the way his voice vibrated with emotion, but he couldn't control it. He looked away, into the flames. "You know nothing."

"I know my father grieved for you. He wrote you letters. You never answered. He was hungry for news of you, and had to get that from your squire. Ask him. Ask Morgan, who was sent with you to keep you safe, to remind you of your heritage and a family who loved you. Did you think it was easy for my father?" Her voice was angry, shaking a little as she said, "It wasn't. I wanted, just once, to hear him talk of me the way he talked of you. Oh, he was good to me. I was cared for, loved in a careless kind of way, but I wasn't a son. I wasn't the son he'd lost, that he couldn't replace. It was said that he wept when I was born, because I was a girl."

She stood up in a smooth motion, hands trembling as

she slid them down her skirts. "I hated you for a long time. And now you're here, and I think I still hate you."

When she turned away, he stopped her, a single word, hoarse and unsteady. "Wait."

She glanced at him, proud, defiant, making him think of Sasha. And he saw how young she was, how vulnerable and afraid, adrift in an unfriendly world, as he had once been. He held out his palm, a peace offering, a gesture that he wasn't certain she'd return. For a moment, there was a long silence. Then she drew in a shaky breath and reached out to put her hand in his. A smile wobbled on her mouth.

"Welcome home, Rhys."

The simple words washed over him in a cleansing tide, and he returned her smile. "It's good to be home."

It didn't eradicate all the pain, or the betrayals, but somehow, the simple gesture from this girl, a half-sister he hadn't even known existed until he came back, did more to ease his inner torment than he'd ever thought possible. Perhaps it wasn't an ending, but only the beginning.

The summer birch had been placed in position in Cwnllew on Saint John's Eve. *Y fedwen haf* they called it, and it was festooned with ribboned wreaths and topped with a weathercock complete with gilded feathers and flowing ribbons attached to its tail. A banner floated beneath the weathercock, and hefty village lads guarded the slender pole from theft by a neighboring village.

It was all in good fun, Cailin told Sasha, but the village that lost its summer birch was disgraced for ages. "But if we can manage to steal *y fedwen haf* from another village, then we'll be held in high esteem."

"And they call me pagan," Sasha muttered with a shake of her head. She eyed Cailin when the girl erupted into peals of amusement. "Am I still regarded as a witch?"

"Nay, a faerie." Cailin grinned. "It's your witching eyes."

"I'm getting weary of hearing that." She glanced across the bailey again, for what seemed the hundredth time. Rhys was still talking with some men she didn't know, though one of them she remembered being called Sir Nic-las, a man who had once been thought to be against Glen-lyon. Apparently, he had decided to join Rhys, if he had ever been against him. Sir Robert's suggestion of a tour-nament and Midsummer celebration had drawn many sup-porters, and the keep was crowded to bursting with guests.

Her gaze drifted over the knights and soldiers idly, not-ing that only a few were armed. Rhys. Sir Robert. Sir Clyde. The others carried dining daggers, but no lethal swords swung at their sides. A tremor of doubt quivered through her suddenly, a flash of premonition and evil, then it was gone. She stood, abruptly cold, as if a chill wind had washed over her. A vague stench remained, as if the wind had blown decay and death over the bailey. Caught by the force of the impression, she stood still and silent.

"Will you come to the *ffatio* tonight?" Cailin asked, and Sasha turned blinking to look at her.

"What is that?" Her voice sounded odd, and she cleared her throat.

"At midnight, all the unmarried women go to the well to wash a garment. According to legend, while you beat the garment with a bat staff, you say several times *Sawl ddaw igyd-fydio, doed i gyd-ffatio,* and then—"

"Wait. What does that mean?"

" 'He who would my partner be, let him come and wash with me.' It is said that a master met his servant at the well, and the maid was advanced to the head of the table to *cyd-fydio* as lawful wife instead of servant." Cailin's smile was impish. "Try it on my brother."

Sasha looked down at her hands, and the flowers she'd been stringing for a wreath. She'd crushed one of them between her fingers. She shrugged carelessly. "What makes you think I want to be your brother's wife?"

"I don't need the sight to know that. But don't worry—I won't tell."

Her head jerked up, and she met Cailin's eyes. The girl did not look away, or flinch, but returned her gaze stead-ily. Not many people could do that, save Rhys. Or Elspeth and Biagio, and only when they did not care if she knew their thoughts. Cailin kept her thoughts in Welsh, a deliberate act. Could she possibly know? Sasha frowned.

But before she could say anything Cailin was moving away, changing the direction of the conversation, talking about the festivities. "Sir Brian said that he's going to draw the lots to see who jousts against whom in the lists tomorrow. I told him he could wear my colors if he likes."

Because she didn't know what to say about Brian—no doubt he'd told Cailin a great many things about elf queens and faeries—Sasha said, "I have all the arrangements made for my surprise. Did Biagio tell you?"

"Just that he thinks you're going to end up in trouble over this. He claims all your brilliant ideas end up with him bleeding and you running for your life."

"A few have, but not all." She shook her head, throwing off the earlier pall. "He just never listens to all the directions. He thinks he knows it all, and then—well, you can imagine how some things have turned out. This will go well and amaze everyone if he'll just do what I tell him."

"Hmm. I can't understand why you want to do this. It sounds dangerous to me, and I don't even know all the details."

"It's not dangerous at all. I saw it done once in Cyprus. It was very impressive." She paused. Torture would not wring from her the reason she wanted to do it so badly. How could she admit to anyone that she wanted Rhys to be overwhelmed with admiration for her cleverness? Perhaps if he were, he would finally tell her how much he cared, that no woman would ever compare to her. It might fill the emptiness that still ached within her.

Sighing, Cailin perched atop a bench, swinging her feet against the wooden sides. Sunlight glinted in her hair. "Cyprus. I've never left Wales. Not that I really want to. I like it here."

Sasha gave her a disbelieving glance. "I can't imagine that."

"Can't you?" Cailin smiled. "Isn't there somewhere you want to go and never leave?"

She thought for a moment of her home, the whitewashed towers and minarets, the way the sun turned the gilded turrets to rose gold as it set each evening, and the soft breezes and strong fragrance of orange trees and burning incense. She remembered the mosaic tiles that lined the main courtyard, a huge fountain carved in the shape of a fish spouting water from its mouth, and the bright, living fish swimming in the fountain pool. There had been green plants and scrollwork, hanging silk curtains that drifted and billowed in the breezes, and the musical sound of stringed instruments playing delicately. Yea, she thought of it still, but not as often now. There were other memories, too, things she recalled without knowing how, flashing scimitars and burnooses stained with blood, screams and a head in a silver bowl. And then her father, all gentle affection, casual and careless, calling her *zaharat*.

But somehow, instead of clinging to those scenes with pristine clarity, other images intruded on her memory. Rhys the first time she saw him, a sun god on a black horse, riding in an English forest with his hair backlit like a halo, handsome and arrogant, and so completely breathtaking that she'd not been able to think. Then came images of the meadow, whitethorn above them, blue sky and Rhys's smoke-gray eyes, his hands working subtle magic on her and transporting her into another realm so that nothing else seemed to matter.

It was a betrayal of the prophecy to think of Rhys instead of her legacy. And yet, there were times when she couldn't help but wonder what it would be like to be with him always, to never leave his side.

"Sasha?"

Jerking her attention back to Cailin, she shrugged. "I've thought about it, and the only place I'd never want to leave is my home. It's what I was born for, and I intend to return."

Cailin smiled. "Then I wish for you what you wish for yourself. Shall I conjure up a spell for it?"

"Don't let Sir Brian hear you say that. I'll end up burned at the stake as a witch for influencing you." She wedged the final flower into the wreath of twined vines and handed it to Cailin. "Here. Use it to decorate the stick you planted in the ground."

"*Y fedwen haf*," Cailin corrected with a laugh. "If you're going to stay in Wales, you should at least learn some of the language."

"It sounds too much like spitting to me." She shaded her eyes with her hand, watching as Biagio approached. "Ah, I think he must have finished our preparations."

Reaching her, Biagio scowled. "I've got a bad feeling about this, bella. And anytime I have a bad feeling—"

"You've eaten too much. Don't worry. Did Elspeth finish my costume?"

He nodded, a gloomy expression on his face. His eyes moved to Cailin and he smiled faintly, then looked back at Sasha. "If his lordship takes exception to this, I'm going to tell him it was all your idea. Fair warning—I won't protect you."

"What a surprise. The echoes of your last denials are still ringing in my ears."

"You're quite, quite mad, and I hope you come to your senses before it's too late." He sighed. "But I'll be there."

"I knew you would. You never fail me."

Biagio looked up and past her, and a breeze lifted a dark strand of his hair, blowing it across his face. She was struck, suddenly, with how much older he looked. In just a short time, he'd taken on the harder edge of maturity, with a deeper voice, a faint shadow on his jawline, and that definite masculine arrogance. He was growing up. He would no longer be her companion in daring escapades, but one of those annoying male voices of admonition that threw shadows on such marvelous adventures.

Before she could yield to the sadness of how they'd both changed so greatly, he was looking back at her with a slight grimace. "The lord and master approaches. Run, while there's still time."

Cailin laughed, a soft sound, and put a hand over her mouth. He looked at her, smiling and appreciative, an appraising sort of regard that held a wealth of speculation. Sasha lifted a brow, then looked past him.

Rhys approached, his tall frame making her heart leap with anticipation and something else she dared not examine too closely. She put on her brightest smile and went to greet him.

"It looks as if all is going well, my lord."

"Yea." He smiled down at her, an intimate lift of his lips that seemed to be for her alone, soft and tender. Putting a hand on her elbow, he looked up at his sister, then Biagio. "Pretty children. Will you all be at the bonfire this evening?"

"I would never miss a Saint John's Eve bonfire," Cailin said promptly. "And I promised Sir Brian I would go with him at midnight to dig up Saint-John's-wort. He says the roots are good for keeping witches and demons away."

"I fear that he's influencing you too greatly," Rhys said, but he was smiling. "Has he given you charms yet?"

"Three."

"I'm not surprised." Rhys slid his arm around Sasha's waist, his gaze moving from Cailin back to her. "There's to be another meeting of the barons, so I'll see you later at the bonfire."

"That's all right. Biagio and I planned to meet Elspeth." She smiled. Things couldn't have worked out better. She'd wondered how she would manage to avoid him. "I'm certain I'll see you there, my lord."

As Rhys walked away, Biagio stared at her narrowly. *Magic, bella? How do you always manage to get your way?*

She smiled serenely. It did seem to work out that way.

CHAPTER NINETEEN

A huge bonfire lit the bailey. Flames flared high, sending up showers of sparks and curls of smoke, and villagers and castle folk alike danced gaily around the blaze. There had been dancing since early afternoon, though now dark shadows crept over the bailey and village below, cast by the towers and turrets above. Children shrieked and dogs barked, and the air was filled with festivity and laughter.

Rhys watched from a small dais erected under a tree in the bailey. It had been decided that all weapons would be left at the castle gates, and the men and soldiers roaming the grounds had nothing more than small dining daggers with them. There had been few protests, surprisingly enough, for most visiting barons saw the sense in it. And it freed everyone to enjoy themselves without worry of betrayal. Not that his own men weren't armed, for of course, order had to be maintained. Already, a few men too full of drink had been dragged below to the dungeons to sleep awhile.

But aside from that, there had been no confrontations

or disorder. The meetings were going well, and his vassals swore to his standard. He and Sir Niclas of Raglan had met privately, and Rhys believed him when Sir Niclas said he would never have come to Gavin's aid. It had all been a ruse, a device by John and Gavin to weaken the strength and authority of the barons under the Prince of Deheubarth, to establish John's own dominance over the Marcher lords. And it had failed. Now he was firmly established here, lent credibility by the strength of his neighbors, given benediction by the appearance of the Prince of Deheubarth. For the prince had arrived a few hours before, his retinue streaming behind him, his very presence a gracious blessing and confirmation.

It was going well.

Relieved, yet somehow ill at ease with the smooth progression of events, Rhys gazed at the crowd and thought of all the things that could go wrong. A chance word, a squabble between barons, an insult, could propel matters toward disaster. And yet there was no hint of trouble.

"It's finally going right, and you want to worry," Brian muttered when he asked once again if all the guards were in place. "Nothing is going wrong, Rhys. Even your lady is behaving with proper manners."

Amused, Rhys slanted his knight a glance. "You sound surprised."

"Yea. Other than a few incantations, I don't expect her to do anything too dreadful."

"She enjoys goading you. I told you that. You let her do it to you, so I can't really feel too badly about it." He paused, then shifted in his chair and glanced down the length of the dais to where the prince sat in regal splendor. Giving his status proper due, Lord Rhys of Deheubarth had been given the place of honor, a seat above the others, accompanied by members of his retinue. Older now, the prince seemed to be enjoying himself immensely, and had remarked on Glenlyon's hospitality.

"Where is she?" Brian asked after a moment, scanning the crowd. "I haven't seen her or your sister for a while."

He shrugged. "I saw her earlier. She went to change into

proper garments, she said. You know how females are, always fussing about gowns and jewelry."

Brian frowned. "I never thought of her as caring much about those things. She seemed just as content to wear nothing as—grant pardon, my lord. I shouldn't have reminded you of that."

"No," he muttered, "you shouldn't." Curse her. Brian was right. She never cared about proper attire. So where was she?

"I think the entertainment is about to begin." Sir Robert came up behind them, his weathered face creased with satisfaction. "There are tumblers and acrobats as well as others, my lord. Shall I give the signal for them to begin?"

It was still light, though the shadows were growing quickly, and he nodded. "Yea, Sir Robert, give the signal before it's too dark for everyone to see well."

At the end of the bailey, but directly in front of the barons' dais, a platform had been erected. It was far enough above the ground that those at the back of the crowd could see, and people began to throng toward the area as musicians mounted the platform and began to play. Torches were lit, casting leaping light over the stage. Tumblers catapulted their bodies across the stand in a series of cartwheels and somersaults, bodies twisting agilely into near impossible positions. Small dogs barked and leaped through hoops, whirling like furry dancers, and palms banging wildly against taut sheepskins provided accompaniment. Bells jangled, stringed instruments twanged, and the air was filled with noise and laughter.

Rhys looked through the crowd again but still didn't see Sasha. He'd thought she would be at the front of the crowd, for she'd reveled in the recent activities. A good thing, as he hadn't been able to give her as much attention as she seemed to crave. But there had been so much to do of late, the meetings, the summons, the hundreds of details that couldn't all be left to Owain to complete—and he'd still been with her at night, though late, sliding into the wide bed to drag her under him, waking her with kisses and heated caresses, ignoring her sleepy protests until he felt her begin to respond—yea, he'd not completely ignored her.

Brian made a strangled sound, and Rhys glanced at him. He was staring toward the stage, eyes wide and riveted, and Rhys followed his gaze. Then he scowled. Up on the stage, in a whirl of voluminous cloak and loose dark hair, stood Sasha. Biagio was with her, a collage of gay colors and garments that he recognized: blue cape, scarlet jerkin, varicolored hose, and a new cap with bells sewn along its dangling length. Curse them. He hadn't given permission for her to be part of the entertainment. He hadn't even been asked. Or advised of her intention. His hands curled into fists atop the arms of his wooden chair, and he fumed silently, unwilling to let anyone know he had been ignorant of her conduct.

Holding up her hands, Sasha called for quiet, and oddly, the noisy crowd fell silent. She smiled, glanced around them, a sweep of dark eyes and lush lashes, the smile mysterious and frightening. Some people gasped, others murmured, but all were mesmerized as she swayed across the stage and indicated a tall, silk-draped structure.

"A miracle for your entertainment," she said into the hush, "a feat of magic to dazzle and amaze you. My handsome assistant will show you that there is nothing inside the stall but silk curtains, a container of only air and . . . magic. . . ."

Magic. Was she mad? So many viewed her askance, leery of her witching eyes and fey reputation, and now she was tweaking their noses with a blatant display of magic on Midsummer Eve . . . she was liable to end burned as a witch before the night was over, but he could do no more than sit and watch in stunned silence as she strutted across the stage as blithely as if she were a princess in her court.

Biagio made a great show of fluttering the curtains, lifting them and shaking them, the bells on his long cap jangling accompaniment. He was a blur of color, dark hair and flashing teeth, jewel-bright garments and graceful motions. When he'd proven how empty the silk structure was, he paused, sweeping the crowd with a lingering gaze, smile still curving his mouth.

Sasha stepped forward and surveyed the people gazing up at the platform. "I shall need more help with this feat, for it is very involved and requires witnesses to prove the power of magic. Ah, you, Sir Knight, come up onto the platform with me, if you please. Doesn't he look strong and daring? Capable of withstanding magic?"

Spatters of laughter sounded, some of it uneasy, all of it fascinated, and Rhys narrowed his eyes as he recognized Sir Bowen climbing onto the high platform. What did she think she was doing? His hands tightened into fists and he leaned forward, tensing.

"My lord," Brian murmured at his elbow, his voice betraying his own awareness of the danger, "all are watching you."

It was true. Spectators glanced at him and then the stage, and he knew his reaction would be well noted. So he sat back, forced himself to relax, putting a smile on his face as he plotted Sasha's imminent punishment for being so bold and foolish.

And then she was calling up another participant, and Cailin stepped onto the stage as well. Brian wheezed in horror. He half rose to his feet, and Rhys put out a hand. "Sir Brian—all are watching you."

His mocking reminder was not sufficient to restrict Brian, who slung him a swift, horrified glance, and pushed his way from the platform. So much for watching calmly. He turned back to look at the stage, where Sasha was grandly displaying Biagio inside the curtained structure. She had Cailin and Sir Bowen inspect it closely, showing to those watching that it was only a flimsy silk booth. They rounded it, lifted corners of material, shook it.

When they stepped back, the crowd was hushed. Slowly, every move a graceful glide, Sasha lifted the hood of her cloak and covered her hair. It concealed her completely from head to foot, flowing around her in a dark river of black, so that the only visible signs of her human form were her hands emerging from the folds. A slender hazel branch swished through the air and motioned for the silk curtains to be drawn around Biagio as he stood in the center of the booth. Quiet shrouded the crowd. Sasha

glided across the stage, her voice lifting in a patter of
meaningless sounds, high and lilting, words of enchantment, evoking spirits and magic and mystery. A shower of
white flower petals flew into the air, some drifting on a
sudden gust of wind, others falling like new snow across
the platform and onto the crowd closest to the stage. A
concerted gasp went up, then that breathless waiting
again, a tension that gripped them all as she wove her
magic in song and suspense.

Cailin and Sir Bowen stood to the side, silent and tense.
A rattle sounded, clattering metal rings attached to a taut
circle of sheepskin, light and tinkling, bells and cryptic music. It found a cadence, grew louder, the thumping beat of
a palm against the sheepskin finding the tempo of a beating heart, steady and rhythmic, drawing the net of tension
tighter and tighter. The black cloak swirled, swept across
the platform, briefly disappeared in a drop over the platform's edge, then reappeared a few feet farther down,
moving more stiffly now, a jerky walk from the other side
of the silken tent. Around and around the cloaked figure
circled, chanting nonsensical words in a higher singsong.

Suddenly, a white dove streaked skyward, wings beating
against the air as it rose higher and higher. More gasps,
then the cessation of the bells and sheepskin drum. Another swift move, a slash of the hazel limb. Then—shocking—the silence exploded with sound, and the stage was
wrapped in a blinding fog. People screamed, falling back
in panic, then, as no one else on the stage moved, their
curiosity won over their fear.

At a beckoning from the cloaked form, Cailin and Sir
Bowen moved forward and drew back the silk curtains.
The booth was empty.

Before anyone could move, a shout drifted down from
above. Heads turned, mouths dropped open as people
gaped. Atop a wall overlooking the bailey, perched on a
stone step of the tower gate, Biagio waved a greeting. Bells
jangled on his cap, his blue cape swirled, and his shapely
legs pranced in varicolored hose. A blur of white teeth,
dark hair, and scarlet jerkin, mocking and triumphant, an
instant transport from place to place in full view of the

assembly. He strutted like a peacock, leaped nimbly over a parapet, then vanished into a sudden puff of smoke.

Before anyone had recovered from their shock, there was another explosion and a swirl of smoke atop the stage, and all eyes turned to see Biagio sweep them a low bow. He looked up, gaze skimming over the stunned faces of the crowd.

"For your pleasure and amusement, lords and ladies, an entertaining illusion. We hope you enjoyed it."

When he lifted an arm and pointed, heads turned to the tower wall, and there stood another Biagio, a slender figure in blue cape and scarlet jerkin, waving impudently and laughing. Sasha. Atop the stage, the cloaked figure let the hood fall back, and Elspeth nodded to the crowd. A jest. An illusion as he'd said, a trick after all. A deft switch of players. Not magic, just strange deception.

Among the applause, relief.

No less relieved was Rhys, who wasn't the least bit superstitious. And with the relief, was fury. White-hot fury. An instant's error, and there could have been a wild riot, a panicked reaction from a mob no less dangerous because it was contained in castle walls. Even soldiers—supposedly logical and clear thinking—had been known to panic at the suggestion of the supernatural and magic. He'd not forgotten their reaction that day in the weald, when a small figure in a hooded purple robe had barred their path and scared their horses.

"Remarkable entertainment, my lord," the Prince of Deheubarth leaned forward to say, "most remarkable."

"Yea," he managed to say, "I must go and commend them on their performance. By your leave, my lord. . . ."

He was stepping down from the dais, making his way through the crowd. People, released now from the tension of terror to laugh and talk of the amazing feat and how none of them had been at all frightened, parted to clear him a path. Someone gasped, and he wondered what was in his face that drew such a reaction when Midsummer magic apparently had not. . . .

• • •

Laughing, Sasha moved swiftly through the shadowed
gloom. No one had lit torches here yet, and the narrow
staircases of the tower gates were dark. Oh, the looks on
those faces—and Rhys. Would she ever be able to forget
his expression? Even from so far away, his stunned reaction was evident. But what had everyone expected? She
was the Elf Queen, a faerie, one of the Tylwyth Teg. At
least she wasn't out dancing in the moonlight in the midst
of a ring of mushrooms and cowslip blossoms.

The bells on the cap jangled noisily as she skipped down
the steps, one hand grazing the stone walls for balance,
her attention focused on her feet so that she wouldn't mis-
step. It would hardly be very inspiring for the Elf Queen
to be found at the bottom of the steps with a broken leg
after managing to awe an entire village with her performance.

She reached the bottom and stepped into a faint pool of
illumination thrown by a rushlight. It sputtered in a holder
over her head, spraying sparks. She paused. Now which
way was it? She'd gone over and over it before the trick,
knowing there was little time to switch places with Elspeth
and manage to magically "appear" on the tower wall.
Now that it was all over, she could go and collect her
accolades. Oh, they would all be so admiring, so effusive
in their praise, and what would Rhys say then? Would he
join them? Would he finally see that she was much more
than just a warm body in the night?

A twist, a turn, shadowed walls and lengthy corridors
empty of guards and soldiers, and she was standing in an
unfamiliar, dark chamber. A single torch hissed in an iron
holder. There was the soft, subtle echo of a distant clang,
as if an iron door had swung shut, then nothing. It made
her think of the dungeon suddenly, and the furtive,
stealthy noises that had inhabited her days and nights,
closing in around her.

Attuned to a growing tension that loomed in the dim-
ness, she heard the first scattering of thoughts, attended
by a sense of pervading evil. She took an involuntary step
backward. Her heart raced. Something wicked drew near.
Dark, forceful, drawing energy it came closer.

Midsummer Eve . . . Cailin's laughing warnings, her teasing predictions of evil spirits and demons, suddenly took on substance. It was the borderline hour, the hour between day and night, not one season or the other, the time when spirits freely roamed. Dull bells and muffled footsteps, all the whispered tales and remembered myths of tortured souls and anguished howls . . . but she did not believe. She knew better than most that the inner torment, the human evil, held far more power over this world than any of the other world forces.

And yet, and yet . . . the approaching malevolence was dark and powerful, a twisted curl of malicious hatred and enmity. It left her breathless, staggering, weak enough to reach out for support. Her hand grazed the stone wall, damp roughness scraping her fingertips as she hastily tried to erect her mental barriers against the advancing wickedness.

She was on her knees, dazed and shaky, concentrating on resistance, while around her the blur of light and shadows spun faster and faster in a rapid arc that left her faint. Drawing on all her inner resources, she steadied herself with an effort, slowly strengthening the barriers enough to allow her to rise to her feet again.

"What have we here?" a rough voice mocked, a black menacing drift from the shadows, slipping up and around her, a web of spite and relish. "I believe it's the Elf Queen. . . ."

She looked up and wasn't completely surprised to see Sir Clyde step from the darkness around him. The clang of a sword accompanied him as he stepped into the glow of the torch, his broad, flat-featured face a blur of light and shadow. He came forward, but behind him another shadow lurked, hidden from her vision.

But not from her inner sight. Not from that perception that *knew*, always knew. And now her gift arrowed in with swift and unerring precision on the shrouded form hanging back.

She laughed, softly, a laugh to match his wicked leer, an effort to throw them off guard. "Step into the light, Sir Gavin. Don't be shy, for I know you well. . . ."

He did, his eyes black flames, his lips drawn back in a cruel sneer. A free man. No chains. No cell walls to hold him—nothing but space and opportunity surrounding him.

"I should have hung you at once, I think," Gavin remarked, a silky purr in the shadows. "But perhaps there's a use for you after all. Take her, Sir Clyde. Bring her with us. We'll use her as a shield, and when we've managed an escape—" he smiled, "we'll leave her body for my cousin to find."

Sir Clyde looked at her, uneasy and distrustful. "I think it'd be best to kill her now."

"Thinking is not one of your virtues," Gavin snapped. "If it was, my cousin would never have taken the keep in the first place."

Sullenly, "I told you. He kept his plans private until the last minute. There was no time to warn you. Not without being killed for it."

"Really." Gavin shrugged casually, then there was a swift move like a striking snake as his hand flashed out and held her by the wrist, fingers tightening cruelly. "Do not think to fly, little dove. We're not through with you yet." He turned to Sir Clyde. "Bring the torch."

She twisted, knowing it was futile but compelled to try. He'd expect it. And she had to do what was expected, all the while plumbing his mind for his intentions, seeking an escape, a way out of his dangerous trap.

But it was difficult to penetrate the dark haze of his mind, the twisting channels like the turnings of a rat, tunneling this way and that through a labyrinth of thought fragments and fears, hate and evil—it left her numb as he dragged her with them.

Down, down, through dank, fetid passageways where she dared not look at the stones beneath her feet, slick with slime and ooze, malodorous refuse and muffled squeaks. . . . She shuddered, and Gavin laughed softly. Pale light sputtered and flared, casting demon shapes against the wall that looked, in her fevered fear, like Satan's imps. And when it seemed as if he'd taken her far below the surface of the earth and into the very bowels of hell, Sir Clyde was shoving open a door, and fresh air that smelled of oak and wine washed over them.

She blinked. More light here, though still dim. Rows and rows of wine casks against cavern walls, cool air and oak spice. The storage cellar. But how had they arrived here from the castle walls? There must be an entire maze beneath the keep. A rabbit warren of hidden tunnels.

Gavin gave her a shove, and she stumbled forward, striking her head against a corner of stone. Lights exploded in front of her eyes, tiny brilliant suns that shimmered and spun. Dazed, she was vaguely aware of being dragged carelessly across uneven stones as Gavin moved with swift, grim determination.

The blow to her head inverted her thoughts, and instead of focusing on her own blind fear and apprehension, she was suddenly, sharply aware of Sir Clyde's. It was almost palpable. Shaping and forming, the dark fear loomed over them, wearing Rhys's face. Clyde was terrified of him. Deeply, irrevocably, afraid. There was no defined reason for it, only the foreboding of what would happen were he discovered to be a traitor, and a few swift, vague images of another man who had betrayed Rhys ap Griffyn. His mind immediately rebounded to another subject. But it was enough.

Lifting her head, she focused on Sir Clyde.

"Have you thought about what Lord Rhys will do when he discovers your betrayal, Sir Clyde?" Mocking, soft, taunting, she fixed her eyes on him intently. "Dying like that is said to be painful . . . and lengthy."

"Shut your mouth," Gavin growled, jerking hard on her arm. He drew her close to him, his arm cutting off her wind as he curved it around her middle. "Open the passage my cousin so thoughtfully cleared for us, Sir Clyde. And be quick about it. If the guards discover I'm gone, they'll raise the hue and cry."

"It takes at least two men to open that door," Sir Clyde said, his eyes narrowed and his mouth thinned with terror. "Not even Lord Rhys could manage it alone."

Gavin swore, grating, "You talk about him as if he could move mountains. He's just a man, like any other.

His blood is red and spills just as readily. Here. I'll lend my weight to it, and we'll move it aside."

Shoving her ahead of him, Gavin pressed her against the rack of wine casks, using her weight as well. She threw up her hands just in time, wedging them against oak, rough wood splintering into her palms. Caught between two immovable forces, she barely managed to breathe as he flattened himself against her, and she heard the faint, groaning creak of wood and rusty hinges. Lightheaded, breathless, she drew in an aching breath and snatched at the wavering blur of vision.

At the edges of her perception, a slight intrusion hovered, faint at first, then growing sharper, and then she heard it: *Faithless daoine sidhe . . . she'll betray Rhys if she can . . . I told him, I told him, but he'd never listen to me . . . when I catch her, then he'll see that I was right, that she never meant to stay. . . .*

Brian. And he was so intent on proving her betrayal that he was walking into a trap. She had to warn him. He might be her only chance. But how, how could she warn him without letting Gavin know he was near?

Twisting suddenly, wrenching loose and ducking under Gavin's straining arm, she managed to take two steps away before he caught her, his hand snagging in her hair to jerk her viciously back. She screamed, a piercing shriek that reverberated off the stone walls and ceiling, bouncing back in waves of sound. Gavin struck her, hard, the back of his hand catching her cheek and slamming her to the stone floor.

"Stupid bitch. Where do you think you can go? Sir Clyde—push it the rest of the way open. We need to hurry . . . hurry, curse you."

As Gavin pinned her to the floor and tears blurred her eyes from the blow, she heard Brian's sudden thoughts, his wary waiting. He'd heard. He'd heard . . .

Panting and heaving, the bulky Sir Clyde finally got the hidden door all the way open. It yawned, a square black hole behind the wine racks, admitting a rush of cool air and dampness. Gavin was dragging her toward it, and she struggled to delay him despite his showering blows and kicks, his angry curses and snarled threats. Sir Clyde's fear and the distant caution from Brian blurred together, a mix of emotions and reactions, the one bleeding into the other.

But Gavin—ah, his intent was focused and fierce, steady and black as the darkest sin. And he did not intend for either her or Sir Clyde to leave this tunnel alive. It would be Gavin, only Gavin, escaping to a waiting horse, fleeing Glenlyon and Wales, riding to Prince John . . .

Her face ached and her lips felt puffy, but she managed to grasp at the edge of the stone wall as Gavin pulled her into the tunnel. Her gaze shot to Clyde, standing just behind her, his expression terrified and anxious.

"He'll kill you too, you know," she said hoarsely. "Do you think he'll let you live knowing what you know?"

Gavin turned and kicked her, muttering a curse and reassurance all in the same breath, pulling her fingers free of the wall. "She'd say anything. Come on. I need you, Sir Clyde. You know I do."

But Sir Clyde had paused, frowning, and that hesitation cost him dear. She heard it before they did, of course, the stealthy intent, the grim purpose, and then a sword came slashing down, catching Sir Clyde across his back and sending him stumbling forward. He turned, tried to lift his sword arm but couldn't. Blood bubbled from his mouth. A puzzled expression flickered across his face, and his movement ended in a loose sprawl across the open door of the tunnel. Fear and despair, then anguished realization ignited in his brain, a blinding flash of light, then descending darkness, and he made a gurgling sound as Sasha turned away, closing her mind to him.

Brian appeared behind the body, bloodied sword in one hand, fire in his eyes. A strange, wild excitement creased his features, and his eyes gleamed as green as a cat's. "Gavin. I see the evil spirits are loosed on Midsummer Eve."

Gavin laughed softly. "Yea, I see that you are. Are you still sucking hind tit, Irishman, or has my cousin granted you something besides his best wishes?"

Brian tossed his sword from one hand to the other, deft and sure, agile and practiced. His mind raced with possibilities and options, and he had a quick, blurred view of the tunnel behind Gavin. Fear sparked inside him, fear of the dark shadows and not of the man in front of them. Brian was more afraid of vague blackness than Gavin's sword. Determined to keep the fight in the open, he taunted his opponent.

"Better hind tit than none, Gavin. That's what you have. Or had. You won't even have life to grieve over your shortcomings much longer." He beckoned him closer, a curl of his fingers. "Come to the killing."

Fists clenching her tightly, wrapped in the scarlet jerkin beneath her blue cape, Gavin dragged her in front of him. "Would you kill his lady?" he mocked.

Brian shrugged. " 'Tis no secret that I've never held her dear. If she must die, then I won't grieve. I've done my best to rid my lord of her since the day she dropped out of the wind."

The worst part was knowing that he meant most of it. There was a detached worry about how to explain it to Rhys, but other than that, no great sorrow. She glared at him, but this was no time for petty concerns.

" 'Twould suit you if I was killed," she spat. She half turned. "Don't listen to him, my lord Gavin. He'd as soon kill me as not."

"So it's *my lord* now, is it." Gavin hesitated, his mind flitting from one option to the next, discarding one after the other as too dangerous. Then he took a step back and saw the same flicker of dismay in Brian's face as she did. There was a subtle change in his posture, and he edged into the waiting darkness of the tunnel. Brian didn't advance, but his eyes registered discomfort and uneasiness. Gavin laughed. "Very well—'tis your turn, Irishman. Come to the killing."

With that, he leaped backward, pulling her with him, dragging her over rough, cutting stones and down the narrow, winding chasm of the tunnel, deeper and deeper into the thick, inky darkness that closed around them like a fist.

Sound in the close space was magnified. It bounced from corbeled walls in eerie echoes: their footsteps and rasping breaths, the muffled grunts and pants, the clink of his sword against stone, the drag of his boots over the floor. He was feeling his way, as the torch had been left behind, and she was dragged helplessly along. Brian's distress grew fainter and fainter, then was replaced by a deep, surging decision as he plunged in behind them.

Now she felt Brian's fear behind, Gavin's dread determination ahead, and between the two she battled her own shattering reactions. Powerless, a leaf in the wind, buffeted by the storms around her, she could only be swept along. Aware that Brian's grim purpose was to rid the world of any danger to Rhys, she knew that should he accidentally miss in the darkness and kill her, 'twould be no great loss.

And so she gauged the distance between the two men, sensed when Brian drew near enough that he considered striking at Gavin's back, and wedged her foot against the wall and shoved. It didn't gain her release, but it did send Gavin careening off balance. He cursed, heard Brian behind him and turned, loosing her as he lifted his sword to meet the impending threat.

As Brian surged forward, she cried out a warning that she barred his path, and somehow he managed to clear her as he struck out at Gavin. The deafening sound of steel hitting stone rang in the close air. Sparks scattered in the dark. Gavin struck toward the sparks, hoping to catch Brian's sword, but it wasn't there. Grunts echoed from both men. Desperation tinged the air, thick and heavy. Sword met sword, more sparks flew. They closed, straining against each other, panting and cursing, threats fusing them into one solid mass of fierce intensity.

Suddenly, a high, piercing shriek came from somewhere in the darkness, a shivering wail that made the hair on the back of her neck stand up. She felt Brian's attention waver, focus on his gripping fear of banshees and demons, and then—devastating and swift—his spurt of surprise at the sliding thrust of a thin blade between his ribs. He grunted—shocked, dismayed, thinking of Rhys and how he'd failed him, despairing for Sasha's fate—then sank slowly to the tunnel floor in a heavy sprawl.

She screamed then, an anguished wail that reverberated

from the walls and ceiling and stones, surrounding them as if a hundred throats had loosed that cry. Surprised by the depth of her own grief, she felt for Brian in the dark, felt the fluttering little breaths he took, labored and fading, damp warmth on her hands that she knew would be his blood. And then Gavin was reaching for her, finding her by feel and not sight, or maybe by the sound of her sobs, pulling her with him, dragging her along the rough floor, his breath rasping and loud.

And then, far ahead, a tiny prick of moonlight, a faint flicker that faded, then renewed. Gavin was a dark shadow against darker shadows, his thoughts narrowed on escape.

Battered, bruised, scraped raw in places, she couldn't offer much resistance as Gavin swept her toward the light. Fresh air drifted into the passage, cool and smelling of wind and trees. And then they were outside. It was dark, though not the tomb black of the tunnel. Moonlight filtered through trees, gleamed on the bare hump of rocks stacked in such an odd shape. She'd seen them before, the cairns erected by primeval men. Panting, on her hands and knees where Gavin dropped her, Sasha looked up through the hanging curtain of her hair.

A familiar whinny greeted her, and she turned her Gift to the dark shape barely visible against the stacked rocks of the cairn. Bayosha. Her mare. Another soft whinny sounded, and Gavin cursed, looking around cautiously. Nothing but the sound of the wind through the trees and two horses. Beside the mare, a sturdy animal waited patiently. Both were saddled and ready, tied to a heavy limb.

Gavin sagged against a rock for a moment, breathing hard from his exertions. He looked toward her, and she smiled. She saw herself as he saw her, a feral curl of her lips over white teeth, hair loose and hanging in front of her face, contempt and hatred in every line of her body. He enjoyed creating fear. It gave him the sense of power that he craved.

He straightened, a lean, vindictive threat, dark haired and thin faced, all cruel smile and burning eyes as he approached her. Lifting his sword, he brought the tip up under her chin to tilt her head back. She had to look up at him. He was cold steel and lethal promise, yet she refused to cower, refused to give him what he craved. She met his eyes and laughed.

"Little man, do you fear the dark? Do you fear the other side? You should. It waits for you. I have the sight you know. A Gift. I see them—can you? Winged demons, crawling, slimy things, maggots, and hungry dragons—they wait for you, Gavin of Glamorgan. . . ."

Despite his fury, fear crept up his spine, making him shiver, filling his head and body with cold dread, and he couldn't check a glance around him before he looked back at her. "Evil bitch. You would know about maggots and demons, wouldn't you. You're one of them."

She smirked. "Aye. So I am. Sir Clyde told you, didn't he? Ah, I hear that he did . . . What's that? A lucky guess? Nay, 'tis not luck that gives me the power to hear you, Gavin, lord of darkness and death. Shall I tell you what you're thinking now? How you wonder if I'm right? If Sir Clyde was right, and all the other rumors you heard. Yea, you wonder if I'm the Elf Queen, and if I can truly weave magic spells. Wonder no more."

Drawing her legs slowly under her so that she crouched, she saw herself again through his eyes: a wild-looking creature staring up at him, holding him transfixed with her gaze and her game. Then she focused on the horses. Bayosha was easy, a simple transferral, a high, crooning song, and the mare began to snort and plunge at the end of her tether. Gavin's attention swung from Sasha to the horse, and he moved to grab at the reins with one hand. Now the other animal began to snort, eyes rolling wildly, hooves lashing out, making Gavin swear and leap out of the way.

When he looked toward Sasha, she smiled. "Shall I call down the powers of darkness now? Are you ready for them? I can summon the wind and the rain and thunder and lightning if I like." Rising slowly to her feet, holding his attention with her soft, hissing words, she read his intent before he could move and stepped quickly to the other side, avoiding his swift reach. All her senses were trained on this one man, on the difference between life and death.

He waited only for the slightest of chances to use his sword or dagger.

And because she could not be distracted if she meant to survive, she didn't hear anything until the voice came from behind her, soft and deadly and sliding into the soft night air like the sharpest sword: "Touch her and you die, Gavin."

Rhys. Her attention wavered, slid away, and Gavin made his move before she could avoid him. In a smooth, swift coil like the striking of a cobra, he swung around and encircled her, his arm curving around her waist and bringing her up hard against his chest. He laughed.

"I'm in your debt, cousin. She seems adept at avoiding me." He held up his dagger when Rhys took a step forward. "Ah ah—if I die, I take her with me." He drew the blade lightly from just under her ear down her neck, and she felt a stinging warmth where it touched. "Just a little blood now, but you and I both know how much blood there would be if I were to dig a little deeper."

Rhys had halted at once, and now he stood, moon silvered and taut, a vibrating promise against the yawning darkness of the tunnel behind him. Even with her head back against Gavin's chest, she could see the pale sheen of fury in Rhys's eyes, the hot glitter that leaped in their depths.

"Let her go, Gavin. Your quarrel is with me."

"Oh, aye, if I let her go, you'd spit me like a boar on the end of that sword. I'm not that big a fool, cousin."

Silence fell. Gavin's breath was a harsh, rasping rattle in her ear, his thoughts spinning around and around, seeking escape, seeking victory. And then he found it, an idea that splintered the darkness of his thoughts, a final, agonizing choice that he grasped like a weapon.

"You've played chess, cousin. Yea, I know you have. You've been a pawn at times." Gavin laughed again, a rumble at her back. His sword hilt pressed painfully against her ribs. "Well, I have your queen. What will you lose to save her? What will you yield to keep your queen safe?"

Silence again, taut and stretching. A night bird called,

the wind rustled tree branches overhead, and in the distance there was a shout. And then a single word in reply: "All."

Even Gavin was taken aback. "All? All of what? A castle, a bishop, a knight—a king? All, cousin?"

"All. If the queen is lost, all is lost. The most simple player knows that." Rhys lowered his sword slightly, the tip pointing to the ground. "Loose her and I will yield all."

Sasha stared at him. Hot tears stung her eyes. In that moment, in that split second of time too swift to blink, she saw the truth in his face. He meant it. He would yield all for her.

Incredulous, his mind a blank numbness, Gavin repeated, "You will yield all for a woman?"

"Nay, not for a woman. For that woman. For the queen." Rhys jerked his chin up. "Take Glenlyon. It's a cold pile of stones. I can build another. Or I can take another, perhaps in a land where the wind blows soft and the sun always shines on fountains and silk. But every chess player knows there's only one queen."

"Swear it," Gavin said hoarsely, "swear it on your sword and your knight's oath, Rhys ap Griffyn, swear to me that you will yield Glenlyon for the lady's life."

Holding up his sword, Rhys clasped the hilt and met Gavin's gaze. "I swear it on my knight's oath that if you loose the lady, I will yield Glenlyon to you."

For a long moment there was tense silence. Gavin stared at his cousin, hardly daring to believe, yet knowing the value of Rhys's sworn oath. Then he laughed softly. "John will give it to me anyway."

"John is not king."

Gavin shrugged. "He will be."

"Even if he were, I know how to deal with John. King or prince, he's the same man." He gestured with the tip of his sword. "Let her go."

"You're mad, Rhys ap Griffyn. If I release her, I'm dead."

"Try me." There was a grim certainty in his words. "I gave you my word. My knight's oath."

Gavin drew in a shuddering breath. He wanted to believe. Sasha could feel it, hear it, over and over, a spinning circle, but he didn't trust. He gauged Rhys by his own measure, knew that he would lie to save a life, if only his own, and he did not believe his cousin. There was only one advantage he held: the girl in front of him. And as long as she was alive, he was alive. That much he knew for certain.

Backing toward the horses, he shook his head. "I'll take her with me, cousin. If you mean to keep your word, you won't follow me. Once I've reached England, I'll release her. I swear it."

"No." Rhys stepped forward, his sword shifting to the ready. "I won't let you leave with her, Gavin. She stays."

Shaking his head, Gavin took another step back, dragging her with him. His sword was a pressure against her ribs, the dagger still at her throat a cold weight against her skin. "I don't trust you that far. I know better."

She had to do something. She would be caught in the middle of their battle. So she focused her talent and energies on the horses, on the already nervous mare just behind Gavin. In a corner of her mind, she became aware of fear, of the watchful regard of the man approaching, the smell of sweat on him, the taste of the bit, the sweet scent of grass—and over it all, the smell of blood on the man. . . . Closer and closer, a threat, a reminder of vicious blows and pain. . . .

Screaming, rearing, the mare lashed out, her forelegs thrashing in the air as she rose to the reach of her tether, and one hoof caught Gavin's shoulder, spinning him, loosening his hold on Sasha.

She was ready and threw herself from his grasp. The sharp edge of the blade slipped to one side, and she was free. There was a shout, a hoarse cry, and she turned around.

Moving with the pouncing lunge of a lion, Rhys was on Gavin. One one knee, Gavin flung up his sword to parry the blow, but the force of the downward stroke drove him back, steel sliding on steel, until he twisted desperately to one side. Agile, daring, only chance left, Gavin gave a mighty swing of one arm to push the locked swords to one

side, bringing up the dagger he still held in his other fist.
Sasha screamed.

Moonlight glinted on the smooth strike of the blade, a
quick flash toward Rhys's unprotected belly. She was
stumbling forward, mindless, knowing only that she had
to stop it somehow, couldn't let Rhys be killed like Brian,
and then, in a swift motion, Rhys untangled his sword
from the clash, swung it around in a sweeping arc, catching dagger and hand in a clean swipe. Gavin screamed.
Still clutching his sword in his right hand, he made a futile
effort to bring it around, but Rhys was too quick. A savage
blow of the sword's edge caught Gavin, and Sasha turned
quickly away, unable to watch the end, unable to see another death.

It was over. Only a faint grunt, a sigh, then a dark
shroud, and it was over. There was a soft thud of something falling into the leaves, and Sasha realized that she
was on her hands and knees, sobbing. Dark silence. No
clashing thoughts, no rending emotions. Just this, a shuddering release.

Behind her, she heard the arrival of Owain, Sir Bowen,
and Sir Robert, quick whispers in the night, assurances
that all was well. Others came, and she knew that Gavin
was being taken away, heard Biagio ask for her, heard a
soft, gentle reply and reassurance. But she couldn't move,
couldn't react, couldn't bring herself to face anyone. Not
now. Perhaps not ever.

She didn't know how long she knelt there, her knees
pressed into the damp earth and leaves, hair a stringy curtain in front of her face. But her breathing had slowed,
and the world slowly began to regain focus. And then
Rhys was beside her. A solid presence. Silent, strong,
steady. Waiting for her. She looked up, and he smiled
slightly.

His hand lifted, brushed hair away from her eyes, thumb
dragging over tear tracks. "Are you hurt, flower?"

No. She wasn't hurt. She was exhausted, drained, uncertain, but she wasn't hurt. She managed a faint smile
and shook her head, a drift of hair falling over her cheek
til he patiently pushed it aside again.

"Good." He was silent, then said, "You have Biagio to thank for coming after me. I might not have made it in time if he hadn't found you."

"Oh . . . Rhys . . . Brian is—"

"Is arguing with Biagio about whether wine or beef broth is better for a man wounded in the belly." He shrugged when she looked up at him. "He's only wounded. One of his charms deflected Gavin's blade, apparently. And he's alive enough to argue with Biagio. I left them to it, not having time to waste settling arguments." Silence again, soft and this time comforting. After a moment he said in the musing tone of one who has discovered something about himself, "I would have done it, you know."

She didn't have to ask what he meant. A tiny hope blossomed again, the one she'd been carefully cultivating for weeks. "You would? You would have yielded Glenlyon for me?"

"Yea. Before he could blink." His thumb explored the dimple at one corner of her mouth, a light touch, a caress. Her heart was so full that tears threatened to spill, and she couldn't speak. She gazed up at him, at the moonlit face and shadowed features, the light gleam of his eyes barely visible in the gloom, and put her hand over his. He smiled. "I never would have thought I would consider such a thing. But I couldn't let him hurt you, flower."

"It was worth it all, to know you would have left Glenlyon and Wales for me."

Rhys looked faintly surprised. "Flower, I would have yielded it in an instant for you, but I would never have left it to him. It's one thing to yield up a keep, and quite another to abandon it. I could have won it back as soon as you were safe."

"But you said—"

"And I meant it. Every word. I would have yielded up keys and keep for you. But I never give away what's mine. Never. I keep it. Remember that."

Piqued, she stared at him. She didn't know whether to be angry or resigned. After all that had been said an done—well. It wouldn't do at this point to quibble small details. After all, if it had been her, she would have lied like a Trojan, told Gavin anything he wanted to hear. It would hardly be worth it to get angry over something like this. And she hadn't told him everything, either. Not yet. But she would. Somehow, she thought he would understand it all. It was another legacy, a special legacy, a Gift from her mother to her. Yea, she'd tell him. . . .

She looked up, taking a deep breath. Her gaze fell on a length of green-and-purple silk tucked into the leather baldric holding his sword. She reached out, touching her discarded scarf lightly. "You wear my colors."

He smiled. "Yea, so I do. At last. And just in time to fight the most important kind of tourney for you. For us."

Startled, she looked up at him, and read in his eyes a much deeper emotion than she'd seen there before. Oh, if only her Gift would aid her now, would allow her to see into his deepest thoughts and know his true feelings. Quivering, she looked away, then back at him.

"I must tell you something that you may not want to believe, my lord."

A wry smile curled his mouth. "I'm not certain I can stand any more truths right now, flower."

"This is important. It concerns—everything. The past. The present. The future. Will you hear it?"

Rhys sighed and nodded. "Yea, I will listen, though I may regret it."

"I hope—I hope you will not regret it." She took another deep breath for courage and blurted out, "I have an unusual Gift, my lord. I inherited it from my mother, Lady Elfreda of Mersey. 'Tis my only legacy from her, but 'tis one that has served me well at times."

His brow lifted. "And you have this gift you claim with you now?"

"It's not a Gift—that you can hold in your hands, let us say, more a talent. I am told that only the females in our family inherit this Gift, and those who use it unwisely are oft accused of being . . . witches. Demons. Even elf queens."

Rhys stared at her narrowly. "You dabble in magic?"

She shook her head, weary and drained, yet filled with

the need to tell him everything, to know now if he would reject her or keep her with him. "Not as you may think. But I do possess the talent to know what others are thinking, my lord. It has oft been a curse as well as a Gift, especially when I've used it foolishly." When he recoiled slightly, she added desperately, "But I cannot see into your mind, Rhys. You alone have remained a mystery to me. Even when I cannot understand alien tongues, I'm still able to see into the hearts and minds of others. But not you. When I've tried—and believe me, I *have* tried—I'm met with only a blank, brilliant wall of silence. You are too strong for me. That's how I knew you were the one of the prophecy."

For a long moment, he was silent. Owls hooted softly in the treetops. The horses nickered, stamping hooves into the soft ground with muffled sounds. In the distance the low rumble of noise from the castle and village could be heard. Finally, he looked up at her with a shake of his head.

"Brian was right. He sensed that you were different."

Her heart fell. He didn't want her. He believed her, but now he didn't want her. Would never want her. Blindly, feeling her world crashing around her, she tried to rise but stumbled slightly. Rhys caught her.

"Sweet flower, beautiful flower, brave flower, do you think I would love you less because you have this special gift?"

Then he was dragging her up against him, his hands curling around her arms and his face close to hers, murmuring, "You're mine, flower. Only mine."

She smiled, a quivery, hopeful smile. "Yea, lord. Only yours."

"My lady."

"Your lady."

"My love."

She sighed, and tears wet her eyes. As they trickled down her cheeks, she nodded. "Your love. Your only love, as you are mine."

"And that cursed prophecy? Will you abandon it for me?"

Just like a man, to start making demands the moment you gave them what they wanted. She looked up at him. "I can't."

A flash of something exploded in his eyes, and his mouth thinned into a taut line. She said hurriedly, "I can't abandon it because you are the answer to the prophecy. Elspeth told me to repeat it over and over, and think about it, and I did. The prophecy promised me that I would regain that which was lost to me. And now, I think I have—I lost peace and happiness. But it's being returned to me just as the prophecy said—by a griffyn. By you."

After a moment he laughed and pulled her against his chest. His hand moved to tangle in her hair, and he slowly pulled her head back to gaze down into her eyes. "And will you be my lady? In love and marriage?"

"Yea, lord, in all ways. I will be your lady, and I will never betray you." Her hands moved to touch the curving scar on his cheek, the sweet line of his mouth, then flutter over his ears to brush back pale hair. "I will tell you all the truths you want to hear. Do you know that my real name means happiness?"

He grasped her fingers in his and kissed the tips. "I don't know your real name, flower. What is it?"

"Farah. It's Arabic. My mother named me."

Rising to his feet, he pulled her up with him. "Farah. I'll have to get used to it. You'll always be 'flower' to me."

Swinging her into his arms, he strode to the horses and settled her atop Bayosha. He held her there, smiling. Moonlight streamed through lacy branches overhead, gleaming on his face and in his hair. She bent and kissed him, and when she straightened, he whispered, "I love you, flower."

"And I love you."

A bird called softly in the night. Midsummer Eve. A time of magic. A time when elf queens and faeries lured handsome knights to lands of lasting peace and happiness, where there were no worries, and where feasting lasted for all eternity. Maybe there was something to that tale after all . . .

To My Readers

Forgive me for taking liberties with the language of medieval times, but if I had written this as the people really spoke, none of us could have read it. So I improvised, trying to find a balance and cadence that would be true to my characters and their times, while still portraying what they felt and thought. Certain characters and stories lend themselves to certain manners of speech, and so I used what I thought they would say, in whatever mode it would have been at the time.

I hope you enjoyed *The Magic*.

Juliana Garnett

About The Author

Juliana Garnett is a bestselling author writing under a new name to indulge her passion for medieval history. Always fascinated by the romance of *knights in shining armor*, this Southern writer is now at liberty to focus on the pageantry and allure of days when chivalry was expected and there were plenty of damsels in distress.

Ms. Garnett has won numerous awards for her previous works, and hopes to entertain new readers who share her passion for valorous heroes and strong, beautiful heroines.